THE TWO WOLVES

A DYING TRUTH EXPOSED, BOOK THREE

WHICH WOLF WILL THEY FEED?

MARCUS ABSTON

CHAPTER 1

The Power of Words

IN ALBERT BROOKS'S LIVING ROOM, his family sat before him. His daughter Liz, whose six-year-old daughter, Elisa, lay against her chest, held onto several old letters incased in plastic film. She stared at the written history of her ancestors, her eyes big as she looked up at her father.

"Daddy, I don't deserve to read these," Liz said. The sunlight outlined her mouth, which curved down, expressing her shame.

Albert's eyebrows lowered. "Why would you say that?"

Liz bit her lip, then looked at Albert and shook her head. "I'm ashamed. I forgot so much, and I shouldn't have. Christina and Elisa should've at least known which tribe we descended from. I couldn't do the one thing you asked of me. To pass on the truth." She handed the letters to Albert.

Albert looked at Liz, his face blank. "I'm pretty sure I've asked several things from you, including to keep your GPA above a 3.5."

Liz grinned.

Albert's wife Coney cocked her head, side-eyeing Albert. "Albert."

Albert shrugged with a half-smile. "What?"

Liz grinned. "Daddy, I was being serious. I'd rather you tell us the rest."

Liz's daughter Christina sat down next to her and lay her head on Liz's shoulder.

"Annabelle really fought for her freedom," Liz said. "She escaped the Brown plantation, leaving behind her family, Judy Mays, and her sisters. She made it to Mercy, Missouri, with the help of Ruthanne and Elizabeth. Made new friends and fell in love for the first time with Benjamin. Then all of that was destroyed by Mr. Hildebrand murdering Benjamin and her unborn daughter Benita. She didn't even get time to mourn with Ruthanne's and Elizabeth's brothers finding out about the bounty on her. If it wasn't for John and Samuel taking her to Indian Territory, who knows what would've happened."

Albert nodded. "It must've been hard for her. Though she had Aunt Grace and Aunt Lizzie, she had to take her own steps to heal. She had to deal with Nancy Hicks, other Cherokee, and Indian agents. Despite this she still pushed to live her life, and even fell in love again. I know this much from her writings. Her marriage to John even surprised her. She didn't believe she would fall in love again so quickly." He looked around the sunlit living room at the faces of his other children, who sat before him on a couch and chairs. "Liz asked me what happened to Annabelle and the others. Our family was entering a war they didn't see coming. At this time, Annabelle's faith had been strengthened by the help of Elder Joyce. David was now her full responsibility, and she was now Momma A to him. I believe the letters from her friends Elizabeth, Marilyn, Rebecca, and Ruthanne helped her as well.

"Annabelle and John were married December 9, 1849 and gifted with Grace's room. The next day, Annabelle went to work at the supply store, smiling the entire day. An olive-skinned woman named Victoria Coleman, one of Lizzie's childhood friends, entered the store. She was half Cherokee and French. Being Tsula's height, she was shorter than the other women, except Lizzie, and she had her wavy shoulder-length hair put into two braids."

"Good afternoon, I hope you're enjoying this weather. It is warm for this time of year," Victoria said in Cherokee.

Lisa replied, "Hello, Victoria. How have you been? I haven't seen you in a few weeks."

"I've been sick, but I'm feeling well now. I was here to get a few supplies and to see Lizzie, but I see you're working today."

"Yes, Lizzie is at home helping Tsula sew some new clothes for David. He's growing fast."

"I will have to come by your home and see that sweet boy. He reminds me so much of Camille."

Annabelle walked out of the storage closet with Grace.

"Ah, there she is, the new Lightning family member!"

Annabelle replied, "Hi, Victoria. It is good to see you."

Victoria displayed her dimpled smile and said, "It's always good to see you too. Lizzie was excited you and John were allowed to get your marriage license."

Annabelle and Grace looked at her, their eyes wide.

Victoria's brow drew together. "Did I say something wrong?"

Grace answered in her native tongue, "Oh, no...you said nothing wrong. So you came here for Lizzie?"

Victoria sighed. "Yes, I did, but I will see her later. I also came to buy a small sack of cornmeal."

"I can go get a sack for you." Grace went into the storage closet while the other women continued talking.

Annabelle enjoyed Victoria's visit. She was almost the complete opposite of Lizzie. Grace brought Victoria the small sack of cornmeal, and Victoria said her goodbyes.

When Victoria left, Annabelle hummed and thought, *Wow, Lizzie actually approved of our marriage.*

February 1850 arrived with a lighter snow, giving the Lightning-Strongman men opportunity to hunt for turkey and deer. Much to George's dislike, Lizzie joined them on several hunts. George and Lizzie argued every time she joined the men. During the end of February, the family went on another hunt and found a flock of turkey. The family slowly approached the flock, and as Lizzie took aim, the men fired their rifles at the flock. Two of the turkeys fell, one killed by Michael and the other killed by Lizzie.

Lizzie ran toward the dead birds and picked them up, giving one to Michael. She kissed Michael on his forehead and walked back toward the house. George and the other men followed her across the snow-peppered prairie.

"Whoever marries Lizzie will need nine lives like a cat," George said in Cherokee.

Samuel cackled, and John shook his head. The men followed Lizzie closely.

As she approached the house she heard a horse nay. She moved onto the main dirt road and looked to her left at Brock and Hunter.

"Ah, Miss Lizzie Lightning," Brock said. "I see you're taking advantage of the land."

"I'd rather be inside near a fire, but I have a family to feed, Mr. Jackson," Lizzie said. As she stood before the two men, George and the others walked up behind her.

"Well, look what we have here, the whole family," Hunter said.

"When do you ever see just one Indian?" Brock asked.

The two men cackled.

George replied, "Mr. Jackson, Mr. Sawyer, nice to see you. We're on our way home. As you can see, we had a good hunt today."

Brock replied, "I see, now which one of you gentlemen here made the kills?"

"My son Michael took one of the good shots, and my niece made a good shot with her bow."

The men signaled their horses to move past the family and mockingly huffed. "It must be embarrassing for a woman to have to make kills for you men. She should be at home cooking, cleaning, sewing, or nursing. Though I doubt she'll be nursing anything soon."

Lizzie's nose scrunched, her brow furrowed, and she side-eyed the white men.

"My niece is talented with weapons like her sister and my daughter. I'd be a weak man to kill their talent because it's more common with men. Something you white men are so quick to do."

Brock stopped his horse and turned. "Careful now, Mr. Strongman. Your niece is a rarity, but even women like her get domesticated. Or they die a lonely death. It would be a shame for such beauty to go untouched."

Lizzie's grip tightened on the dead turkey she carried. She turned toward the family house with her eyes locked on Brock and stomped away.

"I like my cousin's idea," Samuel said.

Samuel jogged slowly to Lizzie, and the two walked together. The others remained silent as they walked past Brock and Hunter, the two men leering at them.

⸻◆⸻

"I see what you mean, Brock. She wanted to take a shot at you," Hunter said. "What a dangerous breed."

"She is quite the specimen, but eventually she'll get the message," Brock said. "You either become a part of the greatest civilization in the world or risk being erased from history. I'm interested in seeing what the redskin chooses." The men rode off on their horses.

⸻◆⸻

Later in the day, John exited the kitchen as Annabelle picked out some grass caught in David's hair. She tapped the little boy on his shoulder once she finished, and he ran outside smiling. She noticed the slight furrow of John's brow. "What's on your mind?" she asked.

"We ran into the Indian agents before we came home," John said. "Those men test my spirit."

Annabelle slowly rubbed her hands. "What did they do?"

"Insulted us and told us Lizzie needs to be domesticated. I'm proud of her, though. She didn't let her temper rule her."

Annabelle could hear Grace and Tsula enter into the kitchen through the back door.

"I've never trusted any of the Indian agents before, but those two have a lot of darkness in them," John said.

"Annabelle, I know you're out there," Grace shouted. "Come on in and help us cook. John isn't that special." Annabelle grinned.

"I better go before Tsula starts talking too," Annabelle said.

John smiled and kissed his wife. "I'll have you tonight."

"Mm-hmm." Annabelle then giggled and walked around John to enter the kitchen, where she saw two dead turkeys on the large kitchen table. She noticed Lizzie's eyes were fixed on one of the dead birds as she prepared it. Grace handed her a wooden bowl filled with spices to prepare to cook the turkey.

"Maria is getting slowed down by Lisa, so let's get most of supper done to make them feel guilty," Tsula said.

Grace frowned. "Tsula."

"What? I'm just picking on them...nothing wrong with a little fun."

"We're making cornbread too. So first help Annabelle and Lizzie with the turkey and then help them with the beans and cornbread."

"You changed the menu to slow us down."

Grace leered. "Maybe that'll teach you a lesson. Now, get started."

Tsula smacked her lips and walked over to Annabelle, who smiled. As the women prepared supper Lizzie's frustration was felt while she focused on one of the turkeys with hard swings of a cleaver slicing into the dead bird.

Even now Lizzie is unintimidated by the agents...she's something else, Annabelle thought.

Two days later Annabelle, Grace, and Lisa traveled toward the supply store, but Annabelle abruptly felt nauseous and vomited on the dirt road.

"Annabelle, what's wrong with you?" Grace said.

"I don't know. I've been a little ill the past few days," Annabelle said, and she vomited again.

"We need to take her back home," Lisa said in Cherokee. "It must've been what she ate this morning."

Grace replied, "That can't be. We ate the same thing. I should also be feeling sick. Annabelle, Lisa will walk home with you and see if you feel better throughout the day."

When Annabelle and Lisa returned home, Annabelle said, "I'm so confused. I don't become sick like this."

Lisa replied, "Maybe your body didn't like the food even though it was good. Don't worry about it. You'll be fine."

The two women walked to the supply store once Annabelle felt well a few hours later. Annabelle and Lisa entered the store to hear a humming Grace. "Oh, good...are you feeling well, Annabelle?" Grace asked.

Annabelle answered, "I'm feeling much better now."

Grace smiled at Annabelle as she hummed.

"Why are you smiling like that?"

Grace's mouth curved higher. "I think I know why you were sick and why you feel well now."

Annabelle's brows drew together, and she side-eyed the other woman. "What do you know?"

"When did you have your last bleeding?"

Annabelle's mouth dropped. "I don't know. I've been so focused on all the chores, David, John, and customers. No, no, I can't be pregnant. I have never become sick during a pregnancy."

"Sometimes it happens, and sometimes the sickness doesn't happen. Doesn't change that you're carrying a baby now."

Annabelle shook her head. "I need more time."

Grace giggled. "We will see as your belly starts to grow." Annabelle rolled her eyes at Grace as she pressed a hand against her stomach.

"This is exciting!" Lisa said. "When are you going to tell John?"

Annabelle replied, "I need more time. I think I'll tell John in a week."

Lisa gasped. "A week, I've never been able to keep a secret for that long."

Grace replied, "Lisa, you will keep your mouth shut. It's not like the baby is coming out soon." Grace looked at Annabelle, who looked at her fingers still trying to count back and laughed to herself. Grace mumbled, "I'm sure David will be excited to finally have a brother or sister."

During that night, Annabelle lay next to John filled with excitement, but unsure how to tell him.

Days passed as Annabelle discussed her pregnancy with Grace and Lisa. A week passed and the planting season began. She soon started to show, making her question if she was showing earlier than her past two pregnancies, or if the pregnancy were farther along than she'd originally thought. Annabelle waited for John outside of the large house while he finished planting. John walked from the barn alongside Samuel as they said their farewells to Jacob and approached Annabelle.

"Annabelle, can you teach this man how to work harder?" Samuel asked.

Annabelle giggled. "I can try."

John playfully hit Samuel with his hat when Samuel walked off into the family house.

"You look tired and hungry," she said.

John responded, "Your smile gives me strength. Were you waiting for me?"

Annabelle grinned. "There was something I wanted to tell you before supper."

John smirked. "It must be good; your smile is telling a story. Did the Indian agents die?"

Annabelle laughed and slapped John on his chest. "No, silly. I have something a lot better to tell you. I'm pregnant."

John's jaw dropped, his eyes widened, and he shouted with

joy. He picked Annabelle up and twirled her around. "How long have you known?"

Annabelle giggled. "Not too long. I wanted to wait and make sure. Grace and Lisa know, I couldn't hide it from them."

John grabbed Annabelle's hand and kissed it. "Then it's time to tell the others." He ran to the house, much to Annabelle's shock, while she held his hand. John excitedly opened the door and shouted, "I'm going to be a father again!"

Tsula shouted with excitement, giving Annabelle a hug. She placed a hand on Annabelle's stomach, continuing to shriek. "David, come here! Come feel your new baby brother or sister."

David excitedly ran over and touched Annabelle's stomach. "There is a baby coming?" he asked.

"Yes, there's a baby coming," Annabelle said.

David hugged Annabelle and asked, "Can I name him?"

The family chuckled as Annabelle knelt down and rubbed David's cheek. "Maybe, and I see you want a brother."

David grinned and shook his head.

"Later in the year, we will find out if the baby is a boy or girl."

Samuel patted John on his shoulder. "If we're lucky it will be a boy. There are enough women around here."

John chuckled as he hugged his cousin.

"Well, we better make sure the crop this year is as strong as before," George said. "I'm happy for you, boy."

John replied, "Thank you, Uncle George."

As the family ate supper, Annabelle's pregnancy was the main topic of excited conversation. Lizzie even showed great interest. When Annabelle ate, Lizzie abruptly placed another corncob on her plate.

"Don't hold back on your eating. I want to have a strong niece," Lizzie said.

Annabelle was surprised by Lizzie's loving gesture. The family laughed as Lizzie continued eating.

Speaking Cherokee, Michael said, "We need another boy around here."

The men cheered, but the women booed him. The cheerful

conversations reminded Annabelle of her second pregnancy. However, she could also feel fear building up in her. The fear made her feel determined to protect her baby. She would rather die than to lose another baby.

The news of her pregnancy spread quickly among the family's friends. Two months passed as Annabelle enjoyed the changes that came with her pregnancy. Soon the family decided not to allow her to walk alone. To her surprise, Lizzie volunteered to walk with Annabelle. They were sometimes joined by Victoria.

Her visits remained focused on bringing water to the slaves on the Thompson farm and the Tate farm. Jacob's father, Mr. Tate, always greeted Annabelle, Lizzie, and Victoria with a welcoming voice. His daughters, Florence and Piper, were thrilled to see Annabelle's pregnancy progress. For Annabelle, visiting the Thompson farm was the most rewarding for her. Mr. and Mrs. Thompson welcomed Annabelle with open arms. Annabelle was more excited to see Doll, one of the Thompson's field slaves she'd befriended. The older woman eagerly welcomed the young women, and she was excited for Annabelle. Seeing Doll carry around her eight-month-old daughter made Annabelle anxious. The father of the baby girl remained a secret, to Mrs. Thompson's displeasure; she was angered when another Cherokee man approached Doll, and she became protective of Doll.

The situation gave Annabelle mixed feelings, though Doll was happy. Annabelle encouraged her not to bear any more children. The beautiful Georgia was another baby barely resembling Doll. This fact increased Annabelle's fear that Mrs. Thompson's suspicions might turn onto Mr. Thompson, exposing the truth.

———◆———

On May 9, 1850, the Lightning-Strongman family welcomed David's sixth birthday. Though David was excited about his birthday, he cared more about spending time with Annabelle. Seeing Annabelle change over time excited the little boy. As the family sat outside enjoying the weather, Tsula sat down next to Annabelle.

"You're getting huge. Are you sure you're not carrying twins?" Tsula asked.

Annabelle looked at Tsula with narrowing eyes, but then her eyes enlarged, and her gaze went down her stomach.

"Annabelle, I was joking."

"You made my heart race," Annabelle said.

The two women snickered as Tsula patted Annabelle's back.

"I'm happy for you and John, but I'm happier for David," Tsula said. "There are so few children here around David's age. It'll be good for him to have someone to love and play with."

Annabelle smiled. "I think he'll make a good older brother."

"I think he will too. If it is a girl, though, let's teach her how to sew before Lizzie throws a bow and arrow at the child."

The two women laughed as they watched David play catch with Grace and Lizzie.

August 1850 arrived with intense heat. Annabelle hated the timing of her pregnancy. Though Annabelle felt spoiled throughout her pregnancy, she often wondered if her happiness was temporary. Nancy, John's ex, who had attempted to harm Annabelle with a rattlesnake, showed obvious envy, but Annabelle purposely tried to avoid the woman, whose father was white and mother was Cherokee and white. Even in church while she sang hymns Nancy gave Annabelle evil stares. Nancy's attitude increased Annabelle's determination to protect her unborn child.

Nancy's envious behavior toward Annabelle prompted Pastor Bluebird to scold Nancy. However, the greatest threat to Annabelle's family was Brock and Hunter. The Indian agents showed great interest in Annabelle once they noticed her pregnancy. One day when Annabelle, Lizzie, and Grace helped a Cherokee man put supplies on his wagon, Brock and Hunter walked into the store. The Cherokee man said nothing to the Indian agents.

"It seems your store is doing well as usual," Brock said.

"Mr. Jackson, what brings you here?" Grace asked. "Shouldn't you and Mr. Sawyer be out keeping the peace between us and the encroaching white men?"

"What a nice vocabulary you have, Miss Lightning, impressive. But please keep in mind it was the white man that taught you how to speak properly instead of your indigenous gibberish."

Grace replied with a smart tone, "My momma taught me how to speak properly, whether it's Cherokee or the lesser English."

"My, my, you and Miss Lizzie are certainly sisters. How can the peace last when Indians like yourself are so disobedient?"

"Maybe if you and Mr. Sawyer left, y'all could tell your Secretary of Interior that we're doing fine here in Indian Country."

Annabelle came through the back door with a basket of eggs and Lizzie behind her. She abruptly stopped, and Lizzie stepped in front of her.

"Miss Annabelle, Miss Lizzie, always a pleasure," Hunter said.

"Mr. Sawyer and Mr. Jackson, are you here out of kindness or avoiding the heat?" Lizzie asked.

The men laughed as Lizzie and Annabelle walked to the counter.

"So even brave men like yourselves can only take so much heat...what a shame," Lizzie said.

Brock replied, "Miss Lizzie, you always have something to say. If you keep this up, you'll never learn how to actually be a lady. You should learn from your Cousin Lisa with her interesting accent. Even though I'm sure your savage language twisted her tongue, at least she shows some capacity to become a lady."

"You keep telling me how to be a lady. I think it's clear you have never had a lady. Tell me, why isn't your wife living with you anymore, Mr. Jackson? I can't imagine why not."

The two men looked at Lizzie with pressed lips. "Careful now, slave shackles can't tell the difference between a nigger and a prairie nigger," Hunter said.

"I think Miss Annabelle even understands that. You know, after you have that child you could sell it for a high value," Brock said.

Staring at Brock, Annabelle's eyes narrowed.

He continued, his voice filled with sarcasm, "Looks like I said something I shouldn't have, but it's reality. How safe do you think that half-breed will be?"

Annabelle responded, her voice now deep and her brow furrowed, "Safer than the Negroes in the South, that much I can say."

Brock cocked his head and leered. "Ain't nothing like a mother's wrath. Your kind is suited for separation. Very different when you see a white mother separated from a child than a Negro woman. You Negroes move on and make another and another, but a white woman. The connection is so strong she don't want a man to touch her after having a child taken away."

Annabelle scowled. "You have twisted words for a so-called Christian man, Mr. Jackson. I would say there is much you still need to learn, if that's what you believe."

"I think it's time for you and Mr. Sawyer to leave, Mr. Jackson," Grace stated.

"Well, my apologies if my words hurt. We can't change the roles we are meant to play in this world," Brock said. "Let's continue our rounds, Mr. Sawyer."

"Indeed," Hunter said.

Annabelle's anger boiled over when the men left the store. Abruptly Annabelle started to cry. Grace and Lizzie attempted to calm Annabelle as she wept.

"I'm sorry. I shouldn't be crying, but that man really upset me," Annabelle said in Cherokee. "To say I should sell my baby. I'm tired of these evil men."

Lizzie replied, "Don't worry about it; that will never happen. Those men have nothing better to do but to try to kill our spirits. We won't give them the pleasure."

Grace half-smiled while listening to her sister.

Annabelle held onto what Lizzie had said throughout the day.

As Annabelle put on her nightgown and sat in bed with John that evening, she told him what had happened in the supply store. John became furious with what the men had said. Annabelle had never seen John angry like that, but she told him what

Lizzie had told her. John sat in the bed with his arm around Annabelle and kissed her on the cheek.

Later that night, John watched Annabelle sleep. "We don't have everything, but I'm happy we have each other," John whispered. "Thank you Jesus for directing my spirit."

As time went on September arrived, and the family maintained their ways. During this time Annabelle's involvement at the supply store became infrequent, and to her dislike she stopped her water runs. Annabelle also spent a lot of time looking at the letter Ruthanne had written her announcing Marilyn had given birth to a son in April.

"It's almost time, isn't it, little one?" Annabelle spoke to herself.

In late September, Annabelle, Grace, and Lisa had just closed the store when Buck Scott entered.

Buck's chest stuck out, and he kept his chin uplifted as he stopped in front of the counter. "Good evening, ladies, I needed a whole chicken," he said.

"Good evening, Buck," Grace said. "Lisa can go get the chicken for you quickly."

Lisa went out to the chicken coops as Buck stood before Annabelle and Grace holding his walking cane.

Buck replied, "Miss Annabelle, I imagine you're ready to have your child."

Annabelle replied, "Yes, I am. It would be nice to have my body back."

Annabelle and Buck lightly chuckled.

"I hear you and Nancy have decided to see each other," Grace said. "How is giving your time to Nancy going?"

Buck boastfully replied, "I believe things are going quite well. She is a respectable lady. She seeks a husband who treats her well, and I believe I could be such a man. I believe she'd say the same about me."

A smirk arose on Grace's face while she looked at Buck. "You seem sure of yourself. I would say that's a good thing about you," she said. "It is a sad thing seeing a man with no confidence."

The hazel-eyed man shifted his gaze from Grace. "Why, yes, I also believe that's important for a man to be. Maybe if—"

Lisa abruptly plopped a sack with the dead chicken in it on the counter. "Here is your chicken, Buck," Lisa said. "He was the one chicken we've been waiting to get rid of."

"Thank you," Buck said. "Well, here is my payment. I guess I need to be off now, or I will be late. Enjoy the evening, ladies."

Buck walked out of the store with the chicken, and the women cleaned the store before they left.

"I'm surprised by Buck's attitude toward me," Annabelle said in Cherokee. "I hope others will change like him."

Grace replied, "I don't believe Buck has let go some of the beliefs he was taught by his father, but it is nice to see him treat you with more respect. Let us hope the hearts of others continue to change. Breaking the wrongful beliefs of others takes more than the words of a truthful man...it takes the Father changing the hearts of people. That's what I believe."

CHAPTER 2

Joseph

THE FIRST WEEK OF OCTOBER 1850 passed, and the seasons changed. On October 9, 1850, Annabelle, Grace, and Lisa took a walk to enjoy the beautiful changing landscape. An unexpected pain hit Annabelle, and she balled her hand into a fist and squatted.

"Oh, no, it's time," Annabelle said.

"We're not too far away from home," Grace said.

Grace and Lisa quickly helped Annabelle go back to their home as her contractions increased. Lisa ran to the fields and told John Annabelle had gone into labor. John rushed to the family house where they'd taken Annabelle. John impatiently waited at the supper table as Annabelle's labor increased. "What if Elder Joyce doesn't get here in time? Do you know what you're doing, Grace?"

Grace poked her head through the cracked bedroom door. "John, stay in your seat and wait. This won't be my first time dealing with a birth."

"Elder Joyce helped Camille give birth to David, not you."

Grace's brow furrowed. "John…"

John rubbed his face. "I'm sorry. I trust you." He exhaled. "What if it's a girl? I haven't been thinking about enough girl names. Are you sure she's not ready to push?"

"John, if you keep this up!" Annabelle moaned, and Grace immediately went back into the room.

John stood from the table and quickly walked around it. He'd reached for the door handle when Grace's head poked out of the door again. "Is she pushing?"

Grace clenched her teeth. "Get out."

"But I—"

Grace stepped out of the room and pointed to the front door. "Get out before I lose my temper. You keep asking questions that aren't helping. Now get back to the fields." Grace pushed John, coaxing him to leave, and she went back into the sunlit bedroom.

Grace and Lizzie helped keep Annabelle comfortable while her contractions increased. Tsula arrived at home with an anxious Joyce, and the two went into the bedroom the moment Annabelle had finished going through another contraction.

"I leave to get Elder Joyce and y'all put her in my bed!" Tsula shrieked. "One of you is washing my sheets after this."

Grace commanded, "Tsula, you and Lisa prepare supper for the boys. We don't know how much longer this is going to take."

"By the feel of it, dear, you're almost completely open," Joyce said. "Lizzie, get me a chair. This may take some time."

Lizzie went to the living room and fetched a chair, then placed it in the bedroom. Four hours of labor went by with coaching from Joyce. Sweat rested on Annabelle's forehead as she moaned and gave one last good push.

Lizzie lifted up a gasping baby. "It's a boy!" she shrieked.

Grace cut the umbilical cord under Joyce's direction, cleaned him off, and wrapped him in a small brown blanket.

The baby boy cried as Lizzie handed him to Annabelle.

Tears covered Annabelle's cheeks as she said, "My baby boy, look at him. Such a beautiful baby boy with good strong lungs, listen to him."

The women expressed their awe, and the bedroom door slowly opened. John stood in the doorway and then calmly approached Annabelle.

"You have another son, John Lightning," his wife said.

John beamed as he wiped tears from his eyes. Annabelle handed the baby to John, and John looked at the newborn with deep love. "My new son, look at him, a handsome boy like a Lightning man," John joyfully said. "He has my eyes." John turned around, noticing David standing at the supper table wearing a shy smile. "Come say hi to your baby brother, David."

David entered the room and approached the baby slowly while everyone watched. "Hi, little brother, I'm happy you're here now," he said. "He is so small." The family giggled as David looked at his little brother with widened eyes. "Momma A, what is his name?"

Annabelle looked at David, and her mouth arched into a big smile. "Well, me and your daddy talked a little about it," Annabelle said. "I like the name Joseph. That way as he grows, he is always reminded to be an honest and caring person."

John nodded while he looked at the baby. "Joseph it is," John said. "Joseph Lightning, welcome to the world."

John handed Joseph to Annabelle, and David walked up to them. Joseph cooed when David touched his small hands. The family watched with love as Annabelle held her baby boy. Later, Tsula escorted Joyce home after Annabelle seemed well enough to walk to the small house. News of Joseph's birth was a celebration for many who knew the family.

Two months passed as Joseph grew, and for the first time Annabelle had been blessed with the gift of raising and bonding with her own child. On Grace's twenty-third birthday, the family celebrated at supper time. Samuel and Lizzie put in extra effort to catch a turkey, which was Grace's favorite meat. The family sat down and enjoyed each other's company, passing Joseph around. Annabelle watched with a big grin as Joseph smiled at his aunts and cousins as they held him and played with him.

Look at my handsome little man; he has my smile, she thought.

This peaceful time reminded Annabelle of how everyone treated Rebecca's twins, and it comforted her knowing her son had a family to protect him.

CHAPTER 3
Origin, Wildcat

I N JANUARY 1851, ANNABELLE REMAINED at home to raise David and Joseph. Grace, Lisa, and Lizzie ran the supply store. Tsula helped Annabelle with Joseph and knitted a thick blanket for him. Annabelle was now in the role of being more of a listener when the other women came home.

To Annabelle's surprise, Lizzie always was the first who wanted to pick up Joseph. Lizzie's increased kindness bewildered her, even though she expected Lizzie to love her nephew. Over the months, Annabelle pondered if God had changed her, or if the other woman's unsympathetic nature had changed because Joseph was a baby. She wanted to ask Grace but always felt Lizzie's behavior was connected to a darker reason than her being teased and refused to risk asking Lizzie herself.

In late March, after her birthday, Annabelle approached Tsula as she played with Joseph. "Tsula, I've wanted to ask you something for a long time," Annabelle said in Cherokee.

"I think I look better in the summer when my skin is darker," Tsula replied. "It brings out my lovely smile."

Annabelle giggled while Tsula grinned at her. "I don't think I will ever meet someone like you in my life again."

"Well, I was hoping that was the question. What did you want to ask?"

"What happened to Lizzie when y'all were children? The way Grace still talks about her...I didn't believe she was as kind as Grace said, but seeing her now, I can see it."

"John never brought up anything?"

"He's only said their father's death hurt her. I know it's a sensitive subject. It's why I didn't ask Grace, and I'm definitely not asking Lizzie."

"Yeah, it might be too soon to ask Lizzie herself." Tsula took a deep breath. "I guess the truth needs to be told for you to understand. I know it started when we were children. In Georgia, Lizzie was actually very short and always running behind the older kids. I remember she was picked on a lot for being short and well...she had a gap between her teeth big enough to kick a rock through. When we were children, Nancy was even nice, but as we got older Nancy used to tease her a lot. Some of the boys also made it harder for her.

"One day one of the boys kicked dirt at her, and it got into her eye. I was only six, but I remember it well because Lizzie panicked, and cried wiping the dirt out of her eye. Samuel went to the boy that kicked the dirt in her eye, and they argued for a little bit before the boy smacked Samuel. Lizzie jumped on the boy and kept punching him before one of the teachers pulled her off. Dre was his name, and he ran home that day with two black eyes."

"Mrs. Armstrong's nephew?"

"No, this was a different victim."

Annabelle chuckled. "Yeah, sounds like the Lizzie I know now."

Tsula huffed. "I was terrified. From that day Wildcat was born. I had never seen her that angry or knew she could punch. After that I think Lizzie decided to show no fear and didn't hesitate to fight someone who treated her badly. She created her own way to protect herself, and it worked. On the Trail of Tears, Nunna Daul Tsuny, we first lost Kay; she was a runaway slave taken in by a family…she was like an auntie to us. She would cook for us and give us beautiful tight braids showing our scalp. Lizzie loved her. After Kay…we lost my brother William on the way here. She was very sad like me, but I think she handled it by not saying much when we first got here. When Auntie Sarah walked on, I know she took it badly. It did bring out a tougher side of her. But I know Uncle Cliff's death did it.

"When we went to town with my momma one day, my papa and Uncle Cliff started drinking. Papa passed out on the supper table, but we couldn't find my uncle. Lizzie found him behind the barn. He was face down in vomit." Looking at Annabelle, Tsula's eyebrows slanted upward, and her mouth marginally curved downward, forming a small frown. "He was already gone…drank himself to death. Lizzie tried to save him, wiped the vomit off his face. I remember the sadness and shock so strongly. His walking on hurt all of us, but she took it the worst. She began to stutter and cry. First Grace tried to calm her, but that whole night my momma held Lizzie. You know how children can cry themselves to sleep. Not Lizzie…she passed out because she couldn't stop crying and stuttering. From that day is when what Nancy calls the brute appeared. Lizzie has always been a fighter, but that day broke her spirit…made her worse. I think she decided in her heart to never become close to anyone else easily."

Annabelle sighed. "I'm sure Grace felt the same way. It must've been hard."

"Starting at twelve years old, Grace ran the store when my momma couldn't. Uncle Cliff would sometimes get too drunk during the day to work, and Lizzie always did the heavy labor as a child. Carrying the corn, beans, or anything else we were selling. To this day she still lifts like a man, and I know you've seen that. It's why she's so strong. I think after her first fight Uncle Cliff taught her fighting moves, and she started wrestling with the boys. She also learned how to hunt from Uncle Cliff. While John and Samuel were kept in the fields to farm with my papa, Uncle Cliff wanted to spend time with her. He would take her, and they'd hunt. He was a great hunter and kind. Two years after Uncle Cliff died, my momma passed away from sickness. Lizzie closed her heart again when my momma walked on, and she didn't speak for three days. So now you know why Lizzie is Lizzie. You happened to meet her when she was going through a rage moment."

Annabelle frowned. "No wonder John is always hesitant to talk deeply about their father. It's amazing Lizzie can show love at all...they were just children."

Tsula shrugged. "Yeah, like I said, she's a fighter, but she's also a lover. I've learned a lot from that short-tempered, short woman." The women cackled as Tsula played with Joseph.

Months passed, along with David's seventh birthday, and the summer set in. In June 1851, Annabelle returned to working at the supply store. However, she refused to leave Joseph alone. She had John make another bassinet that stayed at the supply store.

———◆———

One day during this time, Nancy entered the quiet store. As Grace and Lizzie quickly moved things around the storage room, Nancy heard Joseph cooing and approached the bassinet that sat behind the counter.

Nancy leaned over and stared at Joseph. "Well, there you are, the baby of Annabelle," Nancy grumbled. "You would get John's eyes, but you're only a color or two lighter than your mother. What an interesting cross you are."

"What are you doing, Nancy Hicks!" Lizzie's voice echoed.

Nancy's eyes widened, and she leered. "My, such a protective tone, Lizzie. I was merely looking at the Negro boy."

Lizzie aggressively marched up to the crib with Grace walking right behind her. She picked up Joseph and stood before Nancy. Joseph smiled at the spiteful woman.

"He's so oblivious as to what he is, and look at you, Lizzie, carrying him like he's yours. What's his name?" Nancy asked.

"My nephew's name is Joseph," Lizzie said. "I suggest you

watch what else comes out of your mouth, or your blue bonnet might end up in your throat."

"Still a brute, even with a baby in your arms. How typical, it's clear you'll never be a proper wife."

Lizzie sarcastically replied, "I'm sorry my life isn't dependent on being a wife—my roots go deeper than yours."

Nancy fixed her malevolent blue eyes on Joseph and looked back at Lizzie. "I imagine your roots must...having a nigger for a nephew must test you."

"Nancy Hicks, if you ever call my nephew a nigger again, I will beat you with a stick after Lizzie stuffs your bonnet in your mouth," Grace growled. "Don't test us Christian women."

Annabelle came into the store with a sack of fresh-picked soybeans. "Nancy, when did you get here?" she asked with wide eyes.

Nancy replied, "I have only been here a moment. I see you have a healthy baby boy. I'm surprised you haven't been to the church since he was born."

"I haven't been to the church because it was cold, and I wanted to make sure he stayed healthy."

"Hmph, I guess your plan worked. I would like my supplies now so I can go."

Nancy handed Grace a list of supplies and then called Paul inside to help Lizzie with them. Nancy stood in the doorway watching Lizzie and Paul put the supplies in the wagon.

"Miss Lizzie, thank you so much for what you did for me," Paul said. "I healed up real good because of you."

"It was nothing, Paul," Lizzie replied.

"No, you helped save me. I know better. Thank you," he said.

Lizzie put the last sack in the wagon and wiped dust off her hands. She went to the store's door.

"Take care, Miss Lizzie."

Lizzie looked at Paul and turned her gaze back to the door, but then she turned back to him while she sighed and half-smiled. "Paul."

Lizzie moved past the taller Nancy as the two women locked eyes.

"You know you don't need to speak to him if it bothers you so," Nancy said.

"I have no problem with his speaking to me. I don't feel like being bothered by anyone today; that's different than disliking someone. Remember it was a slave who saved you, Nancy Hicks."

Nancy clutched her reticule and watched Lizzie walk by. "We're going home right now, Paul," she commanded.

"Yes, ma'am," Paul replied as he helped Nancy get into the wagon.

———◆———

Annabelle came out the store with Joseph and watched Nancy ride off.

"Well, think of it this way, she said Joseph was an attractive, healthy baby," Grace said. "I think that's the best you will ever hear from that woman about Joseph."

"Yeah, I agree."

The encounter with Nancy troubled Annabelle, and it made her wonder how the Indian agents viewed her son. Annabelle kept Joseph inside to keep him out of their sight. Annabelle and John were fearful of the agents, and they wanted to keep peace for their family.

———◆———

At the end of June, John left with Samuel for their first summer trip to Mercy. The men made their typical greetings, giving a pregnant Ruthanne Annabelle's letter detailing Joseph's birth and events in Tahlequah. John and Samuel also came across Marilyn on their brief visit to Allen and Rebecca Keys. She gladly showed them her new baby boy named Benjamin.

John and Samuel returned to Tahlequah with only one letter for Annabelle. She read the letter, which was written by Rebecca.

Annabelle, 1851 is turning out to be another interesting

year. I and the others are excited to hear about Joseph's birth. I'm sure John has probably told you he saw Marilyn and the baby. Daniel is the father, and they have named him Benjamin to honor Benjamin. I hope that rests well with you; as with you, it took Daniel time to adjust to losing his friend. Of course Marilyn's entire pregnancy was seen as unacceptable in the church. Two months ago, Pastor Avail agreed to marry them in secret. I'm sure Ruthanne had plenty to say to Pastor Avail. Marilyn's pregnancy was pardoned by Pastor Avail, who revealed to the deacons that some of her family greatly dislikes her husband. Keeping the husband's identity secret was to keep the peace. Though some still disagreed with the secrecy, any future pregnancies will not have Marilyn accused of fornication. Ruthanne is also pregnant, and her emotions are everywhere. Be grateful you're not here for that. We love you, dear, God bless.

◆

Months passed and Joseph's first birthday arrived with the harvest season. As the family spent time together, John walked outside carrying Joseph, and David followed.

"Come sit with me and your brother," John said.

David sat down next to his father.

"You look like you're happy today."

David smiled at his father and spoke in his native tongue, "Today was the day I got my brother. I have someone else that loves me now."

"You always will, but I want you to also understand that part of your purpose in life now is to protect your brother. Love him no matter what happens in life, and he'll always love you back."

"I will always love him...why would I stop loving him?"

John chuckled. "There will be times when you and your brother will argue and fight. I went through the same thing with your aunties and cousins...especially Auntie Lizzie. A strong family is a family that stays together and loves each other. Right now we have a strong family."

David's lips tightened while he frowned. "I still remember Momma. Is that okay?"

"It's a blessing that you remember her. You were young when she walked on into heaven. She never wanted to leave you, but the Father saw it best for her to move forward before we did. I know it's unfair, but you have been blessed with another momma."

"I love Momma A. She always gives me good hugs. I'm glad you found her."

John placed his hand on David's head. "There's more to that story. I'll tell you when you become older. Heaven has many mysterious ways. What I can tell you is there's always more than what we can see."

Annabelle went outside as John sat with his sons. Listening to John's calm voice as he spoke to David, she placed her hand on her heart and smiled.

In November of 1851, the Lightning-Strongman family struggled to give extra supplies to other Cherokee in town. The cause of the shortage was a deadly disease affecting over a third of the crops in the nation. As the family struggled to give what they could, the marshal entered their store one day. He was a tall, olive-skinned man with broad shoulders.

"I'm always surprised how this family tries to give so much to the tribe," the marshal said, approaching Tsula. He looked at Joseph playing with a ball in his bassinet behind the end of the counter.

"Hey, Luke, did you come in here just to say that, or were you looking for me?" Tsula asked in Cherokee.

Annabelle giggled while she poured cornmeal into a small sack.

Luke pressed his lips together. "Tsula, how many times do I have to tell you? When I'm working, please call me Marshal Luke, you stubborn woman."

Tsula put her hand on her hip. "Don't confuse me with my

cousin, Luke Fields. I'm respectful. I'm so respectful, I kill your chickens for you when you come here to buy some meat. I know it's hard for you to take a life, such a lover."

Luke shook his head. "Not today, Tsula Strongman. I won't get pulled into one of your games. Mrs. Annabelle, how are you doing?"

Annabelle replied, also in Cherokee, "I'm doing well, Marshal Luke, enjoying this day with my little boy and keeping an eye on him."

Luke looked at Joseph. "He seems like a happy baby. It must make you proud."

"It does. He gets a lot of love. I need to find a way to keep him from being spoiled. Lizzie is probably the worst when it comes to giving him whatever he wants."

Luke chuckled. "Well, yes, I can see how that would be an aggravating job. You must have patience to deal with the family you have."

"What does that mean?" Tsula barked. "Watch what you say, or I might tell Grace about the free corncobs I've given you before."

"Sometimes I can't tell who is worse, you or Lizzie!" Luke replied. "Where's Grace? She can control you."

Annabelle quietly giggled as Tsula and Luke stared each other down.

"I think I need to leave. You're not pulling me into another stupid argument, woman." Luke waved at baby Joseph, and Joseph waved back. "Enjoy the day, Annabelle."

Luke opened the door, and the cool winter breeze rushed inside.

"Go out in the cold and keep running away. Eventually you'll get tired," Tsula said.

Luke looked back and smiled at Tsula. "I'm not running, and I'm not playing your game today."

Tsula smiled back, and Luke went out into the cold weather.

Annabelle giggled while she took a sack of cornmeal into the storage room.

"What's so funny, Annabelle?" Tsula asked.

Annabelle answered, "Nothing is funny. I was watching. It's fetching."

Tsula picked up Joseph and kissed the baby. "There isn't nothing fetching going on."

Annabelle scoffed. "If you say so, Tsula. I know he likes you."

"Well, that's his loss. My heart already belongs to a handsome little man. Isn't that right, my little Joseph?" Tsula gave Joseph kisses on his cheek, making him laugh. "That's right, you have my heart, you little angel."

Tsula focused on dancing with Joseph in her arms while Annabelle stood in the storage room doorway watching. She felt overjoyed watching Tsula hold him. Later, the women cleaned up the store and waited for Grace to return from Joyce's home before closing the store.

January 1852 arrived during a brutal winter, making it difficult for the family to get to the supply store. Grace was determined to make it to the store once the storms ended. Her tenacious nature inspired the other family members to take the tough walk into town with her, much to George's disapproval.

George was concerned they were giving too much. He also greatly disapproved of Lizzie joining the men on some of their hunts. He believed Lizzie should watch the children and let the men do most of the hunting.

During the hunts for which Lizzie stayed behind, she would look out the window while carrying Joseph. She grimaced and stomped her foot when the men kept returning empty-handed. Some of the chickens had also died from the brutal winter, adding to her frustration. Grace talked with Lizzie about suppressing her pride.

During the second week of March in 1852, the men had gone into the fields one day to make decisions on where to place the new crops. On this day, Lizzie left on her own to hunt. Annabelle, who had been playing with Joseph at the time, saw Lizzie going toward the prairies. Annabelle told Lisa, and the two women searched the farm for Grace as Tsula watched over Joseph.

———————◆———————

Lizzie traveled through the wilderness with her bow drawn, looking for rabbits. Lizzie grunted, ripped off her white bonnet, and let it fall to the ground. "What was I thinking, bringing this stupid thing?" she complained.

Soon after, a rabbit came into view, and she aimed as she sat in the tallgrass. The sound of a snapping branch broke Lizzie's concentration. She turned around.

A white man with a poorly shaved face stood nearby, holding a rifle. The average-built man leered at her and went down a slope, followed by another white man with two scars under his chin. That man also had a rifle; he was shorter with a stocky build.

"Look at what we find here instead of some small game, Cole. A nice little Cherokee woman," the short man said.

"Now, Matthew, let's not get ahead of ourselves here. She probably don't even speak English," Cole said.

The two men laughed between themselves, and Lizzie slowly turned to leave.

"Wait a minute, beautiful. Don't leave so quickly," Cole said.

"What do you want?" Lizzie asked, turning back.

"How about that, Matthew? She speaks English. We're out here looking to have a good time. You look like you had the same idea we had. It gets a little tiring eating bread and pork for most of the winter."

"True, that does sound like a boring winter. Well, have a nice day, gentlemen." Lizzie came out of the tallgrass when Cole moved toward her. She lifted her bow. "Please don't do that."

"You seem to have some trust issues, Miss Indian. Don't be that way. We just want to talk. There's not much else to be doing out here."

Lizzie side-eyed the men. "I doubt that's the only thing you want to do. Your eyes tell a story, Cole."

Matthew laughed. "She's has you figured out now. She's one of the smart kind. I think your liking these Indian women is blinding you."

"Oh, shut your mouth. These Indian women, they all like to act like they don't have no interest, but I guess you're right. How about we change this game a little? What is your name?"

Lizzie replied, "There's no reason for you to know my name."

Cole looked at Lizzie. His eyebrows slanted downward, and his right eye squinted. "I think you need to watch what you're saying now. What is your name, woman?"

Lizzie smacked her lips. "It's not for you to know...goodbye."

Cole cocked his rifle. "Please keep testing me. You'd be surprised how quick my temper grows, little lady. Now, put down the bow and arrow."

Lizzie slowly placed them down.

Cole moved forward, his rifle aimed at her, and Matthew walked beside him. Lizzie turned around as Cole circled and stepped closer.

"The nerve of an Indian woman telling me what she is and ain't going to do...I promise you, if this was the South, you wouldn't be talking like that," Cole said.

As Lizzie faced Cole, Matthew grabbed Lizzie from behind with both arms. "I got her," he said.

Lizzie tried to shake the stocky man off while Cole kept his rifle aimed at her.

"Wow, she's strong," Matthew said. "Feels like I'm holding a man."

"I suggest you stop, or I will shoot and end things now," Cole said.

Lizzie stopped struggling, and Cole stalked toward her. He ran his fingers through the top part of her hair. "Look at this hair. It would be better if you did it like a civilized woman, not in one raggedy ponytail. Now, what is your name?"

"I'm not telling you my name. What difference would it make?" Lizzie said.

Cole stared at her from cold blue eyes, then slapped her.

Lizzie glared at Cole with furious, dilated brown eyes.

"Woo-wee, you should see the look she's giving me, Matthew," Cole said. "You think you something special, don't you? You ain't nothing but a prairie nigger needing to be tamed."

"I'm not a prairie nigger. I'm a Christian woman, and you're nothing!" Lizzie yelled.

Cole slapped her again and rubbed her face with the back of his hand. "You have no real value out here. You see, Matthew and I live in one of the good towns outside of this land. We know how to use land. You Indians still don't know what to do with land given to you, and I think you never will."

Lizzie chuckled. "We love the land and respect it. That's something your people have never understood. Probably never will until everything is gone."

"I never heard a savage say that. I think she believes she can speak like that because they dress like us now." Cole leered. "What if I rip that dress off? I bet that smooth brown skin is going to show me who you really are."

Matthew replied, "I'm sure it will."

Cole cackled. "Let's take a look now." Cole put down his rifle and reached for the top part of Lizzie's dress.

Lizzie screamed, "Don't touch me!"

"Hold her strong now, Matthew," Cole shouted before grabbing the top part of her dress and tearing it.

Lizzie struggled as the dress ripped. She kicked Cole in the knee, making him fall and howl in agony. She thrust her head back and into Matthew's nose.

Matthew screamed and released Lizzie. "Argh, my nose, my nose!" Blood gushed out of his nose and covered his hands.

Lizzie's quiver fell off when she ran, but Cole grabbed the bottom of her dress, causing her to fall.

Cole jumped on top of Lizzie and wrapped his hands around her neck, choking her. "I bet you feel better than the others, you rebellious little whore. Matthew, get over here and help me!"

Matthew deeply inhaled through his mouth, replying with a

higher pitch, "I think she broke my face. I can't breathe out of my nose. The blood won't stop!"

"You're a special one, aren't you?" He clenched his teeth and choked Lizzie as she gasped for air. "That's right, stop fighting. This won't take long."

Lizzie kneed Cole in his stomach with such force that he was unable to breathe, and he released her. She pushed Cole off of her and took in a big gasp of air.

Matthew charged Lizzie with his bloody nose, but Lizzie quickly grabbed Cole's rifle. She took aim and fired a shot into Matthew's shoulder. Matthew gave an anguished scream as Lizzie ran toward Matthew and hit him with the rifle's stock, knocking him to the ground. Lizzie tossed the empty rifle into the tallgrass and walked away as Cole pulled himself up, holding his knee.

"Where the hell do you think you're going?" he asked.

Turning back, Lizzie rushed at him and tackled him back to the ground, punching and kicking as they hit the ground. Cole tried to fight her off, but Lizzie's ferocity made it difficult. He attempted to punch Lizzie, but she wrapped her legs around his ribcage, making it hard for him to breathe. He grabbed a pile of mud and slapped Lizzie with it, blinding her right eye.

She screamed.

He reached for a nearby stick as she tried to rub out the mud, and he hit her head with it, knocking her off. Lizzie crawled away, struggling to regain her balance. As she crawled away, Cole struck her in the thigh.

She screamed again, and he struggled to stand while she attempted to crawl away. He stood just as Lizzie had barely gathered herself. He reared his hand with the stick to hit Lizzie again, but she kicked Cole's knee with her other leg, knocking him down.

Cole growled, "Never thought you'd be so much trouble. I was going to have a little fun with you, but now I think I'm going to kill you after."

Lizzie kept rubbing the remaining dirt out of her eye while she crawled. "I won't let you shame my body or take my life."

"Nothing but a prairie nigger! That's all you are, and I'll prove it!" Cole tried to stand, but through her blurred vision Lizzie saw his knee buckle, and he fell forward on all fours and groaned. He rubbed his knee, gritted his teeth, and forced himself to crawl toward her.

Pain pulsated through Lizzie's leg. Cole caught up to her, and he reached his shaking hands around her throat and squeezed. Her vision blurred, making it hard to fight back. She struggled to push him away as she reached for her quiver.

Cole sat on top of Lizzie and punched her in the stomach. "I'm going to enjoy this!"

He reared his fist back to take another swing as Lizzie's hand reached into the quiver. She took a swing at Cole with her tomahawk, slitting the lower half of his throat. His blood poured out over Lizzie and his clothes, and he stumbled back as he held his wound. He fell over to his side, his eyes wide. She heard Matthew exhale, noticing him slowly moving.

She forced herself to stand, holding her tomahawk, and looked at Matthew. Her grip tightened on the weapon, and she took two steps toward Cole. Feeling cold and merciless, she stared at a terrified Cole as he held onto his bleeding neck. She let out a brutal shriek and stabbed Cole in his chest, then she pulled her tomahawk out of the dead man's ribcage.

Matthew gasped. Lizzie locked eyes with him, and she slowly approached. "Please calm down, Miss. I'm sorry things went too far, we scared you," Matthew said, his eyes wide. "Please, I won't tell anybody who did it...we was wrong. God knows we were wrong, please, forgive me."

He stood and backed away as Lizzie drew closer to the man. Cole's blood dripped down her face, neck, right hand, and off her tomahawk.

"Please forgive me, like you said, you're a Christian woman. You shouldn't be like this."

"Are you a Christian man?" Lizzie asked.

Matthew stuttered, "Y-yes, ma'am, I-I am."

"It wasn't very Christian of you and your friend to try to rape me. Now, was it? Where in the gospels does it say it's okay to rape me because you think I'm your lesser?"

Sweat ran down Matthew's forehead. "I'm sorry. I want to go home to my family."

"Where do you think I was trying to go?" Lizzie said in a malevolent tone.

Matthew kept looking around for his rifle but didn't see it. "Help, someone please help me!"

Lizzie moved faster as the stocky man walked backward, scanning around him for the rifle.

"Lizzie! Stop it!" Grace yelled.

Lizzie stopped and looked back, seeing Annabelle and Grace on the upper slope. Annabelle placed her hands over her mouth at the sight of blood on Lizzie's green plaid dress. Lizzie shook her head and turned toward Matthew.

"Please help me. We wasn't serious," Matthew said with a higher pitched voice and widened eyes. "Please, Lizzie, calm down."

Lizzie moved toward Matthew again. "You have no right to call me by that name," she growled, her grip tightening on the tomahawk.

"Please, stop her! She's crazy!" Matthew hollered.

Lizzie shrieked and ran after Matthew. Matthew tried to run down the grassy hill, but Lizzie stopped chasing him. As he ran, he looked back and lost his footing, rolling down the hill. He fell onto the lower prairie as Lizzie watched.

The terrified man landed in front of the grazing bison herd. He looked up at the animals, panicked, and ran.

The bison thought of Matthew as a threat and bullied the man as he ran through the herd. Two of the bison led a minor charge, barely missing the man. Others bellowed at the man and charged after him as well. Matthew tried to dodge them, but he ran into a bison, which stepped back and rammed him. Then the other bison in the herd trampled him. Shaking, Lizzie stood on the hill, her tomahawk in hand as she watched the man get trampled to death. Grace slowly approached her sister as she heard Matthew scream, and she looked down helplessly as the herd crushed him.

"Lizzie, what happened here?" Grace asked quietly.

Lizzie, her clothes and body blood-soaked, turned around to look at her sister. "I want to go home," she said, her voice weak.

She walked away from Grace, still holding the bloody tomahawk. She marched past Annabelle, who stood speechless. Annabelle looked at Grace, who picked up Lizzie's bow and put the arrows in the quiver, and they turned toward Cole's blood-soaked dead body.

"We need to leave now; there isn't nothing we can do here," Grace said.

The women quickly followed Lizzie as she trudged home with a limp.

"Lizzie, what happened back there?" Grace asked in Cherokee. "Lizzie, look at me!"

Grace followed her dazed sister and heard Lizzie murmuring to herself. Grace stepped in front of Lizzie and gently placed her hand on Lizzie's right hand, convincing her to drop the tomahawk.

"Lizzie, focus what happened, why did you kill that man?" Grace asked.

Lizzie shivered. "They...they tried to rape me!" she bawled. Grasping onto Grace, she wept. "They tried to rape me! I tried to walk away, but they threatened to shoot me, and they tried to rape me. I lost control. I killed that man!"

Annabelle's and Grace's jaws dropped, and their eyes widened. They rubbed Lizzie's back, wiped the tears off of her face as she cried with anger etched in her voice, and made her take deep breaths to calm her. The women quickly escorted Lizzie into the small log cabin, and she took off her blood-soaked dress. Her heart still raced as she sat on a bench.

The door opened and Lisa entered. "Hey, I saw y'all walk in—What..."

Lizzie shivered on the bench and looked at Lisa.

"What is this, Lizzie, what happened to you? Are you hurt? What happened to her?" Lisa asked.

"Two white men tried to rape and kill her," Annabelle said.

Lisa tightened her hand into a fist and knelt down next to Lizzie. "You made them pay for it?" she asked.

Lizzie whispered, "Yeah, I killed them."

"Lizzie, you killed one of them, but that other man ran into the bison herd. It wasn't your fault," Grace said in Cherokee.

Lizzie turned around. "That's a lie...it was my fault. I was in that area longer than them. I knew the herd was there. I chased him into the herd, believing he was too stupid to stand still. I was right."

Grace's eyes swelled with tears as she soaked a towel in water. "We have to clean this blood off you," she said. "Annabelle, take some of the firewood outside and make a small fire. When that's done come for the dress and put it in the fire."

Annabelle replied in Cherokee, "Okay, what about her tomahawk? It's still outside."

"Bring that to me first. We have to do this quickly," Grace said. "Nobody but us can know of this. Tsula can't know about this, because she talks too much. She has a good heart, but her temper causes her to tell things she shouldn't. I think you need see Elder Joyce about this, but it's your choice."

Lizzie agreed for her to see Joyce, and Annabelle rushed outside to grab Lizzie's tomahawk. She brought it inside, and Grace told her to place it in a bucket. Grace and Lisa helped Lizzie clean herself off while Annabelle set the fire. As the fire burned, Annabelle went inside the house, grabbed Lizzie's bloodstained dress, and tossed it in the fire. Lisa cleaned Lizzie's hair, and Grace cleaned off Lizzie's tomahawk. Grace exhaled and rubbed her neck because they were unable to hide the wounds on Lizzie's face. The women went to the other house to prepare supper with Tsula, and Lisa hummed while the other women were mostly quiet.

Tsula noticed the bruising on Lizzie's cheek. Lizzie's hand

shook while she cut the duck. "What happened to you, Lizzie? It looks like your cheek is swollen?" Tsula asked in Cherokee.

"I was out looking for some rabbits when I slipped down one of the hills," Lizzie replied. "I'm fine, I heal fast."

Tsula squinted. "If I didn't know better, I'd say you got into a fight, but okay."

Grace and Lisa looked at each other and frowned.

"Well," Tsula continued, "if one of those little cuts turns into a scar, you should make a brave story so people don't laugh at you."

"I'm not doing such a thing. I fell and it will heal fine. Only weak people are worried about what others think of them."

Tsula lifted an eyebrow, and she leered. "So when Jacob told you the two of you were friends and you got angry at him, you were a weak person?"

Lizzie stopped cutting up the duck and stabbed her cutting board. Annabelle and Lisa jumped. Lizzie stormed out of the kitchen.

"Okay... that was still too soon," Tsula said.

Grace went over to Tsula and smacked her on the back of her head. "You run your mouth too much!" Grace yelled. "You need to learn how to be more sensitive. Or do I need to start talking about you and Marshal Luke?"

Tsula frowned and went to Lizzie's cutting board, cutting the remaining duck for her.

During supper John and the other men noticed Lizzie's wounds, but they accepted Lizzie's story. The family conversed as they ate supper, but Lizzie remained silent. Annabelle had handed baby Joseph to Lizzie in an attempt to cheer her up. The family stopped eating as Lizzie wiped tears from her face.

"What's wrong with you, Lizzie?" George asked in Cherokee.

Lizzie replied, "Nothing, I'm fine...I'm happy."

George frowned. "Are you sure? There is no reason for you to hide anything if something is wrong."

Lizzie rubbed her cheek against Joseph's. "Nothing is wrong, I'm happy to have Joseph with me."

"What babies do to women! Even Lizzie is crying when she's happy now," George said.

The family lightly laughed. However, Lisa caressed Lizzie's hair and kissed her on the cheek. During the night, Lizzie struggled to sleep, her fear now replaced by anger.

A week passed as the women of the family struggled to make peace with what had happened. One day as the women strolled into town, Brock and Hunter stopped them. Brock demanded the women all walk home because the entire family needed to be questioned on a murder. The women reluctantly marched back to the family house and allowed the men inside to avoid suspicion.

"Well, now, the whole family is together," Brock said, his voice dripping with sarcasm. "This is a rare treat indeed. Now, I'm going to be brief in this unwelcome finding. Some white travelers on their way back to their town found the body of Cole Pepper...a US citizen clearly murdered by two barbaric attacks."

A playful Joseph shrieked with excitement as he chased a ball.

"David, come get your brother and stay in the room like you were told," Annabelle scolded in Cherokee.

David ran and picked up Joseph and went into the men's bedroom.

"Well, now, look at that half-breed," Brock said.

Hunter replied, "He looks barely Indian, a healthy-looking baby boy. Impressive."

"Indeed, what a shame we're just now seeing the child, especially since the child population is now rising," Brock commented.

Annabelle glared at Brock.

"Well, back to what's more important. There are five families closest to the murder scene. Your family is the last to be questioned. We've already asked the Tate family, Thompson family, Sunshine family, and Cornstalk family. I want to know if any of you knew there was a dead white man in the prairie about a mile north of here? The man had been noted as missing."

Sweat trickled down Lizzie's back while her family remained silent.

"We know nothing of this," George finally said. "We are good people."

Brock rubbed his chin while he stared down his nose at George and huffed, replying, "Mr. Strongman, even good people hide terrible secrets. Isn't that what your pastor teaches you? That no man is completely righteous."

"We're made righteous through Jesus, and we're aware that we are still capable of making bad choices. No man is perfect."

"I stand corrected, Mr. Sawyer."

Looking at Brock, Hunter chuckled.

"I tell you more of what we know for sure," Brock continued. "Mr. Pepper was murdered with a tomahawk or a large knife, and I don't see any of the white settlers out here doing such a brutal act. You savages are waiting for the right moment to rebel."

"Don't come here insulting my family," John yelled. "Not one of us has murdered any man. If that's all you came here for, then you can leave."

"Well, I care little if I have insulted your family. Matthew Hefner, who had three small children, is also missing. We found him trampled to death by the bison, but he also had a bullet wound in his shoulder. Now, what do you want me to think of that?"

John's voice rose, "The answer is there, two white men get into a fight, one dies and the other gets himself killed. How simple is that?"

"A small possibility, but I know you Indians...even your women are dangerous." Brock rubbed his chin. "I have good reasons for believing it was one of your people, or even one of the more dangerous tribes north of here."

John stood up while he scowled, facing Brock. "You white

men have killed each other for centuries, but you come here and question us! As if you white men are of pure heart."

"Calm down, John," George replied as he signaled for John to sit down.

Hunter replied, "Such a temper! It's easy to see Lizzie is your sister. A woman like her...I'm sure she has a dark side to her."

"I believe that's enough, Mr. Sawyer," Brock scoffed. "We're gaining nothing from this." Brock locked his eyes onto Lizzie. "Though I agree that Miss Lizzie Lightning certainly represents what's wrong with you people. When you give a woman too much freedom, that's what you get."

"You can leave now," Lizzie said, her voice deepening on each word.

"Now one of the women speaks," Brock said. "You Indians keep on protecting the law breakers here. I guarantee you all will be in chains. Maybe intelligence will arise one day, or some chains might get on that healthy half-breed. They do respond better than you full bloods and sell for a better price."

Lizzie erupted from her seat, but Grace and Lisa pulled her down.

"You're nothing but a coward!" Lizzie shrieked. "Scared because your fathers could never control us, and you can't either."

Brock scoffed. "My beauty, the fact that you're no longer in Georgia or the South shows how much we do control you. Let's be off. Time will tell the truth eventually."

The two men walked out of the house and talked between themselves as they got on their horses and rode away. The family later discussed the murders over supper while Annabelle and the others held onto their secret. Grace had convinced the others the men would rebel if they knew the truth.

———◆———

A month passed, and the Indian agents made their presence known throughout Tahlequah and the other Cherokee towns. Annabelle worried about the attention, but John was determined not to let the men intimidate him. One day, John moved through

Tahlequah carrying a chicken cage to the supply store when he saw his friend, Cody Morningstar.

"I haven't seen you in two months, Cody," John said in Cherokee. "How are you?"

Cody looked up and struggled to stand. "It has been some time...since I saw you, John," Cody slurred. "How is life?"

John frowned when he smelled the alcohol on Cody's breath and clothes. "You're drunk and the sun isn't even high. You need help, Cody."

"I'm good." Cody grasped his bottle of rum. "This helps me make it through each day. Before you talk about my drinking maybe you should think about your uncle's."

"We're trying to work with him so he quits. Try going to Elder Joyce or Pastor Bluebird if you don't want my help. I hate seeing you like this, doing nothing with yourself."

"You want me to start following Jesus like you now? I never thought I would see the day you would give into the white man's ways for a woman."

"I haven't given my life to Jesus for Annabelle or any of my family. I had to listen and realize the truth is written in that book. The Father spoke to me and gave me a vision of the truth. That helped me make the choice for my spirit. Because white men have used the Bible for evil reasons does not change truth in the book."

"You still betray our ancestors by accepting it."

"What if the old ways were missing the truth, and evil men who lived far from us were shown the truth and brought it to us? Does their corruption change the truth?"

Cody slurred, "No, but I hate them, look at what we're left with out here."

John sighed. "I know, but please don't allow your own hate to kill you. Love and freedom are through believing Jesus. Please don't make the mistakes I have made, letting this pain blind you from the truth. Please believe me. Following Jesus doesn't kill the Indian, Jesus strengthens us to rise above the hate, and believing does free us more than the old ways ever could."

Cody shook his head. "I have a hard time believing that. How can they claim they're following the Creator when they do nothing but hate and control people?"

"Don't let their actions blind you. Open your heart, ask to be shown the truth. You should speak to Elder Joyce about her awakening if you don't want to talk to Pastor Bluebird."

Cody placed his hand on John's shoulder. "Maybe one of these days I will. We will see each other again."

John smiled. "You're always my friend. We will see each other again."

Cody smiled and went away.

John walked to the supply store in deep thought and handed the chicken to Annabelle.

"What are you thinking about?" she asked.

John answered in Cherokee, "Nothing."

"You don't look like nothing is on your mind."

John shifted his gaze from Annabelle. "I have nothing to say."

Annabelle scowled. "Then go back home to the fields." She moved toward the back door.

"Don't be mad at me."

She looked back at John, her eyes narrowing. "Who said I was mad?"

She went outside and closed the door. John grunted and went home. Hours passed while John worked the fields with George, Jacob, Michael, and Samuel. While John put up the horses with Jacob, he heard Annabelle talking. John came out the barn and saw her under the redbud tree with Joseph.

John approached Annabelle and sat down next to her. "How did the rest of the day go?" he asked.

"It was okay, Mrs. Armstrong came by after you left. I was certain she was going to take Joseph home with her." Annabelle chuckled. "She was there for maybe thirty minutes playing with him."

John pulled a blade of grass. "I saw Cody today."

Annabelle's eyes widened. "We haven't seen him for over a month now. How is he?"

"He was drunk when I saw him. I tried to guide him to Jesus in some way, but I think I failed. He's lost and angry. I don't want to see him ruin his life like my father."

"Then we will keep praying for him and help him when we can. I don't want to see him destroy himself either."

John sighed. "He's a good man. I don't know how I can help him."

Annabelle gave a half-smile. "It isn't your place to save him. It is the Father's place. Trust him, and trust his timing."

"How are you so patient?"

"I think I learned from Grace, and I had to wait for you. It was worth the wait."

John grinned and put his arm around Annabelle as Joseph played in Annabelle's lap. The young couple watched a pronghorn herd and later went inside to join their family.

———◆———

When June 1852 arrived, John and Samuel prepared the wagon for their trip back to Mercy.

Annabelle handed John her letter. "Every time you and Samuel leave for Mercy, I wish I could go with you," she said in Cherokee.

"I hope one of these days you'll be able to visit with us," John replied.

Annabelle kissed John, and the men later rode off to Mercy.

CHAPTER 4
Hidden Struggles

A FEW DAYS LATER, THE YOUNG men arrived in Mercy, noticing the town's atmosphere had changed. The town's people seemed far less welcoming, but the men ignored the people and entered Mr. Boston's store.

"Well, there are two faces I expected to show up soon," Ruthanne said, standing in one of the aisles.

Samuel replied, "Mrs. Ruthanne, it's good to see you."

"It's good to see the two of you, and I'm glad y'all arrived when you did. I only work two days during the week now since I had the baby."

John replied, "Then good timing it is. I do have a letter for you from Annabelle."

"Good!" Ruthanne said as she walked to the counter and reached for her reticule. "I had decided yesterday to keep this letter with me until I saw you, John. Rebecca and Allen are gone with the children for two weeks on a political mission."

"How is your husband?" John asked.

"He is doing well. He has been busy trying to keep peace in the town with so much political tension here. It was hard enough for him to protect Marilyn and her baby boy. Thankfully, his color is lighter than Daniel's."

"We were going to Miss Marilyn's store after leaving here," Samuel said.

Ruthanne chuckled. "Marilyn is actually at my home watching my daughter Belle and her son Benjamin. Mr. Boston, are you feeling better now?"

Mr. Boston coughed, "I'm doing quite well now, Ruthanne."

John heard the landing of a walking stick as the older man moved toward the front of the store.

"Well, look who's here. John Lightning and Samuel Strongman, it is a blessing to see you boys," Mr. Boston said.

John replied, "It is good to see you, Mr. Boston."

"How are Annabelle and your sons doing?"

"They are well. Annabelle will be pleased to know you're doing good."

"Well, I'll return, Mr. Boston. I need to help them find Marilyn," Ruthanne said. "Mr. Fluffs, come here."

The large, green-eyed cat came trotting from the back and approached Ruthanne. She petted the long-haired cat's blotchy gray-and-white pattern and left the store, leading John and Samuel.

Ruthanne took the men to her home, a two-story brown brick house with two large living room windows.

"What a nice home you and Pastor Avail have," John said.

Ruthanne replied, "Thank you. Peter's father actually helped us pay for most of it. He was so excited we were getting married that he even bought us a horse. Well, come on in. I'm sure Marilyn will be surprised to see y'all." The three walked inside and heard the playful laughing of a toddler. "Marilyn!"

Marilyn walked out of the living room to the staircase. "John and Samuel, it's a surprise to see you!" she said.

A toddler ran to her and held her, laughing.

"Well, this is Benjamin. Say hi, Benjamin," Marilyn said.

"Hi," Benjamin said in a playful tone.

The men smiled at the hazel-eyed boy. "Daniel must be proud to be his father, that's Benjamin's father's name, right?" Samuel said.

The two women looked at John and Samuel with wide eyes.

"So we are clear, almost no one in this town knows Daniel

is the father," Ruthanne said. "Since Daniel is mulatto, it would put his life at risk. I should have known Annabelle would tell you. It must be different in Indian Territory."

John replied, "We're sorry for saying too much."

Marilyn replied, "No, no, it is fine. Thank you for kind words. Daniel is very fond of Benjamin."

Belle began to cry.

"Belle, is it time for you to be changed, or do you just want attention?"

"I'll get her," Ruthanne said.

Belle stopped crying once her mother picked her up and walked toward the men, taking off her white bonnet. "Here is my little nine-month angel, Belle," she said.

John replied, chuckling, "She has your eyes, Annabelle will be excited."

"One of these days I will come to Indian Territory. I would like to see her and your son."

John nodded. "At the right time I think that would be a good thing."

Ruthanne grinned. "Besides, I would like to share baby stories with Annabelle eventually."

The group laughed and talked for a short while. John later gave Ruthanne Annabelle's letter, and Ruthanne gave John her letter. The two men left with Marilyn and Benjamin, going to her store to get perfume for Annabelle and Lizzie.

◆

At the same time John and Samuel were in Mercy, Grace and Lizzie went to Elder Joyce. Lizzie's frequent nightmares had become too much for her, and she'd backslid into her old ways. The sisters were welcomed into the pine-scented home, and speaking in their native tongue, they were greeted inside with the smell of burning sage.

After the two sisters sat down, Joyce said, "Wildcat, I can feel the confusion in your spirit, the pain you keep pushing down in your soul. Learning the truth shocked me, but you come here split-minded, Lizzie Lightning...with your sister forcing you to come."

Lizzie replied, "I've prayed for release from my nightmares, but the day keeps replaying when I sleep. I can't sleep on my back anymore. I'm scared someone will try to choke me."

"You're looking for freedom from this terrible moment. Sometimes it takes time to heal spiritually from evil incidents like what you experienced. Do you feel guilt for what you did?"

Lizzie leaned forward. "I feel no guilt for what I did to those men." Her eyes shifted from Joyce to the ground. "But that's also what scares me...all I felt was anger and the desire for revenge. I don't remember all of it. That scares me the most."

"When I fought in that white man's war, I felt no pity for the men I fought against. I felt my strength only came from me and the love I had for my family. I had raised my children and much to their disagreement, I fought in that war for them. I've seen many evil things, and I have done many evil things as a warrior. Moments like those don't leave the mind easily."

Lizzie grabbed her braid. "I want to feel free from all of it. Every nightmare reminds me I could have died there, and my family would've never known what happened to me. I look at my nephews and the thought of not being able to hold them scares me."

"You must accept the truth. I believe that's part of the problem. You never believed that you would have to take a life. You protected yourself. But have you forgiven them?"

"I haven't forgiven them." Lizzie's voice deepened with each word. "They don't deserve forgiveness for what they did to me. How can I give them forgiveness when they deserved to die?"

"If you hold onto this sickness of unforgiveness it will destroy every part of your life. You will become a slave to hate, and the evil spirits will rejoice in your failure."

Lizzie's voice rose. "I don't want to say it was okay! What they did to me!" She wiped a tear from her face. "I can't be weak!"

Joyce folded her hands. "You have to let this go. Forgiving those men won't ignore the evil they did to you. It will free you to move forward. How can you love if you have so much anger in you? I have seen those eyes before, believing that being alone will protect you from experiencing pain."

Lizzie shrugged. "I don't want a man. I want nothing to do with men from this day, and every day after this! I don't need them or their love in my life."

Joyce's eyebrows slanted upward while she pinched a side of her mouth. She shook her head. "You can't even say that with a strong voice. It's your pride. Show what those men didn't show to you. Love, kindness, and respect."

Lizzie's gaze shifted to the floor.

"I'm so proud of you for fighting to control your anger."

Lizzie's eyes shifted back to Joyce and widened.

"Your sister is proud of you. Don't let all of that work be destroyed by your hurt pride."

Lizzie sniffled but tried to stop herself.

Joyce slapped her knee. "Enough of that…let go of that pain," Joyce commanded. "There's no shame in your crying here." Joyce stood up from her rocking chair and approached Lizzie.

Lizzie bit her lip. "I can't, I don't want to look weak. I'm tired of these white men coming to Tahlequah. I want them to leave."

Joyce held Lizzie's hands, and Lizzie stood before the old woman.

"We say this to free you," Elder Joyce said. "Not to excuse what those men did. Repeat after me, Lord forgive us our sins, for we also forgive everyone that's indebted to us. And lead us not into temptation, but deliver us from evil."

Lizzie repeated after Joyce. Tears broke free and poured down her cheeks.

"Let the anger and hate go…you have so much good in your heart. Don't let it be killed."

Lizzie held onto Elder Joyce and wept as Joyce hummed and embraced her.

"Grace, hug your sister," Elder Joyce instructed.

Grace hugged Lizzie, saying, "I love you."

Lizzie cried harder.

Elder Joyce picked up the burning sage. "I will say a prayer of healing and protection over you," she said.

Joyce prayed and waved the smoke over Lizzie and sealed the prayer in Jesus's name. Grace put her arm around Lizzie, who wiped her face again.

Seeing her actions, Joyce chuckled. She whispered under her breath, "That stubborn child...so determined to be seen as strong. Father, please help her understand her strength comes through you...not her pride."

Two days later, John and Samuel arrived back in Tahlequah with supplies and perfume for Annabelle and Lizzie.

"Welcome back. You look happy," Annabelle said in Cherokee.

John replied, "I am happy, I'm returning back to you and the boys. I believe this is what you're looking for."

John handed Annabelle her letter from Ruthanne. Annabelle kissed John and quickly went to the family house. Annabelle sat down at the supper table and placed a whining Joseph in her lap to calm him down.

She anxiously opened the letter from Ruthanne. The letter detailed the Keys' political involvement as abolitionists and told her that Mr. Jefferson, the church treasurer, had passed.

Annabelle felt sad when she read that Peter wasn't taking the old man's passing well, but it pleased her to know Marilyn and her son were doing well and that Elizabeth had left Mississippi with Robin. She sighed, feeling the loss of Mr. Jefferson.

"Rest in peace, Mr. Jefferson," she said.

CHAPTER 5
Molly

ONE DAY IN AUGUST OF 1852, Maria entered the supply store and spoke with Annabelle and Grace. Annabelle had grown fond of Maria and hoped Samuel would ask her to marry him soon.

As the young women talked to each other, a white woman wearing a red-and-white Victorian dress and white bonnet covering her ringlet-styled hair stepped into the supply store. It was uncommon for them to see a white woman in Tahlequah.

The young woman's green eyes widened when she entered. "Good afternoon, I wanted to purchase some flour," she said.

"I will see the two of you later today," Maria said.

"Bye, Maria," Grace said.

Maria walked past the white woman and left the store.

"I was told you Indians could speak English well in this store, but wasn't sure if the stories were true," the woman said.

Grace replied, "I speak English. My sister-in-law Annabelle speaks English too."

"How lovely, my name is Molly Hills. My husband Reverend Hills isn't far behind."

"That must be nice, having a reverend for a husband," Annabelle replied.

"Well, he is a servant of God. I think that's the best you can do. If you don't mind my asking, where are you from? Your English is surprisingly good."

"I'm from here; this is my home."

Molly lowered her eyebrows. "With a strong southern accent like that? I doubt it."

"Where are you and your husband from, if you don't mind my asking?"

"We're from Pennsylvania. We traveled from Tennessee."

Grace replied, "That's very far from here."

Molly replied, "You've been to Tennessee! That's quite surprising. I was told your people don't travel far."

Grace chuckled. "My family traveled through from Georgia when I was a child. That's why we have a southern accent. Something your people seem to forget easily."

"I remember hearing the stories, but I was too young to have seen it myself. It was a sad moment in our time."

Grace put her hand on her hip. "Why are you and your husband here?"

Molly smiled. "We're missionaries, and we've come to help spread the Lord's word, and help Indians become more civilized. Are the two of you believers in Jesus Christ?"

"Yes, we are. There is a Pentecostal church not far from here my family attends."

"That's good to hear. I hope my husband and I are able to help the rest of your people follow God and leave behind the old savage ways. It's necessary for the people to do everything civilized, for women to do what women are supposed to do and men to do what they're supposed to do. It is a simple way of life."

"I think your heart is in the right place, but you sound like every white person I have ever met. So quick to tell us what we're doing wrong. What will be next? Will you tell me my first language is uncivilized and shouldn't be spoken? You're welcome here, but there's a lot you need to learn."

Molly gave a half-smile. "Well, I guess that's a warmer welcome than what the Choctaws gave me. I never thought I would hear that from a tribe that supports slavery."

Grace bit her lip as she looked at Molly. "Though some of my people may support such evil, my family does not. Don't accuse us of such beliefs."

When Molly realized she had insulted Grace, she said, "My apologies, it's hard to determine who is for slavery and who isn't. The slaves here are much different than what I'm used to seeing in the South. The fact Annabelle felt so comfortable to speak to me is proof."

Annabelle replied, "I have gone through many things, Mrs. Hill. I have no interest in trouble."

"Please, call me Molly."

Lizzie entered the store with a dead hare. "Look what I caught, no chicken tonight," Lizzie said in Cherokee. Lizzie glanced at Molly and sneered. "I'm going home to cut him up now."

Molly put her hand to her chest and said, "My word, did she really bring in a rabbit from the wilderness like a savage? I see much work needs to be done here for some of the women."

"Who are you?" Lizzie asked in English.

Molly gasped. "You speak English, what a blessing! Well, I'm Molly Hills. I'm a missionary with my husband Reverend Hills."

"So few white women come here. I've only met ten over the years, and you make eleven. Maybe you're different than the others and might learn there is more to you than following your husband around and pushing out babies."

Molly's mouth dropped. "How can someone like you speak English so well but have such a rude nature!"

Lizzie smirked. "You know...if you want to spread the good word you can't be so weak. I'll see y'all at home." She turned and left the store.

Grace rubbed her forehead, saying, "My little sister. I'm sorry; she can be difficult sometimes."

Molly replied, "I must say she is a different character. I'm sure once she accepts Jesus, she'll be an entirely different woman. Plus some lessons in manners."

Annabelle and Grace grimaced as they looked at the naïve woman.

Reverend Hills later walked into the store, brushing his brown beard with his hand, and greeted them. "My, what a well-kept supply store," he said. "I hope my wife has kept all of you good company."

"She has been a pleasure," Grace said.

"Such good English as I was told earlier. Are you a woman of faith?"

"Yes, I am, Reverend Hills. All of us here are Christians."

"Well, I hope to spread the good word to all of Indian Territory. The Lord cares not about the color of his children's skin, but about the condition of their hearts and souls." His gaze fixed onto Annabelle. "Oh, you have a slave?"

"No, sir, this is my sister-in-law, Annabelle."

He brushed back his brown hair. "Well, that brings a smile to my face, and you are a beauty."

Annabelle grinned and replied, "Thank you, Reverend Hills. It's interesting to learn that you and your wife came from Pennsylvania. It must've been quite the adventure, sir."

His blue eyes widened. "Your speech is remarkable for a Negro woman. You give me even more hope that we can make a change. The more Indians we pull away from their old savage ways, the more peace and harmony we'll have in the land."

Annabelle's grin slightly dropped. "Well, I'm sure your intentions are good."

"Creating balance is the only way. Women have their roles of cooking, caring for children, and other house duties, while men should deal with the politics and providing."

"I'm guessing that means hunting too," Grace said.

"Well, yes, hunting is no place for a woman. There should never be a reason to use a weapon designed for a man."

Grace exhaled. "There's a lot you need to learn about my people, but I'm happy to have met you, Reverend Hills."

Reverend Hills smiled and adjusted his vest. "I do look forward to learning about your tribe. Is your husband the owner of your store?"

"I'm not married, and this is my family's store. We own it together."

"A family that's able to move as one is a beautiful thing. I do look forward to meeting more of your family."

"Oh, I've met her younger sister," Molly said.

"Is that so! I'm sure she's quite as welcoming as these ladies."

Lizzie's family quietly exhaled under their breath.

Reverend Hills continued, "Well, it's time to go eat a good lunch. You ladies have a blessed day."

"You too, Reverend Hills," the women said.

Reverend Hills turned to the front door, but then immediately looked at Molly. "Oh! Did you get what was needed, dear?"

"Yes, I have everything," Molly replied.

"Oh, good, good." Reverend Hills waved at the women and walked to the front door.

Molly waved at the young women with a big smile. "Have a good day."

"You too, Molly," the women said. Molly exited the store while Reverend Hills held the door. Annabelle's mouth curved up a little while she saw them leave even though Reverend Hills had demonstrated the same ignorance as his wife.

———◆———

As time passed, Annabelle gave water to the slaves. It became common for her to see the Hills on her way to the farms. Grace often traveled with Annabelle to be safe. The Indian agents kept the tension in Tahlequah, with their frustration over not finding who'd killed the two white men.

Pastor Bluebird preached to those in the church to put all worries on the Father and not allow the evil actions of others to change them. Annabelle worried that Lizzie wouldn't handle the pressure of keeping the secret, but Lizzie seemed happier.

Two days before Joseph's second birthday, Annabelle and Grace left to see Victoria. Victoria loved Joseph, and she welcomed Annabelle and Grace to her home to get a pair of pants she had made for him. She also wanted Annabelle to meet her cousin Eli Five Killer another old friend of the Lightning-Strongman family that had arrived from North Carolina.

Afterward, while the women went home with Joseph holding Annabelle's hand, they noticed Tsula and Lizzie in front of the family house. Both women were equipped to practice archery. Joseph ran ahead of the women to Lizzie and gave her a hug as she kissed him on the cheek.

"You stay here with Auntie Lisa," Lizzie said in Cherokee. "Me and Auntie Tsula have to go."

Tsula kissed Joseph on the cheek, and he ran toward Lizzie laughing. Lizzie picked him up.

"He's so precious when he runs to you," Tsula said. "That will change when he realizes how crazy you are."

Lizzie frowned. "Crazy, who are you calling crazy?"

Tsula smirked. "It isn't healthy to live in denial."

Lizzie smacked her lips, opened the front door, and put Joseph down. The toddler walked inside, and Lizzie closed the door.

"Keep talking," Lizzie said. "I see how you and Luke look at each other, and play stupid games with each other. Be careful. He might find another woman."

Tsula's nose crinkled, and her eyes narrowed as she glared at her cousin. She went back to the front door when Lizzie placed her bow in front of Tsula.

"Don't be that way," Lizzie said. "I didn't mean it."

Tsula turned around and went toward their practice grounds. "Hmph, I don't see why I have to come with you. I don't feel like doing this right now. Normally you go on your own, so why am I coming?"

"You haven't shot an arrow for fun since the spring, and maybe I want someone with me. And Lisa really wanted to spend time with Joseph," Lizzie said.

Tsula rolled her eyes.

"Hey, you two," Grace said as she and Annabelle slowly approached the house.

Tsula continued to the practice grounds. "I'm being kid-napped," she said.

"She whines more than Joseph," Lizzie said.

"No, I don't."

"Yes, you do."

"Whatever, Wildcat. I'll be sure to give your future husband a survival list when he's alone with you."

"Can't stand you."

Tsula looked back at Annabelle and Grace, who were about to go into the family house, with a big smile.

"Wildcat said she can't stand me," Tsula shouted. "I think I've won her love."

"I love you too." Lizzie rolled her lower lip to hold back a smile.

Annabelle and Grace laughed and went inside the house.

———◆———

Later in the day, Lisa played with the boys and decided to pre-pare things for supper. Lisa told her father that she was taking David with her to get water from the well, and she left Joseph with George. She smiled while she worked and felt comfortable leaving Joseph with George. She wondered if she would feel the same if she left her own children with George someday.

Lisa returned with the water buckets, allowing David to stay outside and play. She walked through the side door of the house and brushed off her blue calico dress. She slipped through the kitchen and heard George playing catch and laughing with Joseph.

"You're such smart little boy for a half-blood," George chuck-led. "I wish you hadn't gotten your momma's nappy hair. I don't know what your papa was thinking marrying your momma, but I guess that's what love does to people. I guess when I pass, I'll have to leave all I have to the others. I can't pass on property to a Negro. If you only looked more like your papa, we would be able to do such a thing. I hope my children don't make that mistake, bringing home a Negro. I love you, boy, but you're enough."

Lisa's heart dropped along with her dimpled smile, listening to her father, and she felt her emotions rise. Lisa took a deep breath and entered the living room with her arms stretched out. "Joseph, come here!" Lisa said in Cherokee, her voice playful. Joseph excitedly ran toward Lisa, and she picked him up. "I will be outside with the boys, Papa, until the others return to help me cook."

"Good, I hate sitting here for most of the day. My arm is feeling stronger now. I think I'll be able to go back into the fields and help them with the harvest tomorrow."

Lisa replied, "That's good, Papa."

"Lisa, Joseph...he is a smart boy. I should have known better, considering John, and Annabelle being so smart for a Negro."

"Did you think he would be dumb?"

"Well, no...just not completely like us, but I was wrong about him. He almost reminds me of Jacob."

"Yeah, good hearts are what should matter."

Lisa walked away as George sat back in his rocking chair, and he looked at his Cherokee Phoenix newspaper. He then frowned and stood up to watch Lisa with the boys.

❖

Days passed until it was time for Joseph's second birthday, and Maria joined them as a new member of the family. Maria and Samuel had gotten married two weeks before Joseph's birthday. Samuel temporarily moved in with Maria's family.

Celebrating Joseph's birthday, Annabelle sat at the supper table next to John, and Lizzie held Joseph in her lap. Everyone was excited to have Maria with them for the first time as a Strongman. Grace sat in her chair observing the cheerfulness of her family. Grace looked at Lizzie holding Joseph, hating the thought that their happiness was temporary, but she decided to let go of her worry.

❖

More than a month later, Lisa entered the large barn to feed the horses while George, John, and Samuel went hunting for wild game. As Lisa fed the horses, the barn door slowly opened, and Lizzie came inside.

"I should be out there with them hunting for you," Lizzie said. "Today is your birthday. You should have something else besides chicken or beef."

Lisa giggled, saying, "Let them have their way. It's my birthday...that's what I ask of you. Will you braid my hair before supper?"

"Yeah, I'll make two braids for you this time." Lizzie gave Lisa a hug and went back home.

Later in the day, Lisa returned to the barn to brush the horses as the other women prepared supper. While Lisa brushed Big Boy, the barn door opened and Jacob entered.

"Hey, beautiful," Jacob said in Cherokee. "Have you been enjoying your birthday?"

Lisa quickly approached Jacob with the horse brush in her hand. "What are you doing!" Lisa asked. "Did anyone see you walk in here?"

Jacob shook his head. "No, I'm sure nobody saw me walk in here."

Lisa walked past Jacob and cracked open the barn door, looking to see if anyone else approached. She crinkled her nose. "You have to be more careful, Jacob. I don't want to risk our being alone like this. My birthday has been a good day."

"What's wrong? You've been acting worried for a while. Are you nervous about telling your papa about us in January?"

"I don't think that's a good idea. I'm worried that my papa still isn't ready to learn the truth. I'm sorry."

Jacob frowned and came up to Lisa. "What makes you say this?"

"I heard him say something about Joseph, and it hurt. It really hurt to hear him say what he said, even though I know he loves Joseph. I'm unsure if he'll ever see him as Cherokee. If he sees Joseph that way, how will he look at our love for each other?"

"If you want to wait a little longer, I will wait with you, but I'm not going to remain silent if we reach five years together. I want you to give me some strong babies."

Lisa giggled and hit Jacob on his chest. "No, I told you I'm not giving you babies until we are seen as husband and wife. We had two scares. That's enough."

Jacob scoffed. "No, you had two scares. I was excited. I was hoping to see a good-looking Cherokee baby."

Lisa chuckled and pushed Jacob toward the door. "You need to leave, Jacob Tate." Lisa then kissed Jacob on his cheek. "Thank you for coming. Maybe later we will spend some more time together."

Jacob looked back and smiled. "I will always wait for you."

Lisa smirked and opened the barn door. "Fool me once, Jacob Tate. Those words won't work this time."

Jacob moaned and looked outside before he left the barn. Lisa followed and closed the barn door. She watched Jacob go home and went toward the large log cabin. When she was about to open the front door, Lizzie opened it.

"You have good timing," Lizzie said in Cherokee. "Look at you with your big smile, brushing the horses really means a lot to you."

Lisa shifted her gaze away from Lizzie's face. "It has always made me happy, you know that. Did the boys catch anything?"

Lizzie rolled her eyes and turned to walk away. "No, sorry, chicken will be our main meat again."

"It's okay, I'm sure y'all cooked it good." Lisa followed Lizzie inside.

The family later sat down for supper. They laughed together and talked about various things while Lisa kept replaying in her mind what Jacob said. As Lisa sat at the table with her family, she realized her father might never accept Jacob as someone she loves.

All I can do is hope and have faith Papa will open his heart.

On February 25, 1853, Eli greeted Grace as she left the supply store. As they strolled past Tahlequah's city hall, Grace noticed many of the council members leaving.

"Why are so many of the council here right now?" Grace asked in her native tongue.

Eli replied in Cherokee, "They must've had an emergency meeting."

"But for what purpose?"

Mr. Gross exited the courthouse to walk home.

"Eli," she said, "I need to speak with Mr. Gross. I feel like I need to ask him something."

"Tell me what you learn later. I can see you want to talk with him alone."

"Thank you for understanding."

Eli nodded and went away.

Grace immediately walked after Mr. Gross. "Mr. Gross, Mr. Gross."

Mr. Gross turned around and adjusted his black frock coat. "Ah, Grace, how are you today?" Mr. Gross asked.

"My day is going well. I noticed a lot of the council left. What's going on that so many of you would be leaving at the same time?" Grace asked.

Mr. Gross sighed. "I imagine you won't leave me alone until I tell you."

Grace grinned. "You know me well, Mr. Gross. Please tell me. It must be serious."

"Over the last two weeks three Cherokee children have been kidnapped, and we have no idea where they were taken to. All the kidnappings happened away from Tahlequah on the edge of our territory. One kidnapping was witnessed. White men took an eight-year-old girl, and they rode off with clothes covering their faces."

Grace's face twisted with a furrow forming in her brow. "Why haven't these terrible things been told to us? Why is the council keeping this quiet?"

"We're announcing it today, and it will be written in the *Cherokee Phoenix* to make our people aware. We are trying to keep the peace and keep the amount of fear our people will have low."

Grace scratched her head. "That's the dumbest answer to a problem I have heard. Tell the truth—you and the others are scared to speak out to the United States. Our children are being taken, and you want the people to be calm?"

"Grace, we have to cooperate with them. We have to, and that's the best solution we can come up with."

"How about getting some men and tracking them, or are you, Chief Ross, and the others scared to hunt down kidnappers? Do you think they took the children to the South?" Mr. Gross sighed. "What would make you think that?"

Grace's voice rose, "Where else could they get away with taking an Indian child? Those white people don't see much of a difference between us and Negroes. The council is too prideful to admit that truth until it's one of their daughters."

Grace turned and stormed away as Mr. Gross yelled, "In what way do you propose we stop this? In what political way do you propose, Grace Lightning, that we stop this?"

Grace turned back around with clear rage in her brown eyes. "There is nothing political that can be done. I say Luke and some good men should ride through and bring those children back home whether or not it takes a fight. The message needs to be sent clearly that we're not going to tolerate their hate anymore."

"If it were only possible to do such an act without encouraging the US army to come here in full force...we will do what the other tribes are doing. We will send a group of men through certain areas that may have the children, and we will bring them home."

Grace growled, "Those white men will never let those children go without a fight."

Grace walked away as Mr. Gross watched, scowling. Grace

later told her family, and they decided David and Joseph would never be allowed to play in the prairies away from home.

<hr>

Months passed with other changes affecting Annabelle and her family. In early March, Buck Scott and Nancy Hicks got married. Tsula found the marriage amusing, declaring that Nancy had rescued Grace from Buck's persistence. Grace attempted to avoid the topic, knowing it would give Tsula more to talk about.

During the spring, the Lightning-Strongman family decided to make another house next to the small one for Samuel and Maria. The construction of the house excited Annabelle because it meant having Maria close to the family, an answer to Annabelle's prayers. Tsula showed the most excitement about having her twin move back home.

As time passed life seemed to have calmed down for Annabelle. The bond between the young brothers seemed unbreakable, bringing joy to Annabelle's heart.

In June of 1853, Rebecca, Ruthanne, and Marilyn wrote to Annabelle in one letter, telling her all was well in Mercy. Rebecca also informed Annabelle she and Allen had now become committed to aiding the Underground Railroad, but this needed to remain secret for their safety. Annabelle understood the Keys were putting their lives at risk and prayed for them every night.

CHAPTER 6

The Good and the Bad

JULY 25, 1853 GREETED THEM with a strong summer breeze. Lizzie's more welcoming nature had returned, though Annabelle believed Lizzie's twenty-fifth birthday to be the cause. Lizzie spent most of the day with her nephews, wearing the new green-and-orange calico dress Tsula had made for her.

Before supper, Lizzie sat under the old redbud tree with the boys, and Annabelle wandered toward them. "David, Auntie Grace wants you for a moment, and take your brother with you," she said.

"Yes, Momma A," David replied.

Lizzie glanced at Annabelle and twisted her mouth. "Why did you send them away?"

Grinning, Annabelle sat down next to Lizzie.

"Why are you smiling?"

Annabelle took Lizzie's hand and placed it on her belly. "This is my birthday gift to you. It will arrive in a couple months."

Lizzie shrieked with excitement as she felt Annabelle's belly. "How far are you?"

Annabelle squinted. "I think three months, I haven't even told John yet. I started showing about two days ago."

"Well, let's go tell them. I want to see John's face when you tell him!" Lizzie quickly got up and grabbed Annabelle by the arm, forcing her up. "This time, it'll be a girl!"

Annabelle thought, *God, for my sanity let it be a girl. Let Lizzie have her way this time.*

Lizzie escorted Annabelle to the house with a big grin. "I know you must be excited. We'll have to cook extra for you."

The two young women entered the house and moved toward John, who sat at the supper table.

"Annabelle is pregnant again!" Lizzie exclaimed.

Annabelle's jaw dropped, and her eyes anchored sideways on Lizzie. She looked at John, shrugged, and smiled.

John and the rest of the family celebrated the exciting news with Lizzie's birthday. As the family ate supper, Lisa picked at her food and fed Joseph in her lap. Lisa locked eyes with Annabelle, forcefully grinning at her while she held Joseph. Annabelle understood Lisa's smile, and she hoped that Lisa would find love.

———◆———

A month later, Maria announced her pregnancy, and the family cheered and congratulated Maria and Samuel with hugs and kisses. Annabelle was especially excited to have some of the attention taken away from her.

Maria stayed home with Tsula, watching the boys and helping with washing clothes, sorting food supplies, and other house chores while Annabelle, Grace, and Lisa managed the supply store. Lizzie maintained her busyness, switching between the supply store and helping finish the new house.

Annabelle and Grace took Maria with them to the farms when they took water to the slaves. The experience was shocking for Maria, though she realized the slaves were not treated badly, and they walked home singing hymns.

The harvest festival arrived with the Lightning-Strongman family not only celebrating a good harvest, but also celebrating the completion of the new house for Samuel and Maria. As the celebration continued through the night, Annabelle noticed

Tsula and Lisa were constantly scanning the crowd for George, and Lisa kept drumming her fingers on her thighs.

"Hey, Lisa, come with me. I would like to talk with you," a Cherokee man said.

Lisa replied in Cherokee, "I have no time for you right now, Tony Fisher."

"How about we talk when I come by the supply store later to get some supplies for my father?"

The others looked at Lisa as they ate corn on the cob. "We always talk, Tony."

"I know, but not—"

"Tony, you're good man, but now isn't the time for you to want to spend time with me. There may never come a time. So please stop chasing me."

Annabelle and the other women looked at Lisa with wide eyes.

Tony nodded and went away.

"Lisa, you could have said that better," Tsula said. "You're not getting any younger. You almost sounded like Lizzie for a moment."

Lizzie glared at Tsula with narrowed eyes.

Lisa's brow lowered, her nose crinkled, and her voice erupted with a growl, "I'm worried about Papa. We messed up losing him in the crowd. He has been doing so well not drinking as much. I don't think he can handle this alone. We should have made him stay home."

Tsula replied, "He would've never stayed home. If we had done that it would have only angered him. Please try to be patient. Worrying about it will only make you uglier."

Lisa chuckled while she folded her arms.

"Aw, there's a smile, but you know I'm still the most beautiful, right?" Tsula said.

Lizzie scoffed. "Please, maybe if you stopped wearing your hair in twin buns like a white woman you would be something to look at."

Tsula side-eyed and smacked her lips at Lizzie, and the women cackled.

Toward the end of the festival, John and Samuel found George drunk and talking to other drunken Cherokee. George shouted his excitement with others, embarrassing the cousins. John and Samuel helped George return home. The men followed the family closely.

"Ah, my boys, my boys," George slurred in Cherokee. "John, you marry a Negro woman, and, Samuel, you marry a Mexican. I never would've predicted such a thing, but your mothers would have loved the women y'all have chosen. You boys do make me proud. You both grew up to be better men than me."

"You're a good man, Dad," Samuel said.

George shook his head. "I'm a broken man, the Father knows I am. I have a Negro for a nephew, and now I'm going to be a grandpa to a half-breed. I wonder if Michael is going to continue the path the two of you have created. It looks like only the women will be marrying Cherokee." George chuckled and coughed.

The men finally arrived home and helped George inside.

"I love them," George said. "John, I love your boy. He is a smart boy; he'll do good for this family."

John replied in Cherokee, "I know you do, Uncle George. I know."

The men escorted George into his room. Tsula and Lisa folded their arms at the sight of him, then went into their room. Samuel later went to his house with Maria, and John went home.

<hr>

John entered his bedroom, met with Annabelle sitting on the bed with her legs and arms crossed. He knew immediately she wanted to talk.

"Well, everyone has gone to sleep. It's going to be a busy day tomorrow," he said.

"Is that right?" she said.

"Yeah, everyone is tired." John avoided eye contact with Annabelle.

He put on his pajamas, and she moved to the head of the bed. John got in the bed next to Annabelle, kissing her on the cheek before lying down.

Annabelle crossed her arms. "I heard what George said."

John sighed and sat up.

"I don't like him referring to our son as the Negro. What will he be calling this baby?"

"You didn't hear everything he said."

She frowned. "I heard enough, John. Joseph is half Cherokee, despite what the laws say. All Joseph knows is being Cherokee."

He sighed. "Uncle George loves Joseph...I know he does have a lot to still work on, but he loves our son. I will tell him not to call Joseph that, and as for the new baby, I'll remind him not to make that mistake."

Her voice deepened, "He better not call him that again, John Lightning. I'm not playing. I'll tolerate him calling him a half-blood like Samuel's and Maria's baby but not Negro. Joseph has a better chance than I did, and I don't want him feeling less important than other family members."

John wrapped his arm around Annabelle. "That will never happen. I promise you that will never happen. I won't allow it. Grace won't allow it, and Lizzie definitely won't allow it. Let's get some sleep. It has been a long day."

She kept looking forward with her arms crossed.

"I promise I'm taking this seriously. Let me hold you until you fall asleep," John requested.

Annabelle unfolded her arms and looked at him. "All right, but George better not make that mistake again."

Annabelle kissed her husband and lay her head on his chest. He sighed, and she fell asleep as he ran his hand over her braided hair.

✦

As time passed, Annabelle and Maria spent much of their time enjoying each other's companionship and seeing their bodies change. A week after Grace's birthday all the women sat in the living room in front of the fireplace and braided each other's hair as David and Joseph played.

Annabelle heard the boys moving the chairs at the supper table around. "Boys, please be careful. I don't want nobody hitting their head on the table again," she said.

Tsula giggled while she undid Annabelle's braids. "Do you hear that, Maria?" she asked. "That will be you in a few years."

The women laughed as Lizzie kept looking back at the boys while she braided Grace's hair.

"So, Grace, you're almost thirty," Tsula said. "I see the way you look at Eli."

Grace critically replied, "Tsula, you're always focused on others. You need to stay focused on your business."

Tsula sarcastically replied, "I do focus on me, but all of you are a part of me. So learning what's going on in your hidden lives is my business."

"You never do know when to shut your mouth," Lizzie said, with her voice deepening and head cocked. She leered. "You need to focus on your play toy like I told you earlier."

"Luke Fields isn't my play toy. I always knew he wanted me. I didn't want the attention at the time," Tsula proudly said. "I'm the most beautiful after all." She rubbed her palm against her cheek and grinned.

The other women laughed hysterically as Tsula braided Annabelle's hair.

"So, Lisa...why do you keep pushing Tony away?" Tsula said. "He's not bad for a man."

Lisa glanced at her sister. "I don't have an interest in him, and that's the end of that story."

"She's guarding herself, meaning there is someone on her mind...who is it?"

Lisa ignored Tsula as she braided Maria's hair.

"You know, Annabelle, that's how Lisa always avoids speaking the truth, by not saying anything at all."

"Shut up, Tsula, for once act like a grown woman," Lisa growled.

Tsula side-eyed Lisa and scoffed. "I'm acting like a grown woman! You're the one that's being childish not telling the truth. It's not like the guy is ugly. I know you, we all know you. Sweet Lisa, mm-hmm, as if you would let any man into your life."

Lisa looked away from Tsula, clenching her teeth while she finished Maria's hair.

"Umm, Tsula, please don't make her mad while she's finishing my hair," Maria said.

"I'm sorry, Maria! Please tell me if I'm making the braids too tight," Lisa said.

Tsula smirked as she looked at Lisa.

"No more of this talk for the day, Tsula," Grace said. "There are other things we can talk about, like baby names for the two new babies."

"Yes, tell us if the two of you have any names for the babies," Lizzie excitedly said.

Annabelle replied, "Well, I do have a few names. I've been thinking about. I don't know if the baby is a boy or a girl."

"What are you hoping for, Annabelle?" Maria asked.

Annabelle sighed deeply and patted her belly. "I want a girl. I think David and Joseph are enough."

The women laughed, and Maria replied, "I'm with you, Annabelle. I want my first to be a girl, though I know Samuel wants a son. I'll give him a son later."

"I hate to say this, but I think you're having another boy, Annabelle," Grace said. "Look how big you are now. The two of you are only about a month apart, but you're huge compared to Maria."

Annabelle moaned.

"I'm sorry...maybe I'm wrong, though."

"Wouldn't be the first time," Lizzie said. "She told our momma I was going to be a boy."

"She wasn't completely wrong," Tsula replied.

The women laughed, but Lizzie gritted her teeth and rumbled while she glanced at Tsula.

Joseph walked to Annabelle and placed his head on her belly.

"You don't care if you have a new baby brother or sister," Annabelle said as she looked at Joseph. "You want someone new to play with. Well, you'll have two new babies to play with."

"Can I hold the babies when they come?" Joseph asked.

"You can, but not alone."

Joseph smiled and ran back to David. The women smiled at Joseph and talked among themselves. Joseph's excitement warmed Annabelle's heart. It gave her more hope if something happened to her. Joseph still had a family who loved him and would protect him.

The year 1853 ended with moderate tension among the Cherokee people. The kidnapping of Cherokee children remained a serious concern. The Seminole reported forty-seven kidnappings. The Choctaw now reported sixty missing children believed to have been kidnapped by white men, and twenty-four now were taken away from the Natchez. The Creek also reported white men, claiming some of the people were runaway slaves, raided one of their mixed towns. The Creek council met with the Cherokee, confirming the town was attacked at night with some half-blood Negroes taken, but most of the kidnappings were children, making it seventy-six known kidnappings now haunting the nation.

———◆———

On the evening of March 19, 1854, Paul entered the supply store as Annabelle and Grace resupplied their inventory.

"Good evening, Miss Annabelle, Miss Grace," he said.

"Hello, Paul. How are you doing?" Grace asked.

Paul grinned. "I'm doing good, Miss Grace."

"Paul, that's enough from you for now," Nancy said, stepping inside as she held her daughter. "Give them the list of supplies we need. You know I don't like being out long with Eve."

"She's a beautiful girl, Nancy," Grace said.

"Thank you, Grace," Nancy replied. "Though it's hardly a surprise Eve would be as beautiful as she is now. I'm surprised you don't have your boy with you, Annabelle."

"The boys are at home," Annabelle said.

"I find it so interesting, your calling David your own," Nancy said with a lifted eyebrow. "I'm sure Camille would be excited, seeing her son calling a pregnant Negro woman mommy. You look like you're due any day now with this new one."

Annabelle smiled, although the expression didn't reach her eyes. "I was hoping having a child would kill some of your bitter mouth. Maybe a good slap in the face would help your progression."

Nancy stared at Annabelle as she cuddled a sleeping Eve.

"Enough, Paul. Give me the list," Grace commanded.

He gave her the list, and she read it as Annabelle and Nancy glared at each other with contempt.

"All right, Lisa, come out of the storage room," Grace said. "I know you can hear us."

Lisa exited the storage closet with her dimpled grin etched across her face. "Hello, Nancy, she is a beautiful girl."

Grace replied, "Here's the list. Show Paul what to grab, and Annabelle, she needs one chicken."

Nancy spoke with a snobbish tone, "Yes, please hurry. I would like to have this done before she wakes up. Annabelle, one chicken...just one."

Annabelle narrowed her eyes at Nancy, then went to the chicken coops, struggling to control her anger.

She went back into the supply store carrying the chicken by its feet, marching to Nancy's wagon. Paul opened up a small chicken cage, and Annabelle put the chicken inside.

"My...that chicken looks so mad, Miss Annabelle," Paul said.

"The chicken knows what's coming," Annabelle said. "You wouldn't be too happy if you were the chicken, Paul."

"I guess I wouldn't be happy, Miss Annabelle. You look like you ready to have this baby."

"This is my last day working at the supply store, and yes, I'm ready to have this child. John is so nervous, he nearly walked with me more than half the way to the store today."

Paul grinned. "He's a good man. I see how he treat you. How is Miss Lizzie?"

"Lizzie is fine. Do you want me to tell her you asked about her?"

"Oh, no, no, I wanted to know 'cause she looked mad the last time I saw her. Pretty women like herself shouldn't be so mad."

Annabelle smiled. "I will let her know you wanted to know how she was doing. She will appreciate it."

Paul shyly nodded and got into the wagon while Nancy waited. The wagon rode away, and Annabelle stepped inside the supply store, giggling to herself as she thought about Paul's kindness.

CHAPTER 7

An Answer to an Abandoned Prayer

THREE WEEKS PASSED, WITH ANNABELLE becoming more excited about the pregnancy. Joyce visited her each day, and she later told Annabelle of the strong possibility that she was carrying twins. The news wasn't well taken by Annabelle, and she wanted to know if there was a way to put her into labor immediately. Joyce assured Annabelle the babies were fine.

On April 17, 1854, Joyce took another stroll to the Lightning-Strongman home and saw Lizzie running toward her.

"I'm coming, Lizzie," the older woman said in their native tongue. "Did y'all get things ready for the babies?"

"Babies?" Lizzie replied.

"I'm sure Annabelle is pregnant with twins. Hopefully this goes quickly. Usually, experienced mothers deliver faster." Joyce rushed into the large house and marched into the women's bedroom, immediately noticing Annabelle's rapid breathing and widened eyes. "Annabelle, baby, you need to remain calm. Every thought that's creating doubt, I need you to kill it."

"I never thought I would give birth to twins," Annabelle whined. "The pain is getting stronger, and I have to push out two!"

"Let go of that fear, Annabelle! You're strong enough for this. Look at who is around you right now. Your family. No more of this 'I never thought.' The Father has given you something special."

Annabelle took deep breaths. Her labor progressed throughout the day, and the time arrived for her to push. Joyce and Grace coached her, and eventually, they heard the strong cry of a baby.

"It's a girl," Grace said.

Joyce cut the umbilical cord, and Grace handed the infant to Lizzie.

Annabelle wiped away a tear and said, "A girl."

"There's the other head—push, Annabelle!" Joyce said.

Continuing to push, Annabelle moaned in agony. She rested a few minutes and then pushed again.

"Annabelle, one more push," Grace said.

Annabelle strained, and out came the other baby, this one quieter than its sister.

"It's a girl! Two girls, Annabelle!" Grace exclaimed.

Annabelle wept as Joyce cut the umbilical cord and Grace cleaned her off.

John came in, and Lizzie handed him his daughter.

"She's beautiful," Lizzie said in Cherokee.

John's eyes teared as he smiled and knelt next to Annabelle, who held the other newborn girl. "You're truly a strong woman."

Annabelle wiped tears of joy from her face as she held her daughter. "Look how God has blessed us. Two girls...I lost my first two, and then I'm blessed with twins with you."

John's lips quivered. He stared into Annabelle's elated brown eyes.

"Do you want the boys in here now?" John asked.

"Yes, tell them to come quickly, but everything needs to be cleaned up."

"Boys come here, come meet your new sisters."

David came in the room holding Joseph's hand. The boys had big smiles as they looked at their new baby sisters. David held the hand of one of his sisters while Annabelle cradled her, and Joseph kissed the other sister on the forehead as John held her.

"Will they be like Auntie Lizzie?" David excitedly asked.

Everyone including Lizzie looked at David with big eyes.

"They'll be who the Father has made them to be, and it is their choice to follow that path," Joyce said. "Who knows, they might be a little like Auntie Lizzie."

"All right, that's enough. We have to give Momma A time to rest, and give them names," John said.

While exiting the room, the boys' mouths curved upward into big grins, and George looked into the room.

"My goodness, more girls," George said. "I see now the boys are not catching up at all after this."

Everyone chuckled.

George approached the twins. "Beautiful baby girls. Have you decided on names?"

Annabelle answered, "I have thought about it and talked to John, though he wants me to name them. The oldest is Rain. John is holding her. I will give the boys something to be happy about with her younger sister. I will name her Jannie since the boys kept calling my belly Jan. Rain will bring life wherever she goes, and Jannie is the quiet storm."

George smiled. "I like those names." He walked out to the living room and sat down in his rocking chair.

"Look at all that hair...too adorable," Tsula said. "Looks like some more hair to be braided later."

"Yeah, I'm a bit surprised by that," Annabelle said. "Look at them. Ready for the world."

Once Annabelle felt rested, she carried Rain to the small house, while John carried Jannie. Joy consumed Annabelle at being blessed with two beautiful twin girls. Rain wore a white gown, and Jannie wore a red one, both knitted by Tsula.

Annabelle sat in the bed cradling both of the twins. John watched, captivated by the beauty of his daughters and his wife.

"How are we going to tell the difference between them?" he

asked in Cherokee. "I think Rain will have to wear that white gown for most of her life."

Annabelle laughed as she looked at John with joyful eyes. "We give them time to be who they are, and I'm sure they each won't like being mistaken for the other. But I agree. For now, I think Rain needs to be kept in white so we know who is who."

A month passed, with David's tenth birthday and the birth of Rosita, Maria and Samuel's daughter. The twins grew healthy and more active. Caring for twins was a real challenge for Annabelle, though the family helped her. Annabelle was determined to remain as scheduled on breastfeeding to reduce stress. She learned the twins fell asleep quicker if they were both in the same crib. She was eager for the girls to sleep through the whole night.

One day in early June, Victoria came by to visit Lizzie. She entered the small house and was joyfully welcomed by Annabelle.

"Look at those beautiful girls," Victoria shrieked in Cherokee. "Wow, they both have John's eyes, and...and...oh, they really don't look much like you at all, Annabelle!" Victoria covered her mouth, and her eyes bulged. "Oh, no, I'm sorry, Annabelle. I didn't mean that in a bad way. I'm just surprised."

"No, it's okay. I said the same thing two weeks ago," Annabelle said. "They have a lighter color than Joseph, and they favor David a lot more. Even their hair is different than my own. I have no idea what I'm going to do with twin girls with long hair, just feeling how smooth their hair is and seeing how much they have already. God help me."

Victoria and Lizzie giggled, looking at the twins.

"I'm sure Tsula will have a fun time with them," Victoria said. "They look so attractive! Can I pick one of them up?"

"Yeah, but be quick. It's close to their nap time. Here, you can hold Rain. She's got some good weight on her."

Annabelle reached into the crib to pick up Rain and handed her to Victoria. Rain cooed as Victoria held and danced around with her.

"This makes me want to get married; what about you, Lizzie?" Victoria asked.

"You only say that because you don't live with them," Lizzie replied. "I can hear all three babies crying at night all the way in my room."

"Poor Auntie Lizzie, are the girls tiring you already?" Victoria teased.

"Shut up, you always have something to say. When they get old enough, I think I will teach them how to hunt."

"Well, look at that...she is so quick to complain but wants them to spend time with her."

Annabelle and Victoria chuckled while Lizzie sat down in a rocking chair trying not to smile. Lizzie and Victoria later left the house when the twins fell asleep. Annabelle was pleased with Victoria's visit and then took the opportunity to take a nap.

In mid-June of 1854, John and Samuel made their trip to Mercy with letters being exchanged between John and Ruthanne. Annabelle wrote her letter, revealing the exciting news that she had given birth to twin girls, and she called them the blessing that was more important than her past pain.

Ruthanne wrote that Rebecca and Allen had given their blessings to Annabelle, and Allen signed his name on the letter. Marilyn had also included a brief note telling her that Allen had been teaching Daniel how to read and write, and they were expecting their second child. Annabelle loved the news but wished she could see them.

Lisa would often trade places with Lizzie and help Annabelle and Maria with the babies. She also worked with the horses and had Jacob visit the twins and Rosita. Watching Jacob interact with the twins fulfilled her and helped to build up the courage to tell her father about their relationship.

Annabelle noticed how Lisa looked at Jacob as he interacted with the babies, and he seemed to love making them laugh. Annabelle had seen this before, but she wondered if Lisa had told Jacob how she felt about him.

In early September, Annabelle returned to the supply store to help Grace and Lizzie. The twins were distracted with the rattles John had brought them from Mercy, and Lizzie's constant interaction. One day, Lizzie noticed Paul driving Nancy to the supply store as she returned there. Lizzie attempted to walk past when Paul stepped around the wagon, but he placed his hand on her shoulder.

"Miss Lizzie, you sure working hard today," he said.

"Don't touch me," Lizzie snarled. "Don't touch me unless I say it's okay. I don't like men touching me."

He stepped back, his eyes downcast.

She sighed heavily. "Look, Paul, when I say don't touch me, it's not because you're mulatto."

"Is there a problem?" Nancy griped.

"No, ugly, there isn't a problem." Lizzie snapped back, storming into the supply store. Upon entering the store she heard Nancy command Paul to help her down with Eve, and she took another deep exhale at the sound of Nancy's voice.

Nancy entered the store, and Eve's hazel eyes glanced around.

"Lizzie Lightning, that was rude and truly uncalled for," Nancy bickered.

Grace looked at Lizzie, and her sister kept silent.

"At least attempt to show some manners while I have Eve with me," Nancy said. "I don't want my daughter picking up some of your disgusting habits."

"I'm sure she'll do quite well, Nancy," Lizzie said, her voice dripping with sarcasm. "How funny she has Buck's hazel eyes, must be a relief to you."

"Lizzie," Grace said.

Nancy clenched her teeth and glared at Lizzie, her blue eyes furious. "You're a constant thorn in my side, Lizzie Lightning."

Rain woke up and cooed.

"Wait a moment...whose babies are those?" Nancy asked.

"They are my new nieces. You missed them since you and Buck decided to make a trip to Tennessee," Grace said.

Nancy's jaw dropped. "Nieces...what do you mean missed them?"

Grace replied, "You know, Annabelle was pregnant. Well, she had twins. It's only been a short time since she's returned to the church."

Nancy approached the cradle and looked at Rain and Jannie. "Impossible, there's no way they're the offspring of Annabelle Lightning. I refuse to believe such a thing."

"Why would you say something like that?" Lizzie asked, agitation coloring her voice.

Nancy scoffed. "Don't play dumb with me, Lizzie. In what way do these babies look like the children of a Negro? Even their hair resembles nothing of Negro blood. How is this possible?"

Lizzie folded her arms. "Is it so hard to believe, Nancy? Annabelle isn't an ugly woman. If it makes you feel any better, they do have her smile."

Nancy rolled her eyes. "John must be proud he has two new children actually representing the tribe."

Lizzie raised her voice, "Joseph represents our people; he is Cherokee."

Nancy scoffed. "A child born to a Negro mother isn't a Cherokee, though it is tempting to call these two here somewhat Cherokee."

"My nieces will represent the tribe far more than your daughter ever could with her hazel eyes. It must bother you seeing two half-bloods more beautiful than your daughter."

"Lizzie, you—"

A sudden squeak from the door caught everyone's attention as Annabelle came inside, sweeping chicken feathers off her dress.

"Ah, these are your daughters?" Nancy asked.

Annabelle replied, "Yes, Rain and Jannie are their names."

Nancy sneered. "Interesting names. Well, I didn't come here

for this. Paul, stop standing over there like a statue and give Grace the list."

"Here is the list, Miss Grace," Paul said, handing Grace the list.

"Thank you, Paul," Grace said. "I see you've decided to keep your hair cut lower this year."

Paul blushed. "Well, yes, ma'am. I think it makes it easier to be strong in the heat. I got my father's hair, so it brushes real good."

Nancy sneered. "Enough; I don't have time for this."

"Lizzie, here is the list. Tell Paul what to grab," Grace said.

Grace handed Lizzie the list, and Lizzie looked at it while she entered the supply room. "I can take this to the wagon myself," she said.

Nancy mockingly chuckled, saying, "That's so you, Lizzie. Instead of having my slave do his job, you insist on doing things the hard way. Still a brute...as always."

Lizzie exited the supply room carrying a sack of beans. "Keep talking, blue eyes," she irritably said.

Nancy pressed her lips together as she held Eve, watching Lizzie go outside with Paul. "Well, I do think it is time for me to leave. I won't lower myself in front of my daughter for Lizzie's amusement. You have beautiful daughters, Annabelle. Maybe they will have a better chance than you, seeing that they look like Indian children."

Annabelle forced a smile while she and Nancy locked eyes. Nancy walked out to the wagon as Annabelle and Grace watched.

"I cannot stand that woman some days...such a bitter witch," Annabelle said.

"I think she'll always be a person that will test all of us," Grace said. "I'm proud of you, though, you didn't say something back to her that was mean. But Lizzie...well, at least she didn't grab Nancy by her hair, so I guess that's improvement."

Annabelle and Grace chuckled.

However, throughout the day, Nancy's words seeped into Annabelle's mind. She already accepted that Joseph would have a harder life than the girls, but she felt Joseph would still have a better life than she did. The thought of teaching her daughters to lie about their heritage terrified Annabelle, but if it meant protecting them, she would do so.

The differences between her children were made painfully obvious. She decided to keep the thought from the children, not wanting Joseph to feel less than his siblings. She later went to Joyce, seeking counsel with what to do about their differences.

Joyce acknowledged the truth that people would treat them differently. However, the older woman also encouraged Annabelle to remain strict in treating all of the children the same.

Annabelle later went to Pastor Bluebird, again expressing her concerns. He reassured Annabelle he would make sure Joseph wouldn't be treated different than the other children, but he warned her to prepare Joseph to be treated differently. She left the church more encouraged but dreading the day she'd have to teach Joseph.

One day in December, David and Joseph ran outside to play in the snow while John and Samuel cut firewood. The young boys played with snowballs. David wanted to end the playing because he got cold.

"No more snowballs, Joseph. We need to go inside so we can get warmer," David said in Cherokee.

"No, I want to play," Joseph replied.

"We can play again later. Come inside."

"No," Joseph whined.

"Come with me now. I promise we'll play later."

Joseph pouted. "You're not Momma. You can't tell me what to do."

"I'm older than you. I can tell you what to do! Now we're going inside...Momma can make us some soup."

David marched to Joseph, grabbed his arm, and dragged Joseph to the log cabin as Joseph screamed.

"Forget it, you big baby. I will eat all the soup. You will get nothing." David let go of Joseph and marched away.

Joseph stood, and his jaw dropped. He reached into the

snow, then threw a snowball at David, hitting him in the back of the head.

"That hurt, Joseph!"

"You can't have all the soup," Joseph said.

David ran after his brother.

Joseph tried to run, but David caught Joseph and forced his face into the snow.

"Stop it! I want Mommy!"

David yelled, "You eat the snow if you want the soup that bad! Eat it!"

"I don't want to eat it! Mommy! I want Mommy!" Joseph cried.

"Shut up."

Suddenly, Annabelle grabbed David and gave him two smacks on his butt with the whipping stick.

David yelped and tried to rub out the pain.

"David, don't ever do that to your brother," Annabelle yelled in Cherokee. She felt Joseph's face as David frowned. "His face is cold. That's enough play time."

David replied with a low growl, "I told him we needed to come inside, but he kept fighting me."

"That's the end of it, David. You're stronger than your brother. You still have to be careful with him at all times. Come inside. I have soup ready to eat."

Annabelle followed the boys inside, where they sat down at the table and ate their soup. Joseph was back to being his normal carefree self, but Annabelle noticed how quiet David was as he ate.

"Joseph, you ate good like a big boy, so you can run to the big house by yourself to play with Auntie Grace."

Joseph shrieked with excitement, running outside and down the snow trail to the big house while Annabelle watched, then returned inside the house.

"I'm done. Can I go back outside?" David said.

Annabelle sat down next to David and moved his bowl. "David, what's wrong? You haven't spoken to your brother," she said.

"He didn't get in trouble like me. He threw a snowball at the back of my head, and it hurt, but I got spanked. He never gets punished like me."

Annabelle put her arm around David. "I'm sorry, next time you tell me the whole story, okay? I love you and I love your brother. I don't want to see the two of you hurting each other. You're a good older brother. I want to see you keep being a good older brother."

David hugged Annabelle and began to cry.

"I know it looks like me and your papa are unfair, but Joseph is still learning. So we have to treat him differently than you, but we love you the same."

"I love you too, Momma A."

Annabelle kissed David on his forehead as she held him. Before supper, Annabelle told John what had happened. Though John took it as boys rough playing, he understood he needed to talk with David. After supper, John went back to the big house, and Annabelle put the twins down to sleep.

John entered the boys' room, looking at David and Joseph playing with each other. "Michael, you were supposed to be telling them to go to sleep," he said.

Michael replied, "I always let them play a little before bed."

"I guess that works. Take Joseph outside for a moment. I need to talk to David."

"Let's go, Joseph."

Joseph got out of his bed and hugged John. John placed his hand on Joseph's head, and then Michael escorted Joseph from the room.

John sat down next to David. "I want you to know I'm proud of you. Auntie Lizzie says that you're reading good now."

"She said that?" David said with a smile. "Auntie Lizzie also said she would teach me how to shoot an arrow if Auntie Grace doesn't."

John looked at David with raised eyebrows. "Um...we will wait a little longer for that. Momma A told me what happened earlier today with you and Joseph. I know right now you and

Joseph will disagree about many things, but the two of you are brothers. He is your younger brother, and part of the job of being an older brother is protecting your younger brother and sisters. Just as it is my job to protect you, Momma A, Auntie Grace, and Lizzie, and everyone in our family. Can I trust you to do that?"

David frowned and looked away from John. "Yes, Papa, you can trust me."

"Why do you look so sad?"

"Momma A gave me two hits but didn't give Joseph any."

John chuckled. "I understand. I used to feel the same way when your Auntie Lizzie would do bad things, and your grandma didn't punish her." John's brow lowered. "There were a lot of times… I'll tell you this. Life isn't always fair. When Joseph gets old enough, I promise he will be getting punished for doing the wrong things. I'm sure there will be a few moments to laugh, but don't laugh at him."

David laughed, and John gave him a hug.

"I love you, Papa," the young boy said.

"I love you too, David. You're a strong boy."

The Lightning-Strongman family lived through another winter, struggling to help supply the poorer people of the tribe. Grace became discouraged, but Eli Five Killer kept her spirit high.

One day in May 1855, Annabelle took the twins with her to the supply store. Lizzie, Maria, and Tsula stayed home to take care of the other children. As Annabelle, Grace, Lisa, and the twins went to the supply store, Rain happily held her mother's hand as they walked, and Grace held Jannie's hand.

Sitting on their horses, Brock Jackson and Hunter Sawyer watched the family. Ignoring all the other Cherokee passing, Brock slowly made his horse trot forward and stop.

"Those two half-breeds that free Negro woman Annabelle gave birth to surprise me," Brock said.

"I don't believe I have seen a cross quite like those children," Hunter said. "Those girls are just over a year."

"When those half-breeds were bred, I was certain eventually

they would look like their mother. Both of those girls already have hair reaching their shoulders and their father's color. These Cherokee become weaker and weaker with their stance on the Negro."

Hunter sneered. "I'm concerned with these two half-breeds. They truly represent the change in Cherokee society. How much longer before we see more children like that? It's near impossible to tell them from the full bloods. I believe more runaway slaves will try this."

"For now, we have no say in this matter. If the Cherokee cannot control their men from being nigger-lovers, it will bring their destruction faster and have them begging us for a solution. These prairie niggers make laws a white man must go through to marry a Cherokee woman, but here we have them making babies with Negro women with little to no words spoken about it."

Hunter rubbed his chin. "I think it's these powerful families allowing Negroes into their bloodlines creates the biggest problem. How can they become more civilized having so many with the blood of a savage and the mind of a Negro? Impossible for them to survive if this continues."

"If these missionaries don't push them further west, they might breed with these Negroes so much they'll end up in chains one day."

Hunter scoffed. "We should continue to encourage them to make their status more clear with the free Negroes."

"No, our concern is all about order and keeping the peace. I'm more surprised with these Indian women willing to birth these half-breeds with Negro men. It's sickening. At least find a good Indian man or do better and get a white man who can raise prominent children."

Hunter shrugged. "Well, the Cherokee have shown some of this."

"Chief Ross is a fool, a Cherokee-Scottish fool. I want to keep more of an eye on the Lightning family. There is something different about them."

"Are you sure that you're not still upset with Lizzie Lightning for getting a faster draw on you?" Hunter teased.

Brock smirked. "I assure you it's not that, Hunter, but I'm certainly looking for a rematch with that smart-mouthed woman. She still needs to be taught some lessons."

The men rode off through Tahlequah, and the Lightning-Strongman family remained unaware of how much interest the family held for the Indian agents.

CHAPTER 8
Thankful

SUMMER ARRIVED HOTTER THAN IT did the previous year, giving spark to a wildfire. The fire was intense, and as a precaution, the Lightning-Strongman family moved a few of their belongings to Victoria's family farm.

Much to the family's relief, a strong thunderstorm stopped the wildfire. The abrupt nature of the fire postponed John and Samuel's trip to Mercy.

On June 23, 1855, the cousins prepared the wagon, and Michael joined them to celebrate his twentieth birthday. The men rode to Mercy and talked about all the good times that had happened over the years. The men arrived at Mercy and drove the wagon to Mr. Boston's store. The men got off the wagon, and to their surprise, Ruthanne had left a note on the door requesting them to go to Rebecca's home.

The men arrived at the Keys' home and knocked on the door. A young teenage Ashley opened the door, and with much excitement, she rushed to give John a hug.

"Mommy, Mr. John and Mr. Samuel are back!" Ashley yelled.

Rebecca came to the door holding a baby boy. "It is good to see the two of you. Who is this nice young man?"

"This is my younger brother, Michael. He was a kid the last time we brought him to Mercy," Samuel said.

Rebecca gave a forced grin. "Well, you men have always had

good timing. Me and Ashley made a batch of cookies. Please come in."

John, Michael, and Samuel entered and saw the twins eating cookies.

"Elisha and Esther, take a seat!" Rebecca said.

The twins quickly took a seat without saying a word as Rebecca walked to their supper table.

"They have grown," John said.

"Yes, in size and in appetite. Ashley, I want you to go get Mrs. Avail. Tell her the Cherokee have arrived."

"Okay, Mother!" Ashley said, then left the house.

Rebecca sat down with the baby boy and looked at the young men with her eyebrows slanted upward and her mouth slowly curved downward. "As you can see, much has happened. This healthy little man here is Isaiah. He and his siblings have certainly been a shining light for us this past week. Be careful with how you tell Annabelle what I'm about to tell you, John."

A few days later, John, Samuel, and Michael arrived back in Tahlequah during a heavy rainfall. The men finished unloading the wagon. Frowning, John entered the small house, greeted by Grace, Rain, and Jannie.

Annabelle knew John was troubled, and when he handed her a letter, she quickly opened it.

In the letter, Rebecca poked fun at Annabelle since the twins didn't look like her, and she wrote that Allen felt the same way about Elisha, but he advised her to treat the children the same.

Rebecca wrote that Marilyn had given birth to a hazel-eyed girl, and Rebecca had given birth to Isaiah two weeks ago, stating he looked like Allen. The letter further stated Mr. Boston had passed three days before in his sleep, and Sierra Nicole had found him. Ruthanne took his death badly, and she decided to take Mr. Fluffs home since Belle adored the cat. In closing, Rebecca told Annabelle Mr. Boston had no known family, so Allen had put in a bid to get the store.

Annabelle looked at John and wept uncontrollably.

John embraced her. "Grace, can you take the girls with you for a moment?" he asked in Cherokee.

Grace took the twins with her.

"I know it hurts," John said. "I know that man did a lot for you, but think how happy he is for you. It will pass..."

Grace was later told and was saddened to hear the man who'd helped them on their way to Indian Territory was now gone. The twins slept when night fell, and Annabelle sat on her bed looking at the lamp. John walked in and sat down next to Annabelle.

She placed her head on his shoulder. "I was hoping one day, I would be able to pay that man back in some way," Annabelle said. She wiped away a tear. "Thank you was not enough."

"Sometimes that's all we are meant to give. We give from the heart, and if you say it right, that's a powerful gift."

She looked into her husband's brown eyes and kissed him. He helped her take off her dress and massaged her back. His hands drifted over her scars as he tried to relax her.

"You know as smooth as my scars are...I can still tell when you touch them. Our children will never know the feeling of a whip or a branch striking their back or legs. If it wasn't for Mr. Boston, we wouldn't have them."

"The Father moves in mysterious ways. You know I first met Mr. Boston when I was a boy, and so many years later you meet him."

"Why did you say that like I'm old?"

"Well, because you were old compared to me."

Annabelle giggled and hit John with a pillow. "See, now, that wasn't fair."

The young couple laughed and spent the night in each other's arms. John's effort relaxed Annabelle in this time of mourning.

Three months passed, and the friendship between Grace and Eli grew. Grace struggled to suppress her feelings about Eli Five Killer.

In October of 1855, Grace, Annabelle, and Lisa were journeying home from the supply store when Eli approached them from a couple of feet down the street.

"Oh, no, I can't talk with him today," Grace said.

Annabelle and Lisa looked around and caught sight of Eli.

"It's Eli!" Lisa said, waving. "You should give him a chance. He is a good man,"

Grace angrily replied, "Then you give him a chance!"

Lisa's voice softened as she displayed her dimpled grin. "I think he is a better match for you than he is for me. He works to help the people and is trying to be involved with the council."

"I think Lisa is right. Is there something we don't see about him that you do?" Annabelle asked in Cherokee. "He is a kind, handsome man. I see the way you look at him."

Grace glanced at Annabelle and Lisa with contempt while the women walked. "I guess I can try."

Lisa laughed. "Try...you have been flirting with him the past couple of months, but you won't give him a chance. It's okay to be scared if that's the problem."

Grace growled, "Shut up, Lisa."

"Hi, Grace," Eli said in Cherokee. "Hi, Annabelle, Lisa."

"Hi, Eli," Annabelle and Lisa said in unison.

"Are all of you on your way home?" Eli asked.

"We were, but Annabelle and I have something to do first," Lisa said before grabbing Annabelle's arm and making her follow.

"Uh, we'll see you at home," Annabelle said.

"Annabelle! Lisa!" Grace yelled. "Ugh...I'm not cooking a thing when I get back to that house!"

"I can walk you home," Eli said. "I'm meeting with Pastor Bluebird today, but at this pace, I'm going to be early."

Grace's tone lowered and she forced a smile. "That's fine, Eli."

The two strolled down the dirt road of Tahlequah as Grace shied away from Eli.

"I learned today one of the kidnapped children had been found on a plantation in Tennessee," Eli said.

"Is the child all right?" Grace asked with a frown.

"She was fine, a little underfed and scared. She couldn't tell us who kidnapped her because the man had his face covered, but he was a white man. He sold her for $600 dollars to a cotton plantation."

"What did the slave owners say?"

"The owners claimed they had legal documents stating that she was their property, but the family made a deal, giving the man $250 dollars since she wasn't born to a mother who had been a slave."

Grace shook her head. "This evil is going to continue. I don't want to become an old woman, and still have to worry about the children in my family. I wish there was a way we could end slavery in our nation. That would help us protect our own better."

Eli smiled. "There's a change happening, and more of us are talking about abolitionist movements. Have you heard of this Underground Railroad?"

"Of course I have, I first heard of it from Mr. Gross. The white people are angry about its existence. I heard hundreds of slaves have escaped through it. An Underground Railroad is hard to imagine."

"I think it's hard to imagine, but it shows how the people really feel about slavery. I also think it shows our people can't end slavery in Cherokee land if we remain lost. I think we have a chance to change things."

Grace tried not to smile as she walked with Eli.

"Wait...was that a smile I saw?"

Grace looked at Eli but tightened her lips. "I think...it's men like you that can make the change. No matter how long it takes, I think it can be done before we become old."

Eli cleared his throat. "I didn't want to only walk you home today, but I wanted to ask you if we could spend more time together. I think you're a good woman."

Grace barely contained her blush. "Eli, I have more important things to do than to wait for you to walk me home all the time." Grace noticed the hurt in Eli's brown eyes. "You have a great heart. I need some time to think about what you said. I'm grateful you would like to spend time with me."

"Well, if me walking you home is boring, how about you teach me how to use a bow? Victoria told me you still practice."

Grace looked away from Eli and the corner of her mouth pinched. "Well, here's my home. Thank you, Eli." Grace sighed and forced herself to smile. "Maybe shooting arrows is a more fun way to spend time with each other. We will see each other again."

"We will each other each again." Eli rubbed his mouth, attempting to hide his excitement, and left when Grace entered her home.

Three days passed, and Grace struggled with her feelings. She decided to go to see Joyce. She told Joyce about the friendship between herself and Eli as the wise woman sat in her rocking chair.

"Grace, listen to yourself. You're creating excuses to not give Eli a chance," Joyce said in Cherokee. "You've been in the role of a mother for so long that you have forgotten how to let go and go down your own path. If you don't want to become married, say so."

Grace replied, "He is a good man. I think he would be better with someone else. I need to just focus on my family."

"You don't even believe that. I see it in your eyes. Child, you're afraid and waiting for everything to fit perfectly. Finding the right person and falling in love never happens perfectly. You're waiting for the stars to all line up and an angel to give you a message confirming Eli. Where's your faith to take a chance?"

"I feel if things do change between me and Eli, I will become distracted. I feel I'll lose a part of myself."

"You won't lose a part of yourself if you're doing things correctly. You are your own just as he is his own. The two of you should work each other. I don't think you're looking for someone to complete you, which is good, but you're afraid that you'll sacrifice too much. In relationships, that's why you create boundaries of what you will do and what you won't do."

"What if he doesn't respect what I say?" Grace asked.

Joyce leaned forward. "If he doesn't respect you, make him

aware he doesn't respect your wishes. If he continues on that path, it is okay for you to move on, and keep your heart open for another possibility. Jesus will show you."

Grace sighed. "I'm in no rush to be married. I know that sounds weird."

"If you feel that you can fall in love with him and have a relationship with him, take your time. Let him know you want to take your time."

"Thank you for your wisdom."

"If you need anything else, you tell me, child. I haven't seen Lizzie outside of church. Has her temper weakened?"

"Yes, she seems happier, but I can tell she does not like to go out to the practice fields alone anymore. She still has that look in her eyes. I think she is counting down until the Indian agents come for her."

"But none of you have spoken of the incident outside of the family."

"No, we haven't, but I think she has too much fight in her. She hides her pain. She even broke the handle off her tomahawk to put a new one on."

"She's attempting to heal, then. Keep giving her time, and I will visit soon. I also want to see the twins again before we have church." Joyce chuckled. "I love the chubby cheeks they have."

Grace stood from the old rocking chair. "I need to go now. It's almost time for supper to be made. Thank you again."

"We will see each other again." Joyce said.

Grace approached the old door and opened it, allowing the sun's rays to filter into the house.

"Grace...Grace!"

Grace turned around.

"If you do choose to give that boy a chance and you grow feelings for him, don't make him wait more than two years for you to allow him to marry you. It does not take that long to figure it out."

Grace sighed. "Yes, Elder Joyce." Grace went outside and closed the door.

Joyce moved to her table and picked up a corncob. She looked at it and chuckled. "That girl, she probably would make that boy wait ten years to marry her if she could."

The year passed, along with Grace's thirtieth birthday. During the winter, a small amount of snowfall made it easier on the family. Lizzie had once again been allowed to go hunting with the men, and they succeeded in killing a pronghorn and waterfowl with her help. The animals were brought back home for a special occasion.

The next day was February 4, 1856, and they spent it celebrating Tsula and Luke's wedding. Clyde Walton even came from Choctaw territory to take part in the festivities as the family laughed and joked.

George seemed pleased with the marriage. His rum had been taken from him once Lisa found it. George and Clyde talked with each other, and Rain tugged on George's trousers. He picked her up, placed her on his lap, and ran his hand through her long wavy hair while he talked to Clyde. The two men enjoyed her playful company.

Annabelle realized George had never shown deep affection for Joseph in that manner. The favoritism was obvious as she looked at Jannie while Lizzie held her.

She thought, *I wish I could cut their hair so they wouldn't be so different from Joseph. I wish that was the answer, but even if I were to cut their hair, it wouldn't change anything.*

Joseph laughed, and Annabelle looked to see Jacob playing with him. She looked at Jacob, and hope blossomed. She felt someone take her hand. She looked over, and John smiled at her, rubbing her hand.

"Everything will be all right," her husband proudly said.

"Your confidence is...a little comforting."

John looked into her eyes with a smirk. "Well, I know what will give you a lot of comfort."

She grinned and giggled. "You need to behave! This day is

about Tsula. Maybe later if the girls fall asleep on time. I want to clear my mind first too."

"What is bothering you?"

"I'm noticing little things, but maybe I'm thinking too hard."

"What are those things?"

"I want to be clear before I say anything. I don't want to create a storm when there are clouds present."

John kissed Annabelle's hand. "I'm ready to listen when you're ready to talk."

Annabelle smiled at her husband and refocused on Tsula's happiness. She wanted nothing but peace within her family.

May 1856 arrived with what George described as a miraculous start with the crops. The family had allowed Big Boy to breed with Queen, and she'd given birth to a healthy foal a month prior.

Lisa told David it was his early birthday gift, and the day after the boy's twelfth birthday, he sat in school, excited about celebrating. In school, David excelled and enjoyed his teacher, Mr. Manley. In his classroom were fifteen classmates, and David was surrounded by wood floors and two large windows that allowed sunlight inside. Mr. Manley's desk sat in front of all the students' wooden desks. When the teacher turned around to write on the blackboard a small piece of paper was put onto David's desk by a female friend.

"What's this, Naomi?" David whispered, speaking Cherokee.

The brown-skinned, straight-haired girl replied, "It's from Lacey."

David glanced at Lacey and then flipped over the sheet of paper.

He read, *What's it like to have a Negro for a momma?*

David looked at Lacy with his eyes lowered and his lips pressed. He sighed and wrote, *No different than your momma.* He flipped the piece of paper over to its blank side and handed it to Naomi when Mr. Manley turned back around to the blackboard.

Lacey got David's response and frowned after reading it. He

noticed her writing aggressively. She passed the paper through Naomi again.

David read, *Don't get smart with me, David. My momma is Cherokee; she isn't Negro. It wasn't being mean to ask.* He looked at Lacey and sighed.

"Is there something wrong, David?" Mr. Manley asked.

David looked at Mr. Manley, wide-eyed, replying, "No, sir."

"Stay focused. We're almost done." Mr. Manley turned back around to write on the board.

David wrote a response while Mr. Manley talked. The note was passed through Naomi and back to Lacey.

She read, *Well, she's my momma. I love her like you love yours. She's very nice. What's it like to have a white daddy?*

Lacey grunted.

"Is there a problem, Lacey?" Mr. Manley asked.

Lacey shook her head, replying, "No, sir."

She wrote a response and waited for Mr. Manley to write more on the board before sending the note back through Naomi.

It read, *I don't like to talk about him. I'm always reminded that I'm not full-blood.*

David frowned. He glanced at Lacey and wrote a response. He was trying to pass it back to Naomi when Mr. Manley turned around.

The two preteens froze as Mr. Manley's lips tightened and his glare fixed on them. The tall, slender, brown-skinned man walked up to them and took the note.

David's heart pumped erratically.

Mr. Manley flipped the note open and read the conversation. He lowered the note from his face. His brown eyes fixed on David and then onto Lacey. "I'll deal with you two after class," he said.

David gulped while Mr. Manley returned to his desk. An hour later, the class was dismissed, and the students went home—except for David and Lacey.

"The two of you are to remain focused in class at all times," Mr. Manley said. "Is that understood?"

"Yes, Mr. Manley," the children replied.

Mr. Manley continued with his speech when Lacey's mother arrived. He spoke with Lacey's mother briefly. The conversation ended with a light chuckle, and Lacey was taken home. David saw Annabelle in the hallway, and Mr. Manley spoke with her.

David thought, *I'm in so much trouble.*

"Mrs. Lightning, David has great potential, and I think this whole conversation was pure curiosity, but he must remain focused," Mr. Manley calmly said.

"I agree, Mr. Manley," Annabelle said.

"Hi," Rain said, speaking Cherokee.

Mr. Manley smiled and replied in the same language, "Hi."

"I'm so sorry, they're at that age," Annabelle said.

"No worries, I'm sure having two-year old twins is a challenge. I would think you've had talks with him about race before. Your being a Negro woman and having children of Cherokee blood."

"I have and I've noticed his increasingly angry responses. I'll work with him. He has to accept some children will be curious, and others will, unfortunately, judge him because of me."

"You're clearly a good mother, Mrs. Lightning. Please keep up the hard work." He looked down at Jannie and Rain with a smile. "I'll be looking for these two in nine years."

Annabelle smiled. "Of course, Mr. Manley."

"Oh, and don't be too hard on him. He did apologize for bringing up Lacey's father."

"Thank you for letting me know." Annabelle's gaze shifted to David through the doorpost. "Come on, David."

David stood up and walked out of the classroom with his head down.

"Apologize to Mr. Manley for disrupting class today."

David looked up. "I'm sorry for disrupting class, Mr. Manley."

"Apology accepted," Mr. Manley replied. "Listen to your momma."

"Yes, sir."

The family left the school and walked home. The twin girls rambled with random words. David remained silent while Annabelle held Jannie's and Rain's hands.

"David, you have to remember some people will ask you about me," Annabelle said in Cherokee. "It's okay for people to ask about me."

"I'm sorry, Momma A. I thought she was trying to be mean at first."

"You're twelve now. Remember to control yourself when people say things you don't like…especially about me. As you get older, you'll find a mountain of opinions exist, but you have to act in love. She hurt your feelings at first, didn't she?"

David frowned. "Yes. I thought she was going to call you a nigger."

Annabelle withheld her frown. "You can't make people change. You have to fight hate with love. Your actions will always speak louder than the words out of your mouth. You have a good spirit, and you're a good big brother."

"I hate how some people treat you. I'm scared of the Indian agents."

"Don't worry about them. You do as we taught you. You stay away from them, okay?"

"Yes, ma'am."

"I'm proud of you for apologizing to Lacey. Even children with a white parent can have a hard time."

"I promise I'll apologize to her again."

Annabelle grinned. "Okay, I always expect kindness out of you. How about we make your favorite chicken stew?"

David's eyes shot open. "Really! Thank you, Momma A."

Annabelle lightly giggled, saying, "You're welcome. I think your Auntie Lizzie has scared all of the rabbits, and it'll make Uncle George happy to have it too. We need to get you big and strong."

"Look, Momma A, my muscles did get bigger." David lifted up his arm, attempting to flex the tiny bicep he had.

Annabelle smiled. "I see, wow, you're definitely getting stronger. I'm sure you'll make Lizzie happy with your improvement." Annabelle leaned over and kissed David on the cheek.

David grinned and walked home with his mother and sisters.

David often wanted to leave the farm but was forbidden. The family was terrified with the possibility of his being kidnapped. Other children, close to the Lightning-Strongman family, were allowed to come to their farm. Annabelle believed their parents were too lenient and didn't take the kidnappings seriously enough.

Two days after her talk with David, she kept watch over David's friends while she sat under the old redbud tree and read her Bible. The children played kickball with each other on the open field next to the large barn.

At this time, Grace approached her. "Annabelle, Tsula has finished making a new dress for Rain. She wants you to see it before she makes one for Jannie."

Annabelle stood with her eyebrows rising while sweeping grass off of her dress. "All right, I'm coming. Can you watch the children?"

"Yes, I'll watch them."

Annabelle went inside the family house, and Grace sat under the tree.

Grace watched the playing children. One girl kicked the ball to David, and he kicked the ball to another boy. The boy missed the ball, and the other children laughed at him.

"What kind of a kick was that, David?" the olive-skinned boy yelled.

"It was a good kick. It isn't my fault you acted slowly, Eric!" David yelled.

Eric replied, "It was your fault. You did that to make fun of me."

"Can we get back to playing?" the girl asked.

"Shut up, Mel. You saw what he did!" Eric said. "Why defend him?"

David angrily replied, "You can't tell Mel to shut up! She wants to play, so stop acting like a little baby."

"I'm not acting like a baby. Maybe we should let Joseph take your place. At least he isn't mean," Eric snarled.

David huffed. "My brother would probably kick the ball into your face."

Mel laughed.

"It would be funny to see you cry like your drunken white daddy."

Mel gasped as the two boys faced each other. "You take that back, David!"

"I don't have to because it's true; he drinks more than my Uncle George."

"Well, at least I don't have a nigger for a mother."

David's eyes widened. "What did you call her?"

Eric stepped closer to David. "You heard me, a nigger, and your little nigger brother. And I think someone else is Rain and Jannie's mommy. They're too pretty to have a nigger for a mother."

David lunged at Eric.

"Stop it, please, stop it!" Mel yelled.

The boys rolled around in the grass punching each other. David got on top of Eric and punched him in the cheek. He was about to take another hit, but Grace grabbed his arm and bent it. David shrieked in pain.

"If you're not your auntie's nephew...get up, David!" Grace roared with a furrowed brow.

She released David's arm, and he stood.

"Let me look at you, Eric." Grace cleaned off Eric's face.

Both of the boys were bruised.

Grace looked at the boys and the tears drying on David's face. "What was this about?" she asked.

"He called my momma a nigger," David said with hands balling into fists.

Grace looked at Eric and took a deep breath. "Don't ever say that word, Eric. Do you understand me? Because as far as white people besides your daddy are concerned, you're a nigger, too. They'll just call you a prairie nigger or redskin instead."

"He called my daddy a drunken white man," Eric said with his voice breaking.

David looked toward the grass, but Grace grabbed his chin and forced him to look at her as she said, "David Lightning, did you say that?"

"Yes, ma'am, I did," David said.

Grace smacked David on his cheek and smacked Eric on his. "If you boys ever say those words again, I will make a whip out of the tallgrass to beat you with. Do you boys understand that?"

The boys nodded with big eyes as Mel watched.

"Now both of you go to the well and wipe the dirt off your faces."

The boys ran to the well as Grace watched.

"Miss Lightning, I'm sorry I didn't stop them," Mel said.

"Sweetie, don't worry about it," Grace said. "Would you like some cornbread?"

"Yes, Miss Lightning."

Grace and Mel strolled to the family house as the boys slowly followed. Grace fed the children cornbread and sent them home.

David had nearly stood when Grace placed her hand on his shoulder and pushed him back down. "You're not free, little boy," she demanded. "Unfortunately, in our family the ability to control anger is limited, but I won't excuse what you did today. I know what Eric said was wrong, but I want you to promise me you'll try harder to control your anger. We don't start fights in this family."

"I promise not to start any more fighting, Auntie Grace," David quietly said.

"David Lightning...that didn't sound like a promise."

David raised his voice, "I promise to try to control my anger and not start fights."

"All right, you can go back outside to the small house."

David left and Grace cleaned off the supper table. Lizzie left her room, yawning and stretching.

Grace huffed, saying, "Your nephew..."

"What do you mean?" Lizzie asked.

"He has a little temper, but I corrected him."

"Oh...well, he'll grow out of it."

Grace looked at her short sister unconvinced and went into the kitchen. "Yeah, that thinking didn't work for you very well," she murmured.

Lizzie lowered her head. "Did you say something?"

"No, Lizzie...but you can come here and help me clean these plates. We need them for supper."

Lizzie grunted and walked into the kitchen. As the two sisters cleaned the kitchen they hummed, and Lizzie began to sing their mother's favorite church hymn. "Jesus, your love surpasses my understanding, and your blood covers my transgressions. In all thy ways I shall acknowledge you, and you shall direct my paths. You are faithful. You are faithful in all of my storms." Grace's heart swelled while she listened to her sister's resonating soprano voice. Grace joined her sister's chorus while they finished cleaning the dishes.

———◆———

In the warm morning, the sound of horses pulling a carriage echoed throughout the area as John and Samuel began a trip to Mercy, Missouri. Annabelle and the others said their farewells as the men left. After a few days Annabelle would stand by the old redbud tree and scan the land as far she could see, hoping for them to return safely with a letter from Rebecca or Ruthanne.

The next day, Grace traveled to the supply store alone to drop off supplies and noticed Mr. Gross going home. "Mr. Gross! Mr. Gross, do you have some time?" she asked.

"Your timing isn't nothing short of miraculous, Grace Lightning," he said.

"Now, Mr. Gross, I thought you would be happy to see me."

"My dear, you know your presence is of no bother to me, it's some of your political viewpoints that test my patience. It's bad enough the US government and these Indian agents keep interfering in Cherokee affairs."

"I know about the ruling on that bill that wanted all free Negroes removed from Cherokee land. Something so serious was not fully exposed to most of us, Mr. Gross."

"Then you know all of the free Negroes are safe. Chief Ross immediately vetoed it, and basically set it on fire. Between that and the growing viewpoints on abolitionists owing to Reverend Jones on the outskirts of our territory, I have my hands full."

"I hear Reverend Jones and his son are quite interesting white men with their viewpoints against slavery."

"Why am I not surprised that you have interest in learning more about this reverend? I have nothing more to say of it. It is bad enough Lillian is showing more interest in releasing some of our own slaves. I won't have my house broken down out of sympathy."

Grace tilted her head. "I understand your frustration."

"I'm not surprised that you do."

"How has the little girl been doing after being kidnapped and given back to her family?"

"That family has done well for themselves. The girl still has nightmares, but I believe she'll grow past them. She has no choice but to grow past the incident."

"I suppose there was no apology," Grace sarcastically said. "Instead of a white man being punished for the wrongful kidnapping of an Indian girl he gets $250 to make up for his property loss."

Mr. Gross placed both hands on his black cane. "Must I remind you our priority is keeping the peace, and that type of attitude will just build the tensions between us and the US."

"Forgive me, but I find it pitiful our elected officials won't stand against this form of evil. Will it take more tears from desperate mothers? How high do the numbers have to be? Five hundred or a thousand…that would put us back to the Indian War days, wouldn't it? Maybe if Chief Ross had the courage to write to President Pierce about this specific issue, things would change, or maybe we will get lucky and the president will drop dead soon."

Grace swung around to stalk away, and Mr. Gross clutched his black cane.

"We're negotiating a solution," he said.

Grace turned with a frown. "Negotiations don't always work, or is our presence in this abandoned land so easily forgotten? Good day, Mr. Gross, please tell Lillian I said hello."

————◆————

The next day, Grace went to their practice fields with her bow and arrows, where Lizzie was attempting to teach David and Joseph archery.

"What are you doing here? Why are you not at the store?" Lizzie asked in Cherokee.

"I'm taking a break while Annabelle and Lisa take water to the slaves," Grace replied.

"Auntie Grace, I can hit the tree!" Joseph exclaimed.

Grace smiled. "I'm so proud of you, and what about you, David?"

"I can hit the tree, and I almost hit the small log hanging from the tree," David said.

"Well, show me what you can do. Both of you take a turn."

The boys aimed, with Joseph first taking a shot and hitting the tree David took his shot and grazed the hanging target. Joseph gave a snaggletooth smile.

"Very good, boys. Auntie Lizzie did a good job teaching you."

Lizzie withheld her grin as Grace glanced at her. "They're fast learners. I've only been teaching them for a month," Lizzie said.

"I guess I'll take a few shots, and you boys can tell me how I did," Grace said. She took aim and hit the target in the center, then hit two other targets in the same fashion.

The boys' mouths dropped.

"Auntie Lizzie, why are you not that good?" Joseph asked.

Lizzie clutched her hand into a half fist.

Grace chuckled, saying, "Auntie Lizzie is good. She isn't always as patient as she could be."

"I'm also not as old as Auntie Grace. She has been doing this a lot more years than me," Lizzie said with an instigating tone.

Grace leered at Lizzie. "See, boys, that's why Auntie Lizzie sometimes misses, but you boys are doing well with her. I will see the two of you later today." Grace kissed both of the boys on their foreheads and began to walk back.

"Why did you come out here?" Lizzie asked.

Grace stopped. "I needed to clear my mind. I was still angry with what Mr. Gross said."

"The bill was destroyed, so we don't have to worry about hiding Annabelle. Are you sure there was not something else in your mind?"

"No, I'm well. I will see you at supper." Grace left while Lizzie watched.

Lizzie grabbed her braid and began to unbraid it, but abruptly stopped, realizing the boys were still with her. "Okay, both of you can keep trying for the next thirty minutes," Lizzie said as she folded her arms.

⸺⸺◆⸺⸺

The cousins later returned to their family with two letters for Annabelle. One of the letters was from Rebecca and Ruthanne, the other from Marilyn. The letters were of a good nature, and Rebecca informed Annabelle that Allen had purchased Mr. Boston's store. Ruthanne wrote about Belle and her newborn Christina in an amusing way, telling how they looked nothing like Peter, but they had his laugh. Marilyn wrote, sharing how she feared for Daniel's safety, making him promise to stop at the Keys' place before coming home. Marilyn also had her daughter leave a paint imprint of her hand on the letter, and she described her children as hazel-eyed angels.

In September of 1856, Rain, Jannie, and Rosita played catch in the short grass between the family house and Annabelle's home. Reverend Hills and Molly walked up to the property, watching the toddlers play. Molly was especially amused by the girls' innocence.

Annabelle quickly came out of the house, having seen them walk onto the property. "Reverend Hills, Molly, it is a surprise to see both of you out here. Is there something you need?" she asked.

"Good afternoon, Miss Annabelle," Reverend Hills said. "We came to spend some time with the family if the men will allow it. We just wanted to go over some of the good word with all of you."

Annabelle saw the kindness in Reverend Hills. "I will get John and George so they can speak with you." She stood to leave but noticed Rain getting up. "Stay there, Rain. Mommy is coming back," she said in Cherokee.

Rain sat down and played with her sister and cousin.

Annabelle left and strolled toward the big barn as Reverend Hills raised his eyebrows. "My word, her ability to quickly change her tongue is impressive. I do believe these children don't know a word of English."

Molly replied, "She is impressive, isn't she, dear, and such a kind heart. Those twins there are Annabelle's."

"Why they look almost entirely like the full bloods. They are impressive children of God. I apologize for not taking those trips with you to their supply store. I see I have missed a lot over these two years."

"There isn't anything for you to apologize for...you felt that God wanted you to preach to others in other towns. At least you have spoken with this family on occasion. That's better than never speaking with them."

Reverend Hills sighed. "I guess you're right."

Lizzie exited the family house.

Molly's eyes widened. "Look, dear! There she is, the one I told you about."

Lizzie quickly approached them. Her eyes showed no fear, and she took off her white bonnet.

"My...so you know her. She does have a strong stature. What would you do with her?" Reverend Hills asked.

"Lizzie is her name. See, it's women like her I want to help."

"Are you sure, dear?" Reverend Hills whispered.

Lizzie stood in front of the toddlers, and they smiled at her.

"What are you doing here?" Lizzie asked. She put her hand on her hip. "I asked a question," she said, her voice deepening with each word.

Reverend Hills replied, "My apologies, my wife Molly and I were waiting for Mr. Strongman and John. Annabelle has just left to get them."

"What do you want with them?"

"Well…why, I wanted to give a sermon to your family today, I believe it is our good Lord's will today."

"What if they say no?"

Reverend Hills frowned. "Well, then, we will respect their wishes. Would you like to hear the good word for yourself?"

"I listen to the good Lord all the time. I pray to him all the time, even when I practice my hunting. I pray for guidance."

"My lady, hunting isn't proper for a woman, and such a young one at that. Surely, there are things in the house that need taking care of, and the raising of children, that's a necessity." Lizzie folded her arms and stared at Reverend Hills. "I see here three very young children. Is that one yours?"

"Rosita is my baby cousin. The other two are my nieces."

Smiling, Molly said, "It must be a handful having three small ones always running around. It must be tiring."

"I feel fine when I take care of them, and they will learn how to defend themselves and hunt like me."

"Is that proper for Christian girls? I mean, are you Christian?"

Lizzie narrowed her eyes as she looked at Molly.

"Reverend Hills and Mrs. Hills, it is good to see you," George said, approaching with Annabelle and John.

"Mr. Strongman, it is a pleasure," Reverend Hills said.

George shook his hand.

Lizzie looked away and picked up Rosita and Jannie. "Follow me, Rain," Lizzie said in Cherokee.

Rain immediately followed Lizzie when she went into the house, and Molly watched.

The men spoke as Annabelle stood behind John and George. Molly remained silent and kept smiling at her.

George and John agreed to allow Reverend Hills to preach to the family for a short time. The family sat down on tree trunks in front of the barn while Reverend Hills preached. Reverend Hills was quite pleased with their being receptive, and after preaching walked with George, John, and Samuel as they talked about crops.

Molly sat with the women and played with the girls in the family house. "Wow, they're such beautiful girls. I like how all their hair is braided; it is beautiful," Molly said.

"Thank you, it takes work, and I'll be happy when they learn how to take care of their hair by themselves," Maria said.

"You're from Mexico, correct?"

"Yes, I am. I was born there."

"Where's the rest of your family?"

"If you don't count the family I have here, my Mexican family is three miles east of here. It works well because Rosita will always know where she came from."

"Why did you allow her to be taught Cherokee? Why didn't you start her with English?"

Maria sighed and looked at Molly. "I wanted her to be able to talk with her cousins first, and I myself speak enough to talk well with others. Once she becomes a stronger speaker, I will teach her Spanish and then English. The original languages of her family are more important to me than the one that's taking over."

Molly bit her lip. "I apologize. I didn't mean to offend you."

"I forgive you. You're far better than the other white women I have met in my life."

Molly half-smiled. "I know things are not what they should be, but it's not all bad."

Maria's gaze shifted to the clouds and back onto Molly. "I've been called a prostitute several times because white women's husbands have looked at me. I've experienced that for years since I started living in this land."

"Why...I couldn't even imagine an insult of that nature being spoken of me at all."

"Welcome to the world of a Mexican woman. I hope you and your husband can make a difference. You seem like you want to."

"Maria, we are ready. Come inside and help me with the soup," Grace said. "Molly, you're welcome to come help us cook if you want."

"I would be honored to help," Molly said.

As the women cooked, Molly helped Lisa with the beans. It warmed her heart to listen to how the women interacted with each other. The women finished cooking the food and served it.

The Hills sat down at the family supper table as guests. The experience was similar to what the Hills had experienced before with other Cherokee families. Though it was rare for them to see a Negro woman legally married to a Cherokee man, it wasn't uncommon for the Hills to see children of Negro and Indian blood. As Tsula led her usual conversations, Lizzie remained mostly silent, with Rain in her lap, mostly avoiding eye contact with the Hills.

"What is wrong with you, Lizzie?" Grace asked in Cherokee.

Lizzie answered in the same tongue, "Nothing is wrong with me. I have nothing to say."

"Liar, you're thinking about something."

Lizzie rolled her eyes as she ate her cornbread and shared it with Rain.

When the sunset was midway, Reverend Hills and Molly left the family home, though Molly remained reluctant to leave wanting to talk with Lizzie. When they left the house, Samuel shook Reverend Hills' hand. The moment the men said their goodbyes, Molly noticed Lizzie watching them. The couple left discussing the good time they'd had with the Lightning-Strongman family.

———◆———

November 5, 1856, arrived, and Lisa celebrated her twenty-ninth birthday. As Lisa brushed the horses, Jacob suddenly entered the barn with John.

Lisa looked up and her heart dropped. "Jacob...John, what is this?" Lisa asked in Cherokee.

"What do you mean? Jacob wanted to wish you a happy birthday," John said. "I walked over with him so we can plan some turkey hunting. It has been a few years since he joined us."

"Sounds like a good idea," Lisa said with her dimpled smile slowly revealing itself. "Jacob, it's good to see you."

Lisa gave Jacob a hug.

"I couldn't miss your birthday. You know that," Jacob said.

Lisa smiled at Jacob, attempting not to blush.

"How is little Jake?"

Lisa giggled. "He is doing well. Queen is a good mother. They're supposed to be finishing the new stall for him this winter."

"I can help you guys with that, John. I have nothing else to do but collect firewood with my dad."

"I think I left big boy's grain outside the barn. Can you get it for me, John?" Lisa asked.

John replied, "All right, because it is your birthday."

John walked out the barn, and Lisa quickly kissed Jacob. "I need you to stop, you clever man. Please be patient."

"Lisa, I have been patient for eight years. If your papa cannot accept our love now, he never will," Jacob said.

"I understand but...fine. This summer we tell him. When John and Samuel return from Mercy, we will tell them. At least by then I will have all the help we will need if my papa over-reacts."

"What are the two of you talking about?" John asked.

"Nothing, just how I wanted the new stall done so he under-stands," Lisa said in Cherokee.

John sighed. "You already told me and Uncle George."

Lisa crossed her arms. "Why can't I tell him too? Now, both of you leave. Jacob, you can stay for supper."

"I like that idea. We need more men at the table," John said.

Jacob's eyebrows shot up, hearing Lisa's request, and he

smiled. "I would like that. I will go tell my pa," he said. "It will make him happy that more food will be at the table for him."

Lisa smiled at Jacob, and he went home to tell his father.

"I'm going to get the boys," John said. "They're back from school, and I'm sure they'll enjoy going on the hunt."

"I'm sure they will," Lisa said. "Mrs. Beads is speaking highly of Joseph. She said he fits in perfectly at school."

"Was there any doubt? He's my son."

"I'm sure he has Annabelle's mind and not yours."

John dismissively waved at Lisa and she laughed.

Soon after, at supper, the family celebrated Lisa's birthday. During the joyous occasion while they laughed and celebrated, Lisa held Jannie in her lap. She looked at Jacob and smiled. Jacob smiled back, but she looked away, trying to stay more focused on what Tsula said.

She was engulfed in the moment and traded toddlers among the women. Smiling, she looked at Annabelle, and when she looked away to give Rain a cheek hug, Annabelle smirked.

⸻ ◆ ⸻

To Annabelle's relief the family had worn out the twins, and they had fallen asleep at the table. After putting the twins to bed, she walked back into her bedroom. Her eyes widened when she saw John asleep. *Oh, he fell asleep trying to wait for me*, she thought. *He must be tired.* She smiled, put on her nightgown, and got into bed. She pulled the bed sheets over her husband and lay down. *I can't get Lisa off my mind. It feels like her joy increases when she's around Jacob.* Her eyes widened. *It can't be because...no, she wouldn't keep that a secret. I mean...ugh, go to sleep, Annabelle, you're overthinking it. They would be fetching together, but then there's Lizzie. Forget it; I'll just pray for Lisa.* Annabelle smiled and said a new prayer that night for Lisa to be loved by a good man.

⸻ ◆ ⸻

In late March of 1857, Grace went to the school to get Joseph. They returned home and gathered a few supplies. Joseph walked with Grace to the supply store carrying a small sack filled with beans. Joseph gave Grace the sack once they reached the store, and he waited on the steps while Grace went inside. As he waited, a wagon pulled up to the supply store.

In the wagon were Nancy and Eve. Paul got down from the wagon and helped Eve get down. The excited toddler ran to the door but tripped and fell. Joseph helped her stand.

Nancy marched toward the children. "Eve, come here," she bellowed angrily.

Eve smiled at Joseph and moved toward her mother.

"Joseph, that was kind of you, but you're not to touch Eve. Is that understood?" Nancy said.

Joseph replied, "I don't understand, Mrs. Scott. I did not hurt her."

"Just do as you're told. Eve can't be making friends with a Negro child before her own kind."

"Mrs. Scott, I'm Cherokee."

Nancy scoffed. "You're a half-breed of the lower kind. You'll never be equal to a full-blood nor a Cherokee with white blood. You're barely above a mulatto. They're barely above full-blood Negroes like your—"

"Nancy Hicks Scott," Grace barked. "I suggest you not finish that sentence, or you will get embarrassed in front of your daughter."

Nancy smacked her lips. "How long before you explain all of it to him?" she said with an instigative tone. "My daughter will know her place, but it seems you refuse to let your nephew know his."

Tsula came out the supply store. "What is all the talk about?" she asked.

"You're incapable of staying out of conversations, Tsula Strongman," Nancy bickered.

"That's Tsula Fields. I did get married, but I know you lack a mind to remember. I'll forgive you this one time."

"Joseph, go inside for a moment and give some feed to the chickens, okay, sweetie?" Grace said.

"Okay, Auntie Grace," Joseph said, entering the supply store.

Grace watched and Nancy began to tap her foot.

"What is it that you need, Nancy?" Tsula asked.

"How nice to see you actually working. I'm so proud of you, Tsula." Nancy sneered.

"What a beautiful girl." Tsula waved at Eve.

She smiled and waved back at Tsula.

"You could learn a lot from her," Tsula said. "I hope you don't turn your daughter into a bitter, dried up cornstalk like yourself."

Nancy gasped and clenched her teeth. "You'll be a terrible mother when that messed-up day arrives. My daughter is a beautiful girl, the most beautiful in the whole nation."

"I think that title belongs to my niece and twin cousins."

Nancy chuckled. "You dare say that those half-breeds surpass my daughter? Why, certainly they surpass their mothers, but to say they'll surpass my daughter is merely a dream."

Tsula crossed her arms, and her head cocked back slightly, while an eyebrow lifted. "I think you need to loosen your bonnet so you can think properly."

"Enough, Nancy. Give me the list so you can go home," Grace said, with her voice rising.

Nancy handed Grace the list, and Paul followed Grace inside to carry out the supplies. Nancy's cold blue eyes locked onto Tsula's spiteful brown eyes while the women remained silent. Paul and Grace loaded the wagon, then Paul lifted Eve into it.

"In some way I wish the two of you a good day," Nancy said as she got on the wagon. "God knows your family needs it."

"Nancy, if you ever talk to Joseph like that again," Grace stated, "I will do to you what Lizzie didn't. I'll make sure the horse crap goes in your mouth."

Nancy grunted and turned around with her arms crossed. "Take us home, Paul."

The wagon was driven off as Tsula and Grace watched.

"I should change my name to Strongman-Fields. My first last name sounds better." Tsula giggled and walked inside the supply store.

Grace remained outside with her arms crossed before reentering the store.

CHAPTER 9

Betrayal

MORE THAN A MONTH LATER, the twins' three-year birthday passed, and things seemed to be unchanged in Tahlequah. The kidnapping of children remained a bitter topic in the Cherokee community. To Annabelle's comfort, Joseph had developed a strong bond with Jacob.

Jacob was what Annabelle felt Joseph needed to see. The friendship between Jacob and John also strengthened her belief. As far as Annabelle was concerned, the boys had strong examples of godly men in their lives, and she imagined the boys grown as loving, God-fearing men.

◆

On April 30, 1857, Lisa finished supper and left to take care of the horses. While the rest of the family sat down together, Lizzie felt bad Lisa was alone. Lizzie excused herself and walked to the barn, staring at the sunset. It seemed right for her to help Lisa take care of the horses instead of leaving her alone. The moment she approached the barn, she heard talking, and she quietly moved to the barn door, cracking it open.

Jacob and Lisa were kissing. Her heart raced as her eyes fixed on the couple. Tears ran down her cheeks. Lizzie's breathing became labored as she listened to them talk and caress each other's face. The couple lay down on a stack of hay and kissed each other again. Lizzie closed the barn door. With her hands clenching into fists, she marched around the barn to the practice grounds. She heard the barn door pushed slightly open and stopped. Her watery eyes shot open, her heart heavily pounded, and she gnashed her teeth. She then heard the door being slowly closed to hide the sound of its closing. Lizzie exhaled and continued to the practice grounds.

As the sun set, Lizzie sat against a tree on the practice grounds, weeping uncontrollably.

"I hate you, Jacob Tate! How dare you go after my sister, my cousin," she cried. "You'll burn for this!" she growled. "She lied to me. I can't believe she lied to me...ugh! How long has this been going on? She could have told me." She screamed and hit the tree with a large branch.

Lizzie returned home emotionally exhausted.

"What's wrong?" Grace asked.

"Nothing, I'm tired and want to sleep," Lizzie said.

Jannie stuck her hands out, and Lizzie picked her up to kiss her. She put the child down and went into her bedroom. During the night, Lizzie stared at Lisa as she lay next to her. Tears trickled down her face.

"You need to tell me why you said nothing when you knew how I felt about him." She stared at Lisa, who slept peacefully, and kissed her on her forehead. "Liar."

Lizzie went to sleep with her back turned to Lisa.

Over the next two months the relationship between Lisa and Lizzie became strained. Lisa even talked to Grace about Lizzie's mood swings, but Grace was unsure why they were happening.

Lizzie brought up relationships more often, but much to her aggravation, Lisa refused to acknowledge her interest in anyone. On July 20, 1857, Lizzie witnessed Lisa take the men food on their break from working in the fields. As Lisa talked with them, Lizzie noticed that when the others spoke to each other and were not looking, Lisa playfully scratched the back of Jacob's neck and snatched her hand back.

Lizzie marched toward the barn. "Lisa, you come help me clean the dishes!" she yelled.

Lisa followed Lizzie to the family house, and Lizzie wiped tears from her eyes while approaching the cabin.

"Lizzie, slow down, it's not even close to supper time, why are you rushing?" Lisa said in Cherokee.

"I'm not rushing. I want to get it done," Lizzie barked.

Lisa groaned, walked inside the house, and helped Lizzie. Lizzie's demeanor calmed down, but she struggled to keep a straight face for her cousin.

Later in the day when the women prepared supper, Lizzie remained mostly silent, trying to suppress her anger. The family ate supper, and Lizzie fed three-year-old Rosita. George left for the outhouse while the family spent time with each other. Lisa later excused herself from the table and went to the horses.

Lizzie eyed Lisa as she left the house and broke the chicken leg sitting on her plate. She gave some of the meat to Rosita. Soon after George returned and sat back down at the table with the smell of rum on him.

George nudged Lizzie. "You're so quiet...focused on Rosita?" he slurred in Cherokee.

"I'm fine, Uncle George. I'm enjoying time with the family," Lizzie said.

"Where's Lisa? Has she been gone for long?"

"Lisa left right after you."

"Lisa should be more patient and brush the horses at a little later time."

Lizzie leered. "I agree, Uncle George."

"You agree with me!" George chuckled. "I think that must be the first time this year you have agreed with me."

Lizzie's eyes narrowed. "Yeah, maybe you should go help her. I think she'll like having you there with her."

"I think I will. I haven't helped her for a long time now. I think it will bring back good memories."

"I think it will."

George stumbled toward the large green barn. The sun outlined the horizon, and as he stood by the door, he heard moaning. George scratched his head and opened the barn door.

Lisa stood between two of the horse stalls with her dress pulled down, and he stepped forward, startling her so that her jaw dropped and her eyes bulged.

"Papa, w-what are you doing here!" Lisa stuttered.

"Lisa, what are you doing? Who's this there with you?" George slurred.

Lisa rushed to cover herself as George stumbled toward her.

"Jacob!" George exclaimed. "What...what is this? Lisa, how could you?"

"Daddy, we were going to tell you next week. Please calm down," Lisa pleaded.

George raised his voice, "Calm down...calm down! You're out here with this nigger giving your body to him like a whore! You shame your momma! And you shame our family behaving like this!"

Lisa cried while she shook her head at George. "I love him! Momma would be proud of me for finding a good Cherokee man who loves me like he does."

"Jacob is a half-breed! You're worth more than he ever will be, but here you are with your dress hanging off your body and spreading your legs like a whore in a city."

"She isn't a whore!" Jacob yelled in Cherokee. "She is one of the bravest and most loving women I've met, and she's been with me for years. I want to marry her." Jacob's head lowered. "I'm sorry we've done things in the wrong way, but I want to spend the rest of my life with her."

"No and no and no," George slurred. "You won't ruin my daughter's life. She won't give you half-breed nigger babies like your slave mother gave your father."

Jacob rushed toward George and grabbed him. The two men punched and grappled with each other.

"Stop it, please, stop it!" Lisa screamed. She grabbed Jacob and held onto him. "Jacob, please, stop it."

Lisa wept as the two men glared at each other and breathed heavily.

"You get off my property, Jacob Tate. If you ever come near my daughter again, I will shoot you dead," George said, as he staggered and stomped his foot.

"I think you need to load your rifle right now," Jacob boldly said. "I will never turn my back on Lisa, not for anyone. Jesus as my witness, I'll never walk away from—."

George pointed at Jacob. "All these years…all these years, I guess you couldn't accept your fate and get a Negro girl. My rifle will be waiting for you, half-breed. Now leave my land before I change my mind."

Lisa stepped in front of Jacob and looked into his eyes. "Jacob, please go," she said. "I love you so much, but I need you to leave."

"I will always love you," Jacob said, then marched toward the door.

His and George's eyes remained anchored on each other until he left the barn.

"Daddy, you've watched Jacob grow up with me, Tsula, Samuel, John, Grace, and Lizzie," Lisa said. "Tell me that you can't see the good-hearted man that he is."

"You have allowed John and Annabelle's relationship to corrupt you," George angrily said in Cherokee. "I will no longer tolerate any of this."

"I heard what you said to Joseph a few years ago. Telling a toddler he's not good enough because he has his momma's hair, and in what way was that showing Joseph love?"

George yelled, "The only true good that has come of that relationship are those twins! Joseph will be seen as a Negro child for his entire life. Nothing will change that."

Lisa shook her head. "All Joseph knows is to be Cherokee. He is a Cherokee child. He has our blood running through his body. You're still so filled with hate, you can't see it. What kind of a

Christian man pushes away his own family because they don't look Cherokee enough? Is that really what you believe, Daddy, or is this the rum I smell on you talking?"

George smacked Lisa. "Don't ever disrespect me like that! I have worked hard to give this family a better life, and you question my beliefs? You want to hear the truth? Joseph is a rare child. He is different than the other half-breed niggers, but that won't make a difference for him for long." His voice rose, "He will always be second to his sisters and his brother."

Tears shimmered in Lisa's eyes. "You're wrong about him being second to his siblings. Those words are the problem that's wrong with our people now, and I'm marrying Jacob. We will go to Pastor Bluebird to receive his blessings."

George struggled to stand correctly. "If you want to be with that nigger...than I'll treat you as one!"

He saw the whip intended for Annabelle on the ground next to a small hay pile, stumbled past Lisa, and grabbed it before walking toward her.

She saw the whip and ran toward the barn door. He quickly cracked the whip and hit her on her back. She screamed in agony but kept running. George chased his daughter and hit her again. Lisa screamed as she pushed the barn door open to rush outside, but George took another swing with the whip. He'd aimed for her back, but the whip hit her calf, and she fell.

"This is what niggers live through! And you want to be a part of it?" George took another swing, hitting Lisa on her back again and ripping her dress.

Lisa screamed as he cracked the whip on her back again.

"Daddy, please stop!" Lisa cried.

George hit her again.

"John, Samuel!" she shrieked.

George continued to hit Lisa again as she cried, and her dress became soaked with blood.

"I never thought I would see the day my own daughter would choose a nigger over her family," George said with tears streaming down his face. "But if I can beat it out of you, that's what I will do!"

George raised his arm to crack the whip again when John and Samuel tackled him. Tsula, Grace, and Lizzie ran toward Lisa as she crawled to the family house with tears streaming down her face.

"What did you do!" Tsula yelled. "Papa, what did you do to her!" She grabbed Lisa's hand and tried to help her stand.

"He caught me with Jacob," Lisa murmured. "I love him...I didn't know how to tell you."

"We have to get her inside," Grace said, her voice rough with anger.

The women helped Lisa up and rushed her to the house while John and Samuel held George down. George wept as he watched Lisa get carried into the house.

———◆———

Annabelle came onto the porch while the women carried Lisa up the steps. "Oh, my God," she said. "Maria, take the children into the boys' room. Don't let them out until we come for them."

"Come on, boys, go to your room," Maria said. "David, take Rain's hand. I will get Jannie and Rosita."

Maria moved the children inside the room and closed the door as the others brought Lisa, moaning in pain, inside.

Annabelle pushed the dishes to the far side of the table, and the women laid Lisa on it. Lizzie tore open the rest of Lisa's dress to address her wounds.

"I'm sorry I never told any of you I love Jacob," Lisa wept. "I didn't know how. I was scared of how Daddy would act. I'm sorry, Lizzie, I should have told you."

Lizzie's lips quivered, her eyes flooding with tears. She looked at the wounds on Lisa's back and noted the fear in her eyes. "Lisa, there isn't nothing for you to be sorry about," she murmured.

Annabelle and Grace rushed to clean the wounds as Tsula and Lizzie helped.

Tsula walked in circles, wiping tears from her face as Lisa moaned in pain. "I don't understand how Papa could do this? Why would he hit her with a whip?"

"He saw me and Jacob together," Lisa faintly said.

Annabelle and Grace looked at each other with bulging eyes while Tsula bit her nails.

"He's drunk," Lizzie said. "I smelled it on him before he left the table."

"How long has this been between you and Jacob?" Grace asked.

Lisa replied, "Eight years."

"Eight years!" Tsula shouted. "You had someone longer than any of us. Proud of you."

Lisa tried to laugh as they bandaged her wounds.

"Looks like three of the cuts might turn into scars," Annabelle said. "I can't believe he did this to you."

The women finished bandaging Lisa.

Lizzie's body shook as she looked at the now-bloodstained table. "It was my fault," Lizzie said with guilt in her voice.

"What are you talking about?" Tsula asked.

Lizzie looked down at the wooden floor. "I saw Lisa and Jacob together two times before. I was the one that told Uncle George you were at the barn. I told him he should help you. I...I never meant for this to happen."

"You jealous, prideful woman," Lisa cried. "I was going to tell all of you after your birthday. Why didn't you say something to me?"

Lizzie yelled, "Because I deserved enough respect from you to know the truth from the beginning! If you wanted Jacob that badly, you could've told me."

"I know why you were angry. You made us believe he rejected you because you approached and kissed him. But that's not the truth. I know he made you vulnerable...because he kissed you first and a day later you kissed him," Lisa growled. "But later he told you he wanted to be friends instead of wanting more from you."

Lizzie's eyes widened, and she took a step back.

"I chose him and kept your secret. But this...you did this! You murderer!" Lisa's voice deepened with bitterness, "That's what you are...a prideful, jealous, murdering—"

"What are you talking about?" Tsula asked.

Everyone's eyes shifted to Tsula.

"Now you go from not talking to talking too much!" Lizzie bellowed with a deep voice.

"That's enough!" Grace yelled.

Tears of anger dripped off Lisa's face and onto the table. "I know you defended yourself, but you killed those white men. Now those Indian agents will forever hunt us because of it."

Tsula gasped and, with her hands covering her mouth, looked at Lizzie.

"I don't want to see your face, Lizzie Lightning," Lisa continued.

Tears welled up in Lizzie's eyes, and she clenched her hand into a fist. "I don't think I can look at you either, sister."

Lizzie stormed out of the house. As she walked to the small house, tears broke away from her eyes and poured down her face. When she approached the small log cabin, she heard John, Michael, and Samuel yelling at George. Drying her tears, she continued to the small house. Once she got there, she felt tears stream down her face again. She kicked a small stick and went inside.

———◆———

"That truth doesn't leave this house, Tsula," Grace said. "Maria doesn't know, and none of the boys know. Is that understood?"

Tsula nodded and wiped tears from her face. Annabelle and Grace slowly helped Lisa off the table in her bloodstained dress.

"We have to keep the wounds clean or they'll get infected," Annabelle said. "I think for the next few days, it is wise you stay inside so we can make sure they don't become infected."

The women helped Lisa go inside the women's room to take off the bloodstained dress. They helped her put on her nightgown, allowing her cuts to remain partially uncovered. Lisa lay in bed on her stomach.

"Where are the children?" Lisa asked in Cherokee.

Annabelle replied, "They are with Maria in the boys' room. They didn't see any of this."

"Good, I want to sleep now. I want to be alone."

"Being alone is the last thing you need," Grace said. "We're here for you through the good and the bad. Today was the bad."

"I will sit here with you until you fall asleep," Tsula said.

The front door opened, and Grace walked out of the women's room. "Michael, why are you not with John and Samuel?" she asked.

"They are walking back right now," Michael answered.

"Uncle George isn't coming back in this house tonight," Grace stated.

"We told him that he is sleeping in the barn. John and Samuel just left him in there. How is Lisa?"

"Go look for yourself."

Michael entered the room as Lisa lay on the bed with her back exposed. He grimaced as he knelt down by his sister's bed. "He told us you were with Jacob in the barn. Is that true?"

Lisa replied, "It's true. That's why he did this to me."

Michael grimaced as he looked at Lisa. "He will never do this again to you. I will kill him before he does this again."

"Don't say that; look at me, Michael. Don't say that."

Michael held Lisa's hand and kissed it.

John and Samuel soon entered the house, and Grace spoke with them. Annabelle and Grace later opened the boys' room to get the children. It had been agreed the children were not to know what had happened to Lisa.

Maria didn't hear much of the arguing, which relieved the other women. Maria and Samuel went to their house to put Rosita to bed. When Samuel told Maria what had happened, she rushed back to Lisa to check on her and wept once she saw the wounds.

Annabelle, Grace, and John returned to the small house with

the twins. They opened the door to find Lizzie sitting in one of the rocking chairs next to a lit lamp. Annabelle and John took the twins to their crib.

Grace stalked toward Lizzie and smacked her. Tears covered her hand as she stared down her sister. She opened her arms, and Lizzie stood to give her a hug. The two women cried as they embraced each other.

"I didn't know he would do that...I didn't know," Lizzie sobbed. "Lisa is going to hate me for the rest of our lives."

"We will heal past this," Grace said.

⸺⬥⸺

The next morning, Tsula entered the barn and put down a plate with a piece of bread and a corncob. "You will have no grits or chicken this morning," she snarled.

"Wait, Tsula, please, give me something to drink," George said in a weak voice.

Tsula grabbed a bucket filled with water she'd carried with her. "Here, this is all you drink!" Her voice rose, "Do you hear me, Papa! That's all...water for the rest of your life."

George frowned. "I'm sorry, Tsula."

"Do you even remember what you did last night?" Tsula asked as she wiped a tear from her face.

"I do remember some of it. I'm sorry, where is your sister? I want to apologize for what I did."

"She is safe; that's all you need to know. The boys will be out here soon to give you clothes to change into. Would you beat me like that? Like you did Lisa?"

George wept. "I'm sorry, I'm a sorry man. I shouldn't have been drinking. I know I caused your sister a lot of pain. I know I did. Please forgive me."

Tears flowed down Tsula's face. She marched out of the barn and slammed the large door.

Tensions remained high between George and the other men while they worked the fields. Jacob's absence helped keep the anger they held for George strong.

Later in the afternoon, Annabelle and Maria traveled to the Tate farm and found Jacob feeding the chickens. The women noticed how distraught Jacob was and talked with him.

He learned that John, Michael, and Samuel had decided to approve of their relationship, but they also requested he was to immediately marry Lisa by the end of the month. Jacob accepted the offer and was told that out of respect, he would not see Lisa for a week, a ploy Grace had come up with so Lisa could heal and to keep tension down.

Annabelle and Maria returned to the farm and told the others Jacob had agreed to the terms.

Annabelle later sat under the redbud tree watching the men work the fields.

Lizzie sat next to her, carrying her tomahawk, and placed it against the tree. "Thank you for helping Lisa," she said.

"You have no reason to thank me, as she is my family too," Annabelle replied in Cherokee.

"I have a dark spirit...I caused all of her pain."

"That's a lie. You didn't know George would do something that evil to her. None of us would ever think he would behave like that to his own daughter. I never believed he could even do that to my own children. Now I have my doubts."

"He's probably going to die like my daddy. Alone...with a bottle in his hand. Lisa probably never wants to see me again until the next season."

"I think in a day or two she'll want to see you. She loves you too much. I think it hurts her more being separated from you."

"I would've thought the same a day ago." Lizzie got up and went to the practice grounds with her tomahawk in her hand.

Annabelle remained under the tree, praying for her family, until she had to check on the children.

Supper that evening was painfully quiet for the family. George was confined to the barn, and Grace took him his supper.

"Momma A, when will Auntie Lisa eat supper with us again?" David asked while at the table.

Annabelle replied, "I think tomorrow she'll feel a lot stronger, and be able to eat with all of us. So don't worry about it."

David half-smiled and ate.

Lizzie remained distraught while she picked at her beef.

———◆———

The next day Grace and Lizzie opened the supply store as Annabelle, Tsula, and Maria remained at home to take care of Lisa and watch the children. Lisa's spirit lifted once Grace told her that John, Michael, and Samuel approved of her relationship with Jacob. Grace also informed Lisa she'd talked to Pastor Bluebird, and he agreed to bless their marriage.

Grace returned to the supply store to finish working, but when they walked home, Grace saw Eli. "Lizzie, I will follow you, but I need to speak to Eli," she said.

"I will keep walking home and wait for you to catch up with me," Lizzie said in Cherokee.

Grace gave Eli a strong hug, and his eyes widened. She explained what had happened. As people passed, they continued talking with each other, and Grace struggled to hide her emotions.

"It makes me feel good that you like me, but I need to focus on my family," Grace finally said.

"Allow me to be there for you," Eli said. "Please don't push me away when you and your family are in so much pain."

"Eli...you can't be my rock. As bad as you want to be, that role belongs to Jesus. I'm grateful to have you in my life, but please let me focus on my family. Please trust me enough to leave me alone for some time."

Eli adjusted his brown vest and exhaled. "I will pray for you and the others, but I will also not remain silent. You always find a way to push me away. You're a good woman, but your heart is so protected that I can't tell what is on your mind."

Grace sighed. "I will try harder to let you in more, but all I ask of you right now is to trust me. Please give me space, and I will be happy to give you more time."

Eli smiled. "I will see you again. We'll see each other in church."

Grace nodded. "Yes, you will."

They went their separate ways, and Grace ran through Tahlequah to catch up to Lizzie.

<hr>

After the men worked in the fields and put the horses back in their stables, John, Michael, and Samuel told George about the agreement with Jacob. George kicked a bucket of water and walked in circles.

"Look at how you're leading this family," George said in Cherokee. "I don't want my daughter in the hands of a half-blood like Jacob. Lisa can find a man that's better for her—not Jacob."

"Jacob has been around us his entire life, and he has worked with us for years," John said in their native tongue. "You're so quick to destroy all of that because they fell in love. I know if Jacob was part white, you would have little to say."

"We have enough half-bloods that have Negro blood…is that too hard for you boys to believe? If we continue like this, we won't be Cherokee anymore. We will be another source of slaves for the white man, and no more Indian."

"You speak with so much hate. How can you honor Jesus with so much hate? Do you know what's hard for me? It was because of Grace and Annabelle I was able to try to see who this Jesus was, not because of you. The past five years have been the happiest I have ever seen you, but you still think like the white man." John shook his head. "Not like a Cherokee."

George huffed. "The idea for Jacob to marry Lisa by the end of the month was Grace's, wasn't it?"

"The three of us came up with the idea, Father," Samuel said. "We talked to Grace about it. She agreed to the idea. After seeing how much Lisa loves Jacob, how can I say no to that? How can you say no to your daughter falling in love with a good Cherokee man?"

"Jacob isn't Cherokee enough," George angrily said. "His

mother was a slave, a Negro slave. Jacob is a half-blood Negro. They will always be lower."

"Momma always taught us a Cherokee is a Cherokee whether he has white or Negro blood in his body," Michael said. "We should still love them because they're our people. Love them like Jesus loves us, and she lived that until the day she died. I won't ruin my memories of her or kill Lisa's heart because you refuse to accept him."

"John, what are the chances of their having children like the twins?" George asked. "What is the chance that the children Lisa would give Jacob will have little or no Negro appearance? Those twins and David will have a better life than Joseph. That's the truth, and I don't want my daughter to watch her children go through that."

John replied, "We will protect them and love them like we're doing now with my children. Will you agree to Lisa's marriage, or will you be an angry old man until you die? Bitter because your daughter fell in love with a good man that isn't a full-blood?"

George sighed, saying with a cynical tone, "I see that no matter what I say, this is happening. If this keeps the peace in our family and helps Lisa forgive me, I will accept their marriage."

The men talked a bit more and entered the family house for supper. The children remained unaware of what had happened and were cheerful while they ate. Tsula refused to look at George and sat at the far edge of the table. Annabelle kept Rain in her lap as she fed her, while Lizzie held Jannie.

"I want to say I'm a fool. I have been a terrible Christian man," George said in Cherokee. "I have no excuse for what I did. It will hurt me the rest of my life. I can't ask for any of you to forget what I did, but I'm asking for forgiveness."

The table remained silent as they looked at George.

"I forgive you, Uncle George," Rain said.

Jannie raised her hand. "Me too," she said.

"What did you do, Uncle George?" David asked.

"Nothing for you to worry about," Grace said. "I forgive you, Uncle George."

"I forgive you, Father," Samuel said.

"I do too," Michael said.

"I forgive you, George," Annabelle said.

"I also forgive you, uncle," John said.

Lizzie stared at George as she fed Jannie. "Never again will this happen," she said with a frown and low tone. "I forgive you."

Tsula ate and wiped a tear from her face. She looked at her father before grabbing her plate and entering her bedroom, closing the door behind her.

"Give her time, Pa," Michael said.

The family ate, and that night, George sat out on the porch looking at the stars.

Lizzie's birthday passed, though she refused to be cheered up by anyone. Grace still made her chicken soup with cornbread. Lizzie reluctantly ate it since Grace refused to let her cook anything.

The day after Lizzie's birthday, Lisa could walk without severe pain in her back, and she put on her dress. In the afternoon, Grace had Lizzie and Lisa sit at the supper table.

"Children, come with me outside for a moment," Maria said.

"No, Maria. I want Tsula to take the children," Grace said.

"Why me?" Tsula asked in Cherokee.

"You'll interrupt while they talk to each other. That's who you are, but the two of them need to say what needs to be said. You will only make them angrier."

Tsula grunted. "Joseph, David, get your sisters and come outside to play." She took Rosita's hand and they stepped outside.

Maria sat next to Annabelle and Grace.

"I feel this has grown to the worst it could, but I won't tolerate strife between the two of you," Grace said in Cherokee. "It ends today. Lisa, tell us everything."

Lisa told the women about the depths of her relationship with Jacob. Lisa struggled to hold back her emotions as she looked at Lizzie. "In the end I always thought if Papa didn't accept Jacob, we would go away to the north," she said. "I know he is the one the Father has made for me. Not being able to show that love...it killed me every day."

Lizzie looked at Lisa. "I'm sorry. I never wanted this to happen to you," Lizzie said in Cherokee. "I'm still mad at Jacob. I think he should have been more of a man and said something. He is the only man I found myself loving, and he knew that. He could've told me it was you he liked, or you could have."

Lisa slammed her hand on the table. "How could I? Do you know who you are? You still like to control all in your life, and when you can't control things, that evil temper of yours comes out."

Lizzie raised her voice, "I've tried my best to control how I feel."

"The truth is, you don't want to control how you feel. You never have and you make others suffer." Lisa's face scrunched. "You're like one of the great storms that rips up the ground."

Lizzie slammed her fist on the table. "What about when I'm in pain? Is it okay for me to show when I'm in pain? You want truth. I like it when people are afraid of me. It protects me when others won't. I'm a fighter! I accept it! When will you stop pretending like you're not? Your thoughts weren't pure when you were with Jacob."

Lisa's pupils dilated, and she growled, "Don't test me."

Lizzie crossed her arms and leered. "Ha, there's the real Lisa. When it really matters, the smile goes away."

"Say what you want. You're nothing but a selfish, jealous, prideful little girl that got mud thrown into her eye one day and—"

Lizzie abruptly stood but Grace quickly slapped her hand on the table. "Sit down and control yourself," Grace yelled. "I will tell both of you what is wrong here. You both let your feelings become bonded to Jacob in one form or another. Lizzie, you have to work on your anger, as always, but now I see it. You think you have to possess what you want, and that's wrong. How are you being a strong woman with a weak mind like that? Unable to let go, unable to take rejection, you've been the happiest I have seen over the past few years, but you destroyed it all because you didn't get your way." Grace turned to Lisa. "Lisa, you've kept this secret for years, and the only thing it brought you was fear."

"And love," Lisa stubbornly murmured.

Grace's left eye narrowed. "What good is something in your life when you can't tell the people that love you about it? You have also grown nasty with your pride. You claim Jacob with your heart but speak of him like he is all in your life. He can't be your main purpose for living." Grace pointed at both women. "Starting from today, Lisa, you won't boast about Jacob so much that it angers Lizzie, and Lizzie won't be difficult to Jacob. Both of you are grown women and need to show it."

Lizzie slowly scratched the wooden table with her nails.

"Now, apologize, because both of you have caused pain to each other."

Lisa turned to Lizzie and sighed, saying, "I'm sorry for not telling the truth to you, and for not trusting you, Lizzie. I'm sorry to all of you."

Lizzie looked down at the supper table. "I'm sorry," she mumbled.

Grace slapped the wooden supper table, yelling, "You look at her, Lizzie Lightning!"

"I'm a grown woman. I'm not apologizing again to her," Lizzie complained as she bobbed her head.

Grace grabbed a large wooden spoon off the table.

"Okay!" Lizzie frowned. "Can't stand you sometimes." She took a deep breath and looked at Lisa. "I'm sorry for not telling you I knew and for only thinking about my feelings. I think that's why you believed you couldn't tell me." Lizzie looked at the healing cut on Lisa's shoulder. "I'm sorry. I'm the reason you got beat."

"Now hug each other. You're sisters, each of our wolf clan," Grace said in Cherokee.

Lisa and Lizzie hugged each other.

"And I'm telling Elder Joyce on both of you! I'm tired, and y'all are grown."

Lisa's and Lizzie's jaw dropped while they glared at Grace.

Later in the day, George apologized to Lisa, though she refused to let him touch her.

While the women prepared supper, things began to feel normal again, though Annabelle knew Lisa and Lizzie were still mad at each other. The conversations among Annabelle, Grace, Maria, and Tsula were overshadowed by the unspoken tension between the cousins. Annabelle felt even the sunrays beaming into the kitchen were dimmed by the remaining tension. The short responses and side-eyeing between the cousins was clear. Even their use of kitchen utensils sounded aggressive toward each other. Annabelle could feel her palms sweat when she heard Lisa cut up the green beans and Lizzie cut up the venison. She thought, *Please, Jesus, let there be peace. I can't tell who's more tempted to throw a knife.* The women brought out the finished dishes and placed them on the dinner table.

Supper became livelier, though Tsula still refused to speak to George. Grace made Lizzie help Lisa clean her healing wounds before bed, and they talked further, helping them forgive each other. During the night, Tsula cuddled next to Luke, staring out at the moon as its light shined through their window.

As the sunrise covered the land, Tsula and Luke walked to the family house. Michael greeted the couple when they went inside.

"Where is Papa?" Tsula asked him.

"He told me he needed a day to clear his mind. He rode off to the Choctaw to spend time with Mr. Walton. He took Ray, so we should be fine in the fields today."

"I see...well, I will get breakfast started. Lizzie, Lisa, wake up and help me cook."

As the family gathered for breakfast, George rode Ray down the dirt trials to Choctaw land. The ride took him four hours, but he was determined to see his old friend. He arrived in the Choctaw's territory and rode Ray past the townspeople. He arrived at Clyde's home and was greatly welcomed.

"What brings you here at this time of day, George?" Clyde asked.

"I needed to get away from the family for a moment," George answered.

Clyde chuckled. "Yeah, it can be that way sometimes. Just don't do things like Peter."

"What did your brother do now?"

"He now has wife number three and two children by her."

"I thought he was still married to Fay."

"He is and says he sees her when she stops complaining so much. Well, enough of that. I know my brother needs to make up his mind and stay with one."

"Yeah, two women, must be hard."

"Now what really brings you out here? So far there has been nothing but good news coming from you."

"I wish it would stay that way. I came because I need a favor, and it won't be easy."

"Speak your mind, George, I'm listening."

George talked with Clyde for some time before returning home. During the journey Ray's reddish-brown coat reflected the sun.

The next day, Florence came by the farm to help make arrangements for Jacob to marry Lisa. Florence beamed and happily spoke about Lisa becoming her sister-in-law, and Mr. Tate had sent word with Florence that he would be buying them a horse as a gift. Annabelle showed off her smile while the women planned for Lisa, and tensions in the Lightning-Strongman family had lessened. The next day was Lisa and Jacob's wedding.

The following morning, the women awakened early to help Lisa clean up, and even Lizzie seemed happy for Lisa.

<hr>

A smile on his face, Jacob meandered down the trail on his horse and saw George.

George stopped on the trail the moment Jacob approached him on horseback. "Jacob Tate, I want to apologize for my behavior before you marry my daughter," George said.

Jacob stopped the horse and dismounted. "Your words mean a lot to me, Mr. Strongman," Jacob said. "I thank Jesus every day for Lisa being in my life."

"As do I, Jacob. I thank the Lord every day for my daughters. I promised their mother I would do all in my power to protect them. They have both grown into good women. I could not be more proud, but even good children make bad choices. You're a good man but not good enough for my daughter."

As Jacob opened his mouth to speak, pain erupted in the back of his head, and he fell to the ground. "Please, don't," Jacob murmured as he reached out to George.

Clyde took another swing, knocking Jacob on the head again, and Jacob's horse ran away.

"That was good timing, George. Quickly get the wagon," Clyde said.

"I thought this boy would come down the trails early. This will teach him a lesson." George ran down the trail to get Clyde's wagon and mumbled, "I'm sorry, Jacob, but I have to protect Lisa. I see no other way of doing this."

George came back down the trail with the wagon, and Clyde tied Jacob's hands with rope. Clyde and George picked Jacob up and place him on the cart.

As the men worked, Nancy walked down the trail with Eve, escorted by Paul. Nancy halted, and the three stood by a large tree on the trail.

"Mrs. Nancy, that's Mr. Strongman, but I don't know the other man," Paul said.

"I'm not blind, Paul," Nancy griped. "I also cannot believe what I'm seeing. Jacob Tate with his arms tied and placed on a wagon."

Nancy and Paul watched as Clyde took a blanket and placed it over Jacob.

"I thought I had seen the craziest things out here, but I was wrong," Nancy said.

"Mrs. Nancy, they killed Mr. Jacob."

"No, I think they're sending him away. His hands are tied, and I can see him breathing."

Paul put both hands on the rifle he held for their protection. "Do you want me to go stop them, Mrs. Nancy?"

"No, I won't endanger myself or Eve. I know who to tell. I'm sure she'll be pleased to hear about what her uncle has done. It's time for us to go."

Nancy, Eve, and Paul returned to the Scott farm, remaining unseen by Clyde or George.

"All right, I'm ready to go," Clyde said. "A few years away will teach this boy not to do what he did again. Lisa will be fine after this."

"I know she will," George said. "I need to go back home now."

"I will talk to you soon in a week or two." Clyde drove off, with Jacob unconscious in the back of the wagon.

As George marched home, heaviness weighed in his chest, and his eyes welled with tears.

He heard a quiet whisper, "Stop the wagon."

He was startled by it and was about to go stop Clyde, but

he stopped and shook his head and inhaled. He returned to the farm scratching his head. Once he arrived home, he remained silent. Hearing the voices of his family made his breathing labored. He stepped out onto the porch and sat down on the steps as the calm summer breeze blew past him. Sweat began to build on his forehead, and he rubbed his hands down his brown trousers.

"Papa, how do I look?" Lisa asked in Cherokee.

George's eyes widened. He turned around and looked at Lisa. "You look very beautiful...like your mother."

Lisa smiled. "All right, let's go to the church. I don't want to keep Jacob waiting."

The family walked to the church and was greeted by Pastor Bluebird. The Tate family also arrived, but Jacob was not with them. Mr. Tate explained Jacob wanted to arrive on his own. An hour passed with both families waiting in the church. Lizzie slowly paced down the pews with her arms crossed while Annabelle and Maria occupied the children. Tsula was speaking with Florence by the pulpit when Lisa returned inside the church. With her hands balled into fists, tears streamed down her face, and she sat on one of the pews. Grace sat down next to her and rubbed Lisa's back. "Something is wrong," Lisa cried.

"Calm down. I'm sure there's a good reason he's not here," Grace replied.

"It's not like him at all. I can feel it in my spirit. Something is wrong."

Grace wiped away the tears on Lisa's face. "Whatever is wrong, we'll figure it out." She swayed with Lisa, who had now pressed her head into Grace's shoulder. Grace glared at the men. Her head made a slight turn to the church's front door, and then rested on top of Lisa's head. The men nodded at Grace and walked outside. At this time, Elder Joyce also sat down on the other side of Lisa and caressed her hair. Grace could hear

Mr. Tate say that he and Samuel would take a ride to search for Jacob.

"I feel your pain, Beautiful Child," Joyce said. "You will persevere beyond this shadow of fear. Give me your hand, baby. We will pray for Jacob no matter where he is." Lisa nodded and held onto Elder Joyce's hand. "You too, Grace." Grace reached over and held the wise woman's hand as she led them in prayer. Elder Joyce then commanded the rest of the women to come to Lisa, and they prayed over her. Samuel and Mr. Tate rode off to the Tate farm and spoke with the slaves but none had seen Jacob. Samuel and Mr. Tate rode down the dirt trails looking for Jacob, but after two hours of looking, they found no signs of the horse or Jacob.

Returning down one of the dirt trails they found a set of horse tracks, but they couldn't tell if it was Jacob's horse. The men returned to the church with no clue as to where Jacob was. The two families later decided to leave the church. When Lisa arrived home, she refused to go inside and sat on the porch.

The rest of the family sat down for supper, and the rays of the sunset illuminated the room. "He must've ran," George grumbled.

"That's not like him," Lizzie said with a frown and her nails slowly scratching the wooden table. "He's a good man."

"What if something has happened to him?" Annabelle asked. "With all these kidnappings going on, I'm worried about him."

"We'll search again for him," Luke said.

"I'm telling you that boy ran," George said as bit into a chicken leg. "The moment he couldn't back out he does this."

Grace's brow furrowed. "Uncle George."

George shrugged. "What?"

"I agree with Lizzie. It's out of his character to not keep his word."

"I think so too, Papa," Tsula said while she picked at her food.

George put down the chicken leg, saying, "Whether he got taken by some crazy white men or ran like I said, it's a tragedy."

"Then how about you speak like it's a tragedy," Lizzie said with each word deepening.

George pointed at Lizzie. "I understand everyone is upset. You're defending him like he's never done anything wrong... acting as if he was going to marry you. It's a good thing he wasn't."

Lizzie's eyes dilated. She grabbed her knife and stabbed the table. The boys and girls jumped as they gasped. Grace saw a tear fall from Lizzie's eye as she stood and stormed to her room with the knife embedded upward into the table. Lizzie slammed her bedroom door, and the family scowled at George.

Grace shook her head, saying, "You have a way with words, Uncle George."

George frowned.

"Finding Jacob will be our priority," John said. "He's my friend, and it bothers me to see Lisa so sad." Annabelle held John's hand and smiled at him, and the family continued to eat. The silence was only interrupted by the toddlers, who began to play with Tsula. The family tried to comfort Lisa before going to bed, but she refused to go to sleep.

During the night, Annabelle was plagued by dreams and couldn't sleep. She got up and looked at the twins while they slept. She slowly caressed both of their heads and half-smiled. She quietly walked down the wooden hallway of her home and went outside. Annabelle wanted to take a better look at the stars, but she noticed Lisa was still sitting outside. She approached the other woman and sat down next to her.

"We finally get freedom, and he disappears," Lisa said. "How fair is that?"

"Life was never promised to be fair," Annabelle said. "I learned that from Elder Joyce, and I've experienced enough life to know that's true."

A tear went down Lisa's face. "I want to die. I know something bad happened to him. He wanted to marry me before I was even ready.”

“Don’t say such things, Lisa. We must have faith we will find him and bring him home safe. I understand how much you love him. I feel the same way about John. How about we pray and get some rest; it will do us no good if you have no strength.”

“Okay, we can pray.”

The women prayed together as the stars shined down on them, then embraced each other and went to bed.

Annabelle believed the moment of prayer strengthened Lisa’s spirit and gave her faith she would learn the truth.

Two days passed. The two families struggled to find any information from anyone in Tahlequah who had seen Jacob. As Annabelle set out plates with Maria, there was a knock on the old wooden door. Annabelle opened the door, and her mouth dropped when she saw Nancy.

“I never expected you to be the one to open the door,” Nancy snobbishly said.

“I never expected you to be one knocking on the door. I guess I should close it in your face,” Annabelle said.

“I guess for this one moment I will ignore my prestige over you. I know something the entire family will want to know, especially Lisa.”

Annabelle let Nancy inside, and the other women gathered around the supper table as the children played outside.

“What is it, Nancy?” Grace asked.

“I know what happened to Jacob,” Nancy answered. “Paul was escorting me and Eve for a morning walk. To my surprise, your uncle and Mr. Walton had Jacob’s hands tied and put him on a wagon.”

Lisa stood up with her eyes widened. “He did what!” she exclaimed with her voice rising.

Nancy sighed. “Then they put a blanket over him.”

Lisa’s knees buckled and she fell into her seat.

"No worries, dear. I saw him breathing, but they must've struck him hard to take him down."

"He's alive?"

"Yes, he was definitely breathing."

Tears welled in Lisa's eyes. "Are you sure?"

"I'm positive. If they had been slower he probably would've woken up."

"He's alive," Lisa cried.

Lizzie's eyes veered from Nancy to her hands while Maria and Tsula rubbed Lisa's back. Nancy's mouth curved downward into a frown.

"I'm sorry I didn't speak of this sooner. I was scared to speak of it, but I see how desperate you are," Nancy said. "I know none of you share my beliefs of what is best for our people, but no one should go through life not knowing what happened to someone they love."

"Thank you, Nancy. Thank you for making the right choice," Lisa said, tremors shaking her body.

"Love is complicated. I know all of you understand that. I hope you find where they took him. I think it's my time to leave." Nancy stood and turned toward the front door. She'd reached to open it when John walked in. "John!"

"I never thought you would ever come back into this house," John said. "Why are you here, Nancy?"

Nancy looked behind John, where Michael, Samuel, and George were a few hundred feet away and coming toward the house. She then looked back at the women. "I think it's better if they tell you than me."

Grace told John the story just before the other men entered the house. George walked in behind his sons, and John looked at Grace with his mouth agape. George walked toward the supper table, and the women glared at him with lowered eyebrows, scrunched faces, and deeply furrowed brows.

"What is going on? Why are all of you so quiet?" Samuel asked. "Why is Nancy here? Maria?"

Lisa stood up from the supper table, and slowly walked to her father. Tears rushed down her cheeks, and she slapped George as hard as she could. "I know what you did," Lisa bellowed. "After all the apologies, you take Jacob away from me?"

George's eyes bulged. "Lisa, I...I did it to protect you," he said holding his cheek. "Jacob will never be right for you."

Lisa growled, "Where is he, Papa? Where is my husband?"

George pointed his pointer finger at Lisa. "That boy isn't your husband."

"Even if I don't get your blessing, he'll still be my husband. If Jesus approves of our love, that's what matters." Lisa's voice rose with each word, "I wanted your approval, but I don't need it!"

"Pa, what did you do to Jacob?" Samuel said with a displeased tone.

"That boy is with the Choctaw to be sold as a slave," George said.

Lisa cried.

Grace stood to hold her. "We're getting him back," she said.

"How did you know?" George asked.

"Nancy saw what you did...you and Clyde," Lisa replied. "You lied to me." She left the house and walked toward the barn.

"I think it is best I leave," Nancy said.

She quickly left the house and was driven home, leaving George to be confronted by his family.

"Right now, I want to tell you how bad of a father you really are, but the first thing this family is doing is getting Jacob back," Grace commanded.

"Grace, I agree, but we are going to have to wait," John said. "If we leave now, we will arrive in the night, and it will be harder to find him." John looked at George. "Your sons, your daughters, and I all grew up with the Tate children. Jacob has done more than he agreed to do originally years ago, and this is how you repay him? I want to say you should sleep in the barn with the horses again, but I think making you sleep here so you can see Lisa's pain is what you deserve."

George shook his head, saying, "Why is it so hard for any of you to see I did this for her? She can do better."

"You did this for yourself!" John yelled. "You sat here knowing the truth, and for what? Because he isn't the man you saw Lisa marrying. What about Jesus's plans for Lisa? Do you know better than the one that gives us rain, the one that gave us the sun and the moon? Her actions don't shame our family, but what you did has ruined our name." He turned and stomped outside.

"Girls, y'all come with me to comfort Lisa. I don't think it is wise for her to be alone," Grace said.

The four women went to the barn and comforted Lisa. Grace later told her they would be going to the Choctaw territory in the morning to find him. Lisa wanted to go, but Grace objected to her going with the men because her wounds hadn't fully healed.

CHAPTER 10
Unexpected Words

THE NEXT MORNING JOHN, LUKE, and Samuel prepared to leave after eating breakfast. The men saddled the horses and led them from the green barn.

Lizzie left the family house and approached the men with her bow and arrows on her back. "I'm coming with you," she said in Cherokee.

John responded, "Lizzie, you're not coming. The three of us can bring Jacob back peacefully."

"I'm coming, John. Some of this is my fault, and none of you are stopping me from coming."

John grunted as Lizzie left to get a horse.

Grace walked toward the men. "I think that's a good idea," she said. "Having one woman with you may persuade them to be nicer. I don't think you could stop her from following you anyway. I'm going to the Tate farm to tell them what we know. Hopefully when you return, you will have Jacob with you."

"I think Mr. Tate will need all the encouraging you can give him, but make sure Florence is there too," Luke said. "Florence is the one person he'll listen to the most."

"Thank you for letting me know," Grace said.

Lizzie rode toward them on Queen. "Enough talk; let's go," she said.

Tsula came out of the house and jogged toward Luke. She

gave him a kiss and said, "Be careful, stupid, we need Jacob back."

Luke chuckled, saying, "I guess I'm stupid to be married to you."

Tsula chuckled and kissed Luke again. "Seriously, be careful. You know not all of the Choctaw like us."

"Are the two of you done?" Lizzie bickered.

"Shut up, Lizzie!" Tsula replied.

"You're slowing us down, Big Mouth."

"I was not, Flour Face, you're so impatient!"

"Enough from both of you children," Grace griped.

"All right, let's go," John said.

The three men and Lizzie rode through the prairie and to the Choctaw territory. During their ride, John prayed to God that Jacob was well. When they arrived in the Choctaw territory, they searched for Clyde and hoped to see Jacob as Samuel led the way to Clyde's home. The group came to an old cabin with a small brittle wooden fence attached to the side of it, containing a few chickens and some haystacks.

Two of Clyde's daughters came out to greet them, recognizing John and Samuel. Both of the long-haired young women were taller than Lizzie.

John and the others rested while they waited for Clyde to return, withholding the full purpose of their arrival.

A few hours later, the group saw Clyde.

Clyde seemed pleased to see John and the others. "What a good surprise to see all of you here," he said.

"I wish we could say the same, Mr. Walton," John said. "We learned yesterday my uncle and you kidnapped Jacob when he was on his way to marry Lisa."

Clyde crossed his arms. "Me and your uncle did take Jacob, but the boy deserved it. How can you defend him after what he did, John? And what marriage?"

"I know you and my uncle see half-bloods differently, but what you did was wrong. We want Jacob back now."

"John, why would you want Lisa to marry a man like Jacob...

Samuel, do you have an answer? Do the two of you believe that having her marry Jacob will hide that he raped her?"

Lizzie dropped her bow and stepped in front of John with wide eyes. "Rape...Jacob never forced himself on Lisa," she said. "Lisa and Jacob had talked about being married for years. They love each other."

Clyde's eyes shifted away from the group and onto the ground. "George...I can't believe that he lied to me," he said, kicking the dirt. "I helped your uncle because he said he didn't want to ruin his friendship with the rest of the Tate family. He didn't want everyone in Tahlequah to know and shame Lisa."

"Mr. Walton, we need to take Jacob home. Where is he?" Samuel asked.

"I sold him to one of our slave owners three miles north. I will get my horse, and we will go there now."

They rode to the farm of the slave owner, and Clyde greeted the man, talking to him in the Choctaw language. The men argued as John and the others watched intensely. Clyde turned around to John and the others with a furrowed brow and a frown.

"Mr. Walton, what is wrong?" Samuel asked.

"He sold Jacob to some Chickasaw passing through town," Clyde said. "They offered him a high price since Jacob looked strong and young. He sold him two days ago for $800, which is double what I accepted."

Lizzie paced and her grip tightened on her bow. "The Chicka-saw...the Chickasaw!" she screamed. "They are known to be brutal to their slaves. This would be like you selling Jacob to Alabama or Mississippi."

"Does he know the man's name? What town he is in?" Luke asked.

Clyde replied, "The buyer was a man named Charlie White, but he does not know which town he is from. It will take time to find Jacob."

"We need to leave for the Chickasaw territory now," Lizzie commanded.

"None of us have been to Chickasaw territory, Lizzie," Luke said. "We only have enough food for one more day. It will take us more than a day to reach the Chickasaw."

"Luke is right," John said.

Lizzie rubbed her forehead and pulled at her ponytail.

"Mr. Walton, will you help us?" John asked.

"Yes, I will help get Jacob back home," Clyde said. "I'm sorry. I was so angry when I believed that Lisa had been hurt. I have no idea how long this will take. I hope this will only take me a week."

Lizzie scoffed, sarcastically replying, "A week."

"Lizzie," John calmly said. "Thank you, Mr. Walton. Please let us know how the search for him is going. I think it will be good if Samuel or I also come with you, at least on some of the searches."

"How will you work your fields? Clyde asked. "You're already missing Jacob and one of you leaving with me will make it harder for you."

"David is old enough to help now. It's the only way we will get Jacob back quickly."

"I understand the need to find Jacob, but if your family starts to lose crops because you or Samuel are not there, it will endanger your family. David is too inexperienced to do it on his own even with your uncle there."

"Every two weeks, Samuel or I will come with you to search for Jacob. If you leave tomorrow, we will give you two weeks, and if you don't return with Jacob by then, one of us will meet you at your home and go to the Chickasaw Nation with you. We have to find him before winter. With the snow, we won't be able to go through the Chickasaw territory safely."

"I agree, and tell your uncle I don't want to see him for the rest of the year. Lying to me to have that boy put into slavery when he did nothing is wrong. I may not fully agree with mixing with the Negroes, but Jacob has always been one of the good ones. I didn't believe it when your uncle told me...I should've gone with my gut believing something was wrong. I will see all of you soon."

"See you soon, Mr. Walton." John said.

John and the others left the Choctaw town, frustrated and concerned with how Lisa would react.

------------◆------------

During this time, Grace spoke with Mr. Tate, who became furious, but Florence kept him calm. Grace promised to have Jacob returned back to Tahlequah immediately and apologized for her uncle's actions. As she returned from the Tate farm, she saw John and the others return without Jacob.

Her heart dropped and she walked faster. George put down a hay bale by the barn, and he approached them.

Lizzie dismounted Queen, her eyes focused on her uncle. She marched toward George, and let her bow fall off of her shoulder to the ground.

Grace's eyes widened, and she ran toward Lizzie, recognizing the look on her sister.

Her uncle said something while he shrugged, but Grace was too far away to hear.

Lizzie punched George, knocking him to the ground. Lizzie howled as she tried to hit George again, but John grabbed her and pulled her back.

As Grace got closer to Lizzie, she noticed the disappointed expressions of Luke and Samuel.

"What happened?" Grace yelled.

John let Lizzie go, and she grabbed her braid.

"The Chickasaw have Jacob!" Lizzie growled in Cherokee. "Clyde sold Jacob to one of the Choctaw, and he sold Jacob to the Chickasaw!" Tears shimmered in Lizzie's eyes and her voice cracked. "I can't tell Lisa...I can't."

Lizzie stalked away, picking up her bow as she went. Luke and Samuel helped George stand, and Grace moved toward her uncle, her watery narrow eyes fixed on him. She gnashed her teeth as he shamefully wiped blood off his busted lip. She shook her head and walked inside the cabin while the men put up the horses.

Grace entered the women's bedroom where Lisa was sitting down on her bed, caressing her hands.

"Lisa, they're home," Grace said in Cherokee.

Lisa looked at Grace with big eyes. "Why do you look sad?" she asked.

Grace's eyes shifted to the wooden floor. "Lisa, they tried to get him, but..."

Lisa's eyes welled, and she started to cry. "This isn't right!"

Grace looked up at Lisa. "I promise, we're bringing him home."

She sat on the bed with Lisa and embraced her while she cried.

———◆———

At the same time Grace held Lisa, Lizzie slumped under one of the old trees on their practice ground. The large tree trunk hid her trembling body. She stared at the horizon and wept uncontrollably.

"Jesus, I can't...I can't do this. Please let it end." She squeezed her bow. "Please, Jesus, I give up. I love him, but she can have him. I promise I'll never do something like this again."

Her tears soaked the green grass around her.

"Please let us find him soon. I'm sorry. I'm sorry for all of it. My heart hurts so much."

Lizzie wept for some time. She later walked by a small pond and looked at her reflection. She cleaned her face and returned home.

Annabelle and the others took the news hard, and they realized they couldn't ignore the children's questions anymore.

David and Joseph were told Jacob had been kidnapped, and they were searching for him, but Annabelle didn't want the boys to know George was responsible.

———◆———

The next day, Florence came to the Lightning-Strongman farm in the morning and was told the terrible news. She went home distraught and told Mr. Tate what had happened. As she went out to the family's fields, Mr. Tate walked out of their house with his rifle and got on his horse.

"Papa, stop! Wait!" Florence yelled in her native tongue.

She ran toward her father, but the horse took off. She rushed to their barn, and breathing heavily, she opened one of the stalls and got one of their horses to pursue him.

⁕

Mr. Tate arrived at the Lightning-Strongman farm and got off his horse. "George Strongman, you come out here," Mr. Tate yelled. "Don't hide behind your family."

John and Samuel exited the barn and saw Mr. Tate waiting for George.

"Mr. Tate, please put down your rifle," Samuel said.

"Samuel, your father has done nothing but cause my boy pain, and he had him sold to the Chickasaw. Your father has a debt to pay."

Samuel put up the palms of his hands. "I know you're hurt, Mr. Tate. We're hurting too. I had one of my closest friends taken from me. The person my sister loves was taken from us. Please put down the rifle."

George exited the barn with his arms stretched out. "You're right, Mark. I deserve to be shot," he said. "My little girl won't speak to me, and the rest of my family only tolerates me now. I ruined your boy's life, and in turn, I ruined an old friend's life." George moved toward Mr. Tate with his arms outstretched.

"Pa, stop this. Your dying won't set things right!" Samuel yelled. "We still have time to make things right."

The men argued, with Mr. Tate's rifle pointed at Samuel and George.

Tsula ran out of the family house. "Please stop, Mr. Tate," she begged.

Florence arrived at the farm as everyone watched. She

stopped the horse in front of her father. "Papa, stop this now," she sobbed.

"He took away Jacob. He needs to be punished," Mr. Tate replied. "Your brother is gone."

Florence wept as she got off the horse. "We don't know that. Please, stop this, Papa. I know you're in pain, but it won't make it right bringing more pain on them. They miss Jacob too."

Mark looked into his daughter's brown eyes and saw the pain he was causing her. He reluctantly put down his rifle and hugged Florence. "I want to make this right. I don't know how."

"Fight my Papa and call it a day," Tsula said. "Lizzie already gave him one good hit. A few more should give us peace."

John and Samuel looked at Tsula with skewed frowns.

"Could that be enough to keep our families at peace, Mr. Tate?" Tsula asked.

"If George agrees," Mr. Tate said.

George nodded and the two men walked onto a patch of grass.

John exhaled and pinched his lips. "Can't believe they agreed to your terms," he said.

Tsula's eyes moved sideways to focus on John. "Sadly, he deserves it, and this will calm the waters," she said.

Samuel glanced at his twin. He shifted his gaze back to the men and watched them fight each other. As both men fought, they tired quickly. Mark managed to get one hit on George, knocking him down. The two men looked at each other while trying to catch their breath.

"Papa, enough, let's go home," Florence said in Cherokee. She approached her father and kissed him on his cheek. "Let's go home. I will make you some soup."

Mark kicked the grass when he walked away and got onto his horse. "You have a good family, George," he said.

Mr. Tate and Florence slowly rode off on the dirt trail, and the others were later told of the incident.

Annabelle was pleased with the outcome between the two

families, and the children remained unaware of who had kid-napped Jacob.

<hr>

Two months went by as Lisa struggled with depression. Tsula braided her hair and tried to keep her spirits up, but Lisa remained depressed. Annabelle attempted to help Lisa break out of her depression by asking her to watch the twins, but it didn't work. Lisa remained almost unattached during her birthday, and as it passed, there was still no clue where in Chickasaw territory Jacob had been taken.

The harvest festival came two days later, and talk of it seemed to upset Lisa. She even refused to help cook supper with the other women. She sat under the redbud tree until Grace managed to convince her to spend time with the family. She later agreed to go to the festival with the rest of the family.

As Lisa stood outside, she became impatient and walked away. Lizzie came outside but didn't see Lisa, assuming she had left to spend time with the horses. As the cool November breeze blew through Lizzie's hair, she became concerned.

Annabelle and the others walked out of their homes and approached Lizzie.

"Lisa isn't with you?" Lizzie asked in Cherokee.

John replied, "No, only us and the children. Grace is coming out soon."

Lizzie panicked and ran to the barn to see that Lisa wasn't there. "Thank you, Jesus, all the horses are there," she said, then ran past her family. "Lisa left for the festival already, but she shouldn't be alone."

John said, "We will follow you soon."

Lizzie's heartbeat increased once she arrived at the festival. The sun had almost completely fallen, and a large crowd had already arrived. She asked people if they had seen Lisa while she searched through the festival. She noticed a man she knew and spoke with him. He told her Lisa had taken some drinks with her and that he'd thought it was weird.

Heart pounding, Lizzie scanned the crowds and couldn't find her cousin. She moved through a less populated area of the festival, where a man with a lamp went past her. She then noticed two people between a couple buildings. She marched over to the dark space and ignored others in her way as she grabbed a lamp from the ground. As she neared, she heard moaning and placed the lamp down.

She gasped at the sight of Lisa with her back against one of the buildings, holding onto Tony Fisher. She clenched her teeth and stalked forward, punching Tony in the eye. He let go of Lisa and fell over. Tony wailed and held his eye.

"Lisa, Lisa!" Lizzie yelled.

"What did you do that for, Lizzie?" Lisa slurred in Cherokee as she struggled to stand. "I was fine."

"You're drunk!" Lizzie barked.

"Lizzie, you crazy woman," Tony yelled in Cherokee. "Did you stab my eye?"

Lizzie's eyes narrowed. "No, be grateful that I didn't."

She helped Lisa stand and escorted her out of the festival.

"Where's our family?" Lisa asked in Cherokee. "I want to see my niece."

"We need to go home. We will see them there," Lizzie said.

As the women continued home, Lisa greeted everyone she saw, then asked, "Why did you hit Tony? I wanted to be there."

"You were shaming yourself. Having sex against a wall with a man you don't love. It's beneath you."

Lisa sobbed as Lizzie struggled to help her keep her balance. "I wanted to feel good. It hurts so bad not having him here, Lizzie. I hate Papa, I hate him so much right now."

Lizzie stopped and hugged Lisa as she cried. "I know it hurts, but this isn't you. Drinking, behaving like a whore. I know it hurts, but think...one day Jacob will return."

Lisa wiped her tears away, and Lizzie helped her walk home.

"I don't want anyone to know about this. I know Jesus is mad at me. I have done so much wrong. I'm reaping what I sowed."

Lizzie put her forehead onto Lisa's forehead. "That's a lie. You don't deserve this pain. I've done many worse things than you, but through Jesus I know I'm free from it. We can only move forward. If we stay in the past, we never heal. I learned that from Elder Joyce."

Lisa sobbed again as Lizzie struggled to help walk her home. Once they returned home, Lizzie sat down on Lisa's bed until Lisa fell asleep.

Shortly after, the rest of the family returned home, and Lizzie told them Lisa was drunk. Tsula immediately entered their room and caressed Lisa's face as she slept. Annabelle and Grace soon walked inside to see Lisa sleeping. The family talked about keeping a closer watch on her.

During their conversation, Lizzie thought, *Should I tell the others Lisa had sex with Tony? No, it would only bring Lisa more pain, and she might not completely remember what she'd done.* While the family talked, John emphasized the next few months could be harder for Lisa because they wouldn't be able to search for Jacob in winter. It was agreed they would pray with Lisa every morning to remind her she is loved. When night came, Lizzie contemplated what to do about Tony.

The next morning Lisa woke up early with a hangover and sat in her bed emotionless. Lisa struggled to remember what had happened the night before, and she stared at Lizzie, who slept next to her.

Grace slowly opened their bedroom door. "Hello, Lisa, are you feeling well?" she asked in Cherokee.

Lisa replied, "My head hurts, but that's all. I'm sorry if I scared you."

"Lizzie brought you home. You should thank her. I need help making breakfast, so wake her." Grace smiled at Lisa and left the room.

Lisa reluctantly got out of bed and nudged Lizzie. The other woman woke and sat up, watching Lisa.

"Do you feel well?" Lizzie asked.

"I have a headache, thank you."

"You have no reason to thank me. We are family."

Lisa's eyes became watery. "Did I have sex with Tony, or is my mind confused?"

Lizzie looked into Lisa's regretful eyes and realized she couldn't lie to her. "You did, but I stopped you. Nothing more happened."

Lisa took a deep breath and ran her hands through her hair. "Tony will tell everyone. Jacob will find out what happened. Did you tell anyone?"

"I won't tell anyone, and don't worry about Tony. He won't talk about it."

Lisa frowned. "Men always tell."

"Jacob didn't tell."

"Jacob was different. How do you know he won't talk?" Lisa's eyes bulged, and she gasped. "Did you kill Tony?"

Lizzie scoffed and stretched while she got out of her bed with the sound of her back cracking. "No....but I know he won't talk. Don't worry about it." Lizzie cracked her wrists as she stretched some more and walked out of their room into the kitchen.

The family ate breakfast together, and Annabelle and the others comforted Lisa. She frowned while she ate. George remained silent and avoided eye contact with his daughter. As everyone else ate, Lizzie finished her grits and grabbed her fried chicken leg before standing. She walked inside the women's bedroom as she ate, then left with her bow and quiver.

"You're going out to the practice grounds this early!" Grace said.

"I'm taking a walk, and I'm going to practice a little," Lizzie said.

"Have fun, Flour Face," Tsula taunted.

Lizzie squinted and grunted. "Big mouth," she mumbled before she left the house.

Outside she walked down the dirt road, and her grip tightened on her bow. A knock on an old house door echoed through one of the Cherokee homes. The door opened, and a black-eyed Tony came out.

"Tony Fisher, there you are," Lizzie said as she walked in a small circle.

"Why are you here, Lizzie?" Tony asked.

"I'm here to make an agreement with you. I know you were not drunk last night."

"What are you talking about?"

Lizzie stopped walking, her eyebrows lowered, and her nose crinkled.

Tony sneered. "No, I was not drunk last night. My night was ruined by a crazy jealous little woman, though."

Lizzie marched up to Tony. "You're not going to tell anyone about what happened. I won't let you ruin her reputation."

Tony pointed at Lizzie. "I don't know what goes through your crazy mind, but she came to me. I didn't force anything...she liked it."

Lizzie's voice deepened. "Lisa was drunk. She barely remembers any of it."

"Are you telling me this to make me feel less of a man? Most of the people in our area now know she had something with Jacob. Your drunken uncle did that."

Lizzie scoffed as she stood in front of Tony, who towered over her. "I'm only going to say this once. You won't speak about last night to anyone, or I will cut off what you think makes you a man."

"You don't scare me. Do you think this black eye scares me?"

Lizzie pulled her tomahawk out of her quiver. The sun reflected off the sharp blade.

Tony quickly backed up, his hands out. "Calm down, Lizzie."

"Please test me, Tony Fisher. I suggest you find a desperate woman fast so she can give you a child. If not, keep your mouth shut. I like you a little, Tony...please don't tempt me." Lizzie put her tomahawk back in her quiver and turned to walk away. "I will see you at church?"

"Yeah, I'm going to church tomorrow," she heard him say behind her.

Lizzie arrived at her home and was greeted by her nephews.

"Let's go to the practice fields." The boys shouted with excitement. At this moment, Lizzie noticed Annabelle by the old redbud tree watching her and the boys. Lizzie gave a half-smile, knowing Annabelle wouldn't be able to see it.

❖

January 1858 arrived with a snowstorm, proving the family couldn't search for Jacob. Annabelle saw the sorrow in Lisa and her sons. During this time, she noticed George's efforts to speak with Lisa, but most of his attempts failed. Over the weeks Lisa spent more time speaking with George. In each conversation Annabelle saw that George slowly patted his knee when Lisa's voice became stern. However, both father and daughter became more relaxed with each conversation. Annabelle smiled when there were a few light chuckles between them. This symbolized the relationship between George and Lisa was slowly healing.

❖

On January 30, 1858, Annabelle and Lisa were in the supply store counting the supplies in the storage room while Grace gave warm water to the chickens outside. Annabelle worked to keep Lisa engaged as the two women talked. A cold wind blew into the store as Brock Jackson and Hunter Sawyer entered.

"Well, it is quiet in here today," Brock said. "Normally, I would see at least three Cherokee in here to get some supplies."

"Good afternoon, Mr. Jackson," Lisa said.

Brock scoffed as he arrogantly approached the counter with Hunter following him. "I never do get tired of that accent of yours, Lisa Strongman."

"It is a unique form of southern accent, Mr. Jackson," Hunter said.

Lisa tightened her lips and cocked her head. She replied, "What do you gentlemen need today?"

"I think Miss Annabelle can get a sack of flour. I can see

you're still mourning over that half-breed nigger. How long you going to wait for a man who disappeared?"

Lisa growled, "It is none of your concern what occurs in my life, Mr. Jackson. You shouldn't even know about it."

"See, this is what I like about these Indian women, Mr. Sawyer. They're so bold."

"I agree, Mr. Jackson," Hunter replied. "It's clear she and Lizzie Lightning are related. It's entertaining to see a savage culture where women have so much control."

"Is it my problem white men like dumb women?" Lisa asked.

The men chuckled as they looked at each other.

"Your kind is certainly something to be watched, but to call our white women dumb isn't true," Brock said. "They simply know their place and respect the rules of a civilized society. Could it be that's why Mr. Tate suddenly walked away? Was he seeing too much similarity between you and Miss Lightning?"

The two men cackled again as Lisa scrunched her face.

Hunter replied, "Mr. Jackson, be proper. Big words confuse them. I think it's a fact Cherokee women are not attracted to real men. They pick men that rely on them."

Annabelle came out of the supply room with a sack of flour and placed it on the counter.

"Mr. Jackson, I heard your wife's name is Katelyn, but also, after leaving you for five years, she returned and left you again for the third time," Lisa said. "I guess that proves me wrong. There are some smart white women."

<hr>

Annabelle looked at Lisa with big eyes while Brock pressed his lips together, and his voice deepened. "You Indians think you're so clever, but I think allowing yourself to be polluted by the touch of a nigger reflects how smart you are. Your value is lowered even by befriending a breed lower than yourself."

Lisa anchored her dilated brown eyes onto Brock. "Mr. Jackson, Jacob's value is far above what you could ever be in your entire life. He is a real man. It must be a blessing for Katelyn to be free of your reign."

Brock lunged at Lisa, but Hunter pulled him back. Annabelle placed her hand on her heart and took a step back.

"Brock, calm yourself. Calm yourself now," Hunter yelled. "You Cherokee women are a bold breed indeed. Miss Annabelle, I hope you haven't adapted such inappropriate behavior."

Annabelle's eyes remained locked on Brock and Hunter. Hunter released Brock, gave her money, and took the sack of flour. Brock kept his blue eyes locked on Lisa as she boldly stood her ground.

"I suggest you behave, Miss Lisa. Behaving like your kin will bring you trouble," Brock said.

Lisa replied with a sarcastic tone, "Goodbye, Mr. Jackson. Take care, Mr. Sawyer."

Hunter patted Brock on his shoulder, and the two men exited the store.

"What was that about?" Annabelle asked.

"I told him it was not my problem white men like dumb women."

Annabelle was stunned, as Lisa hadn't shown such a confrontational side to her since George had whipped her.

As the women organized the store's supplies, Grace went back inside the store. "All of that is done," she said. She noticed the stern looks on Annabelle's and Lisa's faces while they worked. "Is something wrong?"

Lisa looked at Grace and gave a fake smile. "No, nothing is wrong," she said. "We are ready to go home."

Grace looked at Annabelle, but Annabelle shook her head.

Annabelle thought, *I know you can tell she lied, but don't try to pressure Lisa into talking.*

Grace nodded at Annabelle, signaling she understood.

<hr>

The beginning of March 1858 arrived, and the Lightning-Strongman family prepared their fields for the next planting season.

Lizzie traveled down the dirt street of Tahlequah carrying a sack of soybeans while she hummed. As she approached the store, she noticed Molly strolling down another street, and she walked faster to avoid the woman.

"Lizzie, Lizzie Lightning!" Molly cheerfully yelled.

Lizzie cringed when Molly moved through the townspeople to meet up with her.

"Molly, I'm surprised you're not with Reverend Hills," she said.

"My husband is witnessing to some of the people outside of your church. He thought it would be more proper for him to speak to those who pass the church instead of giving a sermon at the church."

Lizzie forced a grin as she continued to the store. "What a thoughtful act; you must be proud."

Molly followed her. "Why, yes, I'm proud of him. He works very hard. Much like your family on your farm, faith without works is dead."

"That's a true word. I've also learned assumption leads to ignorance."

"Those are impressive words, Lizzie. You truly learned a lot in Georgia before you came here."

"We did have a school before it was burned to the ground. It was one of the many things that burned." Lizzie reached the doors of the store. "You don't have to come inside. I'm leaving this at the counter for Annabelle."

"I can wait right here."

Lizzie entered the supply store and gave Annabelle the soybeans. She stepped outside and took a small breath.

"Well, now I can walk home to my family," Lizzie said.

"Good, is it all right that I accompany you? Just for a short time?"

Lizzie forced herself to smile. "That's fine."

The women walked on their way to Lizzie's home, passing several people.

Molly fidgeted with her fingers. "Lizzie, I've wanted to speak to you for so long. You seem to be more closed than the other women in your family."

Lizzie's brown eyes shifted sideways and locked on Molly while they walked. "Does that make me lesser than them?"

"No, I'm just concerned about your salvation. Why do you call God the Creator? Why call our father in heaven by such a lesser name? Are you a believer?"

Lizzie's nose crinkled, and she moved faster. "I speak of him as my people have always referred to him. Because I don't adapt to your people's language, does that make my faith in him lesser?"

"Well, I think it is more proper—"

Lizzie's voice rose, "That's your people's problem! You come here and always try to say your way is better! I believe Jesus Christ is the son of the Creator. The Great Spirit, I will never call him God. After what your people have done to us...white people claim to be Christians, but I have met few showing Jesus's love to my people."

Molly's mouth curved downward, forming a frown. "I believe you...I apologize for doubting your faith. I know I'm still learning, but it does concern me you don't do things like a lady should. Going out on hunts with men, shooting arrows, and I've heard of your reputation as a fighter. Please allow me to help you."

"The only thing white people do is help kill who we are. My people haven't done everything right...the fact we have slaves is proof. But where in the Bible does it say my people's language is uncivilized? That is the right word?"

Molly's gaze went downward. "I can admit my people have made mistakes, but it seems hard for you to admit women have their place and men have theirs. It would make you a better person."

"I'm a much better person than I was years ago. You should be grateful for that."

Molly's brow molded into a small furrow. "In what manner are you being a Christian lady making such a small threat?"

Lizzie stopped walking and stared into Molly's green eyes.

"I'm a fighter. I've experienced things you white women would never be able to handle. You're weak...white women are weak. You don't know what life is like without your men. You wait on your men to do all the work and have no idea what real pain is."

As Molly looked at Lizzie, she took a deep breath. "I imagine it must be hard growing up like that. You challenge me...your words hurt because I stand here trying to understand you. I do understand pain. I've been married to Theodore Hills for twelve years, and I haven't given him children. I've never been pregnant. I'm an envious woman when I see a mother with her baby."

Molly seemed sincere, so Lizzie lowered her guard. "I've only heard of few women having this problem. I guess you do understand real pain, I'm sorry."

"I'm sorry as well. I realize I still have a lot to learn about Indians."

"Yeah, you do."

Molly and Lizzie meandered through Tahlequah, speaking with each other about their differences. It was the first time Molly had listened to Lizzie without judging, and it was Lizzie's first time opening up to a white woman.

Lizzie later told her family about the talks she had with Molly. Annabelle had never thought she'd meet a barren woman, but in her viewpoint, Molly remained a positive force.

* * *

Two months passed as Annabelle's family searched for Jacob. The trips were frustrating for John, Samuel, and Clyde. The guilt weighed heavily on Clyde, and he refused to speak to George. Lisa had found George's hidden rum bottles, and to nullify her pain, she drank at night.

While the moonlight shined down on the family house, Lisa would sit on the steps and get drunk as she lay against the front door and cried. She prayed to Jesus for Jacob to come home alive.

Lisa's family tried to keep her encouraged, but she struggled with her faith. Victoria would often join Lizzie in attempting to lift Lisa's spirit. The young women would take Lisa with them to visit neighboring Cherokee towns.

————————◆————————

During the night of June 29, 1858, Lizzie woke up in the middle of the night and noticed Lisa was gone. She panicked and ran to the front door. She opened it, and Lisa fell backward into the house with a rum bottle in her hand, passed out.

"This has to stop," Lizzie said. She pulled the bottle from Lisa's hand and smashed it on the ground. "What a night," she grumbled.

Carrying Lisa into the house, Lizzie placed Lisa on her bed and kissed her on her cheek. The next day, Lizzie told the others how she'd found Lisa as the other woman slept. Grace became furious and blamed George, then George and Grace argued. During the argument Maria took the children to Annabelle's house to eat.

"I have kept my silence for years, but no more of this!" Grace yelled in her native tongue. "You're to give us every bottle of rum you've hidden."

"I've done well. I haven't been drunk since March, and I will continue to do so."

Grace dismissively waved her hand. "Can't you see Lisa has learned this from you? When my momma died it was me and Auntie Shay barely saving our store. What did you do? You got drunk with my daddy, and what did you do when Lizzie…as a child found him dead! You got drunk, and I kept the family together when Auntie Shay walked on two years later."

George frowned. "The Creator knows I tried to let go of that pain in the wrong way. How long are you going to hold the past against me?"

Grace crossed her arms. "I don't hold the past against you. I'm worried you still live in the past, and your drunken days of the recent past are proof of it. You say I did not let my brother or Samuel lead the family."

"Grace," John said.

Grace's face turned red, her brow creased, and she sharply replied, "No, he needs to hear this! The truth is they were too young to lead. The one adult we did have to lead us was too drunk during most of the day to lead! I never wanted this role!" Grace clutched the wooden supper table. "You forced me into the role! What was left of my childhood was murdered by your selfish, self-pitying ways!"

Annabelle calmly touched Grace's hand, and George sat in his chair speechless while his niece looked at him.

"Please give us all the rum you have hidden on the farm, Uncle George," John said. "We have to do this for Lisa and for the children."

"All right, I can admit the drinking isn't like Lisa," George said as he cleared his throat. "Any bottle she used to find she'd break it immediately. You can come with me if you want, John. I don't feel like I deserve to eat before taking care of this first."

John replied, "I can help you, Uncle George."

George and John left the supper table and went outside so George could show where he had been hiding his rum. Samuel frowned while he picked at his food. Lizzie and Tsula noticed his silent frustration, and Tsula encouraged him as they ate.

A few hours later, Lisa awoke with a hangover and came out of her room. She was greeted by Grace holding a rum bottle.

Lisa rubbed her forehead. "I can explain that," she said.

"This isn't the same bottle from last night," Grace said. "You passed out on the porch, and Lizzie carried you inside."

Lisa sighed, and her brown eyes locked onto Lizzie. "I don't remember last night. I don't know what to say."

"You need to stop this," Lizzie said with calm voice and her brow lowering. "You're scaring all of us."

Lisa's gaze moved downward. "I'm sorry." She felt the sting of tears, then took a deep breath. "I'm ashamed. You should never need to carry me inside our home. I'm just like my father."

Grace and Lizzie frowned.

"That's not true, Lisa," Lizzie said.

Lisa's lips trembled. "Tell the truth. You still love him too, but you're not drowning out your pain with poison. I'm weak."

Lizzie's eyes became watery. "I'm so angry," she said. "I'm struggling...I murdered a duck a few weeks ago."

Grace's and Lisa's eyes widened.

Lizzie closed her eyes and opened them, regret etched in her expression. "When I was out on my own, I took its life, and I cried over it. The duck didn't deserve to die because I was angry. I couldn't even bring it home to cook it because I was wrong. I'd rather get drunk then to take another life out of anger." She gulped. "You were right about me."

"I think is some way we're all not handling Jacob's kidnapping well," Grace said. "Lisa, you're stronger than you believe. Lizzie is right though. We're scared for you."

"I promise I'll try to stop," Lisa said, a tear falling down her cheek. "I don't want to end up like Papa...constantly struggling against alcohol."

Grace smiled. "I believe in you."

"So do I," Lizzie said. "I think you should go speak with Pastor Bluebird or Elder Joyce. Your spirit needs to heal."

Lisa shook her head. "I'm not that bad," she said.

"Lisa," Grace spoke with a calm voice.

"No!" Lisa said, her tone now stern. "I can stop. I don't have a problem. I just need to accept the truth. All I need right now is some water. My head keeps hurting, and I need some time before I even look at Papa. Every time John and Samuel return from the Chickasaw without Jacob, it feels like I'm being whipped again." She turned toward the kitchen.

"That's how it's going to be?" Lizzie asked as she crossed her arms.

Lisa turned around with her eyes narrowed. "Yes."

She marched into the kitchen as Grace and Lizzie watched.

◆

Later in the day Grace spoke with Annabelle, Maria, and Tsula. Annabelle suggested they should pray for Lisa every day before they cooked supper. Grace agreed and before supper she and Annabelle would sit under the old redbud tree and pray for Lisa's healing.

Only after a few days of doing this, Tsula, Maria, and Lizzie joined them. It gave them hope Lisa would return to her former self.

Annabelle was convinced Lisa was experiencing the same thing she did when Benjamin was murdered. Annabelle felt determined to remain positive for Lisa.

A month passed with no sign of Jacob's return, and the Cherokee council's stance remained. Because Jacob had been born to a Negro woman, he was not considered Cherokee. Therefore, no political option existed.

Annabelle felt the same frustration as John, and some of the Chickasaw refused to cooperate. In spite of this, Lisa's happy spirit appeared once again, starting with her laughter, and she began braiding the girls' hair again. She had once again begun to go to the barn by herself to brush the horses and pray. The family realized it was her way of healing and trying to be happy.

Relief filled Annabelle when she noticed Lisa walking to the barn. She hoped Lisa's happiness grew, and she hoped harder for Jacob to be found. She believed Jacob's return was the only way both Lisa and Lizzie could move forward.

On the evening of August 30, 1858, the family ate supper together. Lisa got up and put Rain back in the chair to eat some more.

"Lisa, you ate well today," Annabelle said.

Lisa replied in Cherokee, "I think feeding Rain reminded me how much I like corn and beans."

Annabelle and the others chuckled and ate. "You should sit down a little longer and play with the girls."

Lisa beamed. "I'm not going to stay with the horses long. I will be back before it's time for them to sleep."

Lisa kissed Rain on the cheek and walked outside to the barn. As she went, she glanced at the wildflowers and found herself almost smiling at the sight of them.

Inside the building, she petted Ray and gave him small grains. She reached down to get the horse brush and noticed someone had come behind her. She stood to turn around but felt a blow to the back of her head, and she collapsed.

The horses neighed, and Lisa grasped the hay on the barn floor as her blurred vision cleared. She struggled to stand, fear building inside her. She looked back with wide eyes.

Brock stood in front of her with his revolver in his hand. He had already closed the barn door. "I'm impressed, Miss Strongman, most women wouldn't bc ablc to gct up," Brock said. "Your kind truly is impressive."

"Mr. J-Jackson," Lisa stuttered. "You...what are you doing here?"

Brock leered. "I've been watching you, and you have been watching me. I originally planned for me and your cousin to have a...private conversation. I think you'll do well as her replacement...you were so bold to mock my marriage." Brock sneered. "An Injun woman...a redskin trying to correct me. So why not correct you first and then Miss Lizzie Lightning?"

Lisa struggled again to stand, finally succeeding.

"Aw, now, don't move or scream, or I will shoot you where you stand."

Lisa grimaced. "What do you want from me?"

Brock strutted to Lisa with his revolver fixed on her.

"I asked you a question."

Brock chuckled. "Giving demands when you don't have a weapon, very bold. You and Miss Lizzie Lightning have such disrespect for me and Mr. Sawyer. This is long overdue. Your cousin Grace is the smart one. Though I have no doubts in my mind if she could kill me, she would."

Without hesitation Lisa's voice echoed without fear, "You show us no respect. Why should you get any respect?"

Brock slapped her, and she looked back at Brock with her blazing dilated eyes. She forced herself to stand up straight.

Brock's eyes widened, and his voice became deeper and malicious. "Those eyes, no fear, no respect, just rebellion…I must admit it is as admirable as it is detestable. You told me that my value isn't nothing compared to that half-breed nigger." Brock slapped Lisa again. "How about I show you what your value is? I think you'll make a fine substitute since I failed to get your cousin alone first."

"You don't ever put your hands on me!"

Brock tried to slap Lisa again, but she ducked. Abruptly, she punched Brock in the face. The blow caused Brock to stumble into the wooden stable, and the horses neighed. Lisa tried to run but was still off balance.

Brock chased her and pushed her back down. She tried to run to the barn door, but Brock held the revolver to her head.

"Try it again," he said softly, his voice menacing. Brock wiped blood from his lip and stared at Lisa with vindictive eyes. "We're going to play a game. It's called Indian slave. You're going to do whatever Master Jackson says. First thing you're going to do is take off your dress."

Lisa's face scrunched with disgust, and she scoffed. "That's what this is about, you sick man. The answer is no. I do have that much pride left in me."

Brock clenched his teeth while he looked into Lisa's fearless eyes. "Well, then we will play this another way."

He hit her with the revolver, knocking her face down. He then got on top of her and pressed her down as she grunted, placing the revolver to the back of her head. "A fighter to the end, I never met a woman that fought me this hard."

"You're a coward!" Lisa growled.

"No, I'm an enforcer, and I don't take kindly to rejections, especially from a prairie nigger." Brock reached up Lisa's dress and tried to pull down her under garments, but Lisa struggled.

"Keep on fighting me! I'll end your life here, and then Lizzie will be next! And if that rebellious animal doesn't cooperate, Annabelle's nappy-headed half-breed will be sold along with her. It won't be hard for me to find slave owners that will make fake claims on a young fertile Negro woman, and a healthy Negro boy."

"Joseph is a Cherokee child!" Lisa snarled.

"I will spill your blood and send that nappy-headed half-breed to the South. He'll learn fast where his place is. Now you either do as I say, or your half-breed cousin will be leaving Tahlequah forever. After that Annabelle will be next." Brock leered. "Think about it. How long do you think your rebellious cousin would obey me? She won't last...she'll try to kill me and fail. Afterward, I'll kill her or make her a slave. Either way that half-breed will spend the rest of his life in the South."

Lisa reluctantly put her head down on the hay with Brock continuing to hold the revolver to her head.

"That's what I thought. What is it like loving a half-breed? I wonder what causes a woman to pick a man lower than her." Brock aggressively pulled down Lisa's undergarments, and raped her.

Brock finished, and Lisa quickly pulled up her undergarments.

He leered at her. "Your kind is different." He adjusted his brown trousers. "I've had me a few white women that didn't watch their mouth, and afterward, all I saw in them was obedience. But you... I can see it in those eyes you want to kill me." Brock scoffed. "This is your value. When I make arrangements, you better be there or you can say goodbye to the half-breed. Do you understand me, pretty Indian?"

Lisa looked at Brock, scowling. "I understand, Brock," she said with a rebellious tone.

Brock pointed at Lisa. "Watch that tone. You're the first woman to make me bleed. I guess I shouldn't be surprised you're related to Miss Lizzie Lightning. Must be that pride you Indian women hold onto so desperately."

He exited the barn quietly and closed the door. Lisa grasped the hay on the floor and screamed, punching the hay into the dirt floor of the barn as tears went down her face.

"One of these days, I'm going to kill that man!" Lisa looked up. "Father, why did you allow that evil man to do that to me!"

Lisa cried but realized how much time had gone by. She ran to the family house, drying her tears as she went. She opened the old wooden front door, seeing most of the family had left the supper table. To her right, the twins sat down in the living room with their dolls.

Rain smiled at Lisa and dropped her doll. "Auntie Lisa!" the child yelled. She ran to Lisa and gave her a hug.

Lisa hugged Rain back and took a deep breath to stop her tears from falling.

Michael came out of the boys' bedroom as Lisa played with the twins. "We were worried you were going to stay outside with horses all night," he said.

Lisa replied, "I had no plans of being in there all night. Why spend all that time in there when I have these beautiful faces to play with?" Beaming, she ran her hand through Rain's hair. "Are the boys sleeping?"

Michael replied, "Yeah, both of them are sleeping now."

"Can we wake them?" Jannie asked.

Lisa chuckled. "No, you can't. Where is your mommy?"

"Momma walked with Auntie Grace to our house with some pots," Rain said.

"Michael, can you tell Annabelle the girls can sleep with me and Lizzie? I want to braid their hair," Lisa asked.

Michael answered, "Yeah, I can do that for you."

During the night Lisa braided the girls' hair while they sat on her bed. Lizzie sat across from Lisa and played with Jannie. While Lisa braided Rain's hair, she found herself struggling to contain her emotions. The thought of Brock harming her family echoed in her mind, and a tear went down her face.

"What is wrong?" Lizzie asked in Cherokee.

Lisa replied, "Nothing, I'm happy." She lifted up one of Rain's braids, "Look at this beautiful hair, and these beautiful cheeks." She kissed Rain on the cheek, and Rain giggled.

Lizzie smiled.

Later, as the girls and Lizzie slept, Lisa remained wide awake. She caressed Jannie's braided head as she slept, and while she adored her cousin tears flowed down her face.

She quietly prayed, "Jesus, please protect my family and break me free of that evil man."

She fell asleep embracing Jannie and struggled to comprehend what had happened to her.

Joseph's eighth birthday soon passed, and the search for Jacob continued. Molly's friendship with Annabelle and the others grew during this time. Reverend Hills and Molly often visited the family when they rode past their property.

Though Annabelle thought the only struggle the family was dealing with was Jacob's absence, Lisa had her own hidden war. Brock had raped her three more times since the first encounter, and Lisa felt hopeless. Lisa often thought about killing Brock away from her family's land to make it difficult to accuse someone of his death.

In late October 1858, Annabelle sat beneath the redbud tree and watched her children and the neighbors' children play with each other. The kidnapping of Indian children was still a serious issue.

Annabelle noticed Joseph became more frustrated as the children played tag. Joseph got into an argument with David, but it was common for the boys to fight, so Annabelle ignored it.

Joseph walked away from the others with a frown, and Annabelle closed her Bible as she watched her son walk away.

"Joseph, come here," Annabelle said.

Joseph approached his mother with a frown still etched on his face.

"What is wrong?"

Joseph answered in Cherokee, "The other children always

want me to be the one that chases them. I told David but he said don't worry about it."

"I think your brother is right. Don't worry about it. Be grateful that the other children want to play with you. When I was a child, I only had my friend, her sisters, and a few other Negro children."

Joseph pouted. "If I was full-blood, they wouldn't pick me all the time to chase."

Looking at Joseph, Annabelle lowered her eyebrows, and the corner of her mouth pinched. "What makes you think that?"

"Eric said his daddy said Negroes are only good for a few things, and one is to run. I hear Eric always ask David what it is like to have a half-Negro brother."

"And what does your brother say?"

Joseph shrugged. "He says having me as a brother is the same as Eric and his sister. He said I follow him all the time."

Annabelle smiled at her son. "Sit next to me."

Joseph sat next to Annabelle, and she wrapped her arm around him. "Your brother said those things because he loves you, and he'll always love you. Be proud of who you are even when people call you a half-breed."

Joseph sighed and looked at his mother. "I don't want to be a half-breed. I want to be a full-blood so I get treated nicer. I hate being half Negro. I wish I looked more like Rain and Jannie."

"God gave you to me and your father for a reason. You look the way you're supposed to look. You don't look like your sisters or brother, but you're still loved the same in our family."

"Do you ever think what it would be like to not be Negro?"

Annabelle frowned at Joseph's question, but she realized he was looking for the truth. "Yes, in the past some bad things did happen. Those things made me wish I was a white woman, but then I always remembered I was born a Negro for a reason, and the Creator will always love me no matter how I look."

"Why don't the white people think like that?"

"Because they have been taught to hate and fear, something

we don't do. We love each other like Jesus loves us. Love is stronger than hate, always."

"Are all white people mean?"

"No, not all white people are mean. Think about Mrs. Hills and Reverend Hills. They may not always understand us, but they're not mean white people. They understand what it means to love others that are different than you."

Joseph put his hand on his head. "I wish I could grow long hair like them. I think I would look better with longer hair."

Annabelle chuckled. "I tell you this, focus on being good at school. Mrs. Beads said you're the smartest in your class."

Joseph blushed.

"Also focus on being a good big brother like David." Annabelle took Joseph's hand and placed it on her stomach.

Joseph smiled at his mother, and she kissed him on his cheek.

"Go over to the other children and play," she said.

Joseph ran over to the other children with a smile.

A few weeks passed while Annabelle tried to encourage Joseph. She told Grace about her concerns, and the other woman agreed to make a stronger emphasis on supporting Joseph. However, more distractions arose as Tsula announced her pregnancy, and Lisa seemed to drift away from the family once again.

❖

On November 14, 1858, Annabelle stood by the old redbud tree and wept when she realized the bison herds had been shrinking each year. She knew the wolves and cougars she'd seen preying on the herds weren't responsible. She couldn't understand if her crying was her pregnancy, her worry about Joseph, or Lisa's isolation and drinking. Feeling powerless, all she could do was pray for guidance.

She leaned against the tree looking at the horizon. Soon after, her eyes widened seeing two wolves with gray-tawny coats standing in the sparse woods.

"Oh...it's two wolves...they're bigger than the others," she said.

The wolves stopped moving and looked directly at Annabelle with their amber-colored eyes.

She put her hand on her belly. "They're looking right at me. They can't be the wolves..." Annabelle shook her head. "It was just a story Elder Joyce talked about...it's not them. This pregnancy is making me crazy."

Soon the wolves charged the bison herd from behind. The herd was caught off-guard and stampeded away, but the wolves separated a young bison from the others. They ripped at its hind legs several times.

"No. Not that one!" Tears glided down Annabelle's face. She wiped them away as she watched. "Ugh, I hate this. I cry so easily when I'm pregnant."

She watched the hunt with the herd leaving behind the injured animal. One wolf was particularly aggressive, attacking one of the bison's bloody legs again before leaving it alone like the other wolf. Annabelle believed the aggression was unnecessary. The wolves had already won, with bison blood now soaking the grass.

"I guess that wolf is the evil one."

She turned around and went to her home, unable to watch the wolves finish the kill. She believed the wolves were beautiful animals, but she rarely watched them give fatal bites.

After the harvest festival, exhaustion took over the family. Lisa had gotten drunk during the festival, and she cried as John and Samuel helped walk her home. The others remained perplexed as to why Lisa had regressed. The family believed the pain of not having Jacob with her had grown.

The next morning, George walked out of his bedroom stretching. Tsula sat down at the wooden supper table staring at him. Her lips tightened, and a small furrow formed between her brows. Her fingers lightly tapped on the table.

"You're up unusually early," George said. "How's Lisa?"

Tsula answered with a low tone in their native tongue, "She's having nightmares. She'll wake up not feeling well again."

"I guess it was a mistake to lose track of her in the festival. Most men aren't going to say no to a young woman wanting a drink. I—"

"All of this is your fault, Papa."

"Tsula, sweetie, I apologized. I'm sorry about Jacob. If I could take it back, I would."

"Not once have you volunteered to go out there yourself."

"You know I can't. Clyde is still mad at me, and who knows how Jacob will react when he sees me."

Tsula shook her head. "I'm glad Momma walked on. I'm sure Jesus is shielding her from seeing this in heaven."

"I know I messed up, but—"

Tsula's voice elevated. "But nothing! You broke her. It was your responsibility to protect us and to lead us. But it was Grace that had to do it when Momma died."

George's mouth curved downward into a frown. "I'll do whatever I can to stop Lisa from becoming like me. She's always been a good girl."

Tsula's eyes welled up. "I think you killed the good girl. Because you still have hate in your heart. Never in my life...could I image the thought of hating my daddy. Until last night."

George gulped. "I wish I hadn't bought into the lies I was taught as a young man. I wish I didn't turn to the rum like your Uncle Cliff did. I promise to support Lisa the best I can."

"Actions speak louder than words."

George's eyes shifted from Tsula to the wooden floor.

"Grace has always been there. When she shouldn't have had to be there." A tear streamed down Tsula's face, and she wiped it away. "I'm sitting here pregnant with my first child, but instead of being excited about that, I'm worried my sister won't be here to welcome my baby."

"That won't happen. Lisa is strong."

"Papa, even strong people have a weakness. You attacked

her where she wasn't prepared to lose. Did you even pray about Jacob being a good husband for her?"

George's face blanked.

Tsula sneered. "So you had him put into slavery. A man you've known his entire life. Based on nothing but anger and fear...you're a piece of work."

"I know things are bad now, but like I said, I will support Lisa."

"I hope so. I don't know what I would do if I lost her. We've lost enough."

George nodded. "I never imagined my children would lose so much when they were only children. It'll never excuse my not being the pillar y'all needed."

Tsula stood. "What's done is done. I'm hungry, and I know Lizzie is not going to be in the mood to cook. She's been the main one nursing Lisa."

"What are you making?"

Tsula's eyebrow rose. "Grits and chicken...and before you even ask, no, I'm not cooking for you. You can starve for the day. Or you can eat a loaf of bread."

George frowned as Tsula turned to walk into the kitchen.

"You're a grown man, Papa. You can make something your-self if bread isn't good enough. I suggest you stick with the bread, though, you're getting pudgy. I didn't agree to a fat daddy." Tsula walked into the kitchen humming.

George looked down at his small gut and sighed.

The family took their time to help Lisa heal. Earlier in the month, Lisa refused to go into the barn to celebrate her thirty-first birth-day with the horses. Instead, she slowly rode the dirt trails with Big Boy, isolating herself from the rest of the family.

Lizzie remained determined to keep Lisa from separating her-self. She often left her to watch the children, which was the only thing Lisa wouldn't refuse.

A week after the festival, Tsula and Grace walked down a

trail to visit Victoria. Tsula's long, wavy hair was unbraided like Grace's, and she lightly tugged at it.

Grace slowed down her pace. "What's wrong?" she asked.

"I don't know. I was already feeling a little weird a few days ago, and then Lisa gets drunk. I think all the drama is stressing me out."

"Tsula, I understand being worried about Lisa, but the baby comes first."

"I know...I'm already a slave. My hips are spreading, I can't eat some foods now, and now Nancy makes me even more nauseous."

The two cousins cackled.

"You need to behave."

"I've been behaving. I'm bringing a child into this world married. I think that's a good record. I just don't know why I'm feeling worse."

Grace turned her head, looking down the trail. "I—"

"Grace," Tsula's voice contorted with pain. She squatted and her face scrunched. "Something is wrong."

"Oh, no, okay, we're going home." Grace took Tsula's hand.

The two cousins walked together, but Tsula stopped again.

"What is it?" Grace asked.

Tsula moaned. "I don't know. It's way too early for the baby to come." Tsula eyes teared up. "Something is wrong...I know something is wrong."

"Come on. Once we get home, I'm going to get Elder Joyce."

"Grace, I'm scared."

"Everything will be fine. Remember you said you wanted to walk around like Annabelle to keep your figure. I think you've been doing a great job."

"You think so?"

"Yeah, I do. So let's get you home before you start feeling more pain. Between what is happening with Lisa and your probably eating something your body didn't like, I think you should rest."

The cousins continued home with Tsula fighting pain. She

kept her hand on her belly in an attempt to stay calm. When they approached the family house, Grace called for help. Samuel rushed toward them and carried Tsula inside the big house. Afterward, Michael drove their carriage to Elder Joyce's home with Grace riding next to him.

The women at home worked to comfort Tsula.

"I think something is wrong," Tsula said, her voice cracking.

"Calm yourself. We don't know that," Maria said.

"You know we're here for you, Tsula," Annabelle said.

"I feel so weird, Annabelle," Tsula said. A tear streamed down her cheek, and she wiped it away. "I shouldn't feel this fear."

Annabelle held Tsula's hand. "When Elder Joyce arrives, we'll know how to help you better. We have to hold onto hope... so don't speak like this."

"Thanks, Annabelle."

"I'll be right back. You need some water." Annabelle walked out of the room and went into the kitchen. She leaned against one of the walls and exhaled. She mumbled, "God, please don't let her lose this baby. She doesn't need to experience the pain I did. We're already struggling with Jacob being gone. Please, Jesus, I'm scared for her."

Lizzie walked into the kitchen, and her eyes locked onto Annabelle. The other woman's grief-filled eyes said what Annabelle didn't want to accept. "You—"

"Is this what you experienced?" Lizzie interrupted.

Annabelle's lips quivered, and she frowned. "Almost, but I started to bleed earlier than Tsula."

Lizzie's gaze moved toward the floor and back to Annabelle. "Maybe Elder Joyce can fix this. I don't think Tsula can handle losing a baby. You're stronger than you believe, Annabelle." Lizzie turned around and left the kitchen.

Annabelle closed her eyes and breathed deeply. She went to the well, and tears trickled down her cheek. "I wish I were stronger."

She gathered water from the well and went back inside to comfort Tsula.

When the evening arrived and Tsula's miscarriage was confirmed, the loss was deeply felt, though Tsula tried her best to smile while Elder Joyce assured her she wasn't at fault.

———◆———

The next day after breakfast, Tsula sat under the redbud tree and stared at the prairies.

Annabelle took a deep breath and approached her. "I hope you don't mind if I sit here. You're in my spot," she said in Cherokee.

Tsula replied, "I should have known when I walked over here. The grass was already bent over to accept me sitting on it."

The two women chuckled while they looked at each other.

"If you need anything, I'm here, Tsula," Annabelle said. "I understand the pain of losing a child before you even get to hold them."

Tsula shook her head. "No, I'm fine. You know, Lizzie isn't the only strong one here. I did love someone before Luke. I know how to accept losing something you love. I never thought I'd experience feeling life in me one day, and then on the next feel nothing...this feels crazy. I'm twenty-nine years old, and I lost a baby."

"Yeah, it is a different feeling than seeing someone, and then they're not here anymore." Annabelle looked at Tsula's scrunched face.

"It hurts really bad. I think I could have accepted Luke's death more than losing my child. A child I will never get to hold." Tears fell from Tsula's eyes. She quickly wiped them off her cheeks. "Life is unfair, but I know the Father can bless me like he did you."

"You need to hold strong to what you said. I did lose my children, but later I was blessed with the twins. Two beautiful little girls, I hope they will have a far better life than I ever could. It's also good to grieve."

"I feel like there's enough grief around here."

"You need to let it out so you can heal."

Tsula huffed. "I hate the thought that Nancy is right about me. What if I'm terrible mother? What if that's the reason I lost my baby?"

"Don't think like that. Don't hurt yourself with the words of someone like Nancy. If we are lucky your next baby will be as funny as you are. We need more funny people."

Tsula chuckled as she wiped tears from her face. "Yeah, we do, between Lizzie's and Grace's seriousness, and Lisa now becoming a drunk like our papa. How are the twins going to learn how to be funny? You know you can be funny, but I'm still the most beautiful."

The women laughed and gave each other a hug, and throughout the day, the family encouraged Tsula, keeping her spirit lifted.

A few days later, Lizzie marched to the practice grounds, where David and Joseph had their bows and arrows she had taught them make. She quietly watched them.

Joseph pulled back and released his shot, grazing the wood target.

"You have to hold your bow stronger; don't let it shake, Joseph," David said. "Remember what Auntie Lizzie said?"

Joseph replied in Cherokee, "Yes. What do you think of Auntie Tsula losing the baby, are you sad?"

David lowered his bow and looked at Joseph, his face expressionless. "I'm not sad. The baby is in heaven now, and Auntie Tsula said she'll have a stronger baby next time. Are you sad?"

"A little, I was hoping our new baby brother or sister would have someone to grow up with. Rosita and the twins are the same age."

"The baby will have us. We're the older brothers, and it will always be our job to protect them. The baby will never be alone." Joseph smiled at David as he stood next to his brother. "Watch me hit the target on the high branch like Auntie Lizzie." He took aim with a strong focus, but while he aimed Joseph tickled his ear with a feather. He flinched and missed his target as he released the arrow.

Lizzie smiled when Joseph laughed at David. "What was I supposed to see?"

David sneered. "You little cheater, I should leave you out here alone."

Joseph stepped back. "Why are you getting mad? You've never hit the target before, what is one more miss?"

David grunted, and he reached for another arrow on the ground. "I'm going to tell Momma A if you do it again."

Joseph pouted. "You tell all the time! It was one shot."

"I want my one shot to matter. I'm a warrior, and my skills need to be strong."

Joseph rolled his eyes as he watched David take aim at the same target.

David focused and he missed another shot. Joseph laughed, and David irritably glared at his brother. The boys argued and made fun of each other. Their arguing reminded Lizzie of her and Grace. She stood and approached the boys, who jolted while gasping and didn't say a word. Smiling she took aim and hit the target David had failed to hit twice.

Lizzie gave Joseph a kiss on the cheek, then kissed David on the forehead. "Keep trying boys. I'm proud of you," Lizzie said in Cherokee.

"Thank you, Auntie Lizzie," the boys replied.

As Lizzie left, the boys looked at each other. "I'm going to become as good as Auntie Lizzie," Joseph said.

"Yeah, well...I know I can become as good as Auntie Grace," David said.

Joseph threw his bow down. "You can't get as good as Auntie Grace! Papa can't even beat her, and I watched Auntie beat him!"

David's nose crinkled and he clenched his teeth. "I bet I can!"

"No, you can't! I'm going to ask Momma, and I bet she says you can't!"

David's grip squeezed tighter on his bow. "I know if I ask her, She'll say that I can!"

Lizzie stood by one of the old trees listening to the boys' childish argument. She walked away humming. As she hummed, she prayed for her nephews' protection, hoping their future would be filled with love.

———◆———

Grace's thirty-third birthday arrived, and with it a light snow the children played in. The women spent time together talking about baby names for Annabelle's baby, and the men spent time talking about politics and the crops. After supper, the women decided to braid each other's hair in front of the fireplace while the men played cards.

As Tsula braided Lisa's hair, she noticed bruising on her upper back. "Lisa, how did you get hurt?" she asked.

Lisa replied in Cherokee, "I didn't get hurt. Don't worry about it."

Lizzie said, "It's probably from the last time you got drunk. You hurt yourself and didn't realize it."

Tsula poked the bruise, and Lisa flinched.

"Don't do that, Tsula!" Lisa griped.

Tsula replied, "I'm sorry. I wanted to know if it hurt."

The twins laughed as they sat patiently while Maria and Grace braided their hair.

"Leave her alone and focus on finishing Lisa's hair," Lizzie bickered.

Tsula grunted, and Lisa frowned, but Lizzie knew she couldn't force the truth out of the other woman.

Lisa refused to speak any more about Jacob to Pastor Blue-bird or Elder Joyce because it made her more unable to sleep and short-tempered.

———◆———

On January 5, 1859, Annabelle, Grace, and Lisa went to the supply store while John and Samuel took David and Jacob with them to fix their wood fencing. It helped to keep out the bison and elk, although the deer and pronghorns could jump the fence.

The boys helped carry wood to replace the old fencing, and

John and Samuel showed them how. John watched the boys work after teaching them, and he was pleased with his sons. John's approval motivated the boys, and while they worked, a small pronghorn herd passed.

"David, what do you want to do when you grow up?" Joseph asked in Cherokee.

David replied in their native tongue, "I think I want to be part of the tribal council to help make rules. I did want to be a warrior and fight bad people because Auntie Lizzie is strong and she always said we can't trust the white people. Now I think I can do both. Be strong and make laws to protect us."

"Papa is strong too. Why not think of him when you talk about being strong?"

"Yeah, Papa is strong," David said, "but Auntie Lizzie gets mad really fast, and she gets as strong as a man."

Joseph nodded his head in agreement.

"What do you want to do when you grow up?" David asked.

"I want to visit the cities and see all the different people. I want to see the town, Mercy, Momma talked about so much. I want to see Georgia. I also want to imagine what it would be like to grow up there and not here because the white people make us live here."

David replied, "I would take a trip with you."

Joseph grinned. "You would! It would be fun."

"Yeah, it would, you would need me anyway because you can't aim your bow or use a rifle."

Joseph's smile dropped as David laughed at him. "Shut up! That's why you're getting bumps on your face now and look ugly."

David narrowed his eyes and pushed Joseph. Joseph pushed him back. The two boys grappled each other, and David forced Joseph onto the dead prairie grass. Joseph tried to push David off when David pressed his knee on Joseph's back.

"Give up!" David yelled in Cherokee.

"Never!" Joseph yelled back.

"Give up, you stubborn wolf!"

"I will never give up, you frog face!"

David pressed harder on Joseph's back, making the boy scream.

John's head snapped toward the boys' location. "What are you boys doing?" he yelled.

"Nothing," David said, letting go of Joseph.

Joseph stood up, wiping dead grass off his brown trousers. "See, I wasn't going to quit," he said as he bobbed his head.

John moved to get a full view of the boys. "Finish up, boys, so we get back in time for supper," John said. "Don't make me come over."

The boys looked back at their father with wide eyes and quickly scrambled to finish their job.

Shortly after, Joseph's eyes shot wide open. "No!" he shouted.

John's eyes widened, and he hurried over to the boys with his rifle. He approached his sons as they stared into the prairie. His gaze shifted to where the boys looked, and he saw a large cougar chasing a pronghorn. John exhaled and shook his head.

Joseph looked back, and his jaw dropped. "Papa, come look!"

John thought, *This kid is going to give me gray hair.* He walked closer to the fencing with a half-smile and watched as the cougar caught the pronghorn. "Well, you don't see that every day."

"He's so big, Papa," Joseph said excitedly.

"It could be a girl," David said.

Joseph looked at David, and back to the successful big cat. "This is amazing."

John chuckled. "I don't think your grandma would agree. A long time ago, she got into a fight with one of them."

"I remember Auntie Grace talking about it before," David said.

Looking at the big cat drag away its kill, John laid his rifle against the fence. "Yeah, your grandma's life was spared by the Father. She would tell me the story every now and then. One day I'm sure she became angry with me and showed me her scar on her shoulder."

"Why did she do that?" Joseph asked.

John smiled. "She got tired of my not believing her. My doubt caused her pain."

"Was it scary?"

"No, but I never thought to cross my momma ever again. Your aunties get their strength from her. How many people do you hear about punching one of the great cats and living to tell about it?" John stretched out his arms. "Come here, you two."

The boys stepped up to John, and he placed his hands on their shoulders.

"Life isn't fair, but don't ever turn your back on Jesus because of that truth. With that said, I'm sure the cat took your momma's favorite buck. So we're going to get some flowers and then tell her." John let go of the boys, picked up his rifle, and called to Samuel.

They walked to the family house, talkative and hungry.

John thought, *I hope you're being allowed to watch this from heaven, Momma. I'm a happy man. Even though these two fight, I know they love each other.*

———◆———

In mid-February of 1859 after church, Lisa entered the barn and left the barn door open. Lisa reluctantly stood by the door as the rest of her family took naps or walked into town.

Brock came out of the barren woods to the barn. As he stood before Lisa, she couldn't hide her disgust of the man. Torturing and murdering the racist Indian agent dominated her mind. Brock smirked and entered the open barn as Lisa walked inside behind him.

"I see no matter how many times we do this, you still have the same look in those eyes," Brock agitatedly said. "I think the next time you see me, you better smile."

Lisa side-eyed him, replying, "I apologize if I fail to hide my anger against you. I know when you die, the Father will make you pay for every time." Lisa leered. "In a way, that brings joy to my heart."

Brock smacked Lisa. "What do you savages know? You're the weaker breed. You people make our world weak. Even to this day your people refuse to do everything in a civilized manner. I see nigger-lovers as their masters, I see countless half-breed niggers, and that number keeps rising every year. In what way does God want anything to do with you when you're meant to serve the higher race?"

"If you're so high, why do your people bring nothing but death?"

Brock slapped Lisa again and grabbed her jaw. "You still don't know your place." He pulled out his revolver and placed it to Lisa's temple. "Remember what happens after you're dead."

"I'm sorry," Lisa said with her eyes widening.

Brock scoffed. "I'm sure you are."

"I'll do whatever you want. All I ask is for you to control yourself, and not to release yourself in me again. I won't give you a child. You won't shame me beyond what happens here."

"That was one time." His voice deepened. "I'd never want to create an abomination. I think you need to shut your mouth." He put his revolver back into his holster. "Your lack of cooperation is testing me."

Brock's sour breath made Lisa nauseous. *One day you'll learn the hard way, and I hope I'm there to witness it,* she thought.

She reluctantly took off her undergarments as she looked away from Brock, her brow furrowing. She lay on her stomach and bit her lip.

Brock began to thrust into her.

A tear seeped out of her watery eyes, and she wiped it away.

As he continued, she felt him lose control. "I said, not in me!"

Brock pushed Lisa face first onto the hay, but she forced herself up. Brock put both of his hands on the top her back and pressed her down as Lisa struggled to push up.

"You don't command me!" he growled.

"No!" she screamed into the hay.

He finished, and she kept her head pressed down into the hay, her fingers digging into the dirt floor.

Brock pulled up his trousers. "You take it and do as I say!"

Shivering and breathing heavily, Lisa looked up at Brock, her fingers covered in dirt. "You're an evil man. You will never be loved!"

"Are you speaking back to me?" Brock reached for his revolver.

Lisa gulped with her hate-filled eyes locked on him.

He leered and huffed, and his hand let go of the gun. "Dear Lisa, this isn't about love. I could never love a redskin. It's about taming you. It's pitiful. All you need to do is submit, and I'd be satisfied and stop."

Continuing to leer, Brock kneeled down and placed his hand on her cheek, but Lisa pushed it off.

He smacked her, and his voice deepened, "Keep fighting me, and I'll sell that half-breed kin of yours anyway! I think you know how serious I am about it."

Lisa clenched her hand into a fist, and her gaze moved toward the ground. "I know."

"I'll tell you when your next lesson is. If you cooperate like a lady, I may even forgive Lizzie's transgressions. She'll be indebted to you for life."

Brock slowly poked his head out of the barn door and scanned the land before he left the barn.

Lisa remained on the barn floor, and she shrieked into the hay once he was gone. "I hope I get to kill you one day!"

She stood and moved toward Big Boy, then hugged the horse as she cried, rubbing his head against hers.

Her anger lingered, and though it was not directed at the family, she knew her family noticed her anger. Their efforts increased to lighten her mood through jokes or by leaving the children under her care. However, she now understood how Lizzie could kill.

❖

In mid-March, as Grace left from Joyce's home, Eli approached her.

"How did you know I was here?" she asked.

"May I walk you home?"

Grace tried to force herself not to smile. "Eli, you walked me home yesterday."

Eli cocked his head. "And I will do it again tomorrow and the day after that. Today I was at the right place at the right time."

Grace turned toward at Joyce's home and back to Eli. "Come on," she said.

The two traveled to Grace's home, walking past other towns-people.

"I have given you more of my time since November," she said, "and I even allowed you to come to my home on my birthday. What more do you want?"

"I want your love, if you will let me have it."

Grace was speechless and blushed when she processed what Eli said.

"Did I say something wrong?"

"Well, no...I think you're pushing me too fast. I have to think of my family. Right now finding Jacob is the most important thing. I know you've seen the changes in Lisa. When was the last time you saw her smile...when she didn't have my nieces?"

"I know she is hurting, but does that mean you have to push away how you feel?"

Grace's brow furrowed, and she squinted her brown eyes at Eli. "What do you know about how I feel?"

Eli put his hands in his pockets. "Say that you don't care for me more than as a friend. Say it right now, and I won't ask anything more of you. This last year you have allowed me more into your life. You see me as more than Victoria's cousin. You see me as more than a friend from our childhood."

Grace looked into Eli's eyes. Her heart beat faster, and her breathing became tighter. "I don't want to deal with this right now. How about you focus on Jesus?"

"I'm focused on Jesus."

"You don't seem like it, you keep chasing me. You need to learn how to listen and follow Jesus instead of chasing me."

"How are you listening and following if you push the right thing away because it arrived earlier than you wanted it?"

Grace's eyes widened as she looked at Eli. He took her hand and leaned closer, but she shyly pulled away.

"Don't try that on me, Eli," she said. "And who are you... to say who's right for me! Or how I feel? I can walk alone from here."

"Grace."

"We will see each other again, Eli."

***

Grace walked away, heavily breathing, as Eli watched. Unknown to both of them, Lizzie was watching as she stood by one of the buildings.

Lizzie approached Eli. "Hello, Eli Five Killer," she said.

Eli frowned. "Hey, Lizzie, where did you come from?"

"I was watching and listening. You have a good heart. It's sad Grace keeps pushing you away."

"Your sister is a difficult woman."

Lizzie scoffed. "Most of the women in my family are difficult in some way, but I know how to help you. Come with me, let us talk about Grace."

Lizzie took Eli's hand, and the two walked through Tahlequah.

***

As Annabelle's thirty-first birthday passed, some tension still remained. Lisa's drinking worsened. She found it easy to get illegal rum from men.

A temporary reassignment sent Brock away to the Choctaw, giving Lisa relief. However, fighting between Lizzie and Lisa increased after Lizzie caught her hiding alcohol. Annabelle, seemingly determined to bring peace back, actively searched for any hidden alcohol.

Lisa's sleeping pattern changed, and she stayed up later

than the rest of the family. Lizzie tried to be compassionate, so she stayed up a few nights with Lisa to prevent her from getting drunk while they talked and ate food.

On April 2, 1859, Annabelle traveled, with Lisa and Maria, to the Tate and Thompson farms to give water to their slaves. Annabelle's pregnancy had become more obvious, and she wasn't allowed to walk alone.

Florence welcomed them on the Tate farm. Mr. Tate had been battling depression, but the young women lifted his spirit. Annabelle knew it also lifted Lisa's spirit having a chance to talk to Mr. Tate.

The three women later traveled to the Thompson farm and were greeted by Mr. Thompson.

Annabelle and the other women walked to the large barn where Doll normally worked.

"Doll, are you here?" Annabelle asked in Cherokee.

Doll came out of the barn holding a sack of grains. "Annabelle and Maria!" she exclaimed. "Hello, Lisa. I haven't seen you in a while."

"Hi, Doll," Lisa replied.

Doll put down the sack and with a big grin walked up to the women. She gave all three of them hugs. "Look at you, Annabelle, you're almost ready to have this one," Doll said. "It isn't twins again, I hope."

"I hope not too, but I'm sure this time it is just one," Annabelle said. "I think I would cry if it were another set of twins. I love the girls, but they work too well against me."

"Yes, I'm regretting I didn't give Samuel a son first," Maria said in Cherokee. "Rosita is work. I feel like they can all read each other's minds to plan things. Two weeks ago they tied grass around one of the rooster's necks so they could walk him."

Doll laughed and asked in her native tongue, "Did it work?"

"At first it did, but he pecked through the grass when the

girls were not watching and ran away. All the girls did was probably feed a coyote or cougar."

Doll continued to laugh. "Your girls are more dangerous than mine, that much I can say. Maria, you speak a lot better now. I'm surprised. Did you get tired of Tsula making fun of you?"

"Yes, I did, but Tsula did help me a lot, and now I'm teaching Rosita more Spanish so she can speak better with my side of the family. She is learning much faster than I thought she could."

"I'm glad Master Thompson started speaking English too, but he speaks it mostly to Megan. She's fifteen now. Georgia will be nine years old soon, and she speaks good English."

The women looked over as Megan carried a basket of clothes inside to the large home. The teenage girl now had long brown hair, and her light-brown skin made it clear she was a half-blood child.

"Wow, she's grown since the last time I saw her," Lisa said in Cherokee. "Who was the father?"

"A Cherokee man," Doll replied. "I don't think about it much. Master Thompson has taken on more of a father role for both of the girls. Samantha is also kind to both of them, and Thomas treats them well. Thomas is away at one of the big schools in Illinois now."

Lisa narrowed her eyes. "Megan looks a little like Samantha."

Doll cleared her throat. "Even though Megan is a half-blood, I was surprised how much she didn't look like me, but yes, they look similar."

Annabelle knew Doll was nervous and gave her a hug. "Doll, we need to leave now, we have to return to the supply store," Annabelle said. "Tell Mrs. Thompson we said hi."

Doll replied, "I will…I forgot to tell you she's been ill since last week, but she is doing a lot better now."

Annabelle replied, "Good, I will try to come by tomorrow."

Maria gave Doll a hug. "We will see each other again," she said.

"We will see each other again," Lisa said.

The three women left the Thompson farm, continuing to

enjoy each other's company. As the women walked, they talked about Tsula and Samuel's birthday, which was the next day.

———◆———

Two weeks after Tsula and Samuel's thirtieth birthday. Tsula strolled through the streets of Tahlequah to Elder Joyce's for another meeting with the wise elder. She opened Joyce's front door and entered into the home. She didn't see Joyce, so she stood by the door and sniffed the pine-scented air.

"How does she do it?" Tsula said in Cherokee.

"Do what?" Joyce asked.

Tsula jumped back and fell against the wall. "You were just sitting there! You scared me!"

"I was taking a nap." Joyce stretched and stood up. "You're a special one. No wonder your momma got a gray hair when she had you. Come sit at my supper table."

"If you keep scaring me like that, I'm going to get gray hair early too."

Tsula sat down at the old wooden supper table next to Joyce.

"How is Lisa doing?" the older woman asked. "She's been avoiding me in church for a month, and I haven't been able to visit. There is other drama in town, and it takes time coming out to your family."

"Lisa is still getting drunk. She goes into town now and offers a kiss for a bottle of rum."

"And those fools agree. No surprise there, it's sad to see how much alcohol has become a problem for our people. I wouldn't be surprised if your sister was targeting already drunk men and easily tricking them."

"Most of the time she gets drunk at night when everyone sleeps. Lizzie catches her sometimes, and then they fight."

Joyce folded her hands. "I see...that's proof the problem has grown. And no word on where in the Chickasaw's territory Jacob is being held."

Tsula frowned. "No, they've searched through most of their

territory. The Chickasaw haven't been welcoming to them when they learn they're looking for Jacob."

"I see; this is a bigger problem I'll have to pray harder about. The more time that goes by the less chance they will have in finding him. Your father has created a great problem."

Tsula sighed. "I'm having a hard time talking to him."

"Holding your father captive in your anger won't fix the problem. I'm sure he is suffering every time he sees Lisa."

"I feel he understands what he did was wrong, but saying sorry doesn't feel like he has answered for what he did."

Joyce nodded. "Yes, sorry does not always feel like an apology, but forgiveness must rise above the anger. It allows healing to begin and clears our vision. Forgive, respect, and love your father, and that will help change his heart."

Tsula frowned. "I will try."

"No, do it. Tsula, for the safety and peace of your family, no more trying, you can do it."

"I know...no more excuses."

"Good, I see you've made yourself a new dress. A green dress with small blue circles lined around your skirt, it looks pretty."

"Thank you. It means a lot to hear your approval."

"Now, did you make that dress because you wanted to create something, or did you make that dress to ignore the pain of losing a child?"

Tsula gulped as she looked down at the supper table.

"Take off the bonnet and let me see that beautiful face."

Tsula took off her green bonnet and looked back at Joyce. "I feel much better now. As I told you, Annabelle talked with me, and it made me feel a lot better. Luke has finally calmed down and stopped talking about it. He seems happy now."

"You say one thing, but your eyes are still trying to hide what you really feel. I believe you feel better. The question is, have you let go enough to focus on being blessed with another child?"

"I think someone is knocking on the door, Elder Joyce."

Joyce smirked. "Nice try, Clever Fox, but my hearing is at

least one of the few things that still works well. Now, you tell me the truth, Tsula Fields."

Tsula's gaze shifted around the room. "I think I need a drink or two, and I'll be fine. I'm young...thirty is young."

"Tsula!" Joyce yelled.

Tsula looked at Joyce with big eyes and huffed. "No...I haven't let go. I watch my niece and the twins. It makes me wonder what I missed. It makes me believe I did something wrong. What did I do wrong? Is Jesus mad at me, or do I not deserve..." Tsula's eyes shimmered with tears, but she took a deep breath.

Joyce placed her hand on Tsula's shoulder to comfort her. "Now you're letting the pain go for real. No more jokes or shadows, just you."

Tsula cried and Joyce hugged her.

"Let all of it out, let it go, and trust the Father," Joyce said.

"It was unfair, it was really unfair!" Tsula cried. "I will never get to hold my baby! I haven't felt like this since Momma died."

"You will have another chance. I have prayed for you ever since it happened. In deep prayer I have heard the Holy Spirit speak to me. You'll have another chance. Be patient, Clever Fox."

"I don't know how to make the sadness stop. I'm scared."

"You're doing the right thing right now. It's good to grieve. This is a season. Not what the rest of your life will be. Do you want prayer?"

"Yes, I need a lot of that. And some turkey."

Joyce chuckled and wiped away the tears glistening on Tsula's cheeks. "Okay, Clever Fox."

The wise woman burned sage and prayed for Tsula while she hugged her. The Holy Spirit rested on Tsula, and peace overran her sorrow. After Joyce finished praying for Tsula, the women talked more.

When Tsula left the house, Joyce smiled and said, "Now, remember what we talked about."

"I will trust the Father's plan." Smiling, Tsula went home to spend time with her family.

From that day on she was released from her pain and was willing to look forward to the future.

Poverty remained a problem in Tahlequah. The pressure to feed the family remained a constant worry of the older men. To their surprise, the crops grew healthier than last year, exciting them. George was the most excited, especially since Maria announced at the end of April his second grandchild was on the way.

On May 3, 1859, John instructed David and Joseph to go to the supply store to help organize the supply room while Annabelle and Grace tended the small soybean field and Tsula managed the money. The brothers arrived at the store carrying cornmeal and beans. A wagon with two horses was already there. The boys walked inside the store, attracting the attention of Nancy, Paul, and Eve.

"Hello, boys, I see they're putting you to work," Nancy said. "It is always so entertaining to see you, David. You're looking so much like your father." Nancy sneered at Joseph.

"Good morning, Mrs. Scott," David said. "Thank you."

The two boys moved toward the supply room when Nancy cleared her throat. "Joseph, do you have nothing to say? I know your mother has taught you far better than to remain quiet. It is rude."

"Good morning, Mrs. Scott. I'm sorry for not greeting you," Joseph said.

"Very well-spoken, proof of who your mother is. I suppose that gives some form of hope, being a—"

"Nancy," Tsula said with a low growl in her voice.

Nancy looked at Tsula and remained silent. She then turned her eyes back to Joseph and scoffed. "Well-spoken, Joseph Lightning. Go on now."

The boys went past Paul to the supply room and nodded at him.

"Y'all sure is growing," Paul said.

Nancy replied, "Paul, nobody asked to hear your thoughts right now. Here is the list of supplies we need for now, Tsula."

Tsula replied, "Wow, looks like you don't want to come back for a while."

"I have family visiting from Tennessee. They'll be arriving within a few days. We need to be prepared. The only weakness of being cattle ranchers is most of our crops are for the cattle."

"David, come here," Tsula said with her welcoming smile.

"Yes, Auntie Tsula," David said.

"Here is the list, you and Joseph help Paul put all of these things on the wagon. Be careful with the flour. Do you remember the story of Auntie Lizzie and the flour?"

David replied with a smile, "Yes."

"All right, be careful or I'll start calling you flour face."

David chuckled and went into the supply room.

"What happened to Lizzie?" Nancy asked.

Tsula answered, "That's a story I can't tell. Otherwise, Lizzie might choke me if you learned about it."

Nancy folded her arms and sneered.

"Momma, may I go outside?" Eve asked.

"Yes, but you stay by the wagon and leave the horses alone," Nancy said. Eve walked out the door when Nancy turned around and said, "Don't touch those horses, Eve."

Eve went outside, and Nancy sighed as she touched her forehead.

"Why can't she touch the horses?" Tsula asked.

Nancy snobbishly replied, "She works well with the beasts, but she always gets dirty. It has been somewhat difficult to teach her how to be ladylike. I fear she is influencing her younger sisters."

"Please, those girls are toddlers. I'm sure your family will be pleased to know she is good with a horse. That takes work."

Nancy scoffed. "That's a job for a man, to work with beasts like horses or dogs."

"Nancy, I wouldn't say working or even playing with dogs is

something for only men. I'm sure that if you ran with a pack of dogs, people would not realize you were a woman," Tsula said.

Paul chuckled but stopped when Nancy looked back at him.

Tsula bit her lip and then leered. "I'm sorry. There are still certain moments I have a hard time ignoring your conceited moods."

Nancy huffed. "Your mouth is one of the most unholy things on this earth."

A thudding noise caused Tsula and Nancy to look over. The boys had grabbed the supplies and handed some to Paul.

———◆———

The two boys and Paul exited the supply store, loading the wagon. Joseph noticed Eve watching them. The hazel-eyed girl was rarely allowed to play with the other children, especially Joseph.

"Hello, David. Hello, Joseph," Eve said with a smile etching across her face.

"Hi, Eve," David said.

"Hello, Eve," Joseph said. "That's a pretty dress. It looks like my Auntie Lizzie's."

Eve blushed while she clasped her hands together and said, "Thank you, Joseph. My momma said I have to always look proper. That's what Cherokee women do. You're always so nice, and I like that y'all speak English really good."

"Thanks, Eve. Did your family get more cattle? It looked like it when I walked past your land with Samuel," David said.

Eve's eyebrows lifted. She jumped with a smile, replying, "We did get some more babies!" She grabbed her ringlet-styled light-brown hair. "They are so adorable, but they grow so fast. My momma says we cannot have favorites because we have to eat them or sell their meat to other people. Paul is like me; he doesn't like to kill the cattle."

"No, I don't, Miss Eve," Paul said.

Joseph replied, "We kill chickens, but my momma said it

happens very fast. She said the chickens are too stupid to know what is going to happen most of the time."

David replied, "Yeah, Auntie Lizzie takes the chicken and puts her hand over its head and just chokes it off."

Eve gasped as David reenacted what Lizzie did. "That sounds so mean," Eve said. "My momma says your auntie is a brute."

Joseph replied, "What is a brute?"

"I don't know. I think it's—"

"Eve," Nancy barked. "I gave you permission to come out here and wait, not have conversations. Boys, you may go inside. Paul, take us home."

The boys headed toward the supply store door, but when Paul helped Eve onto the wagon, she waved at the boys.

"Have a good day, boys!" she said.

"Eve, you rebellious child. Sit down," Nancy snarled.

As the wagon rode away, Nancy was clearly heard yelling at Eve from a distance. Eve's kindness was a highlight for Joseph. It helped remove Joseph's insecurity when he was around the other children.

———◆———

On May 9, 1859, David's fifteenth birthday was celebrated. Though it was a happy time, Annabelle noticed Lisa's silence.

Annabelle sat down next to Grace and whispered, "I'm worried about Lisa. She's barely said anything."

"Yeah, I noticed," Grace whispered. "I feel like something else is causing this change in her."

"At first she seemed to be holding onto hope for us to find Jacob. Now she acts like she can't tell us anything."

"That's what's worrying me. She's disconnected from the family. Even during church, Lisa seems unable to relax even when singing hymns."

"I understand her pain," Annabelle said. "The emptiness you feel when someone is stolen from you."

"If this continues, we'll have to ask Elder Joyce to help us some more. We've already asked so much of her. There's going to come a time when she won't be here to guide us."

"What do you think we should do?"

Grace's eye slowly anchored on Lisa and then went back to Annabelle. "Our strongest weapons are prayer and to listen to her. I think we need to keep her from being alone."

"When this baby comes, it'll be hard for me to give Lisa time."

Grace tapped her fingers on her chair. "Maybe your requesting her help with the baby will help. The children are the only thing she's been responding to."

"I used to believe Lisa was determined to remain in mourning, but I think you're right. I guess for now we have to enjoy the day," Annabelle said.

"Yeah, and be amused with this fifteen-year age gap you're about to have."

The two women giggled as they talked and enjoyed time with their family.

Lisa remained on Annabelle's heart, and she hid her worry behind a smile. She thought, *I miss seeing you smile every day, Lisa.*

CHAPTER 11

Not Again

On June 2, 1859, Annabelle, Grace, and Lizzie took the boys with them to bring home some supplies. Maria and Lisa stayed behind to watch the girls while Tsula and Luke visited Victoria. Samuel had already left Tahlequah to meet with Clyde, leaving George, John, and Michael to work the crops.

When Annabelle and the others walked home it began to rain. Lizzie was not pleased but the others laughed it off. Several minutes later, the rain stopped, and they arrived home. The boys strolled inside the family house, but Joseph looked toward the barn, and his eyes widened.

"Auntie Lisa?" Joseph called with a frightened tone.

The three women looked toward the barn, where Lisa lay face down in front of the barn door in a large pool of water. A rum bottle lay nearby her apparently lifeless body. Grace and Lizzie dropped the supplies.

"Lisa!" Grace shrieked. "Lisa!"

Lizzie fell to her knees and shook, with her hands digging into the soaked ground. Grace sprinted to Lisa.

"N-no…not again," Lizzie stuttered. "Not again. This c-can't be r-real."

Annabelle's heart pulsated to her throat. Seeing Lizzie break down made it feel like time had stopped. She turned to the shocked boys and said, "Go inside, get two buckets, and fill one of them with water. Do it now!"

The boys immediately ran to the house.

"Lizzie, come on, we have to help her!" Annabelle shook Lizzie's shoulder and saw tears going down her face.

Lizzie's body seemed frozen by Grace's panicked wailing in the background. Annabelle's eyes teared up, and she struggled to remain calm.

Annabelle slapped Lizzie. "Lizzie! Go help Grace! I can't move like you."

Lizzie's eyes dilated. She quickly stood and ran toward Lisa as Grace struggled to pick her up.

"Please, don't leave us, please, don't leave us," Lizzie murmured as her tears drifted in the wind.

Grace, her face wet and twisted, looked up at Lizzie and cried, "I can't feel her breathe. Lisa, wake up! We need to make her throw up."

Lizzie hastily punched Lisa in the stomach.

Grace gasped. "Lizzie!"

Lisa threw up and gagged.

"Okay, that worked!"

Lizzie angrily kicked the rum jar lying next to Lisa and knelt down. She tried to help Grace move Lisa, then cried as Lisa remained unresponsive.

"Lisa, wake up!" Lizzie wailed.

"She's breathing. We have to take her inside."

During this time, Annabelle jogged to them, relieved to see Lisa breathing. "I can help carry her," Annabelle said.

Grace replied, "No, open the front door and take her blanket off her bed."

Annabelle jogged toward the door, holding her pregnant belly. Grace and Lizzie followed her closely, carrying Lisa.

Maria opened the front door when Annabelle got to the steps. "Oh, my God, what happened?" she asked.

Lizzie replied, "She drank too much. We have to try to get the rest of the alcohol out."

Lisa was brought inside, mud covering her, and Annabelle saw fear in the boys' eyes.

"Put her on the table," Annabelle said. "She'll soak her bed if we put her there."

The women carried Lisa to the dinner table, lay her on her side, and tried to wake her. Grace kept heavily patting Lisa's face, and she moaned.

"David, where are the two buckets?" Annabelle asked.

"They are right here, Momma A. Is Auntie Lisa going to die?" David asked.

Annabelle looked at her sons and could see their eyes welling with tears. "No, but she is sick. You did a good job. David, go to your father and tell him Auntie Lisa is sick. Joseph, you take your sisters and Rosita and go to our house."

The boys immediately did what Annabelle told them, and she took the two buckets to the table. Lizzie kept Lisa on her side, and Grace worked to awaken the unconscious woman. Annabelle placed the empty bucket on the floor while using the other, filled with water, to clean Lisa's muddy face.

Lisa vomited into the bucket on the floor as the women encouraged her to wake and keep vomiting.

While they worked on Lisa, it started to rain again. Annabelle heard John rush inside.

She turned toward John, and he frowned.

"What happened to Lisa?" he asked.

Annabelle replied, her voice cracking with the words, "We found her passed out in front of the barn. She wasn't breathing, but we got her to wake up. She's starting to throw up."

John moved past Annabelle to the table and watched Lisa vomit. "What is happening? Why would she do this?"

"John…"

John stared at Lisa and put his hands on his head.

Annabelle raised her voice, "John!"

John turned around, his eyes wide.

"I think she was trying to kill herself. She smells like a rum bottle. Lisa has never drunk like this before. If it wasn't for Lizzie, she probably wouldn't have started to throw up."

"I'll go tell my uncle and Michael. Something has to change." John went outside in the rain with the sound of Lisa vomiting in the background.

After Lisa gained consciousness enough to respond, the young women helped her take off her soaked dress and put on her nightgown.

Tsula and Luke later returned home to learn what happened. Tsula cried when she saw her sister sleeping. The children were kept in the small house for the rest of the day.

Maria informed the children that their aunt would be fine, but she needed to rest. Annabelle and Maria later took the children their supper and returned back to the family house. The two women later walked inside and sat at the table. George prayed over their supper and sat down, frowning.

Grace gave George a plate of food, but George ignored it. He looked at the rest of the family with his hands folded in front of him.

"I saw my daughter in her room, passed out in her bed because she tried to kill herself," George said. "My little girl, my first-born daughter, almost died today. This is the fault of no one at this table but mine. I took Jacob away from her. I told my little girl she could not marry a good Cherokee man. I'm the one who deserves to die."

Speaking their language, Grace replied, "Uncle George, we have to hold Lisa responsible for her actions. She chose to do this, and we almost lost her."

"The majority of the fault is still mine. She kept her love of Jacob a secret for years because of me."

John replied, "Right now, I think we have to move past the blame. Lisa needs our support, and maybe this time when Samuel returns, they will have found Jacob."

Annabelle said, "Together we're stronger. I believe Lisa needs for us to remain strong."

George replied with a heartened tone, "You're right Anna-belle."

Lizzie responded, "I will walk the roads of Tahlequah tomorrow and speak to every drinker. That's how she has been getting the rum. Uncle George, are there any rum bottles left outside? Please tell us the truth."

George sighed. "There should be nothing left on our land unless Lisa has hidden some. What do you plan to say to the drunks around town?"

Lizzie replied, "I'll have kind words for them. I'll make it clear they're not to give Lisa anything. If they don't listen to me, they'll answer to me. Everyone thinks I'm crazy. I think that'll be simple."

George nodded his approval, and the family ate supper together.

Annabelle felt determined to protect Lisa and help her heal. She couldn't tolerate the thought of losing someone else before their time.

———◆———

The night arrived and Lisa remained asleep while Lizzie watched her. Lizzie fell asleep while trying to pray and began to dream. She looked at her hands, and they were small.

I'm a child again, she thought.

The warm sunlight made the environment feel peaceful. She looked at the old log cabin but turned around and stared at the large green barn. The hairs on her back stood up, and her throat tightened. She slowly walked to the barn.

"Grace," Lizzie said, her southern voice now that of a child.

She moved around the barn and stood by the large doors facing the crops. Her father sat on the ground, slumped back against the wall. Vomit covered his high-collared beige shirt.

Lizzie's legs shook. "Papa?" she said. Her eyes shimmered with tears as she slowly approached him. Tears broke away from her eyes, and she reached for him. She shook him. "You liar!

You're nothing but a drunk and a liar!" Lizzie bawled as she held onto his shoulders.

Suddenly Cliff vomited, and Lizzie let go of him, her eyes widening. She gasped as she looked into his lifeless eyes.

"My sweetest girl," Cliff gurgled.

Lizzie trembled. She was unable to move and gritted her teeth. "No! You're dead! You chose that damn bottle over us!"

Cliff's dead hand grabbed onto Lizzie's arm.

She smelled the alcohol on his breath. "No! Don't touch me! Let go of me!" Lizzie cried.

"You...you're something special. My sweetest..."

Cliff vomited again, and it landed on Lizzie's chest. His lifeless body then fell on top of her.

"No! I won't live this again!"

Lizzie awakened in a cold sweat. She looked over to see Lisa, who was still asleep. She pulled her knees up to her chest, rested her forehead on her knees, and quietly wept. She got out of bed and immediately put on a dress. Constantly wiping away tears, she quietly left the house. She got Queen from the barn and rode to the other side of Tahlequah. She jumped off Queen, and her long unbraided hair bounced down her back. She approached a small house and aggressively knocked on an old wooden door. Her hands shook as she fought to hold her composure.

"I'm coming," Elder Joyce said, her irritation echoing through the door before opening it. "Now who...Lizzie? What has you out here like this?"

Lizzie shook uncontrollably. "I-I...h-he..." She placed her hands on the back of her neck and immense heaving sobs escaped her mouth. "I had ano-another o-one...Lisa s-she..." Lizzie stuttered as she cried. "I ca...I c-can't sleep."

Elder Joyce frowned and embraced the traumatized woman. "It's okay, child, it's okay, Wildcat. You know the Father has you in the palm of his hand. It's okay to still feel pain about your papa. You come on in here, baby. I'll get you some water."

Lizzie began to hyperventilate. "L-Lisa, s-she..."

"Calm down...what about Lisa? What happened to her?"

"S-she tried to k-k-kill h-herself."

Joyce's face dropped. "Is she alive?"

Lizzie nodded.

"Come on, child. Let's clean off that beautiful face. We'll talk about it." Joyce mumbled under her breath, "Lord Jesus, this set her back."

Joyce sat Lizzie down at the supper table. The old woman moved a chair next to Lizzie and sat down. She embraced Lizzie, who put her head on her shoulder.

"Remember it wasn't your fault," Joyce said. "You were a baby...your daddy sealed his fate. There was nothing you could've done differently."

Lizzie then explained what had happened with Lisa. Elder Joyce listened, then prayed over Lizzie while she held the young woman's hand and burned sage.

An hour later, Lizzie returned home. She entered her room quietly and put her nightgown back on as the moonlight outlined her strong body. She slipped back into the bed, and calmly held Lisa's hand. She stared at Lisa with the remanence of tears in her eyes.

"Never again, sister," Lizzie whispered. "I love you."

She prayed a prayer Elder Joyce had instructed her to pray and fell asleep holding onto Lisa's hand.

———◆———

The next day, Lisa awoke late in the morning with a severe hangover. Nausea caused her to slowly move around with a bucket. She was placed under house arrest, and Tsula and Maria stayed home to nurse her back to health. Lisa heard the children playing outside, and she wanted to see them but felt too nauseous to move a lot.

"Why haven't the children come inside?" Lisa asked in her native tongue as she sat down.

Maria answered, "When we found you, the boys saw you and were frightened that you had died. We decided it was best for you to feel well before they saw you. It was hard on all of us."

Lisa took the bucket off her lap while she looked at Tsula and Maria. "I'm sorry. I hurt all of you."

Tsula replied with a saddened voice, "Did you try to kill yourself?" She wiped a tear from her face as Lisa remained silent. Tsula raised her voice, "Lisa, did you try to kill yourself?"

"I was hurting so bad," Lisa said. "At first the thought never came to my mind, but I don't remember much after I kept drinking. I'm sorry. I know I hurt you and everyone."

"What is going on with you? Is all of this about Jacob?" Tsula asked.

Lisa remained silent and her glance shifted to the table.

"Why won't you give me an answer?"

"Lisa, please tell us something," Maria said.

Lisa replied in Cherokee, "I have nothing to say right now."

Tsula stormed out of their home, grunting.

Later in the day, the family greeted Lisa to make sure she was feeling better. The children were still kept in the small house as the rest of the family gathered for supper. The gathering was emotional, and Lisa realized how she had hurt her family. George gave Lisa a tearful apology for all of his actions, insisting he was the one to blame.

George's apology touched Lisa's heart. She gave her father a hug and wept. George's apology was what Lisa needed. It made her want to tell everything, but she refused.

Grace angrily gave her an ultimatum of either speaking with Pastor Bluebird or with Elder Joyce. The two women argued for more than two hours, with the others trying to convince Lisa to seek more help. Lisa reluctantly agreed to see Elder Joyce. The family decided it was best for her to remain at the supply store to help so she wouldn't be alone.

Two days passed, and Lisa became more agitated as the time came closer for her to meet with Joyce. When Annabelle, Grace, Lisa, and Lizzie traveled to the supply store they passed one of the drunks sitting down against one of the buildings. The man looked at Lisa, quickly broke his jar, and stormed off murmuring.

"What is wrong with Ricky? He looked scared," Lisa said.

Lizzie replied, "Nothing, ignore him."

Lisa looked at Lizzie and squinted. While Lisa worked with her family, some of the elder customers lovingly greeted her. The love she received forced her to smile and made her feel valued.

As Lisa and Lizzie loaded one of the wagons with supplies, Lisa noticed Brock and Hunter watching on their horses from a distance. Lisa scowled when she stared at Brock. She put the rest of the supplies on the wagon.

"What are you looking at?" Lizzie asked in Cherokee.

"Nothing," Lisa answered. "That's what they are, soulless."

Lizzie looked at the two men before following Lisa inside the supply store.

✦

"I never get accustomed to the way they look at us," Hunter said. "Especially Miss Lightning. It's almost like she's tempting us to assert our authority here in full force."

Brock replied, "I agree, but I also learned something about these Cherokee. When I give Lisa her lessons, I can feel her rebellion building. However, the mention of separating her from her half-breed kin keeps her in line."

Hunter folded his arms. "So is that an answer to controlling them more?"

"I believe that using the love they have for each other against their will is the best way to civilize them. Our goals remain the same, though some will have to be broken a different way. Seeing them show true authority over their slaves by completely solidifying a true divide between the Cherokee and the Negroes and making sure the Cherokee with white blood remain in power. I believe we can hope to see it now."

"Such a move will take time, at least five years if not more. A new treaty would have to be made. There are too many half-breeds with Cherokee blood in this land. Their constitutional ban on Negroes marrying Cherokee is a joke, and most of the slaveholders are relaxed. I fear more Cherokee will side with the abolitionists. This will become a far safer haven for runaways."

"It is hypocrisy."

"Hypocrisy is the lesser term I would use. Even the Choctaw and Creek have mixed-blood towns now. They won't be Indians if they keep up such sickening behavior. What is it like being with that savage?"

Brock adjusted his cravat. "She is a fighter like her undomesticated cousin. As unnatural as it is, I'll admit it's a bit testing to tame her. It's the look in her eyes. I have no doubt in my mind she'd kill me if she had the chance."

"My word, even when she is following your command to meet you?"

"That woman would shoot me dead with the sun high in the sky if she could. But I can tell I'm finally breaking her spirit. When she starts fully showing respect and obeying like a woman, then I'll consider stopping."

"I think you fancy her a bit. Your own little prairie nigger slave...to replace Katelyn until you find yourself a new wife. I was worried this would happen."

Brock sneered and shook his head. "I have no feelings for that Indian! I want my respect, and she is going to give it."

"What of Miss Lightning? Why didn't you target her first?"

Brock frowned. "The timing never arrived. That's my only reason. I still have Miss Lighting in my sight, but her cousin needs to be fixed first. You could join me and take Miss Lightning. It would be slightly disappointing if you didn't."

Hunter scoffed. "I could never lower myself to such a degree. It's bad enough you touch the other one. Only a white woman is worth my touch. I also believe even if I did succeed in such a thing, that woman would kill me after the act."

Hearing Hunter's response, Brock's eyebrows raised. "I never said you had to do that part of the taming. Very well, I think we need to check the other Cherokee towns before sunset."

"I agree. Other things need to be focused upon. Soon, more

white settlements will come this way. We need to be prepared. Tomorrow, we have to go back to Choctaw territory."

The two men rode away toward the other Cherokee towns. Their demeanors toward the Cherokee people built more resentment against them. The conflict between them and the Cherokee council also increased, and the agents felt the Cherokee had stopped progressing, blaming it on their perceived laziness.

CHAPTER 12
Shackles Revealed

A DAY LATER, SAMUEL RETURNED HOME from exploring the Chickasaw territory, but he had discovered nothing new on Jacob's whereabouts. He was shocked to learn about Lisa's possible attempt to commit suicide, and he was grateful she was safe. Three days later, John and Samuel prepared for their trip to Mercy and left Tahlequah.

On that day, Lisa went to Joyce's home. It made her feel like a punished child. She entered the old pine-scented house and closed the door. The silver-haired elder was sitting at her old supper table alongside a young teenage girl with two braids.

"Lea, go home to your momma for now," Joyce said in Cherokee. "You can come back and have supper with me."

"Hi, Lisa," Lea said.

"Hi, Lea."

The young teenage girl gave Joyce a kiss on the cheek, and she nodded to Lisa as she walked by her.

"I see she's had another growth spurt," Lisa said.

Joyce smiled. "Yes, though Lea is very shy and humble, she's always reminded me of Lizzie. When it matters, she has a strong fighting spirit. You know she is my youngest great-great-granddaughter."

Lisa half-smiled. "Where do you want me to sit?"

"I will come to you. Pick a rocking chair, child." Joyce approached Lisa and sat in her chair. "Now I can see you even better."

As Lisa sat in the rocking chair, she held her hands and shook.

"Calm down, Beautiful Child. You know you're safe here."

"I'm sorry, Elder Joyce. I know I've hurt many people with my actions. My sins have overshadowed who I am."

Joyce smiled at Lisa and placed her hand on top of Lisa's. "I love you, Beautiful Child, just as I love your sister, Clever Fox. The fact you survived what you did to yourself should show you how much Jesus loves you."

Lisa wept. "I don't deserve that much love. I've made so many mistakes, and now I don't recognize my life."

"Lisa, no person is worthy of the salvation Jesus gives us. It is the free gift. The Father has a plan for your life, and you must remain strong to learn more about the path you have to take."

Lisa breathed heavier as Joyce calmly patted her hand. "It feels like my path is becoming darker each month. I don't want to sing the hymns anymore, I struggle to pray, I'm jealous of those in my family who have children. I'm bringing shame to my family."

Joyce cleaned Lisa's face with a cloth. "Beautiful Child, what is really wrong? I know this is deeper than Jacob being taken from you. Lizzie came to me and told me what happened. What has turned you into a bitter woman?"

Lisa took a deep breath. "I'm pregnant. I haven't bled in over four months."

Joyce sighed. "Lisa, you're still loved, and your family will love the baby."

"I don't want the baby," Lisa cried. "I wasn't trying to kill myself...I tried to end my pregnancy. I've fallen so far. I don't know what to say to Jacob if he returns. How can he love me once he sees me with a child that isn't his?"

"I see a loving, kindhearted woman wanting the easy way out. I see in your eyes a woman that loves someone so much she would rather die than to hurt them, but no matter the past mistakes, your trying to take your life is inexcusable. Your trying to take the life of that baby who has done nothing wrong...is the wrong path."

Lisa wiped tears from her face. "I never wanted a baby like this."

"Does that make the taking of life okay? Your life was spared because you have a purpose. That baby has a purpose. I know this is unfair. I know this will be hard. Don't believe that I don't understand."

"This isn't what I wanted in life. It's not my life, and this baby shouldn't be in my life."

Joyce put her soft, wrinkled hand on Lisa's cheek. "The baby ruins what you imagined your life to be, but the Father can bring forth goodness from this wrong. Who is the father?"

Lisa looked at Joyce and bit her thumbnail. "I don't know what to say."

"Lisa...please, don't tell me you're unsure who the father is?"

"I know who the father is, I hate that I know who the father is. Please forgive me. I'm not ready to tell who the father is."

Lisa knew Joyce was analyzing the pain in her eyes. "There is no need to ask for my forgiveness. I will respect your wishes, but you can't keep the truth hidden for long. The child should know who the father is, and it will help you heal. It warms my heart that you came here...you had the choice not to come."

Lisa scoffed. "I think Grace would've killed me if I didn't come. I don't know how to tell them about the baby. I've hurt them so much. I have no right to bring them more pain."

Joyce's brow lowered and her eyebrows drew together. "For you to do something so dangerous. Is there something else you're not telling me about this pregnancy?"

I knew she could tell there was more. I can't lie to her. She can read me, Lisa thought. "Yes, but...I'm...I'm not ready to talk. I still don't believe it myself."

"It's about the baby's father?"

"Yes, ma'am."

"In this case, I will tell the family for you and tell them to respect your ways for now. However, by the time this child is a year old, the entire truth must be told. It will be unfair to the father and the baby for them to be separated if conditions are right. The bitterness left in your heart is also affecting how you're making decisions."

Lisa cringed with the thought of that day to come. The two women got into Joyce's wagon and slowly rode to the Lightning-Strongman farm. When they arrived at the farm, the family was surprised Joyce had brought Lisa home.

Joyce entered the family house, calling for the family to sit with her at their supper table. Lisa remained outside, and she played with the young girls. She struggled with nervousness about how the family would react to the news of her pregnancy. More than an hour passed while Joyce spoke with the adults of the family. The prolonged wait made Lisa feel even more vulnerable.

Joyce left the house laughing, to Lisa's surprise. George came out behind Joyce smiling, but his smile faded when Lisa approached.

"All is well, Beautiful Child. Go inside with your sisters and enjoy your time with them," Joyce said in Cherokee.

"Thank you, Elder Joyce," Lisa replied. She looked at her father. "Did they accept the truth well?"

"Better than I expected. They are upset but will respect your wish, but you need to remain honest with them. The trust needs to be healed." Joyce gave Lisa a hug. "You stay strong and positive. You're not alone."

"I will." Lisa went to the family house, and George's arms reached out, welcoming a hug from his daughter.

Joyce walked to her wagon with the little girls watching her.

"Elder Joyce, one day I will be as wise as you," Rosita said in Cherokee as she approached Joyce.

Joyce chuckled as she got into her wagon. "I'm sure you will. Rosita, Rain, Jannie—the three of you listen to your mommas and love Jesus. You'll go great distances in life doing these things. We will see each other again, children."

"We see each other again, Elder Joyce," the girls said.

Lisa entered the house, taking a deep breath, but was greatly welcomed by George and Michael as they hugged her. They assured her they would help her with the baby if she didn't want the father involved. It warmed Lisa's heart to have their support, but her heart pounded as she looked at the kitchen door. She walked into the kitchen with her heart beating heavily. She looked at Grace and the others.

Annabelle approached her and kissed her on the cheek. "Are you doing well?" she asked in Cherokee.

"Yes."

Grace hugged Lisa and kissed her on the cheek. "Help Maria with the beans," she said. "Today we're making three sisters' soup."

Lisa approached Maria and Tsula, who smiled at her.

"It's good you're cooking with us again," Tsula said.

Lisa looked at Lizzie, but she stared at the duck she was cutting, so she helped Maria prepare the beans. She looked at Lizzie again, but the other woman had a frown and tearful eyes.

"Is Tony the father?" Lizzie abruptly asked in Cherokee.

"Lizzie!" Grace angrily said.

"No, he isn't," Lisa said.

"I would love you even if he was," Lizzie said.

"It means a lot to hear you say that."

Lizzie smiled at Lisa, and the women prepared the food. During supper, the family talked like they did before George had beaten Lisa, and Lisa spoke to them openly.

Two days later, the crowing of the roosters ushered in June 11, 1859. Annabelle was pleased with how Lisa had started to return to her social self. The warm morning air was a sign that the day would be hot, so Annabelle decided to play kickball with the girls before the heat increased. A sharp pain hit Annabelle, causing her to squat.

"Not now," she said.

"Momma, what is wrong?" Rain asked in Cherokee.

"Go get Auntie Grace right now," her mother replied.

Rain ran to the practice grounds while Jannie and Rosita stayed with Annabelle.

"Auntie Annabelle, are you okay?" Rosita asked.

"I'm fine, baby. It looks like today your little cousin is ready to come."

The girls shrieked with excitement.

Annabelle smiled as she looked at the girls and thought, *when the time comes for both of you to give birth, you won't be jumping with joy.*

Grace ran behind Rain. "Annabelle, is it time?" she asked.

"Yes. I had another birth pain."

"Okay, let's take you inside."

Annabelle frowned. "I was hoping John was going to be back by now."

"He might make it back in time, but for now, we have to focus on the baby. What a year this has been so far."

The two women chuckled and stepped inside the family house. During the day, Annabelle's labor progressed. Joyce arrived with Tsula, and Annabelle protested the labor, trying to ignore the pain.

Joyce mockingly scolded her for attempting it. "I know you want John to be here, but the next time you feel pain, you have to push," the older woman said, speaking Cherokee.

Annabelle moaned, but when the next contraction occurred, she pushed. A few more pushes, and Annabelle birthed a little boy. The baby boy cried, much to the joy of everyone.

Grace cleaned off the baby and gave him to Annabelle. "Look at him, a beautiful Cherokee baby."

The women giggled as Annabelle held the red baby. "Children, come here and see your new baby brother."

The boys came in, followed by the twins and Rosita. The children had big grins on their faces upon seeing the new baby.

"Momma, what is his name?" Jannie asked in Cherokee.

"I've talked about a few names with your daddy, but I know traditionally your grandmother would've been allowed to name him," Annabelle said. "Elder Joyce, you have taken the place of a mother and grandmother for so many of us. Would you like to name him?"

Joyce's eyebrows rose when she smiled. "Lord knows I have named many children," Joyce said. "Let us take a look at this beautiful baby boy." Joyce leaned over and looked at the curious infant. "It is a beautiful thing seeing innocence." Joyce chuckled. "Jonathan Lightning."

Annabelle was shocked by Joyce's decision. "I thought of that name when I was pregnant with the twins. I had almost forgotten it."

"Jonny Lightning for a nickname," Lizzie said. "It sounds good."

"What a group you have: David, Joseph, and Jonathan," Joyce said. "Well, I think it is time for me to go. Lisa, I will be looking for you soon."

Lisa nodded.

Joyce left the family, giving them time with the newborn. John and Samuel arrived home that night. John welcomed his new son, and he was told about Lisa's unexpected pregnancy. The men were overwhelmed with the news.

During the night, Annabelle sat in the bed with John while he slept, and she nursed Jonathan. Annabelle reached for the envelope John had brought back with him and opened it. Pulling out three letters, she saw the first was from Rebecca.

In the letter, Rebecca shared her excitement about Annabelle's pregnancy, writing that God had made up for her loss. She also wrote that Mr. Boston's store was doing well and her children were doing great, telling her that Belle was a copy of Ruthanne. She mentioned the Underground Railroad, the kidnapped Indian children, and her fear of a political revolt. She shared the joy her children brought her, commenting that they'll probably drive Mr. Fluffs crazy.

Ruthanne wrote that Elizabeth was married, but she knew nothing more because she wasn't allowed to write often. Ruthanne also expected another child and told Annabelle of how she and Ruben had started speaking to each other again.

Marilyn wrote the third letter, apologizing for not writing as often, and she shared her need to keep things between her and Daniel a secret. Her daughters, Angel and Naomi, had Daniel's eyes. They kept her busy, unlike Benjamin. She also wrote that Daniel's cousin Mary had married a good man named Tim. He was an Osage Indian. Marilyn closed, saying Annabelle was one of the strongest women she knew, and she loved her.

As Annabelle held Jonathan against her chest while he slept, she wondered if the reign of slavery was finally going to end. It would allow Annabelle to return to Mercy to visit and seek out Judy Mays. Her wish for the abolishment of slavery was vocal in her prayers that night.

At the end of June 1859, Grace stood by the old redbud tree watching the bison herds. The decreased number of bison seemed constant. What further concerned her was only one wolf pack remained instead of the four the family could identify, and only two cougars had been seen recently. She was uncertain of how to explain the change.

Grace suddenly heard Rain's laughter and walked to the small house. "Rain, are you scaring those chickens again?" she asked.

Rain replied in Cherokee, "No, Auntie Grace."

"Don't lie to me. It is bad for the wolf clan to be liars." Grace arrived at the chicken coop, and stared down her niece, who had feathers covering her red calico dress. "Clean off the feathers and stop torturing those birds. I swear you and your Auntie Lizzie have too much in common."

"I was not torturing the chickens. They need to learn how to play better." Rain cleaned off the feathers.

"Where's your sister?"

"She is with Auntie Maria learning how to make soup."

"Well...then you go inside to learn how to cook too."

Rain angrily moved past Grace, who gave her a light swat on her butt.

"No angry face," Grace said. "Don't turn that beautiful face into an ugly one."

Rain looked back at Grace, trying to hide her smile. Grace watched her go inside the family house.

In the late afternoon, Grace returned to the farm after clearing her mind on the practice grounds. The moment Grace was about to go up to the front door of the family house, Eli exited the house with a wildflower in his hand.

"What are you doing here?" Grace asked in Cherokee.

"I thought a lot about what you said," Eli said. "The love you have for your family makes me jealous and impresses me. You're right. You have a choice. I would never try to force you to do anything. I want you to listen." He walked off the stairs toward her, making her breathe deeper and her heart race as her eyebrows lifted.

Eli lifted up the yellow wildflower and was about to place it in Grace's hair when she grabbed his wrist. "Stop it, Eli. Please, stop. I need time...my family needs me right now. I can't be selfish and—"

"Grace," Lisa said.

Grace looked past Eli's shoulder as Lisa came toward her with a smile. "I will be fine. Don't make my mistake. Don't keep Eli waiting because the timing is uncomfortable."

Grace looked at Eli. "Please leave us for a moment, Eli."

He went back up the steps.

"I don't know how I can move forward with you in pain like this," Grace said.

"I'll be in more pain if you keep pushing Eli away, and someone else decides to give him the attention he deserves. I know I have you to help me with the baby. Your giving time to Eli won't change that. Please, be happy and stop sacrificing so much for us. You have always led us, and you taught John and Samuel to be good leaders for our family."

"I want things to return to when we were happier. My purpose has always been to help protect the family."

"Our protection comes from heaven. You won't always be able to see the bad things coming, and I think you forgot that. Look at me. I'm pregnant without a husband. You couldn't have stopped this. Tsula lost her baby, and who knows if Lizzie will ever want to marry now. Please let go so your life can begin."

Grace took a deep breath. She stepped around Lisa and approached Eli as Lisa followed her. She looked at Eli with a slight grimace and took the yellow wildflower from Eli's hand. "Okay, I will try for real."

Lisa gave Grace a hug. "You're the greatest cousin and greatest sister anyone could ask for."

While the two women hugged, Lizzie stood in the doorway of the house watching with a smile. She quickly went back inside before Grace noticed her.

Grace thought, *I hope this can work.*

Over time Lisa adjusted to the changes she was experiencing in her pregnancy, while a pregnant Maria encouraged her. July 25, 1859, brought in Lizzie's thirty-first birthday, and her mood lightened as she ate grits and scrambled eggs for breakfast.

When Annabelle nursed Jonathan, she noticed she hadn't heard the twins and walked around the farm looking for them. She saw David standing by the cornfields and called to him. David approached his mother and looked at his baby brother.

"David, have you seen your sisters?" Annabelle asked in Cherokee. "I've looked everywhere for them, and they're not with Rosita."

"I don't know where they are," David replied. "I last saw them this morning. The twins were with Auntie Lizzie."

"Okay, where is your brother?"

"He is with Michael in the cornfields."

Annabelle looked at the fields and noticed the cornstalks moving as Michael and Joseph walked through them. "Carry your brother and come inside for lunch. I can cook you some of the deer meat."

David took Jonathan and followed Annabelle inside as she tried to hide her concern. She hated that Lizzie hadn't told her she was taking the girls.

Not far from the farm was a small stream that fed a large water-hole surrounded by trees and tallgrass. As the sunlight reflected off the calm water, an arrow suddenly went through the water, scattering all of the fish at the surface. A string pulled the arrow back, and Lizzie pulled out a catfish struck by the arrow.

"You're so good, Auntie Lizzie," Jannie said in Cherokee.

The fish shook around, splashing water on the girls. The girls shrieked and put their hands up, trying not to get wet.

"He's still alive," Lizzie said. "Rain, bring me my tomahawk."

Rain brought Lizzie the weapon, and the woman cut the fish's head off. The girls gasped while the fish's body shook.

"It is unfair to the fish to let him suffer," Lizzie said. "If the two of you ever catch a fish, and he is still alive, you cut his head off. It is a dishonor to the Father to torture the fish. Be fair and free the spirit from the body."

Speaking Cherokee, Rain said, "Auntie, I want to try to get one."

Lizzie put the dead fish in a sack. She gave her niece the bow and a special arrow that had string looped into the arrow shaft. "Now, do you remember how to shoot the arrow?"

Rain nodded, and Lizzie watched.

The girl saw a fish and aimed at it. She released the arrow but completely missed the fish. She frowned. "I don't understand. I shoot better than Joseph."

Lizzie giggled and pulled the arrow out of the water. "Now try again. This time, I will teach you." She squatted next to the child and placed her right cheek next to Rain's left cheek. "Now remember to look down the arrow and keep both eyes open. Take two deep calm breaths and aim downward at the fish as you see it. Take one more deep breath as you draw the bow, and release the arrow as you exhale."

As Rain was about to take another shot, an osprey flew down and took a fish. The bird's precision inspired the child to be competitive and take aim again. A few minutes later, Rain tried again. She remained patient and saw another fish. She took aim. She released the arrow and hit it, but it quickly swam away.

"I got it!" Rain said.

"Grab the string, Rain!" Lizzie yelled.

Rain grabbed the remaining string, but she was almost pulled off the waterhole edge.

Lizzie pulled Rain back and grabbed the string, helping her pull the catfish out of the water as it fought back. When she held the fish down on the water's edge, Jannie abruptly cut its head off with Lizzie's tomahawk.

Lizzie looked at Jannie with wide eyes.

"Did I do good?" Jannie asked in Cherokee.

Lizzie stood up and kissed Jannie on the forehead. "You did good, both of you did good, my Sunshine and my Moonlight. Next time, make sure you have the string wrapped around your arm so you can quickly pull out the fish, Sunshine. And, Moonlight, next time wait for me to tell you to chop the fish. Your daddy will be proud of you both."

Rain smiled and picked up the dead fish. Lizzie and the twins returned home with them.

The three arrived home, and Lizzie went inside holding the two dead fish, showing them off to the family.

"Look what we caught," Lizzie said in Cherokee. "We're having fish for supper."

Annabelle looked at the girls' dirty dresses and sighed.

"Momma, I killed the fish!" Jannie said.

"So this is who the two of you were with," Annabelle said. "The next time the two of you want to leave the farm with Auntie Lizzie, you tell me."

Jannie frowned.

Annabelle realized she had overlooked Jannie's accomplishment and sighed, "I'm proud of you. I know that isn't easy to do."

Rain's voice echoed her sister's, "I caught the fish, Momma!"

"Good, now both of you go change into your other dresses. The two of you are not eating your supper in those dirty things."

The two girls pouted and left the house to go change clothes.

"I guess it's a good thing I didn't say they followed me while they were standing here," Lizzie said.

"They followed you? I expect crazy out of the boys, not them."

"Don't be hard on them. Having them with me made my birthday better today, and we are having fish. No chicken today!"

Lizzie walked toward the kitchen.

Annabelle looked at Maria, who was sitting in one of the rocking chairs with a tired expression, and the woman giggled. "Don't worry about it, Annabelle. Rosita would've returned home dirty if she had left too."

Annabelle sighed as she sat down in the other rocking chair, laughing to herself.

A week later, Annabelle sat in the family house rocking Jonathan when Grace entered.

"How are the two of you doing?" Grace asked.

Annabelle looked at Grace with a slight frown. "He is doing great. I think I'm fine, just thinking too much."

"What are you thinking about?" Grace asked.

Annabelle sighed. "It's so stupid. I don't even think it's worth saying."

"If it troubles you this much, you can't hide it."

"Feel Jonathan's hair."

Grace reached over and touched the baby's hair. "I feel nothing wrong with it. His hair is soft."

"Yes, like Rain's and Jannie's. I was hoping this one would be a bit more like me for Joseph's sake. Look at this beautiful boy with my eyes, but that's about the only thing I can see in him that's from me. I'm worried Joseph will compare himself again, now against Jonathan."

Grace's mouth etched into a frown. "We can't worry so much about these things. The best we can do is keep the bonds between the children strong. Give them the same love, treat them fairly."

Annabelle huffed. "I keep telling myself the same thing, but

I know I treat the children differently. I'm harder on Rain than I am with Jannie. I trust David more than I trust Joseph with following instructions. It's easily said, but it is hard to treat them all the same. I'm so worried Joseph will start to think I treat him differently because he looks more Negro than Cherokee."

"I understand you, because it is true...it is hard, but loving them isn't hard. I think that will make up the difference. We have to keep trying. I see the boys, and they have a strong bond like they should, and we have to be grateful for that."

Annabelle half-smiled. "Yeah, you're right." She looked down at Jonathan. "Who knows what personality this one will have? He is calmer than the twins, and that's what I need right now."

The two women giggled and talked before Grace returned to the supply store.

Annabelle needed the conversations. They helped give her new perspectives as she prayed for her children.

During a warm night in early August, Annabelle lay next to John in their bed as Jonathan slept.

"John, are you awake?" Annabelle asked in Cherokee.

"I am now," John said.

She sighed. "I'm sorry."

He rolled over and looked at her. "What's on your mind? It isn't like you to stay awake."

"The others and I have been talking about Lisa. It has been bothering all of us. She won't tell us who the father is. We know she knows who the father is, but we can't imagine who it is."

"I know Lisa knows who the father is, but I also believe she never wanted this person to be the father of the child. I think Lisa was hurting so bad about Jacob she made a bad choice. Now she has to live with it, and we're here to help support her. Don't be tempted into trying to get more from her when she isn't ready to tell us."

Annabelle sighed. "I want to help her more."

"I think being limited to helping reminds us that it is Jesus's place to save and not ours. We can't take over where we're not meant to."

"I hate that you're right."

John chuckled and kissed Annabelle.

She cuddled next to him, and he fell asleep.

Annabelle said a silent prayer before falling asleep. *God, please protect Lisa and give us the patience to listen to what she has to say. Amen.*

———◆———

A few days passed as the summer heat increased in Oklahoma. Lizzie walked through Tahlequah carrying a small sack of soybeans with Jannie, Rain, and Rosita following her. When Lizzie and the three young girls approached the supply store, Brock and Hunter rode their horses down an adjacent street.

The two men saw Lizzie and the three girls. Brock signaled for them to move a little faster to intercept the family.

While they approached, Lizzie noticed them and slowed down, watching the men come nearer to her and the children.

"Miss Lizzie Lightning, I see you have quite the crowd following you today," Brock said.

"I'd say so," Hunter said. "A half-breed Mexican child and two half-breed Negro girls. These twin girls are remarkable creations. It would be almost near impossible to know their mother was a Negro."

Brock replied, "Indeed, Mr. Sawyer."

"What do the two of you want?" Lizzie demanded.

Hunter replied, "It never grows old hearing your demands, though they do test the soul."

"Mr. Sawyer and I were admiring the next generation of your family," Brock said. "It is interesting seeing the half-Mexican has a lighter skin than you, Miss Lightning, interesting."

Lizzie replied with an arrogant tone, "They are beautiful girls. They make me proud."

Brock looked at Sawyer with a leer. "Well, yes, for Indian children they're unique examples," he said. "I hope you're not teaching these promising children any bad habits of yours."

Brock's horse took one step forward.

Lizzie prodded Rosita and Jannie behind her as she stood before the two men on their horses. "The girls are learning how to be Cherokee, not white women. We will be who we are meant to be and not what you want us to be."

"Still set in your savage ways, I see. Be careful, being unwilling to learn new things leads to the weakening of a people."

Lizzie side-eyed the men and gritted her teeth. "I have no problem in learning new things. I have a problem with adopting the ways of other people who don't care about us. Excuse us. I need to keep my word by being on time, and then give them lunch. I'm sure you can understand that much."

Lizzie walked away with the girls following her closely.

Brock cleared his throat, replying, "Well…looks like in some way you're learning some manners. Maybe your preacher has finally listened to our advice on teaching his flock."

Lizzie stopped and turned around with a raised eyebrow. "Mr. Jackson, I simply don't have my bow or arrows with me. Next time we'll have to see who is faster again. I promise to give you a better goodbye."

Brock's grip on the horse's reigns tightened. "One of these days, Lizzie Lightning," he murmured under his breath. He huffed, his eyes locked on Lizzie's.

Brock signaled his horse to turn around as he and Hunter slowly rode their horses away from the family.

Rain's brow lowered. "Auntie Lizzie, what did you mean when you said about being faster?"

Lizzie looked at Rain and smiled. "He didn't believe how fast I was with my bow. One day he was being a bad man, but my aim is faster than his. So your auntie made a grown white man pee on himself that day."

The three little girls laughed while they followed Lizzie.

"That was nasty, Auntie Lizzie," Rosita said.

Lizzie cackled, but she knew Brock still held a grudge against her.

On August 18, 1859, Lisa walked out to the barn after supper, assuring the family she was only out to brush the horses for a short time.

The others decided to trust her, though Lizzie showed an obvious uneasiness about her being alone. As Lisa brushed Queen, the barn door opened and Brock entered.

"I was beginning to wonder if you had seen me signal you with my hat earlier today," Brock said with a confident tone.

Lisa brushed the horse's mane as she looked at Brock. "It's hard to miss your threat, Mr. Jackson," Lisa said, with her voice deepening on the man's name.

Brock strutted up to Lisa, and she turned around, showing her pregnant belly. "What is this? When did you get a child?"

"I was pregnant the last time you visited me a few months ago. It made no difference."

Brock exhaled and rubbed his chin. "Who is the father?"

"The father of the child is of no concern of yours."

Brock smacked his lips when he took off his top hat and slapped Lisa. "You little Indian whore, you need to watch your mouth."

"Now you care? You seem hurt. Is it jealousy or knowing you can't always control me?"

Brock slapped Lisa again, causing her to stumble. "Not that much of a Christian, are you...you little whore. Women like you need to know their place. I should have that nappy-headed little boy sold."

Lisa's voice rose. "That wasn't the deal! And if I'm a whore, what does that make you? You rape me every time you come here. Are you even a Christian?"

His voice deepened. "If I were you, I would be more concerned about the words that come out of my mouth right now."

"I did what you asked of me; but becoming pregnant was never talked about. You white men always seek to control. As I said, I followed all of what you asked of me to protect Joseph. What kind of man does that make you?"

He slapped her again, but she looked back at the irritated man, unfazed by his brutality.

"How dare you question my integrity!" he said.

Her eyes narrowed. "Why do you care if I'm having the child of another man? Don't take your anger out on a child when I have done all you demanded."

"You always give me a little resistance." Brock poked her head. "I guess in your savage mind that gives you some form of honor, but it doesn't." Walking to her side, he puffed while he looked at her pregnant belly. "I never said I would take the boy away if you were exposed as a whore. I find your current form disgusting. I won't demand you until you have the child, and I feel you're able to uphold the agreement." Leering, he cupped her chin with his hand. "Maybe I'll change my mind if you start acting civilized." He let go of her chin, turned around, and put on his top hat.

"Thank you, Mr. Jackson."

Brock looked back at Lisa. "You better remember your place, woman. When I tell you to do something, you do it despite what runs in your rebellious mind. I don't want you." He licked his lips. "You are sweet...but you're no white woman. You're no different than a nigger. The only difference is you still struggle with accepting your place, but I will correct your misunderstanding. Watch your mouth when I approach you again, whore."

Brock left the barn as Lisa watched with a smirk on her face.

"A war is coming your way, Brock Jackson," she whispered. "You'll die by my hand."

Lisa remained on guard the next few days, rehearsing in her mind how she was going to tell her family who the father was or if she should tell them at all.

———◆———

On a hot mid-August day, Michael walked inside the family home with David and Joseph. Joseph grinned when Lisa approached them.

"All of you stink," Lisa said in Cherokee.

Michael replied, "It's hot today and we need water. We need food too."

Lisa gave Joseph her apple she'd taken a bite out of and kissed him on his cheek.

Michael cocked his head. "What about me?"

"I'll bring out some duck and berries for you and David. It looks like my two little men are getting some muscles now."

Joseph blushed while he ate the apple, and Michael placed his hand on top of Joseph's head and smiled.

"Both of them are fast learners. I think we'll have a better crop this year because of their help," Michael said.

"Michael, can we play cards for a little while we eat?" David asked.

"I think we can play some poker for a little bit before the others finish giving the horses some food and water." Michael pulled out a deck of cards from his brown trousers and played with the boys.

Lisa came out of the kitchen with berries and cut-up duck. "Michael, you better not be teaching them how to gamble," she said.

"I'm not teaching them how to gamble," Michael replied. "It's good that they have some skills in playing some good poker."

The boys smiled at Michael.

Lisa shook her head and gave them their lunch. "My little Joseph." Lisa gave Joseph several kisses on his cheek, causing him to giggle.

"I love you, Auntie Lisa," Joseph said.

Lisa playfully touched Joseph's nose with her index finger. "I love you too. More than you know." Lisa whispered in Joseph's ear, "You're my favorite little man. Don't tell your brother."

Joseph's mouth curved up into a big grin. "I won't."

David rolled his eyes. "Don't believe it. I know I'm her favorite and Auntie Lizzie's," he said.

Joseph's smiled dropped from his face, and he looked at Lisa. "Auntie Lisa said I'm her favorite, and I know Auntie Lizzie likes me more."

Lisa lightly chuckled and kissed Joseph's forehead. "Both of you are my favorites."

Lisa went into her room as the boys gasped. They further argued about who was Lizzie's favorite and continued playing poker.

For Joseph, this was the most fun time of the day. He had never beaten Michael or David in a game of poker, but he enjoyed the challenge. After school, he always looked forward to playing cards. He saw Michael as the most playful of the men, and as the two boys and Michael played, they bluffed about what cards they had while laughing and eating.

Lisa smiled and listened to them while she washed the girls' dresses by the back door.

❖

On September 11, 1859, Maria had gone into labor early that morning and with the help of Joyce, she delivered a baby girl.

Afterward, Maria teased Samuel. He now had two girls to watch over, and maybe the next time, he would get a son. The family laughed at Maria's jokes, though she did feel slightly bad the baby was a girl. She also decided she wanted Joyce to name her daughter since both of her grandmothers had passed.

Joyce looked at the infant and Rosita. "I believe the Father is going to do amazing things through this little girl, and she'll go through many changes," Joyce said. "So I believe her name should help guide her on her journeys. We will call her Sky, because her beauty would be forever changing, and her heart will follow Jesus wherever she is meant to go."

As Joyce gave Sky back to Maria, tears of joy flowed down her face. "Gracias, Elder Joyce, I will never forget this."

"It is no problem. I see young mothers here trying their best. That's what makes all of you great mothers. It makes a difference and teaches the children the importance of why they should never quit." Joyce left the family house, and her encouraging words stayed with the women.

Maria cradled Sky, who yawned, and looked at Annabelle, who smiled. "What do you think?" she asked.

"I think she has Tsula's head," Annabelle said.

"Oh, yeah, it's a Strongman trait." The women examined the newborn.

"Looks like she has the same eyebrows as Rain and Jannie."

Maria looked at Sky again. "Yeah, I think you're right. Let's hope she doesn't have the girls' personalities. We need another calm child."

The two women giggled.

"Yes, we do," Annabelle said. "My twins make me rethink having any more children every day."

The two women laughed as they adored Sky.

⸺◆⸺

After Sky's birth, Joseph woke up early and secretly went to the practice fields. Two weeks passed as he snuck to the practice grounds and tried to surpass David.

One early morning in late September, he snuck out of the family house again, but as he went to the practice fields, Annabelle saw him as she walked outside to feed the chickens. She put down the chicken feed and charged after her son.

"Joseph Lightning! Where do you think you're going!" his mother roared.

Annabelle's eyes burned with fury, and Joseph froze.

"I was going to the practice fields, Momma," Joseph said in Cherokee with a terrified tone.

Annabelle snatched Joseph's bow from him, giving him two strong swipes on his butt. Joseph yelled in pain as Annabelle held him.

"I've told you again and again! You can't go anywhere alone!" Annabelle struck Joseph again. "Don't ever do this again, not even to go practice with your bow. Do you understand me?"

"Yes, Momma," Joseph bawled.

"Now you get back in that house and wait for breakfast."

Joseph sprinted back to the family house.

Annabelle saw John standing next to their home. She stalked toward him. "Did you see your child? I can't believe what he tried to do!"

"I saw some of it, and I heard all of it," John said. "Are you sure he hasn't done this before?"

Annabelle took a deep breath and marched past John. "I'm getting the baby."

John put his hand on his head. "I'm sorry. I'll go talk to him while we eat breakfast."

Continuing to walk to the front, Annabelle looked back at her husband. "You better talk to him!" she barked.

She stalked into the house but immediately walked back outside, wiping a tear from her face. "I don't know what I would do if something happened to him. Look how stupid he is, he knows about the children that have been kidnapped."

John gave her a hug. "Joseph is a child, and yes, it was stupid of him. So I will talk to him about it today at breakfast."

"Ugh, these boys," Annabelle growled as she wiped away a tear. "You better correct him."

Annabelle kissed John and walked back into the house to get Jonathan.

✦

During breakfast, Joseph remained upset. David sat next to him teasing him about getting a whooping.

John went inside with Samuel through the kitchen back door and exited the kitchen after briefly speaking to Grace. "Leave your brother alone, David," his father said.

David stopped teasing Joseph, and Joseph gulped as his mouth slowly etched into a frown.

John sat down next to Joseph and placed his hand on his son's head. "I heard you decided to try to go to the practice fields alone this morning."

"Yes, I did, Papa," Joseph said. "I'm sorry."

John's head tilted, and he kept his eyes locked on his son. "You're sorry?"

"Yes, sir, I'm sorry. I didn't mean to make Momma mad."

David watched with big eyes and a smirk, and John cleared his throat.

"It was a brave thing you did, but it was dangerous," John said. "Do you know how angry your momma is right now?"

Joseph replied, "Yes, Papa."

"Why did you try to go out there so early anyway?"

"I want to be better than David."

John and Samuel chuckled.

"I'm proud you want to do better," John said. "I'm sure if your brother does not practice at all, you will become a lot better than him."

Joseph smiled at John while David looked at his father with the corner of his mouth pinching.

"I think I can almost beat you now, David," Joseph said.

Speaking Cherokee, David replied, "Only when the sun becomes the moon will that happen."

Joseph glared at David.

"Keep practicing, Joseph. I'm sure one day you'll be as good as David," Samuel said.

"How about after we finish with the crops today, we can go to the practice fields? I will bring my rifle this time," John said.

Joseph replied in Cherokee, "Are you going to tell Momma?"

John whispered in their native tongue, "Not about the rifle." He hugged Joseph and patted David on his shoulder.

The boys grinned at their father.

Grace came out of the kitchen with three bowls of grits and placed them down on the wooden table. "Did you talk to him?" she asked.

"I did," John replied. "I talked to both of them."

Samuel nodded to Grace reassuringly.

"Why are both of them smiling if you scolded Joseph?" Grace narrowed her eyes. "Never mind...Joseph, don't do that again or Auntie Lizzie and I will also give you a whooping...after your momma."

The grin immediately dropped from Joseph's face.

As soon as Grace left, John patted Joseph on the back.

He kept his word to his sons that day. After working with the crops, Samuel and Michael went with John and the boys to the practice fields, where John enjoyed watching the sibling rivalry between his sons.

Fall came with the first week of October. Changes across Oklahoma showed through the tallgrass changing colors, and the leaves on the trees changed color and fell.

Lisa and Lizzie sat on the steps of the family house watching the children play kickball after Molly had left. A carriage slowly rode down the dirt road, and they saw Eve being driven by Paul.

Eve looked out of the carriage and saw the children playing with the ball. "Paul, please stop the carriage," she said.

Paul stopped the horse carriage.

"Paul, please walk with me to the other children."

"Miss Eve, your momma said to take you to your grandma on the other side of town now," he said. "We need to keep moving."

"My momma said you're to do as I say, and I don't want to go there all day. I love grandma, but she is boring. Now come with me."

Paul got off the carriage and opened the door for Eve.

"Thank you very much, Paul."

Eve and Paul walked to the other children.

"Paul, do I look proper right now?" Eve asked.

Paul smiled at the young girl. "Miss Eve, you look proper for a six-year-old."

Eve smiled. "Thank you."

"Look, Eve is coming to play," Mel said.

"Hi, Eve," the children said.

"Hello, everyone," Eve said. "Can I play?"

"Yeah, you can play. Try not to miss the ball," David replied.

Lisa and Lizzie watched the children with great interest as they played. Paul waved at them, and they waved back.

"You could smile a little and show Paul some kindness," Lisa said in Cherokee.

Lizzie replied, "I'm kind to him."

"If looks could kill, you would be responsible for many deaths."

Lizzie scowled and folded her arms. "First Molly comes here and now Eve." She handed a corncob to Lisa. "Eve is a fetching little girl. It makes you wonder how two crazy people can create a child like that."

Lisa giggled as she bit into the corncob. "That was mean. Leave that little girl alone."

"I've said nothing mean about her. Her stupid mother tests my patience. That poor child and her sisters...what are they, three and four? That family is going to be entertaining when those girls become young ladies."

Lisa and Lizzie cackled and watched the children play for several minutes.

Paul approached Eve. "Miss Eve, I think it wise we go visit your grandma so your momma won't be mad at you," he said with a soft voice.

"Oh, you think she'll be mad at me?" Eve asked.

"I believe it will hurt your momma's heart if we never get to your grandma's home."

"Well, okay. I don't want you to hear her yelling at me today. Bye, Joseph. Bye, David. Bye, Mel. Bye, Rosita. Bye, Rain and Jannie. I have to go to my grandma's home."

"Bye, Eve," the children said.

Paul helped Eve into the carriage, then waved to Lisa and Lizzie.

The carriage drove off, and Lisa leaned onto Lizzie. "Did you smile this time?" she asked.

Lizzie huffed, grabbing a corncob from the pan in front of the women to chew on it.

One day in late October, David and Joseph dropped off two sacks of soybeans at the supply store. As the boys went home past other townspeople, Brock slowly rode down the street, and fear arose in David. The boys were told to try their best to stay away from the Indian agents, but to also be respectful of them.

"Joseph, get on my left side," David said in Cherokee.

Joseph did what David told him to do. The boys tried to walk past as Brock talked to a Cherokee man.

As the boys nearly moved past him, Brock turned his head. "David and Joseph Lightning, come here."

The boys reluctantly walked toward Brock while he ended the conversation with the Cherokee man.

"Look what we have here, the two oldest children of the Lightning family," Brock said with an investigative tone. "I'm surprised the two of you are not working in your father's fields right now."

David replied, "Auntie Grace needed two sacks of soybeans, so we had to bring them."

Brock replied, "Auntie Grace needed them? Hmph...you sound more like a slave, but I guess that should be expected, with your mother being a former slave. How does that feel, having one mother who was a savage, and now having one who's a nigger?"

David clenched his fist as he looked at a leering Brock.

"His momma was a good woman, and my momma is no nigger," Joseph snarled as he stood behind David. "My papa said nigger is an evil word."

Continuing to leer, Brock scoffed.

"Joseph, be quiet," David said.

"I see it now," Brock slowly said as he huffed. "You mostly look like your momma, boy, but you have your father's eyes and the personality of a Cherokee. You certainly are related to Lizzie Lightning. Next time, you watch your mouth, boy, or a whip will go across your back one of these days."

"Auntie Lizzie says you're a coward," Joseph said.

"Joseph, enough!" David snarled, grabbing Joseph's arm and pulling him in the direction of their home. "We have to leave now, Mr. Jackson. It was a good to see you."

Brock turned his horse around and the boys quickly left.

"Your Auntie Lizzie doesn't know how to control her mouth like a woman should," Brock said. "I suggest you not pick up her habits, boy. You ain't no Cherokee as far as me and the law are concerned. You're a nigger like your momma. Did your auntie tell you that?"

Joseph tried to look back at Brock, but David forced him to keep going forward.

"Keep walking," David commanded.

Brock cackled and adjusted his brown frock coat as he watched the boys walk away. Several Cherokee passing by looked at the crooked man with disgust.

"That child will become a problem of mine in the future," Brock said to Hunter as he approached on his horse. "I'll have to kill the fight in that one sometime soon."

"It does appear that way," Hunter said.

"I was wondering what was taking you...I was getting some entertainment," Brock said. "The Negro boy has a lot of mouth on him."

Hunter nodded. "They'll learn their place or go into the ground."

Brock leered and the two men slowly rode to the US Embassy.

As the boys went home, they argued, and Joseph became more emotional as they fought.

"You have to learn how to control your mouth. You're not Auntie Lizzie," David yelled.

"Did you hear what he called Momma?" Joseph yelled. "Why are you not angry?"

"I'm angry, but we have to be careful with what we say to white men, especially the Indian agents. They have a lot of power and can do bad stuff to us."

Joseph growled, "I hate them."

"Momma A says we can't let ourselves hate. It will make us weaker and cause us to do bad things like them. We're not them and should not act like them."

Joseph cried as the boys went home.

David stopped walking and his brow furrowed. "What's wrong, Joseph?"

The younger boy frowned. "Mr. Jackson said I'm not Cherokee. He called me a nigger. I'm not a nigger."

David wiped the tears from Joseph's face. "Stop crying, be strong. You're Cherokee, my brother, and I will always be here for you." David put his fist to Joseph's chest. "I'll always be here, in your heart like Papa and Momma A."

"Thank you, David."

"Don't thank me. It is the truth. Jesus is with us always, and like Jesus, I will always be with you. Remember that."

Joseph nodded, and the two brothers went home. They decided not to tell Annabelle what had happened and spent the rest of the day with their family.

Though Brock's hateful words echoed in Joseph's mind, he believed David's words. His silence was quickly removed by his family wanting him to interact with them. Through all of the jokes, laughs, and smiles, they remained unaware of his troubling thoughts.

October 30, 1859, began as an unusually warm fall day. The rising sun spread light across the land, and Lisa watched it as she stood by the redbud tree. She later went to church with the family.

After they sang one last hymn, Joyce approached her. The older woman prayed for her and encouraged her. Nancy strutted past Lisa and her family with a prideful stride as Joyce and a deacon prayed for Lisa.

Lizzie caught Nancy's judgmental eye roll and stormed out of the church after they finished praying for Lisa. She took off her white bonnet and approached Nancy, who recognized Lizzie's expression. She quickly put her arm through Buck's.

"You think that man is going to save you?" Lizzie snarled. "You know I saw you."

"You need to calm yourself, Lizzie Lightning," Buck said.

Lizzie stopped approaching them and tossed her bonnet on the ground.

"What is your problem with my wife?"

Lizzie pointed at Nancy. "Your wife judged Lisa as she was getting prayer...you little hypocrite."

"I didn't judge her. I pitied her," Nancy bickered.

"You liar!" Lizzie roared. "I know that stupid look on your face when you're judging someone."

"All right, that's enough!" Buck yelled.

A few members of the church watched.

"You leave her alone," Buck said. "You and your crazy temper need to walk home right now."

"Lizzie, this isn't right for no lady," a man said.

"Stay out of it, Caldwell," Lizzie growled. Her eyes fixed on Buck, and she scowled. "Buck, do you want to taste the dirt?"

Buck stuck out his hand. "I'm not going to fight you, and I'm not letting you put your hands on Nancy. Now go home."

Lizzie balled her hands into fists. "You forget who you're talking to, Buck Scott. I will fight a man."

Grace placed her hand on Lizzie's shoulder and stood next to her. "I'm sorry about this, Buck," she said. "Nancy, Eve impresses me. Your daughter has such a kind heart like you did when you were a child. Don't turn her into who you are today. I saw the look too."

Nancy replied, "Grace you...you..." She shrugged and walked toward her daughters, who played on the side of the church.

"How did you know that's what we were talking about?" Buck asked.

Grace replied, "I know my sister, and I could hear her as soon as I came out of the church. Have a good day, Buck." She picked up Lizzie's bonnet and gave it to her.

Lizzie flicked her long braid behind her and put on the bonnet.

"Sorry, Buck," Lizzie said with an emphasis on Buck's name .

Grace wrapped her arm around Lizzie and escorted her sister away. Buck gulped while he watched.

The day continued as Tsula and Lizzie played with the girls outside, and Michael played cards with David and Joseph.

In the small house, Annabelle and Maria talked to each other while Jonathan and Sky slept. The unnatural warm weather prompted George to take John, Luke, and Samuel with him to decide if they needed to expand the fields.

CHAPTER 13
Hidden Pain

LISA REMAINED IN THE FAMILY house while Grace went outside to watch the girls play with Lizzie and Tsula. Lisa prepared the dishes when a strong contraction hit her for several seconds. She dropped several plates.

"Oh, no, not now…this baby better not come right now," she murmured.

The contractions stopped, allowing her to gather herself.

I think I'm okay, Lisa thought.

She picked up the plates she'd dropped and washed them off. As she was cleaning the plates, she felt another contraction. Her heart raced, and she rushed to the front door looking for Grace. She stumbled outside and saw Grace and the others going to the practice fields.

"Grace!" Lisa yelled.

Lisa waved to Grace when she turned around, and the other woman immediately jogged to Lisa.

"What is wrong, Lisa?" Grace asked in Cherokee.

"I think I need Elder Joyce," Lisa said. Her eyes watered, and she sniffed.

"Oh, no, no, don't cry, it's going to be fine."

Lisa frowned. "I don't want to ruin our supper by having this baby now."

Grace shook her head. "Lisa, having the baby now would not ruin anything. Are you feeling birth pains?"

"Yes, I had two of them, and they hurt a lot. How long...oh, no, another one is coming!" Lisa squatted and moaned as amniotic fluid trailed down her leg. "Oh, no, I need to take off my undergarments. The birth water is coming out."

"Okay, I'll help you."

Grace and Lisa quickly entered the family house.

"The baby is coming!" Grace yelled.

Lisa's face immediately scrunched. "Why did you do that?" she growled.

"To save time and so they would stop what they're doing."

Inside the house, Grace helped Lisa take off her undergarments. Suddenly, the door opened, and Tsula came inside.

"Did you say the baby was coming?" Tsula asked.

Grace replied, "Yes. Now, what I need you to—"

Lisa groaned, and her water completely broke. Amniotic fluid gushed onto the floor.

Tsula's and Grace's mouths dropped.

"I'll go grab Big Boy right now!" Tsula said.

Grace helped Lisa get into the bed.

"How is this happening so fast?" Lisa asked in their language.

Grace replied, "I've seen this happen quickly before. There isn't nothing wrong with the baby, I promise. It's time for the baby to come out."

Lizzie rushed inside and stood in the bedroom doorway. "Is something wrong? I've never seen Tsula run like that."

"Well, the baby is arriving faster than normal," Grace said. "The water already came out."

Lizzie looked at wooden floor, seeing the pool of amniotic fluid. She looked back at Grace and Lisa. "Great..."

Several minutes passed while Annabelle, Grace, and Lizzie tried to make Lisa more comfortable. Maria watched over the children as the contractions passed.

Joyce suddenly entered the room. "Lisa, when I prayed for

you, I didn't mean for you to have this baby today," Joyce joked in Cherokee.

Lisa chuckled while Annabelle wiped sweat off her forehead. "I was honestly hoping for another day or two," she said.

Joyce chuckled and checked to see how far along Lisa was in labor. Three hours passed as the contractions and pain increased. Joyce coached Lisa to breathe and push when more labor pains came.

Lisa moaned as the minutes passed, and she pushed out a baby girl. The baby wailed with powerful lungs as they cleaned her off. Grace cut the umbilical cord, and Joyce handed the infant to her mother.

"She is more beautiful than I imagined she would be," Lisa said.

Joyce replied, "She is beautiful and strong. Did you hear that voice? You did a good job, Lisa, good job."

As Lisa held the infant, Joyce sighed and beamed. Several minutes passed as the women helped clean Lisa, then the men and children were allowed to see the new addition to the family.

"I think it is time to give her a name," Joyce said.

"I need a moment. Children, can you go play for a little while outside," Lisa asked.

The children left, excited and waiting to hear the name of their new cousin.

Lisa looked at the men. "I only want the women here with me right now."

"Whatever you want, Lisa," George said.

The men sat down at the supper table and talked among themselves, waiting for Lisa to give a name.

Joyce took her cane to stand before Lisa. She could see a lot was going through the younger woman's mind. "You know you can speak your mind here. Don't worry about what we may say," the older woman said.

Lisa looked at her baby girl and smiled. "I never wanted things to happen like this, and I know...I can't hold anger against my daughter when she has done nothing wrong." Her eyes teared up.

Joyce placed her hand on Lisa's shoulder.

"I want to name her Sunni," Lisa said, "so when I call her name, it will be impossible for me to hate her. I never want to hate my own daughter. I'm afraid if I give her another name, I'll be tempted to hate her."

Tsula cried uncontrollably at Lisa's words. Lizzie took Tsula into the kitchen to calm her down.

"Lisa, what would make you say such a thing?" Grace asked. "Please allow us to understand."

With tears going down her face, Lisa looked up at Joyce. "I hate who the father is," she said. "She will never know the truth."

Joyce nodded and asked in Cherokee, "Then how do you want to spell that name?"

"I don't want her name spelled with a y. I believe children would make fun of her if it was spelled that way. I want to change the y into an i."

"That's a different name, it's a beautiful name," Annabelle said.

Maria replied, "A rare name like that will make her a person to know."

"From this day forward, we will celebrate the life of Sunni Strongman," Joyce said. "You don't want your father and the others here because you don't want them to know the purpose of the name."

Lisa replied, "Yes."

Joyce replied, "Your wishes will be respected as they were before. She is a beautiful girl. Sunni fits well with her. I'm sure she'll be able to make many people smile like her mother has and will again. It is time for me to go. I didn't expect this to go so quickly. I've got a game of cards to play against Lea. She almost beat me last time."

"Elder Joyce, let me walk you outside," Grace said in Cherokee.

"All right." Joyce said her goodbyes, and Grace walked her to her old wagon.

Joyce spoke positively while Grace walked with her. She was confident Lisa was going to be a great mother. She was suspicious the father was not Cherokee.

Soon after, Tsula went inside the bedroom with Lizzie standing behind her. "I'm sorry, it hurt hearing you say that," Tsula said in Cherokee. "I know you dislike the father and it hurts you. Please forgive me for leaving like I did."

"Come hold your niece," Lisa said in Cherokee before handing Sunni to the other woman.

"Look at her. She has your eyes and your dimples," Tsula said. She cooed at Sunni as she held her, and the others explained to her and Lizzie why she'd given her the name.

Tsula and Lizzie promised to keep Lisa's reason a secret, and the women invited the men and the children in to look at the new baby girl.

George loved the name of his granddaughter, and after supper, he went to a social house in Tahlequah to brag about his new granddaughter. That night, Michael surprised Lisa with a crib he had made for her. A day challenged by Lisa's doubts was changed by the love of her family.

During the night, Lisa sat at the supper table while she nursed Sunni with the moonlight shining through the windows of the house. As she nursed Sunni, she hummed as she looked at her daughter.

"Jesus, I said a prayer to you," Lisa whispered. "When I was first raped, I asked you where you were. Why would you allow this? You know I spent every month of my pregnancy asking why? I still believe you should have stopped him because my faith is still hurt. But I'm grateful today, that my daughter is well. This is unfair...I understand evil things happen because the world is broken. All I ask is that you protect Sunni from experiencing what I have. Please protect her from men like her father and teach me to love her every day. Please give me more strength to trust you again. Please help me forgive that man anytime I look at her. That's all I ask."

Lisa entered her bedroom and laid Sunni down in her crib.

"She has a good woman to call mommy," Lizzie whispered.

"When did you wake up?" Lisa whispered.

"I've been awake the whole time. The room smells like a baby." Lizzie grinned. "It makes me want to hold her."

Lisa lay down in her bed and quietly giggled when she faced Lizzie. "I didn't realize the smell was in the room."

"All I can smell is Sunni. A new season has started for you, and I'm happy for you."

Lisa frowned. "I'm not ready for this, Lizzie."

"No one is ready for this when it happens the first time or second time. If the baby would've ruined who you're meant to be, you would not have her now."

Lisa looked away from Lizzie and sighed before facing Lizzie. "I guess I have to believe harder."

"Yes, you do. Don't doubt the Father's love for you. I understand you didn't want this, but you're a strong person. I think you can raise Sunni to be a strong person."

Lisa looked up at the ceiling. "I'm sure the Tate family hates me now. Florence has been the only one to speak to me."

"Give them time. You know Florence runs that family. Be patient."

Lisa smiled at Lizzie and turned over. "Maybe I can. Goodnight."

"Well...goodnight, you have two hours before she wakes up again."

Lisa grunted as Lizzie giggled.

A few days passed with Lisa adjusting to having to wake up in the middle of the night and take care of Sunni. The abnormal hours were stressful for her, but the advice from Annabelle and Maria greatly helped. A few visits from Molly and Reverend Hills also cheered Lisa up. She knew Molly was concerned and tempted to ask who the father was, but she believed Grace had already asked them to respect her wishes. Lisa's thirty-second birthday arrived, and the family made sure it was a joyful time for her.

After supper Lisa sat at the supper table next to Tsula. She watched the men play cards while she quietly hummed at Sunni.

Joseph came up to Lisa with a shy smile. "Auntie Lisa, can I hold her?" Joseph asked in Cherokee.

Lisa smiled at Joseph and glanced at Sunni. "Yes, I will teach you how to hold her," she said. "Now, hold your arms like you're holding Sky and hold them strong."

Lisa gave Sunni to Joseph.

Joseph was so happy he got a chance to hold Sunni he couldn't help but smile. "She is so warm and looks so happy. Hi, Sunni. Hi, baby Sunni."

Tsula and Lisa watched happily as he connected with his little cousin. A few minutes passed, and Sunni began to cry.

"What did I do wrong?" Joseph asked.

Lisa calmly took Sunni from Joseph. "You did nothing wrong. As she gets older, she'll become more comfortable with other people carrying her...like Sky. You did good with her."

Joseph beamed and walked to the end of the table to watch the men play cards. As Lisa calmed down Sunni, she looked up, noticing Annabelle was smiling at her.

Annabelle nodded at Lisa reassuringly.

⸻ ◆ ⸻

When the harvest festival arrived, most of the family left for the event with the exception of Annabelle, Maria, and Lisa, who stayed behind with the babies.

Annabelle felt happy being in their company. "I never thought all three of us would have babies in the house at the same time," Annabelle said.

"Yeah, it's different," Lisa replied.

"You're doing a great job with her," Maria said. "She looks just like you. She even has your smile."

Lisa smiled, exposing her dimples. "Yeah, she does."

"I don't know why, but this reminds me of Mercy. Just sitting around with Rebecca's twins and talking about the future."

"Do you still miss it a lot?" Maria asked.

"I do. Even though I have y'all, it's the memories. How Benita died in my arms...still shakes my spirit."

"I couldn't image it."

"Did you see some of the war, Maria?"

Maria's brow lowered. "I was there when Mexico City was attacked. We lost a lot of good men. I saw those white men raise the American flag in our city. It was heartbreaking."

"I remember being forced here from Georgia, like it was yesterday," Lisa said. "It was very confusing. How can these men come here, and tell us this is no longer our home? It was madness."

"Both of you experienced your homes being attacked while I ran away from the only home I knew," Annabelle said. "I left behind my family, friends...and my best friend. I don't think seeing your home catch on fire is the same as being forced from where you were born."

"I think it depends on the love that was there," Maria said.

"I agree," Lisa said. "I know I'd feel differently if I didn't have any good memories of Georgia."

Sunni yawned loudly, and the women giggled as Lisa checked on her daughter.

"Lisa, you're going to be all right," Annabelle said. "I think before all of them are grown we'll be healed. Truly free from our pasts."

Lisa and Maria smiled, showing their agreement with Annabelle. The women continued talking with each other.

I wonder how Judy Mays is doing, Annabelle thought. *I hope you don't hate me for running away. Even now, I don't know how I would tell you the real reason why I ran away.*

The bonding moment was strong for the three women, and it reminded Annabelle of the good times she'd had in Mercy.

A few weeks later, December of 1859 arrived with a strong,

cold wind. One day in early December, Annabelle and Grace watched Sunni while they ground up dried corn.

"She is such a beautiful baby. I'm surprised she has a lighter color than Lisa," Annabelle said in Cherokee.

"It's funny. She looks almost exactly like Lisa," Grace said. "I'm almost certain her father is a mixed Cherokee. We will see as she gets older."

Annabelle looked at Sunni again. "I never thought of that being a possibility. When do you think Lisa will say something?"

Grace sighed. "Elder Joyce said to give her a year to build up the strength to tell us. We will give her time. Lisa is a good mother. There's no reason to pressure her right now."

Annabelle nodded as they made cornmeal and played with Sunni.

⸻◆⸻

On December 13, 1859, John brought over David and Joseph to help him shovel snow around Elder Joyce's home.

"I like seeing strong young men shoveling snow for an old woman," Joyce said, speaking Cherokee.

John chuckled. "Elder Joyce, it's no problem. Luther told us he was running behind to help you because the snow caused his barn's roof to collapse."

"That son of mine is getting old. He needs to stop being stubborn. I told that boy he needed to clear the snow off the best he could." She shook her head. "David, you've gotten a little taller. Are you going to be tall and handsome like your Pa?"

David blushed. "I think so."

Joyce smiled. "Oh, I like the confidence. I don't think that's you, though, John. I think some of Lizzie slipped in there."

John chuckled.

Joyce noticed Joseph's body tremble. "Come inside, Joseph, and get some warm tea. Then you can come back outside and help your Papa."

"Okay," Joseph said, smiling. He put down his small shovel and followed the elder into her pine-scented home.

"Take off your shoes, baby, and have a seat."

He took off his shoes, walked across the wooden floor, and sat down at the wooden supper table.

The older woman placed a warm cup of tea in front of him, and the boy smiled while his legs happily kicked underneath the table.

"Thank you, Elder Joyce," Joseph said.

"You're welcome, sweet boy. You remind me so much of your papa when he was your age."

"Was he bigger than me?"

Joyce smiled. "He was about the same size as you with the same set of eyes."

Joseph smiled.

"I see you have your momma's beautiful smile. Would you like some honey and bread too?"

"Yes, please."

"Okay." Joyce got a piece of bread and put honey on it. She placed it on a wooden plate and placed it in front of Joseph while he drank the hot tea. "Go on and eat up, baby." She calmly patted Joseph on his back. "I'm sure you'll grow big and strong like your papa."

"Elder Joyce, is it true you fought white men in a war?"

Joyce playfully gasped as she sat down. "Who told you that?"

"David."

"Oh, he was a bad boy to tell you that. Maybe I should give him a whooping for tattle telling."

They both cackled.

"Yes, baby," she said. "A long time ago, I did fight in a war."

"Why?"

"I was trying to do the right thing for my family and our people. I never trusted any of the white men, but the British seemed to be more willing to work with us. Who knows what would've happened if they had won."

"Would we still be in Georgia?"

Joyce sighed. "I don't know, baby. White men have a bad habit of breaking their word. It's a curse among their people."

She playfully nudged Joseph. "And what do you know about Georgia? Your brother has never even been to Georgia."

Joseph giggled.

"For now we have to focus on what's happening here. Trust in the Father. Once we get strong enough, then we can worry about going back to Georgia."

Joseph ate the bread. "I hope I get to go."

"I'm sure you'd love it. I see something so special in you. Like your momma. You keep following Jesus and never allow anyone to kill the kindness in your heart. As you get older you will meet evil men, but never allow them to kill your spirit. You can't control life. You can only control how you respond to it."

"Yes, ma'am."

"You want another piece of bread?"

Joseph grinned.

"Okay, baby, I'll give you one more piece and then you can go back outside with your papa. I don't want him accusing me of kidnapping you." Joyce giggled and fed Joseph.

Afterward Joseph went outside in the cold and helped clear away the snow. Then they said their goodbyes to Elder Joyce and went home.

Joseph adored Elder Joyce, as she was the closest thing he had to a grandmother.

⬩

On December 20, 1859, Eli traveled to the Lightning-Strongman home as a gentle cold breeze passed through Tahlequah. He knocked on the small house door.

"Come in," said a high-pitched voice.

Eli entered the house slowly. "Grace?" he said.

"Look, it's Five Killer," Rain said in Cherokee.

"Rain...you've been told again and again to call him Mr. Eli like he wants," Annabelle scolded. "I will embarrass you in front of him if you keep it up."

Rain lowered her head, then quickly turned to Eli. "I'm sorry, Mr. Eli," she said.

Eli chuckled. "Don't worry about it, Rain. Hello, Jannie. Hello, Rosita."

The little girls smiled and waved at him.

"Annabelle," he said, "I was wondering if Grace was here."

Annabelle nodded. "Grace is in her room reading. You can go knock on her door."

He smiled. "Thank you."

As Eli walked down the hallway to the room, the girls watched and giggled to themselves. He knocked and heard Grace approach the door. His hands became clammy, and his throat tightened. When she opened the door, Grace stood before him.

Her eyes widened and her jaw dropped. "What are you doing here?" she asked in Cherokee.

"Ooooo," the girls said.

"Girls, quiet! And come over here." Annabelle's voice commanded.

The girls immediately quieted and stopped looking down the hallway.

Annabelle signaled for them to sit down and continue sewing, so the girls sat down facing the hallway to watch.

Grace pulled Eli into her room. "What do you want?" she asked as her nose crinkled.

"That wasn't a nice welcome," he replied.

Grace scoffed and narrowed her eyes.

Eli sighed. "Please calm down. I wanted to come here because I have something important I want to say. You know that I came here to live with Victoria because she's all the family I have left." He took Grace's hands. "I'm a grateful man, and I thank Jesus for giving me a friend like you." He cleared his throat. "I love you, Grace Lightning, and after all this time I know what I need to ask. Will you bless me beyond what I deserve and be my wife?"

Grace breathed heavily as she looked Eli. "Wow, Eli...I..." Her mouth curved into a big grin, and she nervously cackled before hugging Eli. "Yes! I'll marry you!" She kissed and hugged him again.

After grabbing Eli's hand, she opened the door and went

down the hall with a smile. When they entered the open space of the house, they stopped. She looked at Annabelle, who sat at the dinner table with a smile.

Annabelle then grunted and tapped her foot against the floor. "I'm sorry. I had to listen."

Grace looked at her nieces and Rosita as the girls grinned at her. "Did the three of you hear what I said?" she asked in Cherokee.

The three girls shook their heads.

"Good, Auntie Grace is getting married!"

The girls shrieked and gave Grace a hug.

"You three can come and tell the others with me. Annabelle, shame on you."

Continuing to beam, Annabelle shrugged. "I couldn't stop myself from listening."

Grace cocked her head with her big smile. "You nosey liar, come on, girls."

The girls put on their cape-like jackets, and they went to the family house with Grace.

Eli watched with a wide-open mouth. "Did she forget I was here? Where is the woman that I know?" he asked. "I think she forgot I was standing behind her."

Annabelle chuckled and replied, "It took you long enough to ask her to marry you, but she's so happy about it she might forget about her birthday coming up. You should go follow them. We'll be cooking supper soon."

"I will...thank you, Annabelle." He smiled. "I think you're right. I waited too long."

He then walked over to the family house and was heartily greeted when he went inside.

Annabelle later joined them, and the family celebrated the engagement. The amount of joy in the household made Annabelle forget the worries in the back of her mind. Even Lisa was active in the celebration. Annabelle hoped for more of these times and for Jacob's return. She heard the howling of wolves during the celebration. Tsula joked that even the wolves were happy for Grace.

During the night, Annabelle found it difficult to sleep because of the amount of joy she felt. Grace's thirty-fourth birthday passed on December 22, and on December 28, 1859, Pastor Bluebird married Grace and Eli. Grace moved to Eli's home with Victoria, and from that day forth, she was known as Grace Five Killer.

A strong snowstorm later arrived in Oklahoma, covering most of the land, and it held the attention of the children. Grace spent some of her time reading the story of Jonah, her favorite Bible story, to the children, and she told them the story of the two wolves. Annabelle memorized the stories by listening to Grace, understanding the need for them to be passed down to the children.

CHAPTER 14
Feeding Wolves

THE WINTER STORMS ENDED, BRINGING in January 1860, much to the excitement of the children. On January 3, 1860, John and Michael took David and Joseph to get firewood from the old forest before it became colder. Though Joseph wanted to play, he grinned when John patted him on his back.

During this time, the girls went outside to play in the snow and threw snowballs at each other. Lizzie watched the girls as she sat down at the supper table. While the girls played, Rain threw a snowball, and it hit Rosita in her mouth.

Rosita shrieked with pain and cried.

"Rosita, you baby, why are you crying?" Rain asked in Cherokee.

Rosita took her hand from her mouth, and blood fell on the snow.

Jannie gasped as she dropped the snowball she held.

"You knocked out my tooth!" Rosita yelled.

Rain gulped at the sight of Rosita's missing tooth and bulging eyes. She trudged toward her cousin. "I'm sorry, Rosita. I think we can put it back in."

"How?" Rosita asked as her brow furrowed. She reached into the snow and threw a snowball, which hit Rain in the mouth.

Rain howled as she held her mouth. Growling, she tackled

Rosita, and the two girls rolled around in the snow, screaming at each other.

Lizzie grabbed both of the girls by their arms. "Enough, no fighting," she said.

Rosita replied with a raised voice, "Auntie Lizzie, Rain knocked out my tooth!" She opened her mouth and showed that her top front incisor was gone.

Rain's eyes dilated. She stomped her foot, and she yelled, "I didn't mean to."

Lizzie gasped when she looked at Rain and said, "Open your mouth."

Rain frowned, opened her mouth, and revealed she was missing a top incisor.

"Your mothers are going to be mad. Go inside to them now! Come, Jannie, you're not in trouble."

Rain and Rosita grunted and went inside their home.

As the girls went, Lizzie noticed the blood spots in the snow, and she found both of the girls' missing teeth. She entered the house and looked at Annabelle and Maria while they sat before the fireplace with Jonathan and Sky.

She made Rain and Rosita stand before their mothers. "Open your mouths," she said.

"What did the two of you...look at this," Maria said with gasp and widened eyes.

"Both of you are missing the same tooth," Annabelle said, her mouth dropping at the sight.

Annabelle and Maria laughed hysterically.

"How did this happen?" Maria asked.

Lizzie replied, "Snowball fight, and then they tried to fight each other after knocking their teeth out."

Lisa walked out of her room with Sunni and raised her eyebrow. "What is so funny?" she asked.

"Turn around," Lizzie commanded to the two embarrassed girls. "Now open your mouths."

The girls reluctantly opened their mouths.

Lisa laughed. "Poor babies, don't worry, your adult teeth will grow in. How did they lose the same tooth?"

Lizzie huffed. "Snowball fight."

Lisa chuckled and gave both of the girls a kiss on the cheek. "Don't worry, it doesn't look too bad. Jannie, are you next to lose teeth?"

Jannie quickly shook her head as the women laughed.

Lizzie rubbed the embarrassed girls' heads and walked away. "Come on, my little wolf warriors. I'll make you some warm soup," she said. "Remember the story of the two wolves. We only want to feed the good wolf so she's stronger than the bad wolf."

The girls followed her into the kitchen.

***

Maria looked at Annabelle as she held Sky, who slept in her arms. "I can no longer tell if I laughed because this was funny, or because I'm too tired to be mad."

Annabelle replied, "I think I'm going to go with tired. I guess I will wait and see when Jannie loses her first tooth. The more I think about it, the funnier it becomes." She shook her head. "Those two knocked out each other's tooth with snowballs. On the first day they get to play outside."

Maria sighed. "It could be worse. It could've been a lot worse between the three of them."

Annabelle chuckled as she rocked Jonathan in her arms. "Yeah, you're right."

The rest of the family was amused once they learned about the girls' little brawl, and George called the girls his three cougars.

Annabelle teased Rain about missing a tooth. She was happy the girls had Rosita. She expected them to grow up to be very close to each other like the women in the family.

***

Weeks passed, and winter lost its grip on the land with the disappearance of the snow. On February 27, 1860, Lisa strolled to the supply store. It was the first day she'd been separated from Sunni. She kept looking back at the trail leading to home. She felt her chest tighten a little, and her hands become sweaty.

She entered the store and saw Mrs. Armstrong's grandson, Kevin. The two talked for a moment while Annabelle stood behind the counter. Kevin left, giving Annabelle and Lisa time to count the money the family had earned during the week.

"You look very happy today," Annabelle said.

"Do I?" Lisa asked. "I feel like I'm in a good mood, but the truth is I'm ready to go home to see Sunni. I've never been away from her for this long."

Annabelle smiled, continuing to help count the money. "Don't worry, I understand how you feel. The truth is you never stop missing them, you become used to it and use the time away to clear your mind."

Lisa chuckled. "I would think like that too if I had twins."

Annabelle sighed. "I never played like a boy like them when I was a child. I did play rough, but those two find a way to do bigger, crazier things. No wonder your father calls Rosita and the twins cougars."

"They're good children, but smart in some bad ways."

"I'm grateful they listen to me. The trees would be missing all their branches if they were bad children. I think that's the interesting part of being a parent. You see pieces of you in them, pieces of other kin in them, and there is something new of their own."

"I never thought of it that way. I wonder how much Sunni may be like me."

"Rain has her good moments, but I see parts of Lizzie in her. That temper is there. I'm thankful Jannie is more patient. Jannie is a silent storm, and her ideas grow until everything comes out."

Lisa thought more about what Sunni would grow into.

"Lisa, I need to count the chickens," Annabelle said. "I'll be right back, and you can go home."

"All right, I'm almost done counting the money anyway."

Annabelle exited through the back door to the chicken coops, and as Lisa counted the money the front door opened. When the sunlight went through the doorway Brock stepped in front of the sunlight, followed by Hunter. The men in their brown frock coats approached the counter.

"Well...there she is, Mr. Sawyer," Brock said. "I was beginning to think you were avoiding me, Miss Strongman."

Lisa gripped the counter. "What do you want, Mr. Jackson?" she asked.

"My word...no good afternoon or hello. These uncivilized manners are worrisome," Hunter said. "I do believe she wants us to leave quickly, Mr. Jackson."

"How is the child?" Brock asked.

Lisa's voice rose as she replied, "My child is fine, Mr. Jackson. What do you do want?"

"Still have a mouth on you, I see. Be careful, things can become much worse. I'm sure you understand that."

Lisa looked at Brock with a cocked head and a lifted eyebrow.

"Our agreement will resume in three days. I'm sure you have no objections to my demands. It seems you have returned to your...former self."

Hunter replied, "She does appear to not have given birth at all, impressive."

Looking at Brock, Lisa bit her lip, but suddenly smirked. "I will keep my word and respect what you demand of me, Mr. Jackson," she said. "With your permission, can you allow me eleven days so I'm rested? The baby has taken a lot of my strength."

Brock's eyebrows raised, but he quickly cleared his throat. "I do believe you're ready right now, but regardless of what you may believe, I'm a gentleman. Ten days, Miss Lisa...nothing more will be offered. If you learn to respect me and Mr. Sawyer, that half-breed boy will no longer be of your concern, and I will end our scheduled meeting in the coming days. I may even forget about Miss Lizzie's reckoning."

"Thank you, Mr. Jackson. You're smart and a kind man. I'm sorry for being disrespectful to you and Mr. Sawyer."

Hunter looked at Lisa with wide eyes.

Brock leered. "See, Mr. Sawyer? Some forms of taming do work. I will see you in ten days. Be careful not to deceive me, or that nappy-headed little boy will be down in Georgia picking cotton."

Lisa calmly replied, "I believe you, sir."

"It seems a change has happened in this one," Hunter said as he stroked his beard. "You may turn into quite the exception of your kind, like the Hicks or Scott family. Good day to you, Miss Strongman."

"Goodbye, Mr. Sawyer," Lisa said.

As Hunter turned around and walked to the door, Brock leaned toward Lisa and caressed Lisa's face lustfully while holding his gold pocket watch in the other hand. Lisa's grip on the counter grew stronger.

"Ten days. Don't disappoint me." Brock adjusted his green vest as he returned his watch to his pocket, then he followed Hunter outside.

"I promise you'll be more than disappointed, Brock," Lisa whispered.

Lisa went outside to Annabelle with a fake smile.

"I'm sorry, Lisa. I didn't mean to take this long," Annabelle said.

"No worries. Did you need help?" Lisa asked.

"No, you can go home to Sunni. Grace will back soon. We will be able to close up quickly since Lizzie was here earlier and moved a lot of things."

"All right, I'll see you at home."

Lisa walked home in deep thought as she wiped the tear that was about to drop from her eye. Before she arrived home, she had an idea that scared her. Throughout the rest of the day, she thought about what Brock had said to her. The possibility of his raping her only one more time was being weighed against the possibility Brock would never let her go.

After three days passed, Lisa became more anxious. She thought of the possibility of running away, but then she thought about Joseph. During the three days, she kept having the same nightmare, and on the third day, she remembered it vividly. When she slept, she dreamed of going into the barn with the sun high, and in the wind, she heard, "The battle isn't yours."

Lisa kneeled down in the barn, and a thunderclap startled her as Brock abruptly stood behind her. She submissively lay down on her stomach. She heard Brock taking off his trousers, and she slowly reached her hand into the hay. Anger and fear rose inside her, and she swung her tomahawk from the hay at Brock.

Suddenly, time froze.

She heard in the wind, "Don't repay evil with evil. Thou shalt not kill."

The calm voices echoed in the wind three times, and a loving hand touched Lisa's shoulder.

She awoke covered in sweat. The dream forced her to pray. She looked over at Lizzie, who slept beside her, and wondered how she'd killed.

———◆———

The next day, John and Samuel went to Choctaw territory to meet with Clyde and search for Jacob again.

As they left, Lisa watched, holding Sunni.

Annabelle noticed the worry in Lisa's eyes and walked back with Lisa to the family house. "Lisa, don't worry. This time, they may find Jacob and bring him home," she said. "Please don't lose faith."

"I think holding onto faith is one of the few things keeping me sane right now," Lisa said.

Later in the day, Annabelle put Jonathan to sleep. She lay in her bed and fell into a deep sleep.

She dreamed of sitting by the old redbud tree, and as she looked around, she noticed a beautiful woman coming toward her with a golden aura.

Annabelle stood and slowly approached the celestial being. "An angel? Constance?" she asked.

"You do have a good memory," Constance said. "Follow me."

The barn doors opened, and the horses were gone.

Annabelle followed Constance inside, feeling something was wrong. "Why am I here? Please tell me you have good news. My family needs good news."

"There have been many things that have happened in this barn; love, laughter, but also anger, pain, and a lot of hate. A storm has been growing for a long time now. You need to be prepared for it. You're not responsible for it, but the evil of one man will challenge you. You're to pray in the morning when you wake up to help prepare you. Lisa is struggling more than you know, and if she makes the wrong choice, it could put not only your family in danger, but the whole tribe."

Annabelle frowned. "Why can't you stop it? I don't know what Lisa could do to cause that much trouble."

"I'm instructed to only intervene by telling you of Lisa's struggle. I'm sorry. I've been told not to physically stop her. A mother will do anything to protect her child and her family. Lisa is tempted to make an evil choice. An act of revenge. You'll see it when it comes. Don't hold back your voice. She is brokenhearted and bitter."

"Why are you now coming to tell me? How long have you been away?"

"I was instructed to follow you the day you fled Mercy and never left. You have beautiful children. I'm happy to see how you have grown as a mother."

Annabelle put her hand to her chest, feeling overwhelmingly complimented by Constance's words. "Thank you, Constance. I only wish I could hear that from my parents."

"Don't doubt the Father in what can be done. In six days, the storm will arrive with full strength. Don't repay evil with evil. We will see each other again," Constance said in the Cherokee language.

Annabelle reached for the angel. "Constance, wait!"

She woke up and immediately leaned against the wall while she sat up in her bed.

Annabelle heard a footstep, and Jannie slowly strolled into the doorway. "Momma, who is Constance?" she asked.

Annabelle replied, "Oh, no one for you to worry about, sweetie. Is Rain asleep?"

"Yes, she is."

"Do you want to sleep with me tonight?"

Jannie nodded and jumped into the bed with her mother.

Annabelle kissed her daughter on the cheek, and the two fell asleep.

Later in the night, Annabelle heard Rain walk into the room. "You can sleep with me too, my little storm."

Rain climbed in the bed and fell asleep.

Annabelle lay next to the girls, savoring the moment and knowing this was not going to last forever.

The next day, Annabelle prayed in the morning and waited for Lisa to say or do something out of character. As the day progressed, she became more frustrated but tried to suppress it.

After a customer left the store, Grace asked, "Annabelle, what is on your mind?"

Annabelle replied in Cherokee, "Nothing, I'm tired. Jonathan had a bad night."

Grace's brow lowered and the corner of her mouth pinched. "We've known each other for too many years. What is it?"

Annabelle sighed. "I was thinking about Jacob. I hope they find him this time. So much time has gone by, and it worries me."

"I understand. I do think about it often, but we have to stay faithful. I know they will find him."

Annabelle smiled at Grace, and later in the day, Annabelle prayed in her mind as she walked home.

Lisa seemed happier as she held Sunni, and her interaction with her daughter made it hard for her to believe Lisa could do something that would endanger the people. Later in the day, as Annabelle ate with Jonathan in her lap, she noticed Tsula taking two corncobs and had two slabs of pronghorn meat on her plate.

The girls giggled while they sat across from Tsula. Lizzie even took notice as Tsula ate her cornbread.

"What are you doing?" Lizzie asked in Cherokee.

Tsula answered, "I'm eating. What are you doing, Flour Face?"

The girls giggled, and Lizzie took a deep breath before she spoke. "Why do you have so much food? You don't eat like that."

"Well...I'm pregnant again."

Lizzie squealed with excitement and hugged Tsula.

Tsula kissed Luke. "Sorry I didn't get to tell you when we were alone."

Luke replied, "It doesn't matter. I'm happy, and you're happy."

George gave Tsula a hug, and the excitement was so strong, Annabelle lost her thoughts about Lisa. She later talked with Tsula, who told her that Joyce's encouragement helped her move forward. It was warming to see Tsula smile for real and be vulnerable.

<hr>

The next day, Lisa felt in her spirit that she needed to talk to Joyce before she did anything else. When she approached the wise woman's home, her hands shook, and before she knocked on Joyce's door, she took a deep breath.

She knocked on the old wooden door and walked inside the home where she was warmly welcomed by Joyce. As time passed, she built up the courage to tell Joyce everything. The truth was hard for her to tell, and Joyce wept with her.

"I want you to know that it takes a strong woman to tell the entire truth. You must continue to walk in love," Joyce said. "Don't allow the evil that has been done to you to change you any more. I know it hurts, but you can rise above it."

"I have a plan so he'll stop coming after me," Lisa said.

Joyce folded her hands. "What is the plan?"

"To have my family catch him in the act and have him kicked

off our land. With all of the family knowing of his threat against Joseph, Lizzie, and Annabelle, they'll be easier to protect."

"Evil always grows when it isn't confronted. I want you to also remember the story of the two wolves. Everyone has two wolves inside of them. One is good and the other is evil. The wolf that wins is the one you feed. Don't feed the evil one."

"I will take your advice. I will tell them tomorrow."

"Give me a hug, Beautiful Child."

Lisa gave Joyce a hug.

"Remember, your actions not only affect you but also Sunni. This is your greatest test," Joyce said.

Lisa left Joyce's home feeling the beginning of a spiritual release.

Throughout the rest of the day, Joyce remained in prayer pursuing wisdom, and she was later joined by Lea. Joyce knew this was the Creator's battle, and she hoped Lisa's family would not be tempted into doing something evil to Brock.

A day passed, and while the women prepared supper, Lisa was quiet.

Annabelle noticed as Lisa cut up the potatoes and kept taking deep breaths. She abruptly put down the knife and took a step back. The others noticed her strange behavior and stopped cooking.

"Lisa, what's wrong?" Grace asked in Cherokee.

"I've been thinking about this for a long time. Now I see that no matter what way I say it...it still hurts me," Lisa said. "I've prayed about this again and again. I know by now that all of you have guessed Sunni's father isn't a full-blood Cherokee. The truth is, her father has no Cherokee blood because he's white, and he has been raping me. It started when Jacob was taken away from me."

Lizzie dropped her knife, and Annabelle put her hand on her heart.

"I'm sorry...I never told any of you about this," Lisa said, her voice beginning to crack. "I was trying to protect us, and I never wanted this."

"Lisa," Tsula said as tears shimmered in her eyes.

Lisa's body shook. "Brock Jackson is Sunni's father. He has been beating me and raping me when I would go to the barn. Most of the time, I wasn't going there to be with the horses. He said he was going to kill me if I didn't do as he said. Then he would go after Lizzie and have Joseph sold." Lisa began to cry. "I don't think he's going to stop raping me."

Lizzie gave Lisa a hug as she sobbed. "I'm sorry...I'm so sorry, sister," Lizzie wailed.

Tsula joined in the hug.

Maria, visibly shaken, approached Lisa with Annabelle and Grace following, and they embraced Lisa.

<hr>

Grace's face turned reddish-brown and she wiped tears off her cheeks. Marching out of the kitchen, she told the children to go to the small house immediately. Her voice was so angry, the wide-eyed children ran to the small house. As she went outside, she called for George and Michael.

At this time, Annabelle realized what her vision was about.

Grace had the men come inside the family house and told them what had happened to Lisa. Annabelle watched as George turned red in the face and immediately apologized to Lisa. They agreed the children and Sunni were never to know the truth.

Lisa told them she had three days left until she met with Brock again. Otherwise, Joseph would be his first target.

George and Michael voted to shoot Brock dead and throw his body into one of the rivers. Lizzie agreed, but Grace strongly objected. She wanted to push them to tell the Cherokee council, but she knew they didn't have the power to remove him immediately. Grace also doubted that the United States government would remove him. Annabelle and Maria agreed with Grace. Tsula believed killing Brock might somehow cause the US government to send more men.

Lisa told the others of her plan to scare Brock away from the family. The family listened and eventually agreed to Lisa's plan even though George and Michael wanted Brock dead.

Annabelle, though suspicious of Lisa's plan, agreed to it.

On March 7, 1860, Lisa strolled through Tahlequah carrying Sunni. As she walked, she was greeted by townspeople she knew.

Unknown to Lisa, Brock and Hunter had spotted her and trotted toward her on their horses. They stopped a distance away while she talked to some women and walked away.

"I'm now more curious as to who the father is of that child," Hunter said. "I'm surprised the child isn't a half-breed Negro of some sort."

"That does attract my attention as well," Brock said.

Hunter raised his eyebrows. "Do you feel some form of jealously?"

Brock scoffed and smirked. "I know you find this entertaining, but there is no man that could make me jealous if he showed affection toward that woman. Especially with all this abolition talk that keeps growing every year."

"Yes, the missionaries are becoming more and more of a problem. The missionaries are so concerned about converting these savages when our very way of life is being threatened. What if the Indians took over? Most would vote for the Negroes to be set free, and then have white men put in chains."

"Those missionaries will be dealt with soon enough. They can preach the good word all they want, but there's no room for the talk of abolition. I say we finish our rounds in this part of town and call it a day."

The men rode their horses through the rest of Tahlequah and then went to another Cherokee town.

❖

On March 8, 1860, Lisa woke up and stared at the ceiling as she took in deep breaths. She stayed home the entire day with Sunni. In the afternoon, thunderclouds passed over, but the clouds didn't release any rain. The loud thunderclaps made her nervous, so she prayed for guidance.

Later in the day, the women prepared supper like they normally would, but they talked about the plan so the children wouldn't hear about it.

Lisa sat at the supper table tapping her finger. She smiled, but Annabelle could tell she the other woman forced herself to appear happy. After supper, Lisa announced she was going to the barn and left the house with Sunni in Maria's arms.

Lisa stood outside and stared at the barn. Her hand slowly balled into a fist. She exhaled and went by the large open barn door, waiting for Brock. Suddenly, she heard rustling in the semi-bloomed woods as he came out of the shrubs. Part of Brock's top hat passed by the edge of the barn's door and waited patiently.

"Look at you, on time as you have been in the past," Brock said.

Brock followed her inside, and she left the barn door cracked open.

"I hope you're a man of your word, Mr. Jackson," Lisa said.

Brock huffed, and he took off his top hat. "I did allow you your ten days. If you keep showing me respect like a woman should, then I may consider what I said. Did you think this would be the last time?"

Lisa looked at Brock with a slight frown.

"Oh, did you actually believe a few nice words would be enough to convince me, or make up for your transgressions against me?"

"I do have eyes, Mr. Jackson. Is this really about my disrespect toward you, or about the way you look at me? I also see the way you treat my people."

Brock raised his voice. "Your people are lacking in discipline. Your people's place is beneath the feet of my people, just as Negroes are meant to work the fields. You know even a few Indians still work those cotton and tobacco fields. They didn't know their place or watch their mouths."

"Maybe when your people learn how to show respect, we will learn how to control what comes out of our mouths. So many of your people call themselves Christians, but so few of them show it. I think you call us savages because it's easier to lie to yourself than to see the truth. You're the savage."

Brock grabbed Lisa's collar and slapped her. "Careful, I might lose control. You don't want to see me lose control. Now take off your undergarments. I don't have all day."

"I don't have any on. I want to get this over with quickly so you can go where you want."

Brock grinned. "You think you're smart. I'll make sure this lasts."

Lisa got down on all fours and breathed heavily.

"No, turn around I want to see your face."

Lisa remained on all fours.

Brock kneeled down and pushed on her side to force her to turn around. "I said to turn around!" he yelled.

The sunlight beamed into the barn when the door violently swung open.

"Take your hands off my sister," Michael said.

Brock turned around.

Michael had his rifle pointed in his direction with Lizzie and Grace standing behind him. Eli also walked up to the open barn door, holding a rifle.

Brock snarled, "What is this? I suggest you rethink what you're doing, boy. Your sister and I were having a conversation."

Michael replied, "We know about all of it now, Mr. Jackson. It's time for you to go."

"What makes you think this is going to stop here? Pull that trigger, boy, and I promise every Cherokee man will be hanged. Please call my bluff."

"What makes you think we are bluffing?" Eli asked. "I think your pride blinds you."

Brock replied with an arrogant tone, "Boy, what do you know about pride? I'm sure your wife over there has killed the pride you did have."

"You're no longer allowed on our land, Mr. Jackson," Grace barked.

"The true leader speaks." Brock sneered. "I'm guessing John and Samuel are out of town then, and your good-for-nothing uncle wasn't man enough to be here."

Grace replied, "Actually, he was afraid that he couldn't look at you without killing you."

Brock leered and looked back at Lisa. "So your daddy isn't just a drunk like the rest of them. Good for him."

"Get up, Mr. Jackson, it is time to go."

"Miss Grace, I may leave today, but what's going to stop me from taking that nappy-headed little boy? Or that beautiful little half-breed baby girl?"

———◆———

The eyes of Grace, Eli, Michael, and Lizzie quickly widened as their jaws dropped.

"No, Lisa!" Annabelle bellowed.

Brock's eyes bulged. He leaned forward and turned around.

Lisa had pulled out her tomahawk from underneath the hay and held it against Brock's throat. Brock looked into Lisa's furious brown eyes and saw the coming of his own death.

"I felt the wind off that one," Brock said with a weak gasp and bulged eyes. "Is the little girl mine?"

Lisa pressed the tomahawk against Brock's throat. A tear went down her face. "She will never be yours...she will never be yours!" Lisa roared.

"Calm down, Lisa," Annabelle said. "Please remember this was not the plan."

"I think you should listen to her," Brock said. "She is very smart for a Negro."

Lisa pressed the tomahawk harder into Brock's neck, and the sharp blade dug into his skin.

"Look, Lisa," Brock said. "I'm sorry. I'm sorry. I didn't listen to you. I'm sorry that I hurt you. I shamed you. Please, don't do this."

Lisa bellowed, "You have no idea how long I have been waiting for this." She looked at the small lines of blood going down Brock's neck and leered. "How does it feel being powerless and knowing if you do the wrong thing it is over? That has been my life for over a year. I should end yours right now."

"Lisa, you're better than this. Let him go," Grace begged.

"Lisa, please...I know it hurts, but listen to us," Lizzie said. "Killing him will only bring us more problems."

"Please listen to us, Lisa," Eli said. "You've won."

Annabelle slowly walked forward, terrified Lisa might actually turn the tomahawk on her. "Lisa, you know I understand what it feels like to be raped many times. I thought about killing that man for a long time, but it wouldn't do me any good. In what way is it right to take this man's life? How do you think Jesus is reacting to this? We're not supposed to repay evil with evil."

Lisa's arm shook while looking into Brock's eyes. "You make my soul sick. Brock, can you tell me why I should not kill you right now? Can you honestly give me one reason why I should not kill you? Don't say because our daughter will need you. She has a grandfather and uncles that will easily take your place."

Brock gulped as he looked into Lisa's fearless eyes. "I have no reason. I believe any reason I say will cause you to kill me."

"Who is the whore now, Brock?"

Brock trembled. "I'm the whore."

Tears streamed down Lisa's face, and her grip tightened.

Calmly Annabelle put her hand onto Lisa's hand, and she got Lisa to slowly lower her tomahawk away from Brock.

"I will never call you Mr. Jackson again. Don't come back here, or the next time, I will kill you, Brock Jackson." Lisa's voiced deepened. "Get away from me before I change my mind. Only Jesus is holding me back."

Brock slowly backed away and suddenly realized he was bleeding from the back of his neck. He looked at Annabelle, realizing she had saved his life. He picked up his top hat and wiped the rest of the blood off his neck.

"Will you ever allow me to see my daughter or tell her who I am?" Brock asked, his brows drawn together.

"Never," Lisa said.

Brock quickly moved past Eli, Michael, and Grace. As Brock went past Lizzie, he glanced at her and huffed.

Lizzie kicked Brock in between his legs, and he fell over, stunned.

"Lizzie!" Grace yelled.

Brock howled as pain shot through his entire body.

Several seconds later Michael helped Brock stand, and the man limped to the woods where his horse waited for him.

"Be careful when you ride past our property, Mr. Jackson. I'd hate to think you were breaking the agreement," Lizzie shouted.

Brock scowled. He looked back at Lizzie as he continued to limp to his horse. He mounted, then the horse slowly trotted onto the dirt road and went away as Brock leaned forward.

Lisa felt a strong surge of relief. The family embraced her and went to the family house with good news to tell George and Maria. As everyone talked and enjoyed the children's company, Lisa sat down in one of the rocking chairs with a blank stare.

Rosita came to Lisa and placed her hand on top of Lisa's. "Auntie Lisa, are you okay?" she asked.

Lisa forced herself to smile and hugged the girl. "I'm fine, Rosita," she said. "I'm a little tired. It has been a hard day for me."

"Some days will be easy, and some days will be hard."

Lisa chuckled. "You're right. I'm proud of how good your English is now. I didn't get good at English until I was twenty-two years old, but you can speak three languages. You're such a smart girl, and I love you."

"I love you too, Auntie Lisa." Rosita returned to the supper table to play with the twins.

Eli walked toward Lisa and sat in a chair. "You're a strong Christian woman," he said. "You almost killed a man who wronged you. I'm sure it would've felt good to end him, but you did a very hard and righteous thing."

Lisa's voice lowered and her eyebrows slanted upward. "It was Annabelle. It was all of you. If I had done this alone, I would've killed him."

"But you didn't, and that makes you strong. Grace wants us to stay tonight. She is afraid Brock will come back for revenge. So we are staying here."

Lisa exhaled and rubbed her hands. "Thank you, Eli. You're a good man."

"Anything for family." Eli smiled at Lisa and went back to the supper table.

Soon after, Lisa looked at the supper table as everyone talked, and Grace smiled at her.

Lisa smiled back.

The next day, Annabelle woke up and cooked breakfast. She realized how long John and Samuel had been gone.

Annabelle thought, *what is going on? They've never been gone this long. They said they were only going to be gone for five days.*

Annabelle entered the family house while the girls ate breakfast. "Grace...John and Samuel have been gone seven days. Didn't they say it would be about five days?"

Grace replied, "Oh, no, you're right. We were so focused on Lisa, I even lost track of time."

"What about Auntie Lisa?" David asked.

"None of your business," Annabelle and Grace said with a serious tone.

David's eyes bulged before he lowered his head and went back to eating his grits. Joseph quietly chuckled.

"If they don't return by tomorrow, I will go to Clyde's myself," Eli said. "Don't worry about it."

Annabelle replied, "All right, one day. How is Lisa?"

Grace answered, "She seems happy right now. She's in the kitchen with Sunni and Tsula."

Annabelle entered the kitchen to find Lisa happily bouncing

Sunni on her hip. It was a happy moment for Annabelle because she understood how freedom felt.

Lisa looked at Annabelle with a big grin. "Look who it is," she said. "It's Auntie Annabelle!"

Sunni smiled.

"Good morning, sweetie," Annabelle said with a baby voice.

Annabelle came up to Lisa, and playfully pinched Sunni's chubby cheeks. The baby giggled and reached out to her, so she picked up the healthy baby, who bounced and laughed in Annabelle's arms.

"She's got her momma's eyes," Tsula said with a high-pitched tone and smirk.

Lisa walked to a counter to help Tsula cook, and Annabelle noticed an entirely different mood from her. The other woman was truly smiling again, and Annabelle hoped this would remain the dominant atmosphere for her family. In the back of her mind, she worried about retaliation from Brock Jackson. She knew how dangerous white men could be. The loss of Benita remained a scar on Annabelle's soul.

Two days passed as the Lightning-Strongman family stayed on guard, not allowing the children to go anywhere alone. Instead of waiting one day to travel to Choctaw land, Eli remained an extra day because he was concerned about Lisa's safety. He promised to leave first thing in the morning to the Choctaw, stating his suspicions regarding how long John and Samuel had taken to return.

During this period, Joyce and Pastor Bluebird were informed about the incident with Brock. Pastor Bluebird insisted on telling the Cherokee council of Brock's crimes, even if Brock received no real punishment, but the Cherokee had no power to banish him from Tahlequah.

CHAPTER 15

Reunited

O
N MARCH 13, 1860, AS Eli rode that morning toward the Choctaw territory, he slowed down his horse.

"You boys had me worried. Welcome home," he said.

By the old redbud tree, Lizzie played with the twins and Rosita when they heard horses coming down the dirt trail. She quickly armed herself with her bow and arrows.

"Girls, you stay right there," Lizzie said in Cherokee.

The girls immediately huddled together, and Lizzie slowly moved up to the dirt trail but then dropped her bow.

The girls watched with raised eyebrows from a distance as Lizzie gave a man a hug.

"Oh, Uncle Samuel, John, and Eli, they're home," Rosita said in Cherokee. "Who is the other man?"

Rain replied, "I don't know."

Lizzie ran ahead of the men with her quiver bouncing against her back shouting, "Grace, Annabelle, Tsula, everyone, come outside!"

Grace quickly came out of the family house and screamed with excitement. She ran to the man and gave him a hug. Annabelle, Maria, and Tsula came outside and looked at the man like they had seen a ghost.

George, Michael, David, and Joseph left the barn and walked toward the group. The girls sat in the grass watching with great interest. The man was bald, with almond-shaped eyes, a strong build, and a small scar on his right cheek.

"Lisa, come out outside," Grace said.

Lisa replied, "I'm coming. I had to get Sunni."

Grace walked up to the front door of the family house and took Sunni as soon as Lisa got to the door.

"Grace, you don't have to be so excited to take her," Lisa said.

Grace grabbed Lisa's arm and pulled her to the crowd.

"Grace, what is the…" Lisa looked at the scarred man and gasped, "It can't be."

"Hi, Lisa," Jacob said.

"Jacob…is that really you?" Lisa asked.

Jacob smiled. "It's me."

Lisa placed her hand over her mouth and began to cry. "Now they find you. I don't know what to say. I'm sorry. I wish I could change things."

"Lisa, there isn't anything to be sorry about. I'm home."

Lisa's face now glistened with tears. "So much has changed, so much has happened."

Sunni giggled, making Lisa's heart drop when she looked at Jacob.

"I don't know how to tell you," Lisa said.

Jacob shook his head. "Whatever it is, I still love you."

Lizzie put her arm around Lisa and sent the boys away. "You knew this was never going to be easy, but you also know whatever happens next, we love you," Lizzie said. "Give her to me."

Grace gave Sunni to Lizzie, and Lizzie nudged Lisa.

"When you were taken away a lot of things happened," Lisa said as she grabbed onto the skirt of her dress and her hands shook. "This…this is my daughter, Sunni." Tears streamed down Lisa's face. Looking into Jacob's eyes, she tried to gauge his reaction. "Please forgive me. I'm so sorry. I never wanted this to happen."

Jacob's eyes widened as he looked at the beautiful baby girl.

"Before you open your mouth, Jacob Tate, there's a lot you need to know," Lizzie said in their native tongue.

Lizzie explained the terrible things Lisa had gone through during Jacob's absence. John and Samuel, listening, were also struck with disbelief and anger.

"You have no reason to be sorry," Jacob said, his voice cracking as he held back tears. "I'm sorry I couldn't be here to protect you. I have no judgment on you, and I still love you and I will love Sunni."

"Jacob, you have no reason to apologize," George said in Cherokee. "All of this was started by my foolishness. May Jesus forgive me. My little girl wanted to marry a good Cherokee man from a good family. I denied her that out of fear. I have failed my family as a leader. All I ask is that you take Lisa as your wife and my granddaughter as your daughter."

Jacob humbly replied, "All is forgiven, Mr. Strongman. I think we've endured enough pain."

Lisa hugged Jacob and wept smiling. "You need to go see your pa," she said.

"We went there first. John and Samuel told me my father was not doing well," Jacob said. "How about we all go inside and tell some old stories?"

"Sounds good to me," John said in Cherokee.

The family rejoiced and entered the family house.

"Girls, come inside," Annabelle said. "Joseph, David, come inside."

The boys ran to the family house smiling. Inside the house, the boys kept asking Jacob questions to learn about where he had been the past two years. The adults lied to the boys and told them Jacob had been rescued earlier, and the women were taking him supplies. He had to remain hidden until the white men that kidnapped him were found. The last trips John and Samuel had made were to help Clyde find the white men and not to search for Jacob. The story was used to hide Sunni's true lineage.

The loving moment was a breakthrough for Lisa. When Jacob held Sunni, he bonded immediately with the baby girl. He was amused that Sunni had Lisa's eyes and smile, and the child remained calm in his arms.

Lisa's eyes kept tearing. She struggled with her mixed emotions and enjoyed the others' reactions to Jacob's return.

Annabelle watched in amazement as she held Jonathan and sat next to John.

She thought, *God, I know what you did for me...but to see what did for Lisa. You've blessed her with more than she was asking for, thank you.*

Later that day, George offered to have another house built for Lisa and Jacob, and he refused to take no for an answer.

Jacob vowed to help George build it, seeing it as opportunity to connect more with his soon-to-be father-in-law.

The next day, Pastor Bluebird went to the Tate farm to greet Jacob, and he was overcome with joy once he saw the younger man.

"The Lord has answered a prayer made by many," Pastor Bluebird said in Cherokee. "I'm always here for you if you need any guidance to help heal your spirit from the evil you experienced."

Jacob replied in their native language, holding back tears, "Thank you for your kind words, Pastor Bluebird. I would like a few more days before talking about all of it. I know I'm a blessed man, and Jesus is good."

"I think it is time to finish what was started so long ago. It's time for you and Lisa to be blessed by the church and seen as one. Lisa and her family are waiting for you right now."

"What!"

Pastor Bluebird reassuringly nodded.

"I don't know what to say."

"I think it's time for us to not keep them waiting, Jacob," Mr. Tate said with a smile.

Florence exited the house with their younger brother, Wren, and older sister. Piper.

Jacob replied in Cherokee, "I agree, Pa, it is time to go."

Pastor Bluebird rode to the church with Jacob and the rest

of the Tate family. The pastor approached the brown-bricked church with Jacob closely following him.

The young man gulped as he walked into the sunlit church. Sweat formed on the back of his neck. He froze at the sight of Lisa standing at the front of the church in front of the pulpit. She had on a green Victorian dress with embroidered white flowers on the skirt, and a blue trim created together by Tsula and Piper.

The entire Lightning-Strongman family was sitting in the front pews along with Elder Joyce, Victoria, and a few other elders. With his throat now tightening, Jacob walked toward Lisa, who had her long, thick wavy hair unbraided.

"I can't put into words...how beautiful you are. Spirit and soul," Jacob said.

"You're my best friend, my lover," Lisa said. Her eyes remained anchored on Jacob. "I can't describe how much I missed you."

"Your eyes give me life."

"Are you two lovebirds ready?" Pastor Bluebird asked with a grin.

Jacob and Lisa turned to Pastor Bluebird, who stood behind the pulpit. "Yes," the two said smiling.

"Marriage is something that takes work," Pastor Bluebird said. "There will continue to be good times and some rough times. However, real love can move the two of you to even greater heights. Sharing your honest feelings, listening to each other, and understanding each other will give you a strong marriage. The most important of all is to make sure you're keeping the Father first place in your lives. The foundation must be him because neither of you are perfect. Lisa comes from a long line of strong women."

The families giggled.

"It is important to be able to let go. This requires trust. You can't love freely without trust. With that being said, a man is to love his wife as Christ loves the church, and a wife is to be submissive to her husband. This does not mean you are lesser,

Lisa. This means you're to allow Jacob to lead and tell him when he's gone and made a mess of things."

The families chuckled again.

"Again, both of these roles truly mean you must listen to each other. Lisa has experienced horrible things. Jacob, it's your responsibility to listen to her needs and help her heal. You can't fix all of the problems, but there's nothing like a husband or wife who's staying with you through the struggle."

As Pastor Bluebird continued, the young couple smiled and listened.

A few minutes later, Pastor Bluebird married Jacob and Lisa. As everyone celebrated more sunlight poured into the church, signifying a heavenly approval to them.

Their marriage was accepted by the church, but not accepted by the Cherokee government. The celebration was moved to the Lightning-Strongman home. The marriage made it seem like things were finally set right.

Over time, Jacob received counseling from Pastor Bluebird to help him further heal from his enslavement. George and Jacob also met with Pastor Bluebird and Elder Joyce together to make sure all was forgiven.

As Annabelle did tasks on the farm, she felt a strong love around their land. She would sometimes watch the men build the new house and allowed the boys to help.

Joseph had a strong bond with his father and the other men in his family, and that's what mattered to Annabelle.

CHAPTER 16
The Two Wolves

Two weeks later, while Annabelle, Lisa, and Grace worked the supply store, Nancy entered. To their surprise, a different slave walked inside with Nancy.

"Good afternoon, ladies, this is Robert. One of my other slaves who's useful...I know y'all have seen him before," Nancy said.

"Good afternoon," Robert said.

"Good afternoon, Robert," the women replied.

Nancy seemed a bit shaken as she stood before Annabelle and the others. "Grace, here is the list of supplies I need today. Robert reads little, unlike Paul. Please be patient with him."

Grace's eyes widened when she heard Nancy's request, and she took the paper. "Come with me, Robert," she said.

Robert politely nodded and followed Grace around the store. He carried the supplies to the door, and Grace let him outside. She stood by the door, watching Robert put the supplies on the wagon.

"Nancy, where's Paul, if you don't mind my asking," Annabelle said.

Nancy replied, "Paul is on my farm healing from a terrible accident two days ago. My little Eve tried to ride one of the horses when we weren't looking. Paul ran to get her when the horse got scared by a snake. The horse threw Eve off, and she landed in the bull pen. That savage bull charged my little girl, but Paul grabbed her and jumped over the fence right as the bull hit the fence. The bull hit the fencing so hard it stabbed Paul in his back through the wood. The dumb bull got himself stuck trying to kill my little girl."

"I'm sorry to hear that," Lisa said. "How are they?"

"Eve is terrified, and her arm is badly bruised, but it is healing. Paul is resting in our home and healing. We're not sure if he going to make it. He lost a lot of blood. He keeps waking up and falling back asleep. He has a bad fever. We have asked Dr. Lewis to look at him."

Annabelle frowned and replied, "I hope Paul recovers. We will be praying for him."

Nancy softly replied, "Thank you. I saw the whole thing. It was my fault. I was supposed to be watching her. Paul might die because he saved my little girl when he could've watched her die." She opened up her reticule, pulling out a piece of paper and a blue wildflower. "Paul for some reason felt Lizzie of all people needed to be cheered up, and this paper is Paul's manumission."

"Nancy, that's so kind of you," Lisa sympathetically said.

"I know I have my ways, and my family has its ways, and my father has his ways. But I can't keep a man...who has been a faithful servant to my family a slave after what he did." Nancy withheld tears while taking a deep breath. "Paul cares about my babies, and he saved Eve's life. I've talked with Buck, and I will be more than happy to pay him to work for us. I believe it is long overdue."

"What you're doing for Paul is an act of love, Nancy," Grace said. "I hope Paul survives so he can thank you."

Nancy replied, "So do I, Grace. Maybe...our people do need to change. All of you have a good day, and if any of you want some beef, we have some for free. Buck shot that bull."

Nancy left the blue wildflower on the counter and walked outside.

Lisa picked up the flower and smiled. "I think Lizzie would've passed out if she had heard Nancy say that," she said.

Grace closed the store's front door. "The Lord does work in mysterious ways," she said.

When the women later arrived home, they told the family what had happened to Paul and gave Lizzie the flower, which Lizzie took.

During the night, Lizzie played with Sunni in her room while Lisa and Annabelle talked. Lizzie made Sunni laugh by making faces at her, and Sunni also kept reaching for the blue wildflower.

Lizzie kept her away from it, and the woman looked at the flower and sighed, whispering, "Do you know. Auntie Lizzie has gotten flowers almost every time from Paul? Auntie Lizzie is so tired of Paul bringing her flowers."

Sunni laughed, trying to reach for the flower again.

"Maybe you see something Auntie Lizzie doesn't see."

A few days later, on April 3, 1860, Lizzie got on Big Boy in the later afternoon, and rode down the dirt trails. She arrived at Nancy's farm, the place the woman's father had built her and Buck as a wedding gift. She jumped down from Big Boy with her quiver and bow on her back.

A slave approached her. "Miss Lizzie, it good to see you. You want me to get Mrs. Nancy for you?" he asked.

Lizzie answered, "Yes, tell her to hurry up and not to waste my time."

"Yes, ma'am. I will immediately."

The slave left as Lizzie leaned against Big Boy and petted his brown mane.

Nancy exited her house and approached Lizzie. "What do you want, Lizzie Lightning?" she asked.

Lizzie answered, "I only came here to see how Paul was healing."

Nancy's eyebrows shot up and her demeanor calmed. "Paul is inside. I will take you to him. Dr. Lewis said the next few days will be very important. Paul has stopped bleeding but he's still in danger of dying if the wound gets infected, or if he is still bleeding on the inside."

The two women went inside Nancy's home and walked through the white hallways to a room. Nancy opened the door, and Lizzie walked inside to see Paul lying in bed with the sun shining through the window.

"Hi, Paul," Lizzie said with her high-pitched southern accent.

Paul turned his head and smiled. "Miss Lizzie, it good to see you," he said with a raspy voice. "Miss Grace, Miss Tsula, John, and Miss Annabelle came by a few days ago."

"Yes, I know. I was busy with the store and my nieces."

"Your family is growing so much. Miss Tsula is having her baby, and Mrs. Lisa and Jacob came by yesterday." Paul coughed.

Lizzie stepped forward and her brow drew together.

"Oh, no, I good, I really am good."

Lizzie rolled her eyes. "You're an idiot. Lying here because you almost got yourself killed trying to save Eve. You're an idiot...but you're a brave man with a good heart."

"I must be dying for you to say that to me."

Lizzie giggled. "Actions do speak louder than words. You showed that by saving Eve. You showed what a Christian man should do or try to do."

"You know my momma...that what she always tell me. Do what is right because people believe you more by what you do than what you say."

"Your momma must've been a smart woman."

"My momma is a mulatto house slave, and my daddy is her master's son. That's why I got the nice hair like you."

Lizzie huffed. "There's no such thing as nice hair. You have to know how to take care of your own. You take good care of your hair. I think I need to leave now so you can save your strength."

"Thank you for coming to see me. You have a good heart."

"Thank you, Paul." Lizzie walked away past Nancy and murmured, "I'm learning how to keep a good heart, Paul."

On April 10, 1860, Lizzie went over to Joyce's home unannounced, though Joyce welcomed her presence. The women talked for some time about the return of Jacob and how well

Lizzie had forgiven herself. Lizzie also talked about her walk with Jesus, but also her constant concern about her family. Constant worry fed into her anger.

Joyce agreed with Lizzie's assessment, and she prayed for her, then poured her some mint tea.

"Continue walking in the path of light, and ask for guidance from the Holy Spirit," Joyce said. "I know that's part of your problem...you can't wait for life to become so out of control that it forces you to pray. I know you remember the story of the two wolves...it is a terrible fight between two wolves. One wolf is evil; he is hate, anger, envy, sorrow, unforgiveness, greed, arrogance, self-pity, guilt, resentment, lies, and false pride. The good wolf is love, joy, peace, hope, humility, kindness, empathy, generosity, truth, and faith. There is a fight going on in the inside of me." Joyce pointed at Lizzie. "The same fight is going on inside you, and inside every other person. Remember the wolf that will win is the one you feed."

Lizzie nodded. "I will always remember that."

"Good. It will help you remember to be Christ-like."

"I guess I have to keep moving forward."

Joyce folded her hands. "Good...because time waits for no one. Wildcat, it takes courage to try to love again...that's something you've always had."

Lizzie put down her tea. "I'm not interested in a man."

Joyce lightly chuckled. "I've heard that lie too many times over the years."

"I promise. I'm not lying. How do you know if it is a lie?"

"I have seen the way you love your nieces, nephews, and younger cousins. You're practicing for what you want in life."

Lizzie sat back in the rocking chair, and her eyes shifted off Joyce to her lap.

"I want you to learn something I didn't learn until my second marriage. The Father didn't make the man to be who you want him to be, but for him to be who he was created to be. You have to trust that he is meant to be who you need and what is best for you."

"I want a Cherokee man when I'm ready."

"What if the right one for you is a mixed-blood or has no Cherokee blood? Will you refuse him when he is best for you?"

"I don't want to give up my culture for a man that will try to make me change."

"I never said you had to. The question was, will you accept what is best for you? I'm not saying he'll be a white man, but will your heart be open to trust the Father?"

"I guess after Jacob, I was done trusting."

"Don't allow disappointments to kill your trust. You know life was never promised to be fair, so don't make it harder by having no trust in anything. The painting is bigger than you."

"I'll try harder."

Joyce's mouth curved downward. "I won't be here forever. When the Father calls me to walk on, you will need to be strong. I don't know if I have fifty days or fifty years left, but I will always be with you in spirit. But you must rely on guidance from heaven on your own so you will have wisdom others cannot give you."

"Thank you for your wisdom."

"You're always welcome here, Wildcat, and you watch your temper around those Indian agents. I heard the Holy Spirit speak to me. We must keep eyes on those men."

Lizzie nodded and left Joyce's home. Joyce's words weighed heavily on Lizzie and inspired her to keep trying. She arrived home to find George and Jacob working on the almost-completed house. As she marched to the family house, she heard the girls laughing as they played. She stopped to watch them for a minute.

Her eyes widened, and she murmured in Cherokee, "Ugh... that smart old woman. Always reading me."

She entered the family house smiling and looking for the babies.

At the same time, Michael was at the supply store with Samuel when someone opened the front door. Michael exited the supply room and smiled at a young Cherokee woman who was standing by the front door. She had caramel-colored skin and kept her long hair in a twin bun style. Her brown round eyes made Michael smile.

"Hello, Michael, I wasn't sure if you were here," the young woman said in their native language.

Michael attempted not to smile when he looked at her. "Hi, Rissa, it's good to see you."

"I wanted to say I had a great time spending time with you last week, and the week before. I know your family has been going through a lot, but I was hoping you could come to the next dance this week."

Michael shyly replied, "I would like that. I had a fun time too. You're a smart woman."

Rissa smiled at Michael. "Thank you. You're a good man and smart. I'll be looking for you later this week."

"Yeah, we will see each other again later this week."

Rissa left the supply store while Michael watched and smiled.

"Look at you. I think you're turning red," Samuel said in Cherokee.

Michael's lips tightened, and he quickly replied, "I'm not."

Samuel walked out of the supply room laughing. "All I have to say is you should have already been spending time with Rissa. She's liked you since the two of you were children. She has a body on her."

Michael grinned. "Yeah, she does...wait, you're married to Maria."

Samuel laughed and patted Michael on the shoulders. "I'm happily married. I was looking to see what you were going to say. Sounded like the truth mostly came out. Let's go home, little brother."

Michael sneered as Samuel walked out of the store. The two men strolled home with Michael grumbling. Samuel eventually stopped teasing Michael and encouraged his brother to spend more time with Rissa.

A few days later in the early morning, Joseph snuck outside to go to the practice grounds. He tried to be quick so Annabelle wouldn't catch him being disobedient, but he didn't realize that Michael watched him.

When he tried to hit targets on the old tree, Michael stood behind one of the old trees on the path watching Joseph. He understood that for Joseph, being as good as David meant a lot, and he enjoyed watching Joseph's effort. He decided to let Joseph practice and learn on his own so he would gain confidence. As long as he was there to watch Joseph, Michael felt comfortable with the boy practicing alone.

April 17, 1860, brought in the twins' sixth birthday, and the girls spoke quickly with big smiles, jumped around, and demanded the playful attention of the whole family. Lisa had baked the girls a small loaf of bread, and they shared it with Rosita. As the girls took time to sew with Tsula, the boys remained outside in the cornfield with Samuel and Michael.

As the boys checked the cornfields for sick plants and ripped off the bad insects, Joseph became impatient. "Michael, does it matter if we keep doing this?" he asked. "It looks like we're going to have a bad crop this year anyway."

Michael laughed and turned to Joseph. "We check all the time to keep the birds out that will eat the corn, and the bugs that'll cause us problems," he said. "We have to keep doing this for our family. We can't trust the white people to give us supplies."

Joseph groaned, "I wish we didn't need anything from them."

Michael looked at Joseph as he worked the cornfields. "How about after we finish here, we play some poker? I can test both of you."

David replied, "That would be fun. I know Joseph will lose. He gets too scared to take a chance."

Joseph replied, "I'm not scared. I'll show you today!"

"All right, enough of the tough talk," Michael said. "It'll be a good time later today."

Michael and the boys finished working in the fields, and they later played poker. John sat down at the table and watched the boys try to beat Michael. The time spent together meant a lot to

Joseph. During one of their rounds, the final hands were put down with Michael having a full house, David having a straight, and Joseph having three of a kind. The others applauded such a close game between the boys, but Joseph sat back in his chair frowning.

David placed his fist on Joseph's chest. "You did good," he said in Cherokee. "I know one day you'll beat me."

Joseph smiled and placed his fist on David's chest. "Thank you, brother."

"I'll play with the boys now so you can go visit Rissa," John said.

The boys chuckled as they looked at Michael.

"What makes you think I want to go see her?" Michael asked.

John huffed and shuffled the cards. "Whatever, be back in time for supper."

As Michael stood up and straightened up his shirt, Tsula exited the kitchen with plates. "Where are you going?" she asked.

"Nowhere," Michael answered.

Tsula put the plates on the table, smirking. "I'm pregnant, not stupid. Go run along and see her. I like her; she makes you turn red in the face."

Michael rolled his eyes and went toward the front door.

"Aw, so adorable! Look at little Michael," Tsula said, grinning.

The boys cackled while Michael left the house.

Tsula turned to them. "One day you and your brother will each bring home a girl, my little Joseph."

"She'll be prettier than what David brings home," Joseph said.

Tsula laughed as David playfully shoved Joseph. The boys continued to play fight before John stopped them. Afterward, the boys spent the rest of day with their family celebrating the twins' birthday.

Over time, Joseph snuck out to the practice fields in the early mornings, and Michael watched him. One early morning when Joseph snuck out to the practice grounds, he turned around thinking he had heard something. He looked for a few minutes and saw someone riding a horse in the distance, then went back to practicing.

He thought, *If I get good enough, then I know Papa will teach me how to use the rifle.*

He took aim with his bow and missed the target hanging off of the tree. Michael remained in the shadows unaware that someone had passed by.

On April 21, 1860, Molly rode to the Lightning-Strongman farm and found the girls. She asked for Lisa's whereabouts, then traveled to the family house and knocked on the door.

Lisa welcomed Molly inside, and Annabelle, Tsula, and Jacob greeted her.

"It is a blessing to see all of you today," Molly said. "Are any of the children around? I wanted to say a few things I know you wouldn't want them to hear."

"None of the children are here," Tsula said.

Molly nodded. "Good. Lisa, I learned from Reverend Hills about you and Mr. Jackson. I—."

Lisa quickly stood up. "How does he know about it?" she asked with a lowered brow.

"Pastor Bluebird told him. We've sworn not to tell anyone else of these horrible incidents."

Lisa sighed and sat back down.

"I want to apologize to you. I've sinned against you because I judged you. I had no right to do such a thing. I assumed you were a promiscuous woman without taking the time to learn the truth." Molly's eyes welled with tears. "Even if you were promiscuous, which I know you're not...no woman should ever experience what you did. I promise Reverend Hills and I will always be around to help if needed."

Lisa gave a half-smile. "Thank you, Molly, that means a lot to me."

"It is evil men like Mr. Jackson that make it difficult to spread God's word. I see this in the other tribes, and it breaks my heart because I don't know how to fix such problems."

"If more of your people admitted to the evil things done to my people, I think that would be the first step to healing. It's hard to listen to the truth from a person unwilling to admit their ways are not perfect."

Molly nodded. "I agree, and you have such a beautiful family. I know that I'm a blessed woman, but in time, I hope to be as blessed as you are."

"You can sit and eat some corn," Tsula said.

Molly giggled. "I appreciate such kindness, Tsula, but I have already eaten. Besides, I've learned to never take any food away from a pregnant woman."

The group laughed.

Molly later said her goodbyes.

After she left, Tsula pushed her chair out from the table. "I never expected anything like that from a white person," she said.

"In some way it gives me hope that things are changing," Annabelle said. "I hope to see a time when slavery will be gone forever."

Jacob placed his hand on Lisa's. "So do I," he said.

Tsula stood, eating a corncob, and entered Lizzie's room, where the other woman was creating an arrow. Tsula sat next to her on the bed. "Did you hear all of that?" she asked.

Lizzie put feathers onto the new arrow and replied, "Yes…it was unexpected. Even for Molly, that was humble of her."

Tsula smiled and playfully nudged Lizzie before she stood and left the room.

Lizzie beamed as she finished creating the new arrow and thought, *Annabelle might be right. How interesting things would be if slavery ended. It's time for a change to happen.*

On April 29, 1860, Annabelle, Grace, Lisa, and Lizzie left the supply store. The day had gone well, with Mr. Gross stopping by as one of the first customers and greeting Annabelle.

Grace and Lisa had worked the counter while Annabelle and Lizzie multitasked. As the women worked, the front door slowly opened, and to their surprise, Brock and Hunter came through the front door.

"I guess the inappropriate looks on your faces sum up your

thoughts," Brock arrogantly said with a slight slur. "Hello, Mr. Jackson and Mr. Sawyer, or good afternoon, Mr. Jackson and Mr. Sawyer, would be appropriate."

Lisa replied with her face scrunching, "How dare you talk about what's appropriate?"

Hunter replied, "Miss Lisa, we're simply making our rounds. I must say I'm pleased that we haven't received any recent complaints from any American citizens about the store."

Brock pointed at Lisa. "I want to talk to this woman alone," he slurred. "The rest of you get out."

"Mr. Jackson, you could offer us all the money in the world so you could have time alone with Lisa," Lizzie said with her head bobbing and voice deepening. "The answer would be no."

"You disrespectful redskin, I'll have you beat."

Lizzie tightened her hand into a fist. "I would like to see you try."

"Lizzie," Grace barked. "Mr. Jackson is obviously drunk. Please take him home, Mr. Sawyer."

Brock replied, "Lisa Strongman, I demand to see my daughter. You either going to respect me and give me my daughter, or I will burn this store to the ground."

Grace moved around the counter and stood before Brock.

Hunter calmly placed his hand on Brock's shoulder. "We've done what we needed to do here," he said. "Don't make a scene. You're in no condition to approach Miss Lisa."

Lisa replied, "He will never be in good condition to see my daughter. Did you think I was speaking words so you would leave me alone? She will never know you. Jacob is her father."

Brock screamed and kicked over a few crates filled with sacks of cornmeal. "You disrespectful whore!" he yelled. "How dare you allow that nigger to raise my daughter...how could she..." He moaned, holding his head.

Hunter stepped toward Brock and whispered in his ear. He looked back at the women. "I will take him home. It has been a rough day for both of us," Hunter said. "I apologize for the mess."

The women scowled at the two men while Hunter helped walk Brock to the door.

"Apologize...apologize to who?" Brock slurred. "To that whore that loves a half-breed nigger, or the nigger standing behind the counter?"

Lizzie ran up to Brock and punched him. Brock fell, and Hunter stumbled, trying to catch him.

"Get out, you hateful man!" Lizzie bellowed. "You're nothing in Tahlequah!"

Annabelle was silent as Hunter struggled to pull Brock to his feet.

"You just hit a US Official," Brock slurred. "I want her hanged!"

"Come on, Brock. We have to leave," Hunter said.

Brock stumbled outside and vomited in front of their horses. Grace followed them and watched, sneering as Hunter struggled to get Brock on his horse. Brock fell on his back, and Hunter helped him stand.

A few townspeople quietly laughed at him.

Hunter was finally able to help Brock onto his horse. He held onto the horse's reins, and the two men slowly rode away.

Some townspeople passing by watched as Hunter struggled to control both horses.

"Are you all right, Lisa?" Grace asked.

"I'm fine," Lisa said. "This was no surprise. He was going to return someday."

"You handled that well," Annabelle said.

"Thank you, Annabelle," Lisa said. "And thank you, Lizzie."

Lizzie smirked, and the women cleaned up the store.

⁌⬥⬥⬥⁍

Later in the night, Annabelle lay in bed with John and talked about what had happened to Lisa. John's nose crinkled and he gnashed his teeth as Annabelle told him that Brock was bold enough to come into the store and demand to speak to Lisa alone. The other men, who'd been told once the women arrived at home, were as upset.

"John, when I see Lisa and when I honestly think about what she went through, my life could've been the same," Annabelle said. "Mr. Brown raped me so many times, and he hit me so many times. Lisa is who I could've been."

John frowned as he listened to Annabelle's words and put his arm around her shoulder. "Don't say that," he said in Cherokee. "I would never let that happen to you."

"You understand well that life is unfair, and we experience terrible things. I know you wouldn't let that happen to me, but if I'm honest, I hurt for Lisa. It's a blessing Jacob has accepted Sunni, but how long will we keep the truth buried?"

"We will keep it buried in our hearts to protect Sunni. The children don't know the truth, and if the truth passes on with us, we will have succeeded."

"You know I would never tell Sunni or our children. It bothers me because the truth has a way of coming to light even when we don't want it to."

"Sometimes the truth is shown in a hurtful way, but I think the best way we can prepare for that is to love Sunni. So she always knows she has a family that'll protect her."

"I guess you're right. Loving Sunni is the strongest weapon we have to protect her. I see the house is almost complete. I'm impressed you and the others are building it so fast."

John rubbed his hand on Annabelle's scars. "You're saying that to make me feel better about getting a splinter in my finger today."

Annabelle giggled. "Yeah, I am."

John laughed and the two kissed each other.

"Does my man need some more care?" she asked.

"Mm-hmm, I need a lot more care."

She grinned. "I don't know about a lot. That's how those twins got here."

He smirked and caressed Annabelle's cheek. "You don't know that."

She grinned. "I know more than you know. Mr. Lightning."

The couple embraced each other and made love before falling asleep.

———◆———

A week went by with life continuing on the Lightning-Strongman farm. On the practice field a redheaded woodpecker was drilling into one of the old trees. A tomahawk hit the tree, startling the bird. The scared bird flew into the higher branches, watching as Lisa approached the tree and pulled out the tomahawk. The moment she walked back to her marker, she saw Jacob coming toward her.

"I'm guessing a lot is still on your mind for you to be here," Jacob said in Cherokee.

Lisa replied, "No, I needed to be here. I haven't practiced this in a few weeks. I don't like the thought of losing my skill."

"I think it would take you longer than a few weeks for you to start throwing badly."

"I used to come out here a lot when I was pregnant with Sunni. I used to imagine Brock's head as the target, and I never missed."

"You know I will protect you."

Lisa folded her arms with her tomahawk in her hand.

"Do you trust me with protecting Sunni?" he asked.

"I do trust you. You're not the problem. The problem is Brock wanting to be in her life and wanting her to know who he is. What kind of a crazy man rapes a woman constantly, and wants to claim the child from the rape?"

"He does have a lot of problems. I promise to always be here for you and Sunni."

Lisa looked at Jacob and half-smiled. "I know you will. I need to create a way to keep Brock away."

"Lisa, let me handle it."

Lisa shook her head. "I know that crazy man wanted to break my spirit, but in some weird way, he thinks he owns me. I never wanted things to be like this."

"I think the real problem is he always had eyes on you, but he also wanted to control you. He thought he was going to rule your life and have you at the same time."

"He's crazy. That's all I know."

"All I know is you need to let us handle it."

"I've told you before. You don't know what it's like! I had no control!"

Jacob raised his voice, "And I was put in chains! Being starved, beaten, and then put into fields!"

Lisa's voice rose. "But did they threaten our lives if you didn't work?"

Jacob's eyebrows lowered and he frowned. "No."

"I'm not saying you didn't have a horrible experience. I prayed for you every day." Anger rose within Lisa as her grip tightened on the tomahawk. "I wish your blood ran through Sunni's body. I wish Jesus would grant me that wish."

"I promise I love her."

"I know you do. But it doesn't change the truth of who her father is, as much as I hate him. The only difference between me and a single mother is she chose wrong. I didn't have a choice. I had a gun pointed to the back of my head."

"I'm your husband. It's my responsibility to protect you."

Lisa closed her eyes and exhaled. She opened her eyes and saw Jacob's frown etch further down his face. "I trust you to protect us." She uncrossed her arms and raised her tomahawk. "But this tomahawk will split his skull if he ever tries to touch me again." She walked past Jacob with the tomahawk in her hand. "I want to go check on Sunni. I trust the girls with her, but I want to watch."

Jacob murmured, "Whatever you want, beautiful."

<hr>

As the weeks passed, the family remained cautious, not allowing the children to go anywhere alone. Joseph still snuck outside in the early morning while Michael watched him. The men had also finished building the house for Jacob and Lisa.

Lisa was thrilled when she got to go inside and see how much effort had been put into building it. The house was bigger than Tsula and Luke's. Walking around the three bedroom house, Tsula smacked her lips and put her hand on her hips. The entire family had checked out the finished house except Lizzie, because she wanted to look last.

As Lizzie walked inside and looked around, Joseph excitedly came to the front door. "Auntie Lizzie, are you going to shoot arrows with us?" he asked in Cherokee.

Lizzie smiled at him and nodded.

"You're the greatest!"

Lizzie chuckled and looked around when a pregnant Tsula entered. "You're the greatest," she said, mimicking Joseph's voice as she playfully clapped her hands and bobbed her head.

"What do you want?" Lizzie asked with her lips smacking.

"I wanted to take another look before Lisa starts putting stuff in it," Tsula said.

"I'm going to ask Uncle George to build me a house on the other side. I need my own space, and the girls need their own."

"What makes you think he's going to do that for you?"

"What does that mean?" Lizzie asked.

"I think if you got a husband, Papa would happily build you one, but you seem to have no interest in trying."

"Shut up, Tsula. I'm so tired of you. Uncle George would do it for me."

"You see, that's the difference between me and you. I get what I want and you don't...most of the time."

"You're lucky that you're pregnant."

"Not really, sleeping is a pain, I think my feet are still swollen, I finally stopped puking in the morning, but I definitely have stronger legs now." Tsula lifted up her dress to show her calf muscles. "See, not too bad. They look almost as good as yours." Tsula leered and exited the house.

Lizzie watched her walk away with a prideful strut. She withheld her laughter, not wanting to give Tsula the satisfaction. "You're not that attractive."

Tsula looked back at Lizzie and leered. "I know...I'm gorgeous."

As Tsula cackled, Lizzie rolled her eyes while inspecting the house.

A few days later, David's sixteenth birthday passed, and tensions built as David was still not allowed to go anywhere on his own.

John reminded David of the kidnappings, but David hated the rules and thought himself old enough to take care of himself. One day in mid-May, David and Joseph were told to take firewood to the now-completed house. While the boys gathered the firewood, David remained in a bad mood. Joseph tried to cheer David up, but he refused to listen. As the boys left the new house, Joseph became angry, feeling ignored by his brother.

"You're a baby, David," Joseph shouted in Cherokee. "None of us can go anywhere alone, so why do you think you should?"

"I'm almost grown," David replied as he folded his arms. "I'm not a child like you. I want to walk around Tahlequah more, not be stuck here with you and the others."

"What if we ask Mel and the others to come over more often?"

"It's not the same. Mel is thirteen and Eric is fourteen. I don't even like Eric that much. It would be a waste of time."

"I think they're fun. You're only mad because Papa said you're not old enough to go on your own."

David kicked a small rock into the woods. "Shut up, Joseph! You don't know anything, you're such a child."

Joseph pouted. "I'm not!" He went to the family house where Grace sat underneath the old redbud tree.

"Come here, Joseph," Grace said in Cherokee.

Joseph grunted and approached his aunt.

"What was David so angry about?"

Joseph answered, "He wants to walk through Tahlequah alone, but Papa said no. I said he was acting like a baby, so now he is mad at me."

"Did he hurt your feelings?"

Joseph remained silent while he looked at Grace.

"Come sit with me, my little corn eater."

Joseph smiled and sat next to her.

"No matter how much the two of you fight, he'll always love you. I know you love him."

"David is mean and ugly, Auntie Grace."

"Well, I guess that makes you ugly too, if ugly means handsome to you."

Joseph bit his lip, trying not to laugh.

Grace smiled. "You know me and Auntie Lizzie used to fight a lot."

"Didn't you and Auntie Lizzie fight yesterday?"

Grace's eyes widened, and she looked away from Joseph. "We did...but it used to be a lot worse. Sometimes things would get broken, but what I'm trying to teach you is that it's normal for siblings to fight and argue. As long as we love each other, that's what matters most."

"Momma said that's what Jesus said is the most important thing to do."

"Your momma is right, and do you remember hearing Pastor Bluebird say something like that?"

"I think I fell asleep last time."

Grace laughed and hugged Joseph. "I'll tell you a little secret. Sometimes Auntie Grace gets a little sleepy too. Come inside. I will give you some catfish and bread."

Joseph followed Grace to the family house and spent some more time with his aunt. He enjoyed her giving spirit.

CHAPTER 17
Coyotes and Cowards

A FEW DAYS LATER NEWS HAD arrived that Paul had healed from his wound and begun to work on moving his arm normally. The Lightning-Strongman family rejoiced for Paul. Paul was now a free mulatto, and he was given a job by Nancy's family. The family went over to visit Paul on their own time. As John was riding down the dirt trails on Ray, he passed one of the waterholes and saw Lizzie sitting by it.

John tied Ray to a tree and approached Lizzie while she dabbed the water with her bow. "I'm surprised you didn't bring the twins out here with you," John said. "They love fishing with you."

Lizzie replied, "The twins love you more, if that makes you feel better."

John scoffed. "Yeah, but it's quickly turning to Auntie Lizzie being the favorite. Rain almost beat me when we shot arrows at one of the old trees. I had to act like I wasn't trying."

"You should go out to the practice fields and shoot more."

"Keeping the crops healthy is too important this year. Our family keeps growing, and we need more food. I do get a chance to practice a few shots with my rifle. Why are you out here?"

"I was thinking before you arrived. I can handle myself."

"I know. I'm worried you're starting to push yourself away from us again."

"Don't worry about that. I've learned to control my anger a lot through prayer and listening to Elder Joyce." Lizzie looked away from John and gazed at the waterhole." I'm nervous about a decision. Elder Joyce asked me to enjoy my singleness, but to seriously think about my future husband."

"I never thought you would let someone pressure you into looking for a husband, even Elder Joyce."

"She isn't pressuring me...she's been encouraging me to do things in my timing, but to also listen to what the Father is trying to tell me. I worked so hard on my anger that I ignore fixing my pride. I'm a proud woman, and I know...being too proud is a bad thing."

"You and Grace remind me of Momma a lot. Momma was not as short-tempered as you, but...she loved us and was a deep thinker like you."

Lizzie half-smiled. "Remember Grace would always question Momma, but I guess that was always the difference between Grace and me. Grace likes to learn. I want my way. I'm sure I got more spankings than both of you."

John chuckled as he took a small pebble and threw it into the waterhole. "Whatever is on your mind, I know it must be important. Try to ask yourself are you making a decision to please yourself or to follow what Jesus is trying to show you."

"Brother, I'm glad you followed Jesus for yourself, and not because of Annabelle." Lizzie grinned. "I've never seen you happier and yeah...even wiser. Momma would be so happy right now."

"Yeah, Jesus has changed me a lot. I wouldn't have bothered to go see Paul a couple of years ago. I wouldn't have cared if he lived or died. Have you seen Paul yet?"

Lizzie's voice became irritable, "I don't need to see him. I don't need that man asking me how I'm doing and trying to give me another flower. I hate flowers."

Lizzie noticed John's brow draw together. "Why are you pushing Paul away?" he asked. "There isn't anything special about going to see him and showing that you're happy he's well now."

"I don't know…he's too nice for me. I don't want anything from him."

John stood and brushed off his brown trousers. "You know when people care about you, they do things without asking for things in return. I think that's what bothers you." John cocked his head and shrugged. "You know he is a free man now."

Lizzie shook her head. "Leave, John."

John put up his hands, walked away, and got onto Ray. "You should see him. I never said more has to happen between the two of you." John slowly rode away.

When John couldn't be seen, Lizzie stood up. She stared at her reflection in the waterhole for a moment, then traveled to Nancy's farm.

As the days went by in Tahlequah, Annabelle was now accompanied by the twins, Rosita, Maria, and Lizzie as she gave water to the slaves. Annabelle was pleased by the girls' humble nature. When the family said their goodbyes to Doll and left the Thompson farm, the girls skipped ahead, with Lizzie close behind them.

"I think these trips are great for the girls," Maria said in Cherokee. "It feels good to at least give them something."

"Yeah, it does," Annabelle said. "I couldn't image random kindness back in Mississippi."

"Judy Mays and her sisters really were your peace at times."

"Yeah, they were. I can't help but wonder how all of them are doing."

Continuing to walk, Maria looked at Annabelle. "I think she misses you as much as you miss her."

Annabelle's brow lowered. "I ran away without leaving her anything. No letter, no I love you. It makes life harder."

"Keep praying on it. You never know unless you ask."

"I always think about how we're the opposite. I ran away from the closest thing I could call a home. You were forced away from your home."

"Sometimes, I do think about returning to Mexico. So Rosita and Sky could see where I had my childhood. I'm afraid of what it looks like now. It's probably best we don't try until they're grown."

"I had a dream about my momma two weeks ago. I can only hope she's well. If it wasn't for her, I wouldn't have run when I did."

"My momma is three miles away from us," Maria said. "I know I'm not as strong as you. I would be going crazy knowing my mother was a slave. If I was you, I'd probably do something stupid, and go try to find her. I'd end up getting caught and put back into slavery."

Annabelle's face went blank.

"I'm sorry, Annabelle."

"There's nothing to apologize for. I think knowing Jesus is with her is what gives me peace. I have to leave it in his hands."

"I'll continue to pray for your momma."

"Thank you. I look at the girls and feel hope. The only things they got from me are my ears and my smile. Everything else is John."

"I don't think so. Rain has your angry look," Maria said.

Annabelle chuckled.

"She does…and Jannie."

"Don't talk about my baby. She's a sweetheart."

"She is, but she's got fire in her too," Maria responded. "She's not quick to show it like Rain. I'm telling you…you should've named Rain lighting and Jannie thunder."

The two women cackled.

"Jannie is not as bad as her sister," Annabelle said.

"No, but she will stand her ground. I think Rosita is learning from them."

"Ha, don't try it. She's got some kick in her too. I think we're doing a good job with them."

"Me too. I'm proud of Rosita. I never imaged having a child who can speak Cherokee, English, and Spanish. I'm glad you asked me to bring Rosita. I don't want her to see the slaves as lesser. I remember you talking about slavery ending before we're old. I hope you're right about that."

The two women smiled at each other. Annabelle enjoyed Maria's positive nature and hoped to learn more Spanish from her cousin-in-law.

———◆———

One day in late May 1860, Grace and Lisa walked through Tahlequah, greeting townspeople.

Lisa noticed Brock and Hunter approaching them on their horses. The standoff between the two women and two men made it seem like no one else was present.

"It seems that you've been avoiding me," Brock said.

"I haven't been avoiding you. I've been living my life, and I have nothing more to say about it," Lisa said.

"There's no need for this rudeness, Miss Lisa," Hunter said.

"I believe that's enough, gentlemen, we need to leave," Grace said.

Brock raised his voice, "No, that isn't enough!" He lowered his voice, "I want to see my daughter."

Lisa's eyes dilated, her hands balled into fists, and she replied, "I told you already! You will never get to know her, and she'll never know you! What crazy man wants to know a child he made by forcing himself onto a woman?"

"I don't want her raised to be a savage. She has my blood. She needs to be raised properly."

"She will be raised as a Cherokee. Not to be part of your sick world."

"Lisa Strongman, don't test me. You're going to bring my daughter to me, and you're going to stop having that half-breed nigger raise her like she's his child. What do you plan to tell her? She has lighter skin than both of you."

Lisa's eyes narrowed. "Your need to control me is a sickness. You've tested me the most...as a Christian woman. There are some days I hope to hear you've been shot and your carcass dragged through the roads of Tahlequah. My daughter does have lighter skin than me, but so do other Cherokee. She won't question her blood when she gets older."

"I think you're in denial. All of you Indians are in denial. Your people will either become more civilized like the rest of us, or your people will be wiped out."

Lisa scoffed. "This is Cherokee land. It doesn't belong to the United States."

Brock replied, "Keep telling yourself that lie! Eventually she'll learn the truth."

Lisa's brown eyes fixed on Brock's face. She put her hand on her hip and took a step forward. "She has my eyes, my smile, my nose, my hair, and my cheeks. What are you going to say to her? Blue eyes." Lisa angrily walked away, with Grace following her closely as Brock watched them.

"Brock, I believe this is a war that you can't win," Hunter said. "I'm still surprised that you care for the child. But Lisa will kill you before you get to that baby girl."

Brock turned back to Hunter with pressed lips. "I don't know why I care so much," Brock said. "However, I will no longer tolerate her disrespect. I'm going to make her suffer for the rest of her life, and I know how to do it."

⸎

On June 1, 1860, as the sunrise outlined Oklahoma, the birds perched on the tallgrass and spread out trees sang.
Joseph had snuck outside once again to the practice fields. Michael quietly watched with a grin as Joseph practiced his shots. Joseph kept grunting with each missed shot. He made another attempt and hit a target with his last arrow. He jumped around with a big smile.

Michael grinned and nodded. He scanned the wilderness and quickly went to the family house to grab something to eat.

As Joseph was about to get the arrows, he heard a branch snap and quickly turned around. Brock stood in the fields staring at Joseph with his right hand behind his back.

"I was watching your skills, boy," Brock said. "Your auntie would be proud to see you hit a target, wouldn't she?"

Looking at the man, Joseph's throat tightened. He gulped and replied, "Yes, she would. I think she's on her way here soon."

"I assume you want to show her your skills, isn't that right, boy?"

"Yes, Mr. Jackson. I can go get her now. I know she's coming."

"No need to be in a rush. I'm sure me and both your aunties will be talking soon."

Joseph looked at Brock and saw what looked to be a bag in his right hand. The malevolent leer etching across Brock's face terrified Joseph. He turned and ran with the bow in his hand.

"Don't run from me, boy! Hunter, stop him!"

As Joseph ran up the trail, Hunter suddenly stepped in front of Joseph, forcing the scared boy to stop.

"Calm down, boy. We want to talk with you," Hunter said. "Didn't your momma teach you to listen to your elders?"

Joseph deeply inhaled, his eyes widened, and he answered, "My momma said I shouldn't go anywhere on my own. I want to go home now, Mr. Sawyer."

Hunter, towering over Joseph, bent over. "You should have listened to your momma, boy."

Joseph tried to run past Hunter. The man managed to grab Joseph's arm, and the boy struggled to break out of Hunter's grasp. Hunter tried to grab Joseph's other arm.

"Let me go, Mr. Sawyer!" Joseph yelled.

Joseph poked Hunter in his eye with his bow, and the man howled, letting go of Joseph.

As Joseph tried to run, Brock tackled him and pinned the boy to the ground. Joseph's bow slid across the grass.

"You have some toughness in you. They'll like that," Brock said. "Now you're coming with us, boy. Stop nursing the eye, Hunter, we need to leave!"

Joseph's heart raced while Brock kept him pinned down. "Momma!" Joseph screamed. "Papa, help—!"

Brock covered Joseph's mouth with one hand and pressed Joseph's head into the ground with his other. Joseph managed to turn his head and bit Brock's hand.

"Ah! You little nigger!"

Joseph kept his jaws locked onto Brock's hand. Brock punched Joseph several times in the head, finally causing Joseph to let go of Brock's hand.

Joseph cried as Hunter forced the sack over his head. "Mommy," Joseph cried in Cherokee.

The men forced Joseph to stand, but Joseph attempted to kick Brock. He hit Brock in the thigh, and the man grunted before striking Joseph over the head with his revolver. Joseph fell to the ground, seemingly lifeless. Brock's eyes widened, and he put his hand on his head.

"What did you do?" Hunter said, wide-eyed with a worrisome tone.

"He's fine," Brock said.

"How do you know?" Hunter lowered his head to listen for Joseph's breath. "The boy isn't breathing."

"I didn't hit him that hard. He's a redskin child; he can take it."

"Did you not hear me? You killed him!"

Brock shook his head. "No! No, he didn't get hit that hard. We're taking him."

Hunter scowled and quickly handed Brock a sack with holes in it for his eyes. Brock quickly picked up Joseph and threw the boy on his shoulders. The men ran toward the dirt trail with brown sacks on their heads. Suddenly, a rifle shot cracked through the air.

Michael grazed Hunter in the arm with the shot. Hunter tripped and collapsed.

The two men returned fire with their revolvers, forcing Michael to jump out of the way. "Let him go!" Michael yelled.

Michael took another shot, forcing the men to run toward the barn. Hunter shot back as he ran toward the barn, forcing Michael back. The men got to the barn, breathing heavily, and Hunter pulled the barn door open to use as a shield while Michael and Hunter exchanged gunfire.

Brock took a shot while holding Joseph, but he missed Michael. Michael attempted to get closer to them using the shed as a shield. He took a step, then slipped on some wet grass and fell.

As he tried to stand, Hunter shot Michael in the upper chest. "I got him!" he yelled.

"Quickly finish him off!" Brock yelled. "I'm going to the wagon."

Hunter leered. He tried to take another shot, but the revolver clicked, revealing it was empty. He gritted his teeth and ran to Michael as the other man tried to put pressure on his wound. Running, Hunter took a swing at Michael with his revolver, but Michael used his rifle to catch the blow. Hunter tried again, but Michael managed to kick Hunter's leg. Hunter's foot slid, and he fell on his chest.

"You disgusting savage!" Hunter growled.

Michael attempted to hit Hunter with his rifle but missed. "Where are you taking Joseph, who are you?" he yelled.

"None of your business, prairie nigger!" Hunter jumped on top of Michael and pressed onto Michael's wound.

Michael cried out, and blood poured from it.

Hunter hit Michael in the head with his revolver, then swung again, but Michael blocked the blow with his rifle. Hunter quickly pressed on Michael's wound again.

The pain weakened Michael, and his grip loosened on the rifle. Hunter yanked the rifle away.

Hunter gasped as the house doors opened, so he raised the rifle to strike Michael. An arrow slammed through Hunter's shoulder, and he howled, dropping the rifle. Turning around, he saw Grace with her bow and arrows, wearing her nightgown. Hunter ran, holding his shoulder. Grace took aim, hitting Hunter in his kneecap.

Hunter collapsed on the ground and started to crawl. "Wait! Don't leave me! Please! They're going to kill me!"

Suddenly a wagon charged down the dirt trails.

Lizzie ran from the family house with her bow and arrows.

"Lizzie, help Michael," Grace yelled in Cherokee. While Lizzie ran to Michael, Grace ran to Hunter with her bow drawn. "Who are you?!"

Hunter rolled around. He lifted both of his bloodstained hands and answered, "Please don't kill me."

Grace squinted when she heard his voice and moved closer to him. "I said, who are you?"

"If you kill me, your whole family will be wiped out."

Grace scowled, kicking Hunter in his stomach and ripping off the brown sack. Her eyes widened, and she grabbed Hunter by the collar. "What are you doing here!"

"Grace!" Lizzie yelled with a grief-stricken tone.

Grace turned around and saw Lizzie holding Michael's head up as she compressed his wound.

"They took Joseph!" Lizzie screamed.

"Who was with you?" Grace bellowed, noticing John and other men running to her aid.

"We need horses now!" John said, running to the barn.

Jacob and Luke followed him.

Grace's grip grew tighter as she looked at Hunter. "Where's my nephew?"

Hunter spit on the ground and looked back at Grace. "I don't know what you're talking about, redskin."

"You liar!" Grace was about to punch Hunter when she heard John, Jacob, and Luke bring out the horses. She turned around and yelled, "John, they took Joseph in that wagon!"

John's brow furrowed, and his nose scrunched. The men quickly threw saddles on the horses. The men snapped the horses' reins and furiously rode down the dirt trails, following the wheel tracks of the wagon.

"You will never get that half-breed nigger back." Hunter laughed.

Grace punched Hunter as hard she could, knocking him unconscious.

"Grace, I need help," Lizzie yelled in Cherokee.

Grace ran toward Michael, but she glanced at Annabelle,

standing in her house doorway. Annabelle followed Grace to Michael as George also ran to him.

Tsula saw Michael bleeding badly and ran to Lisa's house. "Lisa," she yelled. "Michael has been shot!"

Lisa came out of the house with Sunni in one arm and her tomahawk in the other.

As Brock drove the wagon in a panic, he met up with another white man.

"We have to move quickly," Brock yelled. "I have no doubt his family is right behind me."

The man yelled, "That's why we do these things at night!"

"It would've been harder to get him alone! I want them to suffer, and this will do the job."

The man shook his head. "You're a dangerous man."

"They've had their chances. They will know their place. Besides, every nigger whether half or full-blood needs a master. Make sure you tell me what happens when you get to Tennessee, and don't be careless with this boy. He's a smart one."

"I don't take my chances with Injun children." The white man approached the wagon. He removed the sack over Joseph's head, and his jaw appeared slightly unhinged. "Is he alive?"

"What do you mean is he alive? Of course he's alive!"

"He's bleeding from the back of his head. You fool! What did you do?"

"The boy fought back. I had to strike him."

The white man lifted up Joseph's head. "I'm not taking the body of a dead boy. I do have morals and that much respect."

Brock stomped his foot. "He can't be dead."

"Feels different when you kill a child, doesn't it?"

Brock grabbed the man's collar. "He's not dead!"

The man put up his palms, and Brock released him.

"We'll see if he survives," the man said.

"He'll be fine. He's an Indian child."

The men strapped Joseph's body down to the back of the white man's black horse, and the man rode off with Joseph.

Brock rode to his home, abandoning the wagon. With sweat

dripping down his face, he kept looking back while riding away on his horse.

———◆———

John, Jacob, and Luke soon arrived at the wagon. The men saw the two different tracks.

"What do you want to do, John?" Jacob asked in Cherokee.

John replied, "I will go after this trail that's going more to the right. The two of you should go the other way."

Luke replied, "Should one of us follow the trail to get Joseph, and the other go to Maria's family since Samuel is there?"

John replied, "There's no time."

Luke nodded, agreeing with John.

The men rode off on the different trails. As John rode down Brock's trail, he began to pray, "Jesus, please protect my boy. Please protect him. I don't know how I can live with myself if something happens to him. That man Grace wounded was Mr. Sawyer. What craziness is going on?"

Hours passed as John rode through the Cherokee territory. The tracks he followed went onto another dirt trail filled with horse tracks that made it impossible for John to follow his son. He searched for Joseph, his heart breaking with each passing hour.

When the sun had nearly set, John rode Big Boy home. He plodded back to the farm, put Big Boy in his stable, and marched to the family house. He stared at the front door with the horizon outlining his body. Walking through it, he found his entire family gathered at the supper table.

Speechless, John looked at his grief-stricken family and took a deep breath. David looked like he was holding back tears, and John's heart pounded harder. He took two steps to the supper table. He looked at Annabelle with bloodshot eyes.

"John...where's my baby?" Annabelle asked.

"I...I lost track of him...I'm sorry...I—," John mumbled with his voice breaking.

A tear streamed down Annabelle's face, and her eyes bulged. "What did you say?"

"I…I lost track of him. I couldn't find him."

Grace let go of Eli's hand and tightly hugged John, and he broke down in tears. Annabelle bawled as Maria tried to soothe her. The girls clung to Lizzie and cried.

"Please forgive me!" John whispered.

Annabelle stood up, quivering as she approached John, her hands clasping her chest. She hugged John tightly. "There's nothing to forgive."

She then wailed, and John cried.

"You tried," Annabelle consoled. "I know you tried."

As John embraced Annabelle, other members of the family embraced each other.

"Where's Michael?" John asked.

"He is resting," Tsula replied. "He lost a lot of blood, but Lizzie was able to take out the bullet."

Lisa cried. "All of this is my fault! He warned me this was going to happen."

Annabelle's voice bellowed as she yelled, "None of this is your fault!" She rushed to Lisa and hugged her. "We have to get my baby back. We can get him back, and that man outside is going to tell us how."

John turned to her. "Mr. Sawyer is alive?"

"He's tied to the crooked tree," Lizzie said. "We've been giving him water so he would have some strength and not die."

John's brow furrowed. He marched to the kitchen door, and the other men followed him. With each step John took, his rage multiplied. John and the others went outside to stand before Hunter.

The wounded man was tied to the crooked tree, a bucket and bowl sitting in front of him.

"Mr. Sawyer, I was awakened by the screams of my son. I had to convince my wife to stay in our home," John said with a thunderous voice, raising his fist. "Where's my son?"

Albert Brooks looked up from reading off one of the papers incased in plastic. His family, now wide-eyed and silent in the sunlit room, stared at him.

"Before I continue, I need to apologize," he said.

Liz's eyes welled up. "Daddy, why didn't you tell me about Joseph?" She looked at her siblings. "Did any of you know?"

The others shook their heads.

"I guess it goes back to when I said that even painful history should be told," Albert said.

"Our family went through a lot."

"Annabelle was a woman for the ages. She fought so hard to be free and to have a family. This incident brought forth a war."

"I would go to war for my babies," Liz replied.

"The times were different. Things had to be done in a certain way. Our family was already challenged by the two wolves. Lisa had been raped and impregnated, Jacob was kidnapped, Lizzie was almost raped and murdered two men, and Tsula had a miscarriage. Now, Joseph was taken from them."

"Annabelle went after them, didn't she?"

Albert chuckled. "You like the idea of that. God has this way of putting the right people in your life at the right time. Loyalty is tested by storms, and now that you've been told about the two wolves. It's time to reveal the rest of the family's legacy."

Albert reached for an old photo album, and Liz smiled at her father.

TO BE CONTINUED

I hope this adventure was an enjoyable experience for you and that you will visit your favorite retailer to leave a review because your feedback is priceless!

ABOUT THE AUTHOR

Hi, everyone! I'm Marcus, from the south side suburbs of Chicago. I'm a descendent of two Native American tribes. I have two degrees in zoology, love the Olympic games, and I am into Native American history, especially regarding issues that have divided families. Some of the stories I enjoy creating focus on parts of history rarely talked about and revolve around genealogy and interracial relationships, particularly between African American and Native American communities that cause us to reflect on the choices we make especially in our teenage and young adult years. This focus is to help young adults see the bigger picture earlier in their lives. God's greatest commandment is to love each other. I hope to fascinate your minds, to educate, to make you think about your family, and make you reflect on your own choices in life.